THE DEPTHS OF ATLANTIS

To Andi —

Thank you for the support! Love,

Hannah Carter

THE DEPTHS OF ATLANTIS
The Atlantis Trilogy Book 1

Published by Snowridge Press
www.snowridgepress.com

PAPERBACK ISBN: 978-1-958412-08-4

Cover Design by Miblart Design

Interior Formatting by Dragonpen Designs

THE DEPTHS OF ATLANTIS

THE ATLANTIS TRILOGY
Book I

HANNAH CARTER

To God, for giving me the inspiration and dedication to see this book through. And to Chey, who gave a continent a name. Thanks for encouraging my spark of creativity from the start. Know that this book is here because of the support and friendship you gave me to never give up back when I was twelve. ATYNAF.

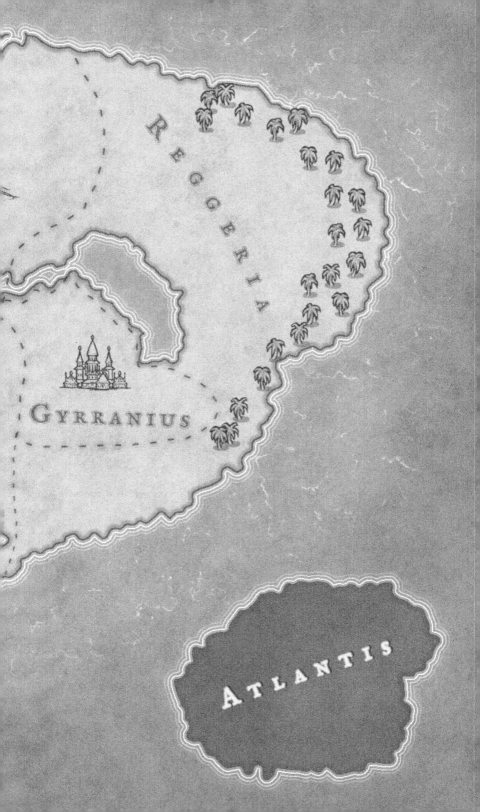

Trigger Warnings:

Depths of Atlantis deals with some subject matter that some readers may find disturbing. While these are real issues that people face, they can be upsetting. Please know that we have tried to portray these sensitively, but understand that everyone has different tolerance levels. As such, some triggers include—

Self-harm
Suicidal thoughts
Concentration camps (mentions + scenes)
Fantasy violence/bloodshed
Death
Anxiety
Depression
PTSD
Child abuse from a parental figure (physical, mental, and emotional)
Kidnapping
War

Some people may also find Reanna's intense self-loathing to be overwhelming. There are also some key moments from Reanna's perspective in which the reader must be aware that these are her thoughts as she struggles with guilt, self-blame, and self-hatred. These sentiments are not the truth of the matter, and should not be treated as fact nor the opinion of the author or publisher.

We hope that you enjoy Depths of Atlantis, and, if you have experienced any of these, know that you are not alone. Many people around the world go through the same things, but fear and shame often tell us that we are isolated, unique in our suffering. If you are struggling, please feel free to send a message to @mermaidhannahwrites on Instagram. If you need a safe place, we can find solace and community together.

Love,

PART I

CHAPTER 1

REANNA

EARTH: PANAMA CITY, FLORIDA

Reanna Cook couldn't sleep. She found it hard to do anything at all, honestly, considering she'd died ten hours ago.

Oh, she hadn't *physically* died, of course. But she had puked in biology, which meant that Trevor Spencer, Mr. "I'm-So-Cool-Because-I'm-Tall-and-Tanned-and-a-Star-Quarterback"—not to mention her arch-nemesis since childhood—was going to think of some *terrible* way to torment her tomorrow.

And the dread of that was what kept her up until 11:46 p.m. Well, that, and the fact that she was seventeen, had no idea where she was going for college, there was a big swim meet coming up in a few days, and she had a pre-calc quiz tomorrow, too.

11:47 p.m. She hadn't even made it a whole two minutes without looking at the clock.

Reanna sucked on her *The Little Mermaid* throw to try and bring some comfort. But when that didn't help, she covered her face and held back the tears that threatened to fall. Stupid biology. Stupid Trevor Spencer. Frankly, she didn't see how he kept *his* guts down while dissecting frogs. Maybe she should tease *him* about being heartless and desensitized to the cruel fate of poor little Mr. Hops-A-Lot Froggy.

In all honesty, she shouldn't have named the frog right before they cut it open. That was probably her first mistake.

Flipping over to her right side, she gazed out at the night sky and the world past her balcony. She'd left her door open a crack so she could hear the gentle waves lap against the shore. The dark, foaming sea, which bore more resemblance to ink right now than water, danced beneath a full moon. There wasn't a single cloud in the sky tonight, so hundreds of stars peeked their celestial heads out to peer down at the Earth.

Reanna gathered up the blanket around her and snuggled beneath it—

Crack.

She stilled under her covers. Had that been a firework? In Florida, it wasn't uncommon for tourists to celebrate their vacation with some kind of illumination, but this was a private section of beachfront homes. Those kinds of noises should be coming from much farther down the shore...

Were there voices just outside her window?

"Mo—" Reanna whispered before she clamped her mouth shut and shoved down her first instinct to bolt into her mother's room. A seventeen-year-old should not have to run to her mom every time something went bump in the night. After all, they lived on the beach. Couples took long, romantic night walks all the time—or at least, that was what Reanna had seen in movies and books. She'd yet to even have a boy hold her hand, though Pete in English class always made moon eyes at her. When he wasn't making moon eyes at every other girl in class, that is.

Reanna closed her eyes and coached herself against the rising tide of anxiety in the pit of her stomach. It was just her imagination;

she'd always had an overactive one. Like the time she thought a robber was stealing their car from the driveway—only it turned out to be a neighborhood kid trying to sneak back home after he'd been out late partying. Or the time she swore up and down that someone was breaking into their house, only to find out that it was two cats getting into a brawl over a ladylove.

But...these voices seemed to be getting closer.

Nope, nope. Forget about her dignity. Time to go get Mom. Reanna threw off her covers and slid out of bed, creeping toward her bedroom door, making sure to always keep the balcony in her peripheral vision. Mom slept just down the hallway—and therefore, so did safety.

Her hand rested on the doorknob now. She would just—

Reanna got out half a scream before it was cut off by a torrent of salty liquid. The water jettisoned at her face from the direction of her balcony with the force of Old Faithful. She stumbled away from the door, slipped, and crashed to the ground. It felt like someone had turned a water hose on the "jet stream" setting and shot her in the mouth; she clawed at her throat and gagged.

Breathe. She desperately needed air. Whatever idiot pathologist had said drowning was a peaceful way to die had clearly never drowned before.

Two invaders approached her, each dressed in silver and blue armor, which seemed to glow faintly in the moonlight. One of them lowered his or her hand. The water slowed down, as if they'd been commanding it.

They grunted at her—no, they were talking—and Reanna realized she recognized the words.

"Come with us," one of them said. The feminine voice spoke halting English with a thick accent.

Reanna choked and coughed until she finally managed to spit out the copious amount of seawater. "I'd rather *die*."

She scrambled to her feet only to be hit by a whirlpool. The force slammed into her nightstand and pushed it down on top of her. The majority of its contents scattered on the floor; her phone skittered under the bed. She shoved the nightstand off and dove for her iPhone—her one lifeline and chance to call 911, even if no one believed her—

"*Faynacore*," the second attacker snarled with a high-pitched voice. Another woman. She latched onto Reanna's leg with a tentacle of water, yanked her backward, and punched her cheek. Reanna screeched and lurched away from her attackers. Tears bubbled in her eyes as the sharp pain blurred her vision. The world swam for a moment, but she had no time to reorient herself before the attackers dragged her closer to the balcony with their weapon of water.

"Mom! *Mom!*" Reanna shrieked, but her kidnappers stifled her voice with another burst of water. Why couldn't her mother hear her? Isabella Cook wasn't *that* heavy of a sleeper.

Reanna kicked at the attacker closest to her and managed to unlatch a few bits of armor from the chest piece. No…not just armor.

A *scale*.

A bright, silver, sparkling, and reflective *scale*, almost magical. Reanna loathed the very sight of it.

"*Mom!*" Reanna clawed her way toward the door, but the water lasso around her ankle tightened. She tried again to scream, tried to grab onto her bed, but she only managed to scrape the leg of it across the floor. In a few seconds, her mom would burst through the door and stop this. She'd come to the rescue, come set everything right, because that's what a mom did.

But, shark fins, if Mom could just hurry it up right about now…

Anxiety ripped through Reanna like a bullet. It soaked her body like invisible blood and made her tremble and go cold.

She'd fought too hard for this life, for this home. The kidnappers could try to take her, but she'd make as much noise as those two male cats when they brawled over their mistress.

"*Momma!*"

The attackers blasted Reanna's mouth and nose with water again. She choked on it. Her body fought to breathe, to stay alive. The soldiers looked puzzled, like they were waiting for something that wasn't happening. They finally cut off the stream of water and released their hold on their prey. Reanna flopped into the pond that seeped across her floor. She swung her foot toward her desk chair and tried to kick it at the attackers as she struggled to get up. One of the brutes flicked their wrist, and a wave bubbled up at their bidding to slam the makeshift weapon against the opposite wall.

The taller of the women grabbed Reanna's ankle with a tentacle of water. The soldiers leaned their heads closer together and whispered in that despicable, guttural language that Reanna had blocked from her memory. She hugged her arms around herself and wished she could summon Spider-Man right off her shirt to save her. Or, at the very least, summon some of Peter Parker's courage, because right now, Reanna had nothing to go on. Her face stung, her lungs burned, and her mouth felt like it was swollen from the sheer amount of salt water she'd consumed.

The shorter soldier nodded. She punched Reanna once more, but at least it was on the other cheek. How mildly considerate. Spots flew in Reanna's vision, and she croaked out an incoherent plea as the taller kidnapper hoisted her over their shoulder.

The second one held a gag made of water across Reanna's mouth. However futile it might be, Reanna still screamed, kicked, and tore into her attackers, determined to break off more bits of their armor and leave a trail. But who would recognize these clues? Who would realize what had happened when Reanna hadn't told anyone about the past? When she thought she'd run away from it for good?

Only now it'd come back to abduct her.

Her kidnappers used another whirlpool to get down off the balcony; below, three figures waited. Two of them gleamed in the moonlight, wearing the same armor as her attackers. The closer they got, the more Reanna could make out the feminine features of the woman in the middle. Her long hair and the skin-tight dress she wore were the same shade as the midnight around them. Her unnaturally pale skin seemed to glow like a secondary moon.

"Certainly took you long enough." The woman scowled at both the soldiers that held Reanna. "I have to clean up what I can of this magical mess, and the rest of you can't be late taking *sweet* Reanna to Arana."

Arana.

Reanna wished they'd killed her. She shrieked behind her gag. Surely someone would hear it and rescue her. Surely one of her neighbors had to be a light sleeper.

The imposing woman chuckled. "Now, Reanna, dear. No need to cause a fuss. I've cast a silence spell, anyway. No one can hear you—not even that woman you call your mother." With one nod from this strange lady, the gag around Reanna's mouth dissipated. The sorceress pinched Reanna's cheeks; long fingernails bit into her skin. "And how rude to call that ugly hag 'mother.' You have no idea how much your *real* mother has missed you. Look at all the trouble she's gone through, sending me…"

"Isabella Cook *is* my mother," Reanna snarled. "More than Arana will ever be."

The woman's eyes seemed to light up as she leaned forward, her mouth inches from Reanna's ear. "You can't undo blood, dear. No matter how much you try. *Oblivisanima vestratur.*"

And then the world was no more.

CHAPTER 2

LAILE

GAIA: DISTRICT OF CAPITAL CITY

"We're off to save a mermaid, the missing Atlantean heir!" Laile perched on a tree branch and swung her legs as she sang. On the ground, Gregory—the grumpy wizard that she had called her best friend since childhood—sat studying the missive from a spy in Atlantis. "We need to find her straight away, or the Council will despair! And all the world will descend into heinous warfare!"

Gregory sighed, folded the note, and tucked it into his pocket. "Do you *have* to sing? Last I checked, the whole world straddled on the precipice of disaster. If we don't rescue this mermaid, the world will totter right over the edge and plummet off the cliff of no return. And for some reason you decide to rewrite folk songs?"

Laile trailed her hands out behind her, searching for a tenuous bond with the dirt below her. Once she found it, she jerked the granules up with magic and solidified them into a diamond whip. As a gem fairy, she could control and transfigure almost all earth-related substances easily. Laile twirled her newest creation around for a moment before she let it dissolve. She'd already made and unmade about fifty of those whips while they waited. "Yeah, well, we've been here for over two hours. I'd much rather rewrite cheesy songs than die of boredom. However, I do have some other suggestions, if you're willing to hear them…" Mostly, they included confessing their feelings and making out. Actually, Laile was good for just making out without confessions, too. But instead, she said, "How about you tell me why you're acting all moody and distant?"

Gregory cleared his throat. "I'm not." Before Laile could press harder, though, he changed the subject.

He'd gotten really good at that lately.

"I'm absolutely sure we have the right coordinates. The spy said they created the portal right here because the veil between worlds is thinnest. They said Arana was planning an abduction around this time and for us to wait. Silently. As in, very little talking. And absolutely no singing."

Laile puffed out her lips. As grateful as she was that the Council trusted her to retrieve Reanna, the missing Atlantean heir, Laile couldn't help but feel that this might all be some elaborate practical joke. "Hey, did my dad give you that missive himself? Or did you get it through a third party?"

"Why does it matter?"

"It *matters* because if one of my brothers gave that to you, we're being pranked. That would be just like Kal to take our real orders and send us on this wild unicorn hunt."

Gregory scratched his head, and Laile wondered if that was a flicker of distrust she saw behind his thick glasses. "Uh…"

A *snap* of air knocked Laile off her perch. She switched into her elemental form—a miniature, diamond-encrusted version of herself—and beat her fairy wings against the air. Gregory held out his hand and caught her. He held onto her until she was full-sized again and on the ground beside him.

"Thanks," she murmured.

He nodded, but he seemed just as distracted by what—or who—had caused that bend in the space-time continuum as she was: a handful of Atlantean soldiers marching out of a portal and carrying a metal cage.

Good. Not too many, just like the note said. A small, covert team—perfect for Laile and Gregory's first taste of Council-sanctioned war action.

"What do you say? I take the two on the right, you take the two on the left?" Laile suggested. She relaxed her fingers, and her diamond whip melted back into dirt. Then she reformed the earth once more, this time into two long daggers. To the untrained eye, it might seem like Gregory waltzed into battle without any protection at all, but if these soldiers underestimated him, they would pay for that mistake.

He nodded. This was it. This was the moment that the Council had prepared them for, the moment that future generations would one day remember. They'd tell of how the great fairy Laile rescued Princess Reanna and triumphed over the Atlantean invaders, all with the help of her husband (well, *future* husband) and sidekick.

"Go!" Laile said.

Gregory raced forward while Laile crystallized and shrank to the size of a thumb again. She flew at the intruders as Gregory cast an *ignis* spell, which sent a fireball hurtling toward the feet of the soldiers. The mermaids might have been able to gain their legs by abusing the magic of their elven prisoners—one of the many travesties Laile would put an end to—but they obviously hadn't lost their intense fear of fire. They lurched backward, dropping the metal cage in their haste, and surged toward Gregory.

That was the soldiers' fatal flaw: they didn't see Laile until it was too late. She expanded to her full size right in front of them, daggers ready. She slammed one hilt into the temple of a brunette soldier. Before the next one could react, Laile whomped the flat side of her other dagger against the back of that soldier's head.

The second woman, a blonde, staggered forward. Laile's orders might be to keep the soldiers alive for interrogation, but that didn't mean she had to go *easy* on the elite mermaids.

Still seemingly dazed, the blonde lost her footing and dropped to the ground, only to dig her fingers into the dirt.

A rocket of water shot up and blocked Laile from her opponent. She reeled back and nearly tripped over the brunette, who seemed to be coming back to her senses. The mermaid had apparently taken a hit to the temple better than expected.

Laile growled under her breath—that was a special talent of hers, given the fact that her father was a werewolf—and kicked the rousing soldier in the nose. The woman slumped once more.

One problem down—

Laile swore as she turned to see a giant tidal wave cresting over her.

She shrank again and zipped out of the way. The blonde soldier's water crashed down on the brunette. A sickening feeling twisted the inside of Laile's stomach, but she didn't have time to hope or pray for the brunette's survival. If she did, she would risk her *own* survival, and she preferred to keep her life, thank-you-very-much.

Laile darted to the blonde and grew right in front of her. This time, she angled her foot at her attacker's face. The force plunged the soldier backward with a bloody nose—a matching set to her friend's.

"*Dormi!*" Gregory yelled.

He placed his hands on the blonde's head. Before she could react, her eyes slid closed, and she thudded to the ground. Laile glanced to her left and caught sight of Gregory's attackers, who were slightly burned and unconscious on the other side of the cage.

"You were supposed to let *me* take that one," Laile grumbled. She released her daggers and let them crumble back into dirt once more. Gregory—who always seemed to be in a haphazard state— looked even more askew after the battle. His rumpled clothes were smudged with dirt, and his glasses perched on his nose off-kilter. Honestly, two out of those three were normal, but he was rarely dirty. Before he could protest, Laile smacked the dust off his shirt while he fixed his glasses. "Are you in one piece? No limbs missing?"

Gregory grunted. "I'm fine. What about yourself?"

Well, if he was so worried, maybe he should check her over, just to make sure everything was okay. Then they could gaze into each other's eyes and—

Hold on. Why was he staring off into space instead of making deep, dramatic eye contact?

Rend and tear it all, she'd waited eighteen years to plant one on him. She supposed she could wait a little bit longer until their mission was complete.

Laile stepped up to the prison's doors. She heard some sort of pitiful and loud bawling coming from inside, like a gryphon that had gotten its tail tromped on. Poor thing. Maybe the princess had been in some weird time loop and hadn't aged a day since she disappeared at age six. That would explain all the crying.

Then again, kidnapping at any age was probably a traumatic event. Laile certainly had no desire to get herself abducted and find out.

"Are you going to open the doors or just stare at them?" Gregory nudged her in the back.

Laile looked over her shoulder and stuck her tongue out at him. "Oh, like you could do better!" She gave the metal handles a few good yanks, but they refused to budge. Locked. No matter. She backed away, intent on crafting a crowbar or some lock-picking device—she hadn't fully thought that through—but Gregory stepped forward.

"Actually, I can." Gregory laid his palms against the doors and intoned, "*Aperidium.*"

At his command, the doors swung open.

"Show off," Laile muttered.

Inside the cage, the prisoner squawked and covered up her face with the sleeve of a ragged, damp sweatshirt. The girl herself was hardly any better than her outfit. She looked like she'd been punched or kicked a few times, but at least it meant she'd put up a glorious fight.

Good. They weren't dealing with a six-year-old caught in a time loop, then.

Laile felt a surge of glee. Here she was, on the cusp of meeting one of her childhood idols, the legendary Princess Reanna. The brave girl who had outwitted her mother, Queen Arana, and escaped Atlantis at such a tender age.

Laile leaned forward and offered her hand to the kidnapped princess. "Come on, get out."

The girl let out another squeak and tried to huddle in on herself. "Please don't hurt me! I just want to go home!"

Laile blinked. Okay, that wasn't exactly the *most* legendary thing to say, but Reanna had just endured a lot. She'd surely pull herself together and be mighty in a second. "Don't worry! We won't hurt you, Reanna."

Tears slipped down the poor girl's bruised cheeks as she grimaced and clutched her head, shaking. Her tangled, wild blonde curls leapt everywhere. "S-stop! Please! Don't hurt me!"

Laile threw a look over her shoulder at Gregory. He stared intently at the bawling Reanna, his brows furrowed, looking very ponderous…and attractive. Laile shook her head and returned her attention to the girl, who was now curled up, her knees pressed against her chin, arms wrapped around her legs.

"Please stop staring at me. I didn't do anything," the girl bleated. She peeked one eye out from beneath her wild blonde mop, made eye contact with Gregory, and then stared at a large rivet on her metal prison.

"Reanna—" Laile began, but Reanna winced again and slapped her hands over her ears. Laile grunted and spoke a little bit louder. "You don't understand. We're here to *help* you! The Council sent us—"

"No, *you* don't understand," the girl whispered. "I'm not the girl you want. I'm not this Re—" She flinched once more. "*That person.* See?" The girl held up her right wrist where a silver bracelet dangled. "The inscription. My name isn't R—that name. It's Gilly."

Laile stared at the engraved bracelet. Her stomach plummeted as she read the words: "*Gilly-Goose, I Will Love You Forever. Mom.*"

Gilly. Her name was Gilly, not Reanna.

Laile slapped her hands over her eyes.

Oh, Composer help them. They'd gotten the wrong girl.

CHAPTER 3

GILLY

UNKNOWN: ???

Gilly found it hard to breathe as the tall, Polynesian-looking girl unceremoniously jerked her from the cage and dumped her onto the muddy ground. Gilly staggered, and a boy, who boasted curly hair and glasses, reached to steady her. She tensed and scooted away from him. He hadn't stopped staring at her since the doors had opened, and, to be honest, it sent her awkward-meter through the roof.

She pinched her wrist—the twentieth time she'd done so since she'd come to a few minutes ago. Each time, she hoped she'd wake up from this bad dream, only to find out that instead, she'd somehow fallen into a *real* nightmare. First, she'd been locked up in a cage while people yelled and banged things around outside, and then these people kept calling her some strange name that wasn't hers.

To be fair, though, she couldn't remember hearing a lot of stuff. Most of the mental files inside her brain seemed to be empty, as if she'd been born in this cage ten minutes ago.

She whimpered once more and stuffed the sleeve of her sweatshirt into her mouth. It was already soaked, but at a time like this, that didn't matter. Her eyes flickered between these two new people, who looked equally frightening in their own ways.

"Who are *you*?" Gilly murmured around the fabric stuffed into her mouth.

"Laile," the lithe, sprightly girl said before she jabbed her finger at Mr. Stares-a-Lot. "And that's Gregory."

Gilly curled her shoulders inward, took a step back, and flailed her arms as she almost tumbled right back into the cage. Mr. Stares-a-Lot—Gregory, as Laile had called him—grabbed her hand and yanked her forward. She purposefully didn't make eye contact with him. He clearly didn't know the proper etiquette about staring: once someone catches you, you look away.

Well, if *he* wouldn't look away, then *she* certainly would, and—

Gilly's breath caught in her throat. Two prone figures lay on the ground. Each wore armor and clutched a sword in their hand. She let out a tiny croak and pointed her finger at the unconscious— at least, she *hoped* they were merely unconscious—bodies. "What did you *do* to them?" she squeaked.

"They're the bad guys." Laile waved her hand as if it were unimportant. "But we just knocked them around a bit. They'll be fine; guards will pick them up later."

Gilly couldn't tell if Laile was lying or not.

Laile directed her next question toward Gregory with a tilt of her head. "Look, the real issue here is, where is Reanna?"

That name again. Gilly clamped her hands over her ears as her brain suddenly felt like it would crack apart. A buzzing filled her mind, as if someone had stuffed her head with a hive of bees. "Stop! I don't know who that girl is, but I'm not her! Can't you just take me home?"

Gregory pushed his glasses farther up his nose. He still hadn't quit that blasted staring. Her internal awkward gauge dipped further into the "danger" zone with every second. "Sure. Where is your home?"

Gilly opened her mouth—and closed it again. "I—I don't know?"

"Who are your parents?"

"Well, I…I have them, you know, everybody has to… Look! My mom gave me this bracelet." Gilly held out her hand for Gregory's inspection once more. He barely glanced at it before he continued his interrogation.

"What's your mom's name, if you're so close to her?"

Gilly clamped her mouth shut. Her brain felt like mush, and she frantically tried to shove the limp pieces together. She *had* a mother…everybody had one. Hers was just… Gilly closed her eyes as she tried to picture what her mother looked like. She couldn't even conjure a fuzzy memory of her. "I…I don't know."

Gilly didn't think the moment could get any worse—but then Gregory stepped forward and put his hands against her forehead. She wriggled, but his fingers clamped tight against her skin.

She closed her eyes and let herself drift to her happy place. She wasn't exactly sure what her happy place was at the moment, but that was beside the point. Almost anything she could picture was better than this. If he didn't quit it soon, her awkward-meter would be broken beyond repair; the needle already danced in "Danger, Will Robinson!" territory. She didn't remember anything ever being quite so unbearable as this—the fact that she didn't remember anything was irrelevant.

It came to a blessed end when Gregory stepped back with a grimace. He shook out his hands and wiped them on his rumpled shirt. "I thought so. Laile, it's a memory spell. They've blocked all her memories."

Gilly's head jerked up at the same time Laile's did, and their voices overlapped.

"Those *shabuus!*" Laile said.

"A memory *spell?* What do you mean, *spell?* You don't mean, like, witches and wizards and—and—Harry Potter and Gandalf—" Gilly knew she was babbling incoherently. But it didn't matter how coherent or incoherent her thoughts were, because nobody paid her a lick of attention.

"*Laile,*" Gregory said sharply. He narrowed his eyes at her.

A blush crept over Laile's cheeks, though Gilly couldn't see why. But at least Gregory was now staring at somebody other than her. Her awkward-meter relaxed back into "keep an eye out; you're probably the most awkward thing here" land. Gilly reasoned, though, that Laile's blush must have had something to do with whatever a "*shabuu*" was.

"Well, they are," Laile mumbled. Then she gripped Gilly's cheeks and gave them a pinch. The strange, irate bunny-girl brought their faces together until their noses almost touched. Her eyes roamed over Gilly's visage as if looking for a sign of life.

Gilly squealed and tried to struggle away—or even voice her displeasure at being handled like this—but Laile's grip held firm. Gilly's awkward-meter didn't even possess a zone for this level of awkwardness.

Apparently disappointed in her search for intellect, Laile released Gilly with a sigh. The brown-skinned girl gestured to Gilly and raised her eyebrows at Gregory. "Sorry to sound insensitive, but we're really on a time crunch here, Greg. If we made a mistake, or if my brother is playing some elaborate hoax on us, then we've got to locate the *real* Reanna and figure out what to do with this girl." Laile jabbed her finger toward Gilly.

Gilly scowled, though her head burned yet again at the mention of that odd name.

Gregory adjusted his glasses once more. "Ah. I see manners aren't going to be your strong suit today. Really, Gilly, she is a pleasant person if she isn't stressed."

Laile muttered something under her breath—Gilly didn't catch it, but she wondered if it was another maybe-swear word like "*shabuu.*" Laile started to pace and tugged on her long brown hair. She muttered to herself while Gregory watched her, looking slightly bemused with a half-smile on his face, though Laile seemed oblivious.

"We've got to fix this memory spell, Greg. Try it. Please," Laile said.

"And what are you going to do?"

"Rewrite another song in my head until I can figure out how I'm going to tell my father—and the rest of the Council—that my idiot brother switched our missives and got us the wrong girl."

"It's only *somewhat* plausible she's the wrong girl. Let me at least try and break the memory spell before we jump to any conclusions."

"Ugh. This is *just* my luck. They're supposed to write about my adventures in future history books, not my *mis*adventures!" Laile swung her arm out and gestured to Gilly. "How am I supposed to start my rise to fame if I accidentally mistook this frizzy-haired crybaby for the *legendary* Princess Reanna?"

Gilly grasped the end of her hair, just a tad bit curious about what it looked like. Unruly, curly, blonde, and, most importantly, ripe for chewing. She plopped it in her mouth, a good replacement for her sweatshirt sleeve.

Gregory turned away from Laile, that half-smile on his face again. "You're making a wonderful first impression, Laile."

Gilly didn't have the heart to point out that he certainly wasn't making that good of an impression, either. "Excuse me. I asked what a—uh—" Gilly's voice cut off as Gregory once more put his hands over her temple.

Gilly didn't care what deity was out there, as long as they answered her prayers for a giant sinkhole, meteor, or sporadic heart attack to kill her—anything to get out of this moment. Unfortunately, death didn't come, so she was forced to endure unbearable embarrassment as Gregory let out a loud exclamation, drew back, and shook his hands as if they were burned.

"Gregory!" Laile's blue eyes widened, and she looked ready to fawn over him. Gregory rubbed his palms together and winced.

"I'm fine." He shook his head. "It's just an extremely powerful memory block. It repelled me at every angle—no, stop fussing, Laile. I'm fine. My reversal spell just backfired is all."

Gilly pursed her lips. She'd been ignored and manhandled without any answers for long enough. "Excuse me! *Reversal spell?* Can someone please tell me what's going on?" Her anxiety increased with each unanswered question. If she didn't get some answers soon, she might just spontaneously combust in a giant fireball of nerves.

Laile and Gregory disregarded her once more, even when Gilly wedged herself between the two. Or…well, it was more of a wedge that respected personal boundaries, something that Gilly actually valued—unlike them. What really ended up happening was Gilly stood self-consciously about a foot away from both of them and gnawed on her hair as she waited for them to acknowledge her.

"All right, so give me the options if you can't reverse it," Laile said, instead of saying what really needed to be said: "*Oh, I'm sorry, Gilly. Of course, I'll answer all your burning questions!*"

"I'm saying, it will at least take my grandmother's magic, which would mean we've got to either find funds for a dragon ship ride to Reggeria—a *long* one, but still our fastest option—buy a magic carpet, walk, get on a bus, or find some other mode of transportation."

What Gregory really should have said, in Gilly's opinion, was: "*I'm sorry for putting my hands on your forehead and making you feel incredibly uncomfortable. Let me make it up to you by explaining all this gibberish to you.*"

But he didn't, so Gilly muttered, "Why don't we teleport?"

She was so used to being ignored that it startled her when Laile answered, in full seriousness, "Right now, only the elves can teleport, and nobody else has figured out how to do it. Just this week, some poor wizard ended up with half his body on some island and half in Simit. I don't know about you, but I prefer both halves of my body attached."

The blood drained from Gilly's face. Somehow, getting an answer was worse than being ignored.

Laile continued as if she hadn't just scarred Gilly for life. "What kind of timeline are we looking at?"

"Too many variables to predict, honestly," Gregory replied. "But we'll need a few days of travel—maybe three or four days if you count the round trip. Factor in however long it might take to break this spell, and, well...worst-case scenario might be a month, though I will admit I'm allowing myself to be a pessimist with that estimate."

"Sorry—I don't think you heard me," Gilly said. "What's a spell?"

Laile stopped her quiet singing long enough to voice her opinions. "We can't do that. By then, Atlantean troops might march farther inland, and their *sha*—I mean, their *queen* threatened to start executing elves if Reanna isn't returned to her soon. Give me a second option."

Gregory took off his glasses, peered at them, and began to clean them. Laile continued to sing under her breath.

Gilly cleared her throat. Maybe they had just forgotten her existence.

Gregory replaced his spectacles on his face. "Well, I have another thought, but you're not going to like it much. We need your mother's alchemy library, and maybe even her skill if I can't mix the correct antidote. Going back home will save us quite a few days of travel time."

He gestured to his left, past the row of trees. Gilly's eyes widened as she glimpsed the hints of a vast city far beyond: curling towers, tall, rounded buildings made of glass, and even what looked to be a giant clock tower, or maybe a bell tower. There were a few hills and trees in between, but a sprawling civilization lay at the heart of the valley.

A tiny breath of awe escaped her lips. This didn't remind her of any city she'd seen in person—but then again, she couldn't remember ever visiting *any* city, small or large, before. However, this one looked like a child's fairy tale come to life, or some idyllic British or German fantasy.

She would not be surprised if a cat in a top hat walked by holding a briefcase.

Laile had fallen quiet. When Gilly turned around, the tall, caramel-skinned girl stood with her hands over her eyes, her mouth twisted in a grimace. It took her another few seconds to speak, and when she did, it sounded like she might cry. "I'm so sick of relying on my parents for *everything*. I *need* to do this on my own. If I just slink back home to *Mommy* and *Daddy*, just like always, and the press catches wind of it—which you *know* they will, because those stupid gossip rags *hate* my dad and therefore me by association— then I could be stripped of my guardianship. *Years* of training— Greg, I've wanted to be nothing else since I was seven. I slaved my entire life for this, worked almost twelve hours a day for who-knows-how-many years…"

"You must have been quite a dedicated seven-year-old." At least one bright side of being ignored whilst having a mental breakdown was that Gilly could give smart-aleck commentary without having to apologize. It was almost like watching a TV show or movie. Although part of her did want to try and deck somebody, just to see if someone would finally pay attention to her.

"I just don't want everything I've done so far to be worthless or for people to think I'm a failure," Laile continued.

"You're not a failure or worthless. We're only eighteen, and this is your first guardianship assignment. There's no way we could know everything out of the gate. Even adults don't know *everything*." Gregory's voice almost sounded soft for a moment, instead of the know-it-all tone he'd been using. He quickly remedied that before he went on, though, and fiddled once more with his glasses, which couldn't have been dirty already. "We didn't intend for anything to happen this way, but this mind-spell block is something we can't undo by ourselves. You're only a failure if you're too prideful to ask for help."

Laile let out a long groan. "I swear, if this is all Kal's doing…but you're right. I guess we'll have to go back."

Gilly plastered a smile on her face, her shoulders tense, everything in her wound up. "Great! Now that that's taken care of, can someone please treat me like I'm a real person and tell me what's going on? What are spells, what's alchemy, why does it look like I'm in some Ghibli storyboard, and where in the world is Reggeria?"

With that, Gilly shoved her sleeve back into her mouth and chomped down. She wished she could bite something—or some*one*—else at that moment.

Laile slowly lowered her hands from her eyes. "Oh, sorry. I'm so stupid. Hope you weren't flipping out too much. Must be really weird to not remember anything."

Gilly gave a thin-lipped smile, which she hoped adequately masked her inner desire to scream. "Nah, absolutely cool. This happens to me every Tuesday."

Laile clucked her tongue and yet again ignored the sarcastic remark. Instead, she pointed to the greenery around them and then to the city far-off in the distance. "Welcome to Gaia, Gilly."

CHAPTER 4

GILLY

GAIA: DISTRICT OF CAPITAL CITY

G*aia.*

A flash shocked Gilly's head as if a star were exploding within her mind. She gasped, fell to the ground, and clutched her ears as she suppressed the urge to rock back and forth. "Don't say that word. Please. Not that word, and not the name of that…that other girl, either. It hurts. It hurts so much," Gilly sobbed.

Laile dropped to her knees beside Gilly and rubbed her back. Gilly shuddered and looked up in time to see Laile and Gregory exchange worried glances.

"I think the spell may have messed with her brain a little too much." Laile tried to force a laugh and failed. "I hope it didn't…uh…you know, jiggle some important parts loose."

Gregory shook his head. "I don't think so."

Apparently, he was unable to comprehend humor—even Gilly could tell Laile had lamely attempted to lighten the mood, and *she* had amnesia.

"I believe she's mentally stable, Laile," Gregory said. At least *he* didn't assume Gilly had irreversible damage. "I would say the name Ga—well, of our world—suddenly awakened a harsh, subconscious memory, which tried to spring forward. Which means that Gilly has memories of this place more than likely, and that she *could* be R—*the other girl.*"

He crouched down beside them, but he didn't touch her—thank goodness. That was about the last thing that Gilly needed when she thought she might explode from the inside out.

Gregory studied her. "But the memory spell suppressed it, which would trigger an extreme reaction to prevent the remembrance of said strong memory."

Though her head still throbbed, Gilly doubted she could have understood what Gregory meant even if she wasn't in debilitating pain.

"But why didn't it work when we said the name of the princess?" Laile asked. "She only freaked out when we said—well, you know."

"If I had to guess? There might be an element of fear involved. If she *is* the princess, then she wouldn't fear her own name. But she might fear this world." Gregory shrugged. "Of course, that theory works if she's this Gilly girl, too. If she's only heard of the princess in passing, then the memories triggered by it would be smaller, and, therefore, less fear-filled."

"If you are the girl we're looking for, then I don't really blame you for having such a strong reaction to Ga—uh, this dimension," Laile whispered. "I wouldn't want to hear the name again either."

Laile still rubbed the curve of Gilly's spine. Though she trembled like a newborn deer, Gilly managed to stand by propping herself up on Laile. The wind buffeted Gilly and the long strands of grass at her feet. The group stood on the crest of a hill, one that would have afforded an excellent picnic spot with a scenic view in better circumstances.

Circumstances that didn't involve being kidnapped, manhandled, and confused.

Gilly's knees buckled under her, but, as waif-like as Laile seemed, the girl managed to hold Gilly up with little effort. "Please...I...I just don't understand, and nobody will explain anything."

Not to mention that her head still felt like a supernova. And she had thought the darkness was bad.

"Understand what? Memory spells? It's simple spellcaster knowledge."

Gilly gritted her teeth at Gregory's know-it-all tone. She wanted to snap at him: *Oh, and I'm supposed to know "simple spellcaster knowledge" when I wouldn't even know my own name if I didn't have a bracelet on? I'm not stupid; I just can't remember!*

But since she couldn't say that, she took her anger out on herself instead. She grabbed a fistful of her blonde curls and yanked. "No, it's not the...uh, 'science' of memory spells. It's the fact that they exist at all. That any of this..." She gestured to the landscape, to the city that looked so picturesque and beautiful with the tips of gothic steeples that towered above the trees, and then to Laile and Gregory specifically. "...actually exists. How can magic exist?"

"Ugh. I feel sick." Laile groaned. "You'd think that the real Reanna—" Gilly moaned, and Laile corrected herself. "Whoops. Uh, *the other girl* would at least have some knowledge of magic."

"Unless all her memories are being blocked," Gregory deadpanned.

Laile snorted, though she still sounded miserable. But the title of most miserable belonged to Gilly, not Laile.

"All right, you got me. Fine. Yes. Unless the memory spell, which means I've got to stop dragging my feet and head back to—" She paused, and her eyes flickered between Gilly and Gregory. "Uh, *home.*"

27

Gregory nodded. "Fair enough. Come on. I'll fly with Gilly."

"Oh, no! I am not flying *anywhere* with *anyone!*" Gilly backed away and held out her hands, as if that could stop whatever voodoo curse he might put on her to fly. She almost tripped down the hill but managed to steady herself before she fell, rolled, and smashed into the trees below. "I just want to go to my home, wherever that is, and I want to remember my life…"

Laile reached out to pat Gilly's arm once more. Now that she'd recovered from the exploding-head sensation, Gilly backed away again and hoped Laile would get the hint: *hands off.*

"Listen, that's what we want, too." Laile's voice sounded cloyingly sweet. "We're going to help you recover your true name and all your memories. Besides, there's no way to get you home now." Laile gave a comforting smile, as if announcing to someone that they'd never see their home again was akin to telling them there was a great sports game on TV.

Gilly squeaked as she tried to think of how to react to that. Part of her was angry and demanded that she argue until she was sent home, but the other part of her wanted to melt into a puddle of tears. The war was so strong inside her that neither side won out, so she simply stood there like an idiot, mouth agape, eyes wide. That, of course, did nothing to counteract their Gilly.exe-is-not-responding theory.

Laile clucked her tongue. If she'd been a Southern woman, that would have been followed by a good-old-fashioned "bless your heart." She reached for a strand of Gilly's hair, but Gilly managed to dodge that by shoving all her wild locks behind her ear just in time.

"I didn't mean it as cruelly as it sounded, promise. We'll get you home; we just…can't…right now." Laile sighed and shifted from one foot to the other. "You can't cross the border between dimensions without elven magic. *Certain people* used the enslaved elves to hop to Earth to get you, but we don't have that option."

Laile gave Gregory the side-eye—maybe she wanted him to jump in—but when he didn't pipe up, she continued. "It's a long story, and since you don't have any memories of...*this place*...it's nearly impossible to explain. But don't worry, because we're going to fix you up a brew that will have you back to your old self, and then I'll explain everything. Promise."

"You keep acting like I'll magically have memories of 'this place' as soon as you 'fix' me!" Gilly snapped. Once her angry side had its day in the sun, though, the weepy side took back over. "What if I'm not Re—" Gilly winced. "I mean—*that girl*? Will you just send me into the wilds of a world that I don't know, completely lost?" She gestured back to the city beyond the forest, with all its quaint-but-terrifying beauty in its mixture of historic and modern architecture.

"No!" Laile protested, but from the way she squirmed, Gilly knew that Laile had no idea what to do if Gilly wasn't truly this Reanna girl.

"We're wasting time debating variables like this," Gregory muttered. "Right now, I've got to put these soldiers into the cage, lock them up until we can send for Council guards to arrest them, *and* charm the door so they can't get out. If I don't, they might wake up, and then it won't matter if you're Reanna or Gilly. They'll kidnap you and take you straight to Queen Arana *again* either way."

Queen Arana.

Gilly gasped as a shiver slid down her spine. Her brain convulsed. Sparks flashed inside her head and exploded in her vision. She reeled forward and lost whatever she had consumed as of late— although she couldn't exactly remember what that had been, either, and there was no way to tell in its current form.

Laile squealed and hoisted Gilly upwards before she fell face-first into her own vomit. Gregory snatched her away and peeled her eyelids back like a doctor to examine her. Gilly moaned and leaned into him.

Laile slid her arms through Gilly's armpits to secure her in place, murmuring soft things that Gilly couldn't hear and that wouldn't make a difference, anyway. She felt as if her mind was a tottering gymnast on a balance beam, and the only semi-coherent thought she could latch onto was that Laile currently sparkled like a diamond. Maybe she used a really shimmery lotion.

Someone shifted in front of her—Gregory? But a blurry, faded-out version of Gregory. Was he near? Or was he actually a mile away? She couldn't tell anymore… "I don't—we need a doctor, Laile! Something's wrong!"

Laile squeaked. "I bet it's the mind spell! She probably has horrible memories of Queen Arana, and—"

Gilly shrieked. Someone screamed, and someone else barked orders, but Gilly's head was too fuzzy to make heads or tails of anything before she drowned in her pain.

CHAPTER 5

LAILE

GAIA: DISTRICT OF CAPITAL CITY

L aile sat in the middle of her mother's alchemy room, bored out of her mind as she flipped through yet another useless, ancient tome. Times like these made her wish she had paid a teensy bit more attention in her parents' alchemy lessons. But every time she tried to brew anything, she only caused another infamous "Incident." Like the whole debacle when she was ten, where she'd attempted to cure her common cold—only to magically enhance it to pneumonia. She'd spent a stint in the hospital as the doctors tried to reverse it. But the true masterpiece occurred when twelve-year-old Laile transformed herself into a bird and had to squawk at everything for two whole days while her parents, Damien and Cynerra Úlfur, tried to undo the charms.

Yes, after the "Incidents," Laile's desire for learning alchemy had been dampened somewhat. Not to mention that she was consistently outshone by many of her siblings and Gregory, so it seemed only natural that she would take the hint and focus on her true talents—which included bossing other people around, hence why she became a guardian.

Still, maybe she shouldn't have given up, if only because she might have been a better help now.

Laile slammed her latest book closed and flopped onto her back with a groan. Hindsight was always 20/20, as Laile's friend Aimee always said. Apparently, that was one of the many Earth colloquialisms that Aimee learned on her vacations there.

"Hey, Gregory...I'm hungry. Want a snack?" She stretched her hand toward where he stood hunched over a book. Laile's mother, Cynerra Úlfur, had been adamant that she had a reversal potion for the memory block. But as for where it was... She'd shoved that job off to Gregory and told him if he'd paid attention during her decade of tutoring, he wouldn't have an issue.

Translation: Cynerra couldn't navigate her own mess and didn't want to be bothered.

"I'm fine." He shut *Fennwick's Alchemic Cures, Volume III* in frustration. "Your mother is a mess, though."

There was a reason that Cynerra was world-renowned for her alchemy skills and not her organizational skills. There was not one clue to what was in any single volume in the library, and most of the books weren't even on shelves but stacked in precarious piles around the room. Oh, yes, they could have bought *updated* spell books, complete with appendixes at any time, but Cynerra's hand-me-down collection held too many memories for Laile's parents.

Laile had dared to buy her mother a newer spell book once. Cynerra had flipped through all the spells, declared she knew them already, and, what—did Laile think Great-Uncle Tomas' copy of *Flamel's Book of Brews* wasn't good enough? Hand-copied and autographed by Nicolas Flamel himself, personalized notes in the margins—

Suffice to say, Cynerra preferred older things, which was why she'd married an older man, too.

Gregory growled under his breath—not nearly as impressive as Laile's growl, though, since his father was a wizard, not a werewolf.

"Ugh. I'm going to throw something if your mother doesn't take an organizational class soon."

Funnily enough, Gregory could be just as much of a slob as Cynerra half the time, but Laile didn't dare say so. He probably wouldn't take kindly to the truth of that suggestion.

Instead, she patted his arm. "Hey, I'm just as frustrated as you, but that's why we both need a snack break before we kill each other. Or worse, my mom."

Gregory raised his eyebrows. Laile sucked in a breath as she met his dark brown eyes. Oh, flying fig-whits—she wouldn't give herself away now. She wouldn't blush, she wouldn't giggle...

To conceal her emotions, she shrank down into her fairy form—the thumb-sized, crystallized version of herself. She flittered over to Gregory's shoulder, careful to keep a hold of his hair so she didn't lose her balance. In all honesty, safety was only *part* of the reason she grabbed his soft curls.

"Still," Gregory muttered. "I can't believe your father lets Cynerra get away with this mess. The Úlfur family libraries were world-famous before your mother came along."

Laile giggled. "Dad says he can have neatness or he can have his Little Tyrant, and there's only one he can't live without."

Gregory grumbled some more things about the mess under his breath, grabbed another thick tome, and heaved it onto the wooden podium. Laile fluttered up to the top of his head and stretched out, her chin balanced on her palms, her feet crossed behind her.

She scanned the page Gregory was reading, but none of it looked important. Most of these seemed medicinal in use—to cure colds or the flu (Laile shuddered in remembrance of the "Incident"), fevers, aches, bumps, rashes, or any physical ails—but none for a memory spell.

"This doesn't make any sense," Gregory said. "Mermaids have water-related magic. No Atlantean can conjure a memory spell on

their own—that ability belongs solely to the witches and wizards…
Or, theoretically, someone well-versed in alchemy and potions."

Laile sat up straighter. "So what? You mean there's a sorceress
or warlock working for Queen Arana?"

"More than likely, since most alchemists tend to be
spellcasters anyway. Not that there aren't exceptions, as your mother
proves."

"Although…what if it's the Council's spy? The one that told us
about the plans to abduct Reanna? They could have been forced to do it."

Gregory rubbed his temple. "Well…I suppose that *could* be it.
But that spell seemed…I don't know. Don't laugh. It just seemed like
that spell fought me—like it held some malicious will. From the
sheer strength of the spell, and my own gut feelings, I'd wager Arana
has an exceedingly powerful spellcaster on her side. Which leaves us
with either a sorceress, warlock, or *possibly* an elf that's sided with
them to escape a concentration camp."

"Great. That's great." Laile sighed, but when Gregory flipped
another page, added, "I don't think you'll find the reversal spell in
there. That's more for pharmaceutical purposes."

Gregory slammed the book closed with more force than was
necessary and carried it back over to the shelf.

"Someone's getting hangry. Bet the snack is sounding good
right about now," Laile teased. She clung on tighter to his curls.
"What's really wrong, Gregory?"

He shuffled through other tomes instead of answering
immediately. After he picked one, he put it on the podium and
relented. "I'm worried, Laile. What if…if this Gilly isn't Reanna?
What if the girl slobbering in her sleep in your guest bedroom has no
clue about Reanna or Arana or…anything? Or what if she is, and she
doesn't give one flying fig-whit about stopping the war?"

"Well—if she *is* the wrong girl, think about this. No one else
will know except you, me, and whoever we choose to tell. Not Arana.

Either way, all we've got to do is convince her to care enough to help us free the elves." Laile's voice dropped to a whisper just in case her parents came in. "And we've got to get her to care enough so that, if the Council rules that we're not to put her in any danger, she'll side with us and consider a few more…*legally questionable* options." Laile nodded. "And how can she not care about stopping the war? If anyone has a reason to hate Queen Arana, it would be Reanna. Besides, I'm sure she'll have a heart of gold."

"She ran away. Abandoned us all." Gregory's flat tone portrayed just how much faith he put into Laile's Council-ordained ward.

Laile bristled and gave one curl a swift tug. True, she didn't know Reanna—or Gilly—personally, but Laile remembered all too clearly hearing her parents discuss the newspapers when she was seven. She remembered the gossip about how the mermaids were cruel and their young princess had run away due to—well, speculations went a little wild there. But no matter the veracity of all the stories and rumors, it hadn't mattered. The stories had solidified Reanna as a hero to the continent of Solis and given Laile a new direction in life: she wanted to be a Council-ordained guardian so she could help people like Reanna.

"She didn't *abandon* anyone. She was six! If you ask me, she was quite a strong person to run away at such a delicate age."

"Any child can run away. Most typically do. That doesn't mean they're strong. It just means they're…pigheaded." Gregory flipped another page, and Laile could sense the anxiousness that oozed out of him, no matter how much he tried to cover it with a calm demeanor.

Gregory, calling someone else pigheaded? That certainly was the dragon pointing out the fairy's wings. Laile rolled her eyes; she absolutely hated him when he acted like this.

Or did she love him? Yes, she definitely loved him…and hated him. Flying fig-whits, why did her heart do such strange flips around him?

"You're not just upset about this memory spell, are you?" Laile twirled one of his curls around her arm.

He responded with nothing but silence, but it was the kind of silence that spoke volumes.

"Gregory—"

"Here it is!" His exclamation dissolved the tension and sent Laile toppling off his head. She flapped her wings to slow her descent and transformed into her full-sized body. She staggered as her feet hit the ground and flapped her wings to try and balance herself. Once she'd successfully avoided falling on her face, her wings disappeared into her back until she needed them next and she stuck her tongue out at Gregory.

"You found it? Where? Can I see?" Laile attempted to wedge herself between him and the station.

Gregory bustled off to gather ingredients. "Can you tell your mom I found it? I'll need her help now."

Ah, errands. How romantic. Forget any love—she utterly hated him. Laile glared at his back as he sorted through the cabinets, working at an impassioned pace. It would be *so* nice if one of those heavy bottles on the top shelf conveniently fell on his head.

But as he came back, arms filled to the brim with ingredients and a half-grin on his face, Laile forgot her plans for revenge. Ugh— those dimples. Why hadn't he asked her out already?

Gregory edged her out of the alchemy station so he could lay the ingredients down. He muttered an *ignis* spell underneath his breath and lit the half-melted candles which rested on the seven prongs that jutted out of the main table. He dumped the first bit of water into the self-heating black cauldron that rested to the side— the *only* new-fangled update Cynerra had made to Great-Uncle Tomas' alchemist station. She'd allowed safety over family heirlooms just that once, for her own children's sake (not to mention the fire codes in their penthouse).

"Right, right. I get it. I'm no longer needed. I'll go get Mom, check on Gilly, and get some snacks." She ruffled his hair, which garnered her a noncommittal and distracted grunt.

She rolled her eyes and went into the family room.

There, her brothers, Mionos and Kal, sat and debated the Council's recent announcement to fund an expedition to colonize the land of Fiastro, an inhospitable desert that boasted the highest temperatures on the continent of Solis—and also the most exotic creatures. At one time, explorers had freely trekked in and out to capture, poach, or kill the animals, but after a series of "Fiastro Fiascoes," as the public dubbed them, the Council banned expeditions in order to protect the indigenous species.

Not to mention to protect the explorers themselves; far too many had never come back.

"It's absolutely not worth it. There are azernos and night lurkers there—and that's just the creatures we know about," Mionos remarked. "I've also heard theories that there are cannibalistic centaurs out there. Maybe even the last remaining unicorn population." He lounged on the couch as he played catch-the-fireball by himself. The flame sputtered and evaporated, though, when a giant black blur leapt on Mionos' stomach. He yelped as their unidentifiable pet, Whisper, stretched out on him.

Whisper had been their mother's childhood pet, although he showed no signs of age in his strange body. He looked like a jaguar by Earth standards, or so said Aimee, but was too tiny to be a jaguar and too big to be a house cat. He was merely Whisper.

Whisper kneaded his oddly-small paws into Mionos' stomach, and Mionos grumbled, trying to shove the animal off. But Whisper was a very persistent, though indeterminate, animal and wouldn't be moved.

Laile plopped into her mother's rocking chair. Even if her alchemy skills lacked refinement, her eavesdropping skills did not.

"That's exactly why there needs to be a colony there! Imagine the adventure. Finally, a region that can be explored—just like in the old days. The danger makes it that much more exciting," Kal said. He seemed to be having a makeshift fencing battle with an imaginary enemy. He hopped back and forth and lunged every few seconds, probably at an invisible cannibalistic centaur. Though the third-oldest sibling, Kal already had several inches on both Mionos and Laile. But the most disgusting part about her younger brother had to be that he was unquestionably a local heartthrob.

Laile almost threw up the first time she'd overheard some girls whispering about his black, tousled hair, "dreamy" dark eyes, and tawny skin.

Mionos rolled his dark brown eyes at their brother's words. Thank goodness *he* was more awkward and gangly and resembled Cynerra, since they both had paler skin. To top it off, he'd dyed his hair a questionable orangish-red color. All of this worked against him and kept Laile from having *two* heartthrob brothers. She'd sooner die, honestly.

"It's a death mission. Azernos can shapeshift into anything, centaurs might boil you for breakfast, and night lurkers can kill you in your dreams. There's a reason it's been off-limits for so long. You know. The 'Fiastro Fiascoes.'" Mionos almost missed a catch, yelped, and rolled off the couch to grab the fireball before it could singe the curtains.

"You're a complete bore." Kal must have lost his fencing match because he flopped backward. He stretched his legs out and took the form of a silver-and-black wolf.

"If you shed on the carpet, Mom will ground you," Laile warned her younger brother. "And, for your information, I'd send you *both* to Fiastro—especially if you switched the missives on me, Kal. And *then* I'd turn your rooms into closets. Or, no! Maybe a hot tub and sauna. Yeah, that'll work."

Kal's voice came out gravelly in his wolf form. "I *told* you already. I didn't switch those stupid missives!"

"Yeah, well, I guess we'll see about that when she wakes up, hmm?" Laile flicked her thumb under her chin at him, a rude gesture she never would have attempted had their parents been around.

"You little—" Kal began.

"Sorry, no time to chit-chat. Have to go get Mom, check on Reanna, and claim snacks for the two of us doing the truly important work in the alchemy room." Laile blew him a kiss.

Kal said something—probably tried to finish an ill-attempt at a retort—but Laile ignored it as she had learned to do in the past sixteen years he had been alive. She crossed the room and opened the door to the guest bedroom, where her comatose rescue slumbered.

Looked like Gilly—or Reanna, whichever—didn't need her, either.

Oh, well.

Laile still needed to find her mom—and fetch those snacks, the most urgent thing a guardian could ever possibly do.

CHAPTER 6

REANNA

UNKNOWN: ???

There was the faint sound of singing. It rose and ebbed as one perfect voice before it separated into two distinct ones. Melody and harmony sang a tune that sounded whimsical yet beautiful.

But there was no color in this world. There was only a deep, worrisome blackness. There were no forms, no images, no dreams to grab hold of.

Then the tune began to form words, which chased away the darkness.

"Well, the old black cat
With his feet so flat
Took the bread from the woman down the street
Now he eats and eats and eats and eats
Only thinking about his treat."

The music dissolved into laughter, cut abruptly off as the world descended back into the void.

Where did the music go? Would it come back? There must be *something* besides this abyss…

And then the world tilted and dissolved into a warm underwater world, a dream—or maybe a dream of a memory.

"Reanna? Reanna, come here."

A much smaller version of Reanna inched forward. Dread seeped into her soul as she swam the familiar "hallway of shame." Portraits of Reanna's great-great-great-grandmas frowned down at her. They seemed just as angry at Reanna as the female guards, who sneered at her as she passed. Sometimes, the guards would also make faces behind her back or pull her hair. They even took her toys when she wasn't looking—although Reanna had no proof that she didn't merely misplace them. Still, she was pretty sure the scary soldiers didn't like her. Even at five years old, she knew that much.

Reanna glanced up from the floor only for a second to look down the wide hallway at her mother. Arana lounged on her throne, rapping out a tune with her long nails against the seashell that formed its right arm.

"Did you forget the rules, Reanna?" Queen Arana asked, her voice as cold as the waters when it was time to sleep. "You ran away from your nurse at bedtime and tried to come into the ballroom." Arana's blonde hair floated in the water, curling around her face and adding to her vicious visage. It looked like a *very* scary ghost, like one in the nighttime story that the guards told from the book that they said not to tell Mama about.

Reanna stuck her thumb in her mouth until a soldier slapped it away. Mama always tried to break Reanna's "childish habit" of putting things in her mouth. Still, the princess managed to tug at her lip with her index finger. "I wanted to see the party, Mama…"

The guard slapped her hand again, so Reanna twisted her fingers together. It just wasn't the same without them in her mouth, though. Her bottom lip trembled, and she glanced down so that her blonde hair covered her face like a curtain of shame. "I'm sorry I disobeyed the rules."

Queen Arana tapped the arm of her chair louder and quicker. "Your insolence shouldn't be tolerated. I should have you banished. You disobeyed a direct order from your queen."

Reanna whimpered. Though she didn't exactly know what *insolence* and *tolerated* meant, she knew they were bad. After all, if she should be banished—which was what happened to the prince who killed his father in a fairy tale the guards read—they had to be bad.

"But I'm feeling generous today," Arana continued.

Reanna didn't know what *generous* meant, either, but it must have also been bad, because *generous* hurt as her mother struck Reanna's blonde head. Reanna collapsed to the floor, but her finger couldn't even make it into her mouth before Arana grabbed her hair and wrenched her upward so that they were face to face. Reanna squeaked, her tail flapping in the water as she tried to escape.

"Do not disobey me! Do you understand? Do you want to be an insolent brat?"

Reanna shook her head and stuck her thumb in her mouth again. Arana swatted it away with a huff. She rolled her eyes upward, releasing Reanna, who quickly swam to her mother's tail and wrapped herself around the fins as the mermaid queen flicked it back and forth.

"You're so...so frustrating, Reanna." The queen paused before she added: "You're so *stupid*."

"Okay," Reanna whispered—she understood *stupid*, at least.

She clung to her mother's tail, even though the sharp scales sliced into her hands. But she didn't want to let go. Not until her mama loved her again, even if she was stupid and in-cents-lent.

Queen Arana heaved a sigh that sounded like she was very, very sleepy. Then she reached down and began to pet her daughter's hair. "Why do you vex me, Reanna? Do you enjoy hurting me?"

"No! I would never hurt you!" Shameful tears bubbled up in Reanna's eyes, but the ocean took them away before they rolled down her cheeks. She stuck her finger back in her mouth. Arana grunted and yanked it back out, her face twisted up in a sneer the whole time—lip curled, eyes narrowed.

Reanna dipped her head. "I didn't mean to veck you, Mama."

Queen Arana snorted, as close to a laugh as she usually got. "Then why aren't you a good girl, Reanna? I wish you would just be a good girl. And stop putting your finger in your mouth or I'll take away your toys." Arana pried Reanna's finger out yet again. "You look so foolish when you do that. It's not proper for a princess."

"I'll try to be a good girl, Mama, really! I love you so, so much!"

Reanna clung to Arana's tail tighter until the queen pried her off. Reanna expected to be sent back to her room, but, to her surprise, Queen Arana opened her arms. Reanna's eyes grew wide, and she rushed toward her mother to tackle her in a hug. Arana stroked Reanna's hair and tilted her tiny chin upward. Mama was so pretty—so why did everybody always say Reanna was so ugly? Both Reanna and her mama had blonde hair, the same oval faces and the same gray-green eyes. Maybe the pieces of her daddy made her ugly—that was why nobody liked her. Some mean lady had once said Reanna's nose was just a little too round and her face a little too chubby.

"I believe you, and I really hope you will be a good girl." Arana twisted a lock of Reanna's hair around her finger. "Don't disobey me again."

"I won't, Mama. Do you still love me?" Reanna clutched at Arana's dress.

"Yes, of course I love you." Queen Arana patted Reanna's head, but she didn't smile. Still, her words warmed Reanna's heart and made her feel fuzzy inside. She had retained her mother's love for another day, a prize in itself.

No matter what, Reanna would make sure to always be a good girl. Then her mother would always love her.

CHAPTER 7

LAILE

GAIA: DISTRICT OF CAPITAL CITY

Cynerra Úlfur watched as Gregory mixed the ingredients together in her cauldron, a pensive look on her face.

Laile sidled up to her mother. "Did you look at Gilly? What did you think?"

Cynerra's blue eyes flickered over to Laile. "I think I trust your assessment. If you say this is necessary, then I'm going to believe you. You're nearly nineteen, not to mention a Council-ordained guardian. Mom's only here to make sure nothing blows up and we don't have any more Incidents." Cynerra wrapped one arm around Laile's shoulders and pulled her close.

Laile popped another nut into her mouth and chewed with a bit more fervor. Being a young adult had to be the most confusing time in a person's life. She could never quite balance the need for her parents' approval with the desire to be independent and separate from them.

The only solution? Eat some more snacks and hope that one day she wouldn't feel like such a little girl, determined to prove herself to a world that seemed against her more often than not thanks to her heritage.

"Laile, can you grab me that mashed flower over there, please?" Gregory scooted his glasses up his nose and gestured to a bowl on the other end of the wooden alchemy table.

"Flowers, snacks...anything else you want me to fetch? I mean, I did take *several* years of extensive schooling to become an official guardian. I'm sure I could at least run some errands for you." Laile dumped the contents of the container into the cauldron...and some berries into Gregory's mouth.

"You want to take over?" Gregory mumbled through the mess in his mouth.

"Uh, no thank you. I'd rather not give myself pneumonia or turn into a bird. Both of those things make it rather hard to dethrone a despot—which is what I *want* to do right now. But since we've got all these boring little odds and ends to accomplish first, I guess I'll stay here and be an overqualified and under-appreciated errand girl." Laile thumped him on the back and returned to her mother's side, right as her father peeked his dark head into the library/alchemist station.

"I'm home," he announced. "I got your message on the witch's stone—"

"*Daddy!*" Laile shoved the rest of her food into her mother's hands and ran into her father's arms.

Forget maturity and her desire to be known as a separate entity from her parents for just a split second. Her dad was home, and she needed to be Daddy's Little Girl for just a second—even if she'd go back to needing her own space once the moment ended.

Laile tackled him and buried her head against her father's brawny chest. She could hear his heartbeat from this angle, and all the important things she'd had to discuss died on her lips. Cynerra Úlfur loved to tell stories about how whenever she needed her persnickety, colicky infant daughter to get some sleep, all she had to do was put her on Damien's chest—and the trick still had some magic left in it.

Damien let out a low chuckle. "There's my girl." He stroked her hair. "I told the Council about the newest developments and, of course, requested that they keep this away from the press. They've asked to see Gilly, regardless of who she is, after she wakes up. I told them it would be tomorrow at the earliest so we don't overwhelm her too soon."

Laile nodded. "I'm so sorry this sets us behind. I hope you got in touch with everyone at the rendezvous point and told them not to expect us anytime soon."

"I did that as well. Don't worry. Consider this a break." He smiled down at her and pressed a kiss against her head. "No matter how hard you think a guardian works, you can't run yourself ragged. You don't have to prove anything to your mom or me—or anybody else that truly matters."

Laile grunted. "You should know better than anyone else that's not true, Daddy."

"It's *because* I know better than anyone else that I can say that. I've fought for equal rights and treatment of werewolves for so long, I've learned that the only people you have to prove yourself to are those who want to hold you down." He cupped her golden-amber cheek in his hands, which were a shade or two darker than her own. "Your worth doesn't hinge on whether or not you do everything completely right the first time."

Damien was the first werewolf representative to ever hold a seat on the Council—something he'd fought to achieve for a long time, since some people still felt like werewolves were subhumans.

And Laile, as both part-werewolf and the daughter of two legends in general, had even *more* to prove. She let out a puff of air. How could she explain the pressure of not only living up to her parents' legacies, but also exceeding the expectations of those that wanted her to fail because of her heritage?

"That's right." Cynerra raised a finger in the air. "It's no fun to do everything by-the-books exactly as it's planned. The fun stuff only happens when you cause just a *little* bit of chaos."

Damien cleared his throat and leaned down. "Don't listen to your mother."

"I heard that!" Cynerra flicked his shoulder.

"Of course you did, you Little Tyrant."

Laile elbowed both her parents as she slipped out of her father's embrace. "Okay, you guys. If you're going to make-out, at least have the decency to not do it around me. I don't need to puke on top of everything else."

"Then don't look. Nobody asked your opinion." Cynerra shoved the snacks back at Laile and swatted her daughter's bottom. Then, with a flourish of her hand, Cynerra made a giant wall of water appear from nowhere and froze it solid to separate her and her husband from the other occupants of the room. As a water fairy, Cynerra's powers more closely resembled a mermaid's magic than her daughter's.

But thank goodness for those powers, or else Laile would be forced to endure a *lot* of awkward situations.

"Done!" Gregory stirred the dark-purple liquid around before he dipped a vial into it. "Laile, do you want to do the honors?"

Laile put down her snacks to take it. The bottle was still hot as she twirled it around. "And where exactly do I put it?"

Gregory looked at her blankly. "Clearly, there's only one orifice this is suitable for. You have to get Gilly to drink it."

"You do realize she's still unconscious, right?" Laile snatched a fruit from Gregory's plate of snacks she'd left on the alchemy station.

"I have faith in you. It's definitely medically possible, just so long as you're careful. You don't even need magic."

Laile clucked her tongue. "Fine. I just hope I don't make her choke or something." She glanced over her shoulder at the water wall. "Okay, you two. Whenever you're ready to be adults again, you can come and join us in Reanna's room."

Laile didn't stick around for her parents' answer. Knowing her mom…she could probably imagine what it was anyway.

Gregory fell into step beside her. Laile kept quiet until they were in Reanna's room, safe from the prying eyes and ears of her many siblings and handsy parents. After all, Reanna couldn't overhear—not over the sound of her own snores. "Hey, Dimples. How are you?"

Gregory drifted over to the window. Laile smiled at the scenery their penthouse allowed them. Perhaps her favorite was the beautiful view of Unity Park, right next to the theater. But all of Capital City looked gorgeous. Laile loved the mix of the old and new—sleek, modern high-rises that mingled with historical buildings and steeples that rose into the air. Blessed Composer Church—one of the oldest buildings in the city—boasted a high bell-tower, which still rang out after Sunday morning worship.

Whimsical stone buildings with thatched roofs could be found right next to a glittering, pyramid-shaped museum. The cobblestone streets added an extra layer of beauty, though most spellcasters preferred to travel in the skies or by carpet than on foot.

Lights blazed in all the shops; twinkle lights lit up the trees in Unity Park; the faint sounds of music drifted from the gothic theater down the street.

Laile never wanted to live anywhere else, and she refused to let Arana and Atlantis destroy this precious home.

She waited a few more seconds before she prodded Gregory again. "Hello, Gaia to Dimples? I asked if you were okay."

Gregory cleared his throat. "Oh, sorry. Just sort of lost in thought. What do you mean? I'm not the one unconscious."

"I don't mean that. I just mean…you've been acting really weird lately. Kind of distant. Zoning out frequently. You know, like just now." Laile settled down on the bed and popped the cork off the bottle. Here went nothing.

"I'm fine."

"Lot on your mind or something?"

A bit of the amethyst liquid dribbled out of Reanna's mouth, and Laile hurried to catch it before it stained anything.

"Just a little bit more than usual." Gregory crossed his arms, his back to her. "I overheard a snippet of Kal and Mionos' conversation in the living room just now. The Council Colonization Charter. If you want my opinion, I think it's foolhardy. Do you know how many indigenous creatures could be put at risk if we do that? Not to mention the loss of human life would be astronomical, whether from animals or the high temperatures and dangerous landscape."

Laile rolled her eyes. "There's a few people I'd still like to send. Some of them are my siblings."

Gregory snorted, and while Laile tried to get at least a fair amount of the drink down Gilly's gullet, she mimicked Gregory's voice in a faux-deep tone, which ended up sounding like a clown. "'What about you, Laile? Are you fine?'" She used her normal voice to mime her own. "'Oh, not really. You know, lots of thoughts and feelings about my first mission going haywire, living up to my own expectations, being caught between childhood and adulthood. You know, lots of things like that, which I can gladly elaborate on since you asked me how I am.'"

Laile twisted the vial around some more and tried to get the last few drops past Gilly's strong gag reflex.

"Er—" Gregory turned to face her. "I'm sorry. I don't…I'm not so good at things like that."

Laile couldn't answer, because finally—*finally*—Gilly took a deep breath, and a peaceful expression settled over her features. Laile tucked the empty container into her pocket and relaxed her shoulders. "There. Done. Let's postpone this little heart-to-heart, Greg. Hopefully, Gilly should be waking up soon, and we'll have all the answers we need."

CHAPTER 8

REANNA

UNKNOWN: POSSIBLY—ATLANTIS

Six-year-old Reanna scurried down the hallway, half-crazed with panic. She had to get out of the room, get somewhere safe—get…

"Reanna!" Queen Arana's voice cut through Reanna's panic like a knife that stabbed her straight in the heart. Reanna reacted likewise; she shot straight up and sucked in a breath.

"Reanna, did you shatter my bust in the ballroom?" Arana's tone was as sharp as an icy barb—such a disturbing mix of emotions that it made Reanna shiver, and she couldn't force herself to turn around and look at her mother.

"Yes, Mama," Reanna breathed, so quiet it could have been blamed on a seahorse.

A roaming guard snickered; her face twisted into a sneer as she passed Reanna. Reanna's lip began to tremble, and she bit it so hard it started to bleed. She blinked and touched the skin there. When she withdrew her index finger, a small trickle of blood marred it before the water carried it away. She pressed her finger against her lip in an attempt to quell the bleeding. "What was that, Reanna?" Arana moved forward and rested a heavy hand on Reanna's shoulder. Her fingernails dug into Reanna's skin, but they drew no blood.

"I…um…yes. I'm sorry, I didn't mean to!" Reanna's excuse rushed out in one burst. She paused only to suck in a breath. "I was just pretending that I was dancing, like at the ball you threw last night, only I wasn't allowed to go, so I played pretend that I was allowed to go, and the prince danced *all* night with me, but then as we were twirling—or, I mean, I was twirling—I accidentally hit your bust, and it fell, and I tried to catch it, and I bruised my arm, because it hit my elbow…"

Reanna offered her mother her elbow as a peace treaty of sorts. The aforementioned bruise had already started turning colors, and a tiny, red line descended from it to her wrist, where a jagged piece of marble had cut her during the experience.

"You should not have been in the ballroom at all!" Queen Arana barked as she shoved Reanna's arm away from her.

Reanna's lip quivered. Arana smacked Reanna's bloody finger away from her mouth. "Stop *chewing* on things—I've told you a million times!"

"Yes, Mama." Reanna fidgeted, unable to look her mama in the eye.

"You know the ballroom is off limits, and yet you always insist on being a *bad girl* and doing whatever you please. And another thing…" Queen Arana's eyes flashed, and she leaned in closer. "All men are evil. You should never want to dance with any man. They are cruel, vile things, ready to twist anything pure and good." She with Reanna's hair for a moment. Reanna flinched, though it seemed her mother wasn't going to yank it—Reanna hated it when she did that. It hurt *so* much…

The queen straightened to her full height and took a deep breath. "There is a reason that we've enslaved men for centuries here, Reanna, and you would be wise to learn this before you go dancing with imaginary princes."

Reanna stuck her finger back in her mouth for a second and sucked furiously. All she could think about was how nice the princes were in her books. Suddenly, all the questions she had been holding back tumbled out. "But what about my daddy? Was he bad? Who was he? Do I look like him at all? Where is he now? Why did you allow the men in for the dance? Why were they all really, really scared when they came in? Where did everybody go after the dance? Why couldn't I come? Why—"

"*Reanna!*" Arana shouted. She grabbed Reanna's shoulders and shook her. "Enough of this senseless wondering, child. Yes, you did get one thing from your father—his incredible dimwittedness! You aggravate me to no end."

Arana shoved Reanna backward, and she *thumped* into a wall. Her head absorbed most of the shock, and Reanna's vision spun. Suddenly there were three Arana's, all of them berating Reanna's *dimwittedness*—which was, apparently, just as bad as being *insolent*.

Arana grabbed one of her guards—or were there four or five?— and pointed at Reanna. The guard smirked and hoisted Reanna up. Reanna's head drooped against her chest for a second, and she blinked, trying to clear her vision. Why did her daddy have to be so dumb-witted? Why did she have to be just like him? She just wanted to be a good girl for her mother. It must have been his fault that Reanna couldn't do anything right, because her mama was perfect.

A few tears slid down Reanna's cheeks, and she sniffed and wiped them away. The guard didn't laugh at her, but she didn't let her go, either.

The soldier hauled Reanna up to the second story; Reanna's tail whacked against the walls. She yelled "ouch!" every time it did, but the guard seemed to be deaf. No—that wasn't right. The guard had listened when Arana gave orders. It could only mean that the guard knew how insolent and dumb-witted that Reanna was, too, and didn't like her.

They finally reached the grand double doors that led into Reanna's room. The guard nodded to two others, who opened the doors wide. The first guard tossed Reanna in on the marble floor. She landed right on her hurt elbow and yipped in pain. All the guards laughed, and one slammed the door behind her. Reanna only paused to gain her strength back before she rushed at the door and pulled on the handles.

"Wait! Let me out! Let me out! I don't like it in here! Mama! *Mama*! There's a scary dolphin in my closet!" This was, of course, not a verifiable truth, but that's what the guards always told her.

Outside the door, the guards roared with laughter, and one of them whistled like a dolphin. They were making fun of her—Reanna was about to be gobbled up whole, and they were out there laughing at her.

Reanna continued to beat at the door and screamed until her voice cracked. Then she sank to the floor and cried. She was so dumb-witted, and it was all her daddy's fault. But she really didn't care…. If only he would come, they could at least be dumb-witted together. Maybe her mama would be mad at her daddy instead of her.

Reanna curled up on the floor, poking at her swollen lip. She winced every time she touched it, but at least it wasn't still bleeding. She sniffed and looked up at her window. Atlantis was already lit up for the night, with strings of lights draped from the top of one spiraled building to the other. Some of the prettiest towers were built to resemble conical seashells, and they stood in shades of purple, pink, and turquoise—all of the prettiest colors—with tops made into giant lights to help mermaids see when the water got dark. Mermaids' eyes, her mama said, helped them see in much darker places than the stupid people up on the ground, but they still needed some illumination.

Reanna swam over to the window. Her muscles strained as she struggled to push open the glass. Finally, it gave a little, and she managed to wedge her fingers under the pane to get a better grip. She shoved it upwards and leaned out her window so she could watch the merfolk pass by underneath. None of them paid her much attention, but why would they? She wasn't that important. Especially not compared to the beautiful city they were looking at. There was the park, with all its white columns decorated with multi-colored strings of seashells and lights. Seaweed danced in the currents while an artist carved a piece of coral.

Oh, and the zoo, far past where Reanna could see. But she could imagine all the hippocampi and octopi and all those other funny animals that ended with "i." And Reanna's absolute favorite—the bookstore that looked *so* big and had so many fun books to read, all charmed with spells to make them not get wet.

Reanna sighed as people dallied right under her window but never looked up. She wiggled her fingers at them, but when they didn't respond, she let her hand drop. She wanted to call out to them, to say hello, but every time, she got too nervous. What if they didn't like her either?

The ocean swept away Reanna's tears as they leaked out of her eyes. Sometimes when she cried, she liked to pretend she had an invisible daddy right beside her who wiped away her tears.

Music wafted up from the streets as an orchestra played somewhere in the distance. Mermaids in fancy dresses swam by. They carried magical icy leashes in their hands while they dragged their man-slaves behind them—just like the men that had come to Mama's ball. The mermen swam along, their heads always low, and they never looked up. It made Reanna sad to think that maybe her daddy had been one of those men once.

She stuck her finger in her mouth. One of the man-slaves lagged behind a bit, and his mistress whirled around and jerked on the leash. Her voice sounded angry as she berated him—right before she made an icy whip with her free hand.

"Stop!" Reanna shrieked as the woman brought the whip down against the man's bare shoulder.

The man didn't make a sound, but Reanna's sobs increased into hysterics. She covered her face; she didn't want to see it, didn't want to hear that awful noise of the ice slapping and tearing at the poor man-slave's skin. She knew what it felt like, and her shoulders started to tingle as she remembered her own punishments.

Why was everybody in Atlantis so mean? Nobody, nobody, *nobody* was ever nice to people, unlike in the storybooks Reanna read.

She turned around so quickly that she bumped her arm against her bedpost. Her bottom lip quivered as she looked at the blood seeping out from her cut arm. She wanted her mama to kiss it, not send her to her room. It had been an accident. Maybe Reanna shouldn't have been dancing, but she hadn't meant for the bust to fall.

Reanna looked at her elbow again...then at the locked door. *Nobody* loved her, or anybody else. What would happen if she ran away? Would anyone even care? Reanna's whole body heaved. The force of her cries made her feel like throwing up.

Reanna wanted her mama to open the door right then. Somebody had to know she was crying, right? Reanna wailed more—*somebody* had to notice. Somebody had to care and want to love her. But those mean guards only laughed, and nobody came.

Maybe her mama really didn't want her. Maybe Arana really wanted a daughter that would be good, not insolent or dumb-witted or stupid—and especially not one who broke things. Reanna's noises turned into quiet sniffling as she scrubbed at her face. Yes, that seemed right. Arana didn't really want a daughter like Reanna. She wanted a good daughter. Nobody would care if Reanna just...vanished, just like nobody cared about her screaming and crying.

THE DEPTHS OF ATLANTIS

It was all that stupid bust's fault. Nobody would ever love her again, not when she'd broken her mama's favorite sculpture. It was probably so, so expensive, and Reanna would be in trouble for that *forever*. Nobody would ever love or hug her again.

Reanna balanced herself on the window sill and looked down at the world below. With one more look behind her, Reanna tilted herself forward slightly…and then a little bit more…

Then it happened.

She swam outside the castle, and the people down below didn't pay any more attention to her than they had when she had waved to them. The woman with the poor man-slave was already farther down the street. Reanna wished she knew enough about her mermaid powers to free that man, but that would probably be another bad thing. She sniffed and swam upwards, closer and closer to the surface, and farther and farther from her mama and the castle.

The surface—that was where she would go.

That was the place for all very bad girls, girls who made their mamas unhappy. Up on the surface, Reanna wouldn't bother anyone. Her mama would be happier without her. *Everyone* would be happier without her.

There was a bright light ahead, something strange and unreal. A song thrummed deep within Reanna's soul, and her shoulders relaxed. It didn't feel scary—the song made her smile. She would reach the light, and she would be okay. Someone, somewhere, loved her.

They just had to.

She could almost hear someone whisper that in her ear—just to her. Just because they wanted her to know she was loved.

The light grew brighter and pierced the darkness. Sound flooded in, so loud that it hurt her ears. The light continued to grow and grow as the ocean faded, as the water sank away, replaced with the blurry images of a room…

…and Reanna jerked upwards, sweating as a scream lurched from her throat.

The tangible memory sank away and left her feeling cold and strange in her own legs. She wasn't six and fleeing Atlantis anymore—she was seventeen, in an unfamiliar place, surrounded by unfamiliar things.

All while an unfamiliar woman approached her with outstretched arms.

PART II

CHAPTER 9

TREVOR

EARTH: PANAMA CITY, FLORIDA

The first period warning bell rang, but Trevor Spencer didn't budge from his spot by the locker. He had a daily rendezvous, and not even a charging linebacker, natural disaster, or teacher could convince him to break it.

He chuckled under his breath, practically giddy with anticipation, if a six-foot-something quarterback could be giddy. He had a good reason to be giddy, though, because of how perfectly yesterday had gone. His longtime nemesis, Reanna Cook, had lost her guts in biology while she dissected a frog. It was like the skies had split open, the "Hallelujah Chorus" had started, and a gift from Heaven had appeared right on his lap...figuratively, of course, because if she had puked on his lap, he would have been more angry than giddy.

As it stood, he had an arsenal of good insults to open with today. He would start by comparing her to the aforementioned dissected frog. Next would come a wisecrack about how every time he saw her, he puked a little in his mouth as well. Mentally, that was as far as Trevor could go, because the rest of the verbal sparring depended on what mood Reanna was in. Hopefully, she would retort with an equally heated barb so that it escalated until they were both sick of the sight of each other in the best way possible. If it was a bad day, Reanna would get all weepy, and her responses would be common one-liners such as "jerk" or "imbecile." Those were the worst days, because there wasn't anything witty he could say back to something as dry as that.

"Come on, Trevor! Reanna probably snuck in the back. You're wasting your time, and you're gonna get a tardy in biology."

Martin Hayes, the cornerback on Trevor's football team, slammed his locker and caused the whole row to jiggle. Martin was nothing if not a brutal force to be reckoned with. A few of their female classmates giggled as he ran his free hand over his cropped black hair. One of them—Carly? Charlie?—tarried the longest, probably hoping to talk to the dark, muscular boy.

Martin either didn't notice her or purposely chose to act like he didn't. After a few seconds, she gave up as her friends tugged her inside the classroom. Only then did Martin take a step closer to the first door on the right and gestured with his thumb for Trevor to come on.

A pause. Martin took another step. Another pause…Martin glared at his resisting friend.

Trevor huffed and rolled his eyes…but still didn't move. "Bet she's too embarrassed to show her face."

"Yeah, yeah, it's tragic. Why do you like picking on her so much? You could be flirting with any of the hot girls in there…" Martin pointed into the biology classroom. "…but instead, you wait around for a girl that isn't even your girlfriend, just so you two can fight about random…junk. You have better things to worry about." Martin strode into the room, shaking his head all the while.

Trevor glanced back one more time to see if Reanna had magically appeared. She hadn't, and there was no one else in the hallway, which nixed his suspicion that she might come to school in disguise. Trevor trudged through the door right before it closed and growled under his breath. His close call garnered a glower from Mr. Boyette, but Trevor was too upset that his gift-wrapped opportunity had been missed to care. He thumped down in his seat, which was also conveniently behind Reanna's. But his metaphorical dartboard didn't lurk there, either.

An irritating, too-peppy trill blasted from the TV as the school's mascot, Shady Shark, danced across the screen in a felt suit. Trevor cringed and massaged his temple. What possessed someone to give up all their dignity and become the school mascot? It was no surprise that the guy within the suit, Sean Davis, had gotten strung up by his underwear on the flagpole two weeks ago. After the torture was over, Hailey Wiseman, the news anchor—and Trevor's ex-girlfriend—appeared on the screen.

All the phones in the classroom went off in a horrible cacophony of alerts.

Every student in the room ignored Sea Breeze High School's cafeteria menu and sports updates as they peered at their phones.

AMBER Alert.

Trevor's blue eyes stalled on the words. His gust twisted around inside him—it couldn't be. Reanna's empty seat didn't mean that…

Local Panama City, Florida police have issued an AMBER Alert for Reanna Cook. Reanna is described as a 17-year-old Caucasian female with blonde, curly hair and green eyes.

She didn't have *green* eyes. Trevor picked up a pencil and notebook to doodle in the margins. In fact, he had noticed way back in fifth grade that they were gray-green, grayer than green on most days, actually. He absent-mindedly sketched them. He was by no means an artist—his only practice really was drawing ugly caricatures of Reanna—but his skill level matched his subject.

He drew wild, flyaway hair that looked like miniature tornadoes coming out of Reanna's head. Perfect. Maybe someone could use it as her lost photo.

Last seen in a Spider-Man sweatshirt and gray sweatpants. That sounded right. She wore that almost every day. *At this time, police do not have a suspect or person of interest. Last seen at her home around 10:30 Thursday night. If you have any information or see someone fitting this description, please call 9-1-1 immediately.*

Whispers flew among the rest of the class as Reanna's life suddenly became as interesting as a cheap gossip rag at the grocery store. Everyone seemed to know *of* their star swimmer, the incredibly awkward vomiting wonder, but who knew how many of them actually knew her. Reanna had seemed to enjoy being invisible everywhere but the swim team.

Daisy, the swim team captain, let out a loud huff next to him. She whipped around in her seat to face the girl behind her and whispered in a voice that hardly passed as a whisper, "That means we've lost our best swimmer. What are we going to do about the state championships?"

"And right after she set that record at our last swim meet," another swimmer moaned. "We were banking on her being here!"

Trevor remembered that match fondly, though he couldn't remember what record Reanna had actually beaten to propel the swim team to victory. Nah—the shining moment in his memory was that he had dumped a bucket of water over her head the next second, and she bought a root beer just to pour it down his shirt. Ah, the good old days. Her face had been all red and scrunched up as she did it, too. She'd even smiled a bit, right before he tossed her in the pool.

As the swim team discussed who they could shuffle around to fill the void Reanna's absence left, Trevor shook his head. Reanna almost deserved his congratulations. She'd been relegated to the same status as the Shady Shark suit, which nobody ever noticed until one of their rivals stole it before a big game.

Mr. Boyette seemed to be the most concerned. He shushed the students and glanced sadly to the empty seat in front of Trevor. Although, come to think of it, Mr. Boyette probably only missed his grading curve. Without his student pet to bolster his test scores, he'd look a lot worse.

Trevor swallowed, and the sides of his mouth twitched. What would Reanna say at a moment like this on a good day?

"*Trevor Spencer, you are an imbecilic moron with the artistic level of a banana.*"

Yeah, that sounded like her, enough that he almost smiled. He started to write that in a speech bubble in his doodle.

Trevor finished his unflattering sketch and glanced over to Reanna's seat. It just wasn't quite as fun if nobody was there to punch him in the shoulder for his hard work. Ugh. Why was no one else in the whole blasted school able to keep him engaged with repartee like her?

The TV screen once more cut to Shady Shark, who seemed even more grossly out of place with his ridiculous dancing. The screen blessedly went dark after a few more seconds, and Mr. Boyette snapped the set off. No one spoke for a moment. Trevor wondered if everyone else was thinking the same thing he was: they'd let them out of school early for this, wouldn't they?

Mr. Boyette finally cleared his throat while he wiped at his eyes. "Students, I...I think..."

"Can I pray, Mr. Boyette?" That came from Julie in the back row.

Trevor rolled his eyes at her and tapped his pencil on his drawing. It was nice to know that Julie had so much concern for Reanna. He hadn't been aware that Julie even acknowledged the shy girl's presence. But he would bet that this show of concern would really boost Julie's chances of becoming Homecoming Queen.

Mr. Boyette nodded his consent, though some of the class began to snicker. Mr. Boyette tried to contain the herd, but Trevor had seen animals better behaved at a zoo. It took five empty threats that Trevor didn't even bother to listen to for the class to get back under control. Finally, when everyone was silent, Julie began to pray.

She prayed for protection and for Reanna to be found quickly—except Julie pronounced Reanna's name as "Ree-auna"— like Rihanna, the singer—instead of "Ree-anna" every single time.

Trevor groaned under his breath while Julie continued her soliloquy. He wouldn't exactly count on that prayer being answered—and not because Julie had mispronounced Reanna's name six times already.

No, it was more likely that Reanna—the great puking wonder, nerd extraordinaire, swim star sweetheart—was dead. The realization left him nauseous, but he didn't dare repeat Reanna's gaffe from biology.

He crumpled up his drawing right after Julie said amen, though he'd stopped paying attention to focus on his all-consuming question:

Who would want to kidnap *Reanna*?

CHAPTER 10

TREVOR

EARTH: PANAMA CITY, FLORIDA

School, unfortunately, was not canceled—but at least football practice was. Trevor would have skipped, anyway. On top of everything else, the late afternoon Florida humidity had soared, which made everything sticky and disgusting. There was nothing that made a day worse than being hot. Since Trevor was already having a bad day, the heat only got on his nerves that much more.

Good thing practice had been canceled, or Trevor probably would have tackled someone…and he was the quarterback.

He took the many, many steps up to his beachfront home, which loomed above him like a horrid blue monster. His house was the smallest space-wise on the strip, but it towered over the beach on huge—not to mention ugly—stilts, with a garage below and steps that led to a wraparound porch.

He yanked the screen door open and threw his backpack down on the floor. He made sure the coast was clear before he slipped and slid on sweaty socks down the hallway.

He finally skidded into his room, still without seeing a single soul. Trevor grabbed a ring off his desk. He would have slipped it on a finger, but it was much too small. So instead, he slipped it into his pocket, feeling as if he had landed on the set of *Lord of the Rings*.

That was the thing he'd tried to drill into Reanna: you could *be* a nerd, just so long as nobody else saw you. And none of the kids at school had ever seen his autographed *Lord of the Rings* posters. Or his custom-made lightsaber. Or his ocarina that he was painstakingly teaching himself to play through YouTube videos. Or figured out that he'd watched every episode of the *Legend of Zelda* cartoon.

Twice.

And as long as no one else ever did, he could have the best of both worlds.

Really, Reanna should have thanked him for all he'd done for her. At the end of the day, he just wanted to toughen her up, make her keep all that weirdness inside so she could live a normal life. Maybe one day she'd even be a cheerleader.

Trevor grimaced.

Ew. Maybe not.

Nobody wanted to see her in a cheerleader's uniform.

He sighed and fiddled with the ring in his pocket as he tiptoed out of his room. He even crafted a story in his mind: Trevor Spencer was not on his way to Reanna's house, but Frodo Baggins was just beginning his trek to Mordor. The ring grew heavy in his pocket. He could already feel its temptations as they called out for him. But he had to stay strong—

"Trevor? Come here, please."

Trevor huffed, all of the mental suspense ruined. He turned to his right and leaned against the door frame, but he didn't take a single step inside the office. Someone worse than Gollum worked there: his father. And if Trevor surrendered to his father's wishes, he might not get out of there for the rest of the day.

Paul Spencer lounged back in his chair with his cell phone pressed against his ear. His other hand massaged his temple, his face twisted into serious lines. Out of habit, Trevor immediately scoured over his memories from the past week to look for a misdeed.

He was fairly certain he'd been a pretty decent human being this week. He had gotten a detention for being tardy, but that was three days ago. No way the office would just be informing Dad of that now.

Grades…no, Trevor was nearly positive that he had all A's and B's, unless he had flunked the history pop quiz. That would have dropped his history grade to a C, but he could have sworn that he did okay. Had he mixed up the Allies and the Central Powers in World War I? Japan had been with the Allies the first time around, he was sure…

Maybe Dad had just decided to make up something to yell at Trevor about.

"Yeah, Jerry, that's fine. Send around thirty percent to missions, but save enough to pay the guys who are coming to fix the leaky roof."

Dad sighed deeply, as if the weight of the world was on his shoulders instead of just his job as a pastor. Trevor almost laughed but caught himself. If he was already in trouble, he didn't want his dad to tack on a charge of disrespect, or Trevor wouldn't ever make it out of the office.

"We've got to stretch to give some to the soup kitchen, too. Their numbers are up, and they're worried about how to feed everyone. Listen, I've got to go. Trevor just walked in. All right. Thanks. Bye." Dad clicked his phone off, stood up, and stretched. A loud pop echoed through the room, and he groaned. "Oh, I'm not as young as I used to be."

"You need something?" Trevor bit back any noise of irritation he was tempted to make, although he did knock his hand against the wooden door frame a few times.

His father's blue eyes darkened. "Jamie told me the news about that little Reanna girl."

Trevor bristled at the thought of his dad spending any time with Julie's widowed mother, but he bit his tongue. They'd already endured quite a few arguments about Jamie, and Trevor had better things to do than point out his dad's awful track record in relationships.

Not to mention, he'd sooner have a Nazgûl for a step-sibling than Julie.

Dad didn't seem to notice Trevor's displeasure. "She wants to hold a prayer vigil at the church."

"For Reanna? Why? She didn't go to church there." Trevor scowled and glanced at the door. So close, yet so far—like getting tackled right before the endzone. "She barely even went to church, period. I'm not sure if Mrs. Cook would like that."

Dad sighed. His grimace rivaled his son's. "The whole community is feeling the loss, Trevor. You could go over and comfort Mr. and Mrs. Cook."

"I could, but I'm not the preacher. It's not my job." Trevor's flippant words elicited a grunt from his dad, just what Trevor had intended.

Besides, if his dad knew anything, he would know there wasn't a "Mr. and Mrs. Cook" anymore—not since Mr. Cook ran off with his secretary. But why would his dad have any reason to notice that? It wasn't like he ever paid attention to anything.

"I thought you would care for once since the poor girl went to your school."

"Just because she went to school with me doesn't mean we were friends. She kept to herself."

Besides himself, he'd never even seen anyone talk to Reanna outside of the swim team people, and that was usually only to discuss some new butterfly stroke technique or something. Trevor didn't know; he wasn't a swimmer. *He* probably wouldn't have even known about Reanna if she hadn't come to VBS the year they were seven.

She'd wandered around, so transfixed by a butterfly that she didn't see a hole in the ground until she fell in it and twisted her ankle. Little Trevor had known right then: one, the girl was an idiot and a danger to herself, and two, somebody had to toughen her up and teach her about life. He purposefully chucked a water balloon at her head right after that.

He'd always hated procrastinating.

"...a seventeen-year-old girl, Trevor! Why can't you ever have some sympathy?"

Well, whoops. Trevor had apparently missed most of his dad's lecture, but whatever. He could probably guess what he'd tuned out by piecing together lectures of the past.

Dad ran his hands through his thick mop of brown hair, which was the exact same shade as Trevor's. People often commented on how much Trevor resembled his father's side of the family with their Native American ancestors. And though Trevor couldn't deny the resemblance—after all, he didn't look a thing like his mother's Swedish ancestors—it irked him to no end to be compared to his dad in any way.

"Sympathy? That's a good one. You didn't have any sympathy for Mom when she left. Or before, really." Trevor jumped up and stomped toward the door. "I'm going to play football with Martin. Don't wait up." He escaped through the front door despite his father hollering at him to stay put. Once Trevor was safely down the zigzagging steps and on the sandy beach, he took a deep breath and turned to his left, counting the houses as he passed them.

One...two...three....four. His personal Mordor was a lot closer than Frodo's.

He took the steps up to the polished white house's front door two at a time. The two-story home was a lot bigger than his own—not to mention a more pleasing color. Trevor knocked on the glass door impulsively.

What would he even say when the owners answered?

A petite brunette opened the door, her eyes red and watering. Trevor winced. Tara Cook: Reanna's older sister—and the person who disliked him the most on the entire planet—besides maybe his own dad. "What do you want?" she snapped.

Great, she was already mad—and way more dangerous than Mount Doom. "Um...Tara?"

Tara glowered at him and crossed her arms over her chest. "Trevor Spencer, you get off my porch this instant. Don't you think you've caused enough trouble?" There was so much acid in her voice that it could eat through metal, and Trevor doubted even his sweetest smooth talking would get a pleasanter reaction out of the twenty-year-old.

"Look...can I come in?" He took a step toward the hardwood floor on the other side of the glass, but Tara shielded him from entering with her body. Despite being barely five feet tall—if that— she always had the mysterious ability to command the room and everything in it.

Tara snorted. "No."

"I would like to speak to your mom." He tried to measure his breathing and remain pleasant. He might deserve a little of her acerbity, but that didn't make it any less irritating.

"No."

"Please?"

"Did you think I wouldn't remember you?" she hissed. "Did you think I'd forget?"

Trevor leaned against his hand, which was pressed against the door frame. He lowered his eyes and his voice, trying his best to plead. "Well...I was hoping you'd let bygones be bygones."

Apparently, not everyone appreciated lessons from Trevor Spencer's School of Hard Knocks.

He glanced up just as she narrowed her viper-like hazel eyes. "Fat chance."

Tara attempted to slam the door, but Trevor leaned in. It caught his shoulder, and Tara smirked. He growled and tried to wrestle past her. Tara planted her hands on his chest and shoved, but he was not only a good foot taller—he was also much stronger. Thankfully, a woman with short, curly black hair walked by and paused to look at the scene. At least if Tara killed him, there would be a witness.

Tentatively, the woman asked, "Tara, honey…what are you doing?"

Tara whipped around, which gave Trevor just enough time to step over her foot and slip inside. Tara elbowed him as he did, though.

"I'm trying to keep this egotistical bully out of our house. He's the Trevor Spencer that always picks on Reanna. He's probably here to gloat."

Trevor held up his hands to prove his innocence. "I'm not here to gloat, although the rest of that is kind of true. And here I thought we were friends, Tara, but now the truth comes out."

Mrs. Cook stiffened. Her deep brown eyes hardened. "What do you want?"

"Um…" Trevor was suddenly dumbfounded. He hadn't expected Tara to be here to ruin all his chances of sweet-talking Mrs. Cook. In retrospect, he admitted it was pretty stupid of him to assume that Tara wouldn't be here. After all, what girl wouldn't come home from college the minute her baby sister was kidnapped?

Trevor's un-carefully crafted plans began to unwind. Ugh—he'd hoped to charm his whole way through this, and then they'd have a heartfelt Hallmark moment that some girls seemed to go gaga over. He fiddled with the ring in his pocket. What was the best way to go about this? Probably not by getting on one knee. Tara might go get a kitchen knife and chase him out of the house.

Unceremoniously, he withdrew the tiny ring and held it out toward Mrs. Cook. "Here…it's Reanna's ring. I figured she'd want it back. You know…when…when she comes back."

Mrs. Cook came over and peered at it; her brow furrowed. "That's her birthstone ring! How did you get it? She said she lost it in the sixth grade, or maybe it was seventh."

"It was fifth." Trevor cleared his throat. "I...took it from her. Just as a little prank, y'know. But then I just kind of forgot about it until I found it a couple months ago in my closet."

"You stole it?" Mrs. Cook demanded. "Reanna always said you were mean, but this—"

"I was a fifth-grade boy, and I thought it was a funny prank. I never meant to keep it. I just...forgot."

Mrs. Cook's glare didn't soften—and boy, did she resemble Tara at that moment—so Trevor tried a different tactic. He stared down at the floor and crossed his hands in front of him. He almost willed tears to well up in his eyes, but that might have been overkill. "I'm really, really stupid, Mrs. Cook. I regret a lot of things I said and did to Reanna." Well, *regret* was a little too strong of a word. From his perspective, everything had been in good fun; it was the School of Hard Knocks program. But now that his only student had been kidnapped and probably killed...well, it made his chest feel weird. His throat tightened for real. "I just wanted to give that to you and tell you that we all miss Reanna at school."

It may have been a false sentiment to speak for the entire school body, but at times like these, Trevor reasoned everyone gave and needed a little false sentiment. It was just standard. Nobody wanted to hear that life at Sea Breeze High was more or less the same without Reanna, minus the swim team's chances at State.

Tara snatched the ring from his hand and curled her fist around it. She narrowed her eyes and licked her lips; Trevor wondered if she could taste the lie he had just spewed. "I'm probably only going to say this once, so listen up. You're a scumbag, a nuisance, and I still don't like you—but thanks for being a decent human being this once."

"See? I knew we could put the past behind us if we tried. Now we're practically best friends." Trevor smirked at her, which only deepened her snarl. He poked her cheek, but when she smacked it away, he sobered again. "I really do hope they find her soon."

And that she hadn't been kidnapped while she chased some stupid butterfly again. If that was the case, he'd relegate her back to pre-school in Trevor Spencer's School of Hard Knocks.

If she even survived long enough to get back.

Mrs. Cook nodded, and Tara, for once, was seemingly flabbergasted. He shoved his hands in his pockets and took a step toward the door. "Well...that's all. Oh...and my dad's church is thinking of having a vigil for her. If you want to come, that is. I know it's not up your alley anymore."

"Thank you." Mrs. Cook exchanged a glance with Tara and gave him a wavering smile. "I'll call your father and ask for the details."

Trevor nodded and slipped out the door. Tension fell from his shoulders as soon as he left Mount Doom—or...

Trevor groaned as a thought hit him.

He should have framed his adventure as Bilbo Baggins, for one reason and one reason only:

Tara made an excellent Smaug.

CHAPTER 11

TREVOR

EARTH: PANAMA CITY, FLORIDA

Trevor wiped the sweat off his face with his shirt—which wasn't on his body—as he walked home. He hadn't really gone to practice football with Martin, of course. He'd gone to a little arcade and blown some money just for the heck of it.

Anything to keep him away from his father.

With his wallet empty, Trevor had decided to walk around town until nightfall. Maybe he'd go swimming or something in the ocean if it got too unbearable. After all, he could only shed so many layers before the police would show up and arrest him.

He passed Reanna's house on his first lap, and—

And backpedaled as he saw a short figure in a blue t-shirt underneath Reanna's back window.

"*Shoot*, shoot, shoot," the person muttered. "I'm too late…"

Whoever it was, they were way too short to be a police officer. The kid probably barely came up to Trevor's chest, if that.

Trevor cupped his hands around his mouth; his shirt dangled between curled fingers. "Hey, you!"

The figure whirled around, the look of a burglar caught in the act—eyes wide, body tensed. Trevor couldn't see very many other distinguishing features, but the kid had brown hair that reminded Trevor of Justin Bieber in his *Baby* era.

The boy gaped at Trevor—and bolted.

A creepy kid, sneaking around Reanna's house the day after she'd been kidnapped? Visions of some weirdo taking pictures for a gossip rag flickered through Trevor's head. Nah—Reanna couldn't be that important, right?

Unless the kid was just a perv.

He chased after the kid. "Wait!" he bellowed.

The boy zoomed past Trevor's house and took a sharp turn to the left. Trevor did the same—and faster. His longer legs gave him an advantage in this pursuit.

"Just wait a second!" Trevor reached out one arm and snagged the kid's shoulder.

Trevor must have jerked a tad bit too hard, because the kid twisted around and *hissed*.

Like a feral cat.

"What—the *heck*," Trevor panted. "Did you just hiss at me?"

The boy's eyes widened. "Excuse me, but I think the question is, why are you chasing me?" The boy slapped Trevor's hand away.

"No, no, I still think the question is why the heck did you hiss at me?" Trevor crossed his arms over his chest. "Or maybe why the heck were you creeping around Reanna's house saying you were *late*?"

The kid's already-pale skin turned a shade of white typically reserved for sheets of paper. Even his freckles disappeared. "Uh—um—"

"I'm waiting."

This seemed to sour the boy's mood even more. "Yeah, yeah, I can *see* that you're waiting. And, by the way, where's your shirt? I think that's the *best* question right now. What, you think you're so good-looking that the world wants to see your abs or something? Because my eyeballs do *not* wanna be subjugated to this right now."

Trevor blinked. A million comebacks and questions formed in his mind, but they all evaporated on his tongue.

They stared at each other. The boy narrowed his blue-gray eyes—Trevor had never seen such animosity in the face of a complete stranger.

Maybe he should call the cops. Then again, cops didn't arrest people for being weird.

"Okay. How about this: if I put my shirt back on, then you tell me your name. If you don't, I'll call the cops right now."

The boy stepped backward. "No—not the cops. *Please.* My sister would literally kill me."

"Then you better get to talking." Trevor slipped his shirt back on.

"Adam." The boy—Adam—huffed. "My name's Adam. And I'm *late* because Reanna was kidnapped, and I wasn't there to stop it."

Trevor snorted. "That's the thing about kidnappings. They don't exactly put out warnings ahead of time. What could *you* do, anyway? What are you, twelve?"

"Fourteen." Adam's fists clenched, and Trevor finally understood the definition of the word *seethed*. The kid's jaw couldn't have been tighter. "I'm *fourteen*."

"Woo. Excuse me. Twelve, fourteen—you're all babies, anyway." Trevor scratched at the back of his sweaty head. "Anyway, point still stands. You can't—couldn't—do anything to save Reanna."

Adam swung a fist at Trevor.

Trevor barked out a broken exclamation as he stumbled backward. His feet got twisted up and he fell, hard, on his backside.

"Shut up! I'm not *useless*. I can—I swear—I'm *sorry* I'm not Mr. Popular-and-a-Star-Quarterback like you, Trevor Spencer!"

Wait—had Trevor even introduced himself?

"But you wanna know the difference between us—other than your sky-high ego? I *care*. I care about other people—about *Reanna*." Trevor picked himself up and dusted his bottom off. "Hey, here's a big question. Why?"

"Uh, because I'm not a self-absorbed jerk, for a start?" Adam scoffed. "I know it's pretty impossible for someone like you to realize other people actually exist and have feelings, but—"

"That's not true."

"If it's not true, then why do you pick on Reanna every single day? Why wasn't it *your* idea to come over here and look for clues or something?"

"Because I'm not Scooby-Doo, for one." Trevor glanced over his shoulder. Good—he didn't see anyone spying on them. "And because it's a job for the cops. Remember them? The people I still might call if you actually assault me?"

Adam punted a pebble off the road. "Then *don't* say I'm useless, weird, stuck in my head, avoiding reality, or that—that I need to face facts and move on, or…"

"I haven't said *any* of that." Although there was a definite possibility that Trevor might say it, eventually, in the course of this strange interaction. "And, for the record—I don't *pick* on Reanna. She's my nemesis. There's a difference. It's a mutual…picking-upon. Sort of an unspoken agreement that—well, it doesn't matter. Point is—no, that's beside the point." Trevor took a deep breath to reorganize his thoughts. "The real issue is—stop lurking around her house. You're just going to get yourself in trouble, and someone is bound to call the police. Consider it a friendly warning." He turned to go, but this time, Adam reached out and stopped him.

"Wait, though." Adam swallowed. "I, um, I could really use your help. I wanna search for Reanna."

Trevor scanned back through the list of words Adam had defined as "off the table." Okay, good—the one Trevor wanted to use wasn't banned. "You're delusional." He held up a hand and intercepted Adam's fist. "And, again, I'd like to warn you about a little thing called *assault charges.*"

Adam licked his lips. When he spoke again, his voice sounded a notch deeper—like he might be trying to channel his inner Batman. Unfortunately, the scrawny kid's deep voice was more on level with Adam West than Christian Bale. "Reanna will be lost forever if you're just going to give up like that. Quitter. Giver-upper."

Trevor sputtered out a laugh, but that didn't stop the quick pinch in his chest.

Ugh. Reanna. So frustrating. She'd never have gotten kidnapped in the first place if she'd take her head out of the clouds more. All his hard work, gone. Vanished like the brain inside Reanna's thick skull.

"Look, Reanna's been kidnapped, and they probably want a ransom. My dad's a preacher, and in case you're wondering, we're not exactly loaded with cash. I can't even shoot a gun, and I don't know where the criminals are. So there's nothing I can do—at all—except go on with my life."

"So if you *knew* who the kidnappers were, you'd help?" Adam stopped his lousy Batman impersonation. "Do you mean that?"

"I never said that—"

"Because I think I know how to figure it out—I've got some pretty good guesses already, but I'm not sure—" Adam blabbered on for a moment. "So? Will you?"

"Will I what?"

"Actually do something to help Reanna that's a little bit more productive than trying to teach her stupid lessons to toughen her up? Which just makes you seem like a big jerk, FYI."

"FYI? Who even says…" Trevor cleared his throat and pinched the bridge of his nose. "Never mind. Do you *really* think—no, no. I'm insane for even thinking about going along with this."

"Yeah, probably. I mean, I'm just some random weirdo, right? But I'm the only one that even cares about Reanna, so I'm your best chance." Adam leaned forward. "And why do you care? No one else at school does. Not even the swim team."

"Because. I…" Adam blushed, and in that moment, Trevor knew.

Lord help him.

"Oh, no. You *like* her. You're blinded by some delusional puppy-love, aren't you? And you're a *freshman*."

"No—it's not—it's not like that!" Adam stepped back and sighed.

He actually had tears in his eyes.

He swiped at them before they could fall, but Trevor saw.

"I just…maybe I'm selfish; maybe I'm the most selfish person in existence, and the most stupid, and stubborn, and—and maybe all those things that my sister and my dad say are true, and maybe I'm not logical in the slightest, but…. I can't. I can't let this go, so I'm really sorry." Adam sniffled.

A genuine *sniffle*.

First Reanna, now Adam—how did all these saps end up in Trevor's lap? And why did it always fall to him to be the one to protect them from themselves? This kid would get himself arrested for sure, if not kidnapped by the same people that abducted her.

"I just—I need to help Reanna. She doesn't deserve this. You have to know that. And—I…I never even got to talk to her." Adam's voice wobbled a little bit. "I never even got to see her smile. Just *once*."

Trevor sighed. "You've got it bad, kid. Risking your own neck just to talk to your one-sided crush?"

Adam scowled and wiped at his eyes. "No. Not that. It's so much more than that."

Trevor sighed—a long-suffering sigh from the depths of his soul. "I'm sure it is. Oh, for crying out loud." He rolled his eyes. "You get one shot to prove to me that you can find some sort of information about Reanna that the investigators haven't found yet. I'll help you do that much—and make sure you don't get arrested. But you have to promise me that if we don't find anything, you'll give up and just...I dunno. Let the cops do their job."

"I..." Adam swallowed. He cocked his head to the side like a little bird. "I guess...okay. Deal."

"All right." Trevor shuffled his feet. "What's your idea? Why are you snooping around Reanna's house?"

"Well...I'm trying to find a way into her room. To look for...stuff." Adam blushed again.

"Okay—nope. If you're looking for kinky stuff, this is when I back out and call the cops."

"No!" Adam shook his head. "Not—you *pervert*. I'm looking for evidence. Something the cops missed or didn't understand or something!"

Trevor chewed on the inside of his lip. "All right. I can maybe get you into Reanna's house—or at least do it for you. No offense, but if we have to scale her trellis, I might be better suited for it."

"Mmhmm. Yeah. Okay, Mr. Star-Football-Player." Adam pursed his lips. "I guess I can agree to that."

"But we've got to wait. Right now, Reanna's mom and sister will be up. So stop being a stupid eager beaver. I'll meet you at Reanna's later tonight, okay?" Trevor pulled his phone out of his pocket. "Give me your number. I'll text you when it's safe."

"Sure." Adam typed out his number and handed the phone back to Trevor. "And, um...thanks." He tried to offer a smile, but it seemed hesitant or embarrassed—Trevor wasn't sure which. "I appreciate it."

"Yeah, well…" Trevor shrugged. "Just say thank you to me at your wedding if we do find Reanna. I expect half the money and half the gifts. Although, if you count all the time I've spent trying to teach Reanna how to be less weird, and if I charge for my services…might as well just address everything to me. I'll make out a list."

Adam rolled his eyes. "Yeah…none of what you said will happen."

"We'll see." Trevor tucked his phone back into his pocket. "Okay. I'll see you tonight. Just…try not to get into any more fights or get arrested before then."

"I'll try." Adam backed away a few paces. "Oh, and tonight…wear a shirt."

CHAPTER 12

TREVOR

EARTH: PANAMA CITY, FLORIDA

T**revor** wasn't sure why he'd agreed to help Adam—beyond the fact that the poor boy reminded him of Reanna, all clueless and hapless. After all, Trevor wouldn't be useful in finding Reanna. In the long run, there was nothing either he or Adam could do besides play detective. But if that was the case, then Trevor was definitely the Remington Steele in their pseudo-investigative-agency: completely clueless and trying his best to bumble his way using charm and good looks. And if that meant he got to be as attractive as Pierce Brosnan in his '80s debut, then Trevor would accept his token part.

Step one on Adam's crazy Sherlock Holmes journey was Reanna's house. Rather conveniently, Adam had also not shown up at their meeting place on time; instead, he sent a text telling Trevor to go on without him.

Some Samwise Gamgee Adam had ended up being—not even willing to come across town, let alone go into the heart of Mordor.

Trevor reached for the lattice fence that ran up the side of Reanna's house but shied away before he could do anything. He kicked some sand at his feet and put his hands against the back of his head. Why was he even doing this? Reanna was dead. Nobody ever spoke the possibility aloud, but Trevor thought about it often enough.

So Trevor was basically risking getting arrested for a dead girl, all because some lovestruck psychopath was trying to star in his own episode of CSI. What had Trevor's life come to?

He huffed and gripped the lattice fence tightly. At the last second, he chickened out again and backed up. No lights shone from inside Reanna's house or any of the ones that surrounded it. He hadn't seen any police cars, either, but that didn't mean they couldn't arrive at any second.

If he got caught, it would be the perfect opportunity for Tara—or, as he would refer to her from now on, Smaug—to kill him.

He grunted and gave his white-latticed enemy a swift kick. Now or never. He scurried up to Reanna's balcony. With his right hand, he strained to reach the railing. His first attempt missed, and his hand swung back around—which upset his delicate equilibrium. He quickly pressed himself against the lattice and held tight. It felt like his heart might explode at any second.

He closed his eyes and prayed for a moment—if he died, he was going to do so with a clean slate. After confessing as many things as he remembered—even some transgressions he'd committed as a stupid kid—Trevor reached his hand back out to the railing. He grunted, his mind so solely focused on reaching the railing that he didn't have time to make a pop culture comparison to help with his nerves.

After what seemed like a precious eternity, Trevor's fingers wrapped around the wood. He tested his weight and said one more prayer.

He released the lattice.

His body dangled in midair.

He swung his left hand over the railing too and heaved himself upward and over. Thank goodness his football coach was something of a weight-lifting fanatic. Trevor could just see himself waltzing into practice tomorrow and saying: *So, Coach. You know those techniques you taught us in the weight room? Turns out they're not only good for winning games. They're useful if you ever want to break into a house in the middle of the night.*

Trevor took a deep breath as he twisted the door open, a bit surprised when he found it unlatched. No wonder Reanna had been kidnapped if even *he* could get into her room.

As he stepped onto the hardwood floor, he had to stop himself from gasping out loud. Adam's last text had implored Trevor to "look for any clues left behind." In the state Reanna's room was in, though, it was impossible to tell what was a clue and what wasn't. Clothes were strewn over the floor and her nightstand was overturned, but her desk and drawers were still standing upright. Her bedsheets were mangled, a *The Little Mermaid* blanket twisted and completely off the bed.

Creeping farther in, Trevor stepped over a toppled lamp and nearly tripped on a book. No wonder they thought Reanna had been kidnapped, even without the ransom note. It did look like a kidnapping scene...unless Reanna had wanted it to look that way to cover up the fact she ran away.

The thought struck Trevor as odd, and he didn't know where it came from. But once the niggling thought was there, it wouldn't leave him alone. It made sense: if Reanna was tired of her life—and who wouldn't be, if they were her?—staging a kidnapping would be a good cover story. Meanwhile, Reanna could have dyed her hair, changed her name, and hitchhiked anywhere in the country, all while the police were looking for her kidnappers.

Or maybe she'd chased some feral, rabies-infested cat around her room, followed it outside when it tried to run away, and...legend said she still searched for it, determined to shower the mangy thing in love and affection.

That would *so* be just like Reanna.

Lost in his theories, Trevor didn't notice another book in his path until he slipped on the hardback and tumbled toward the bed. He managed to catch himself on the overturned nightstand, which rattled as more of the contents of the half-open drawer tumbled to the floor.

He scrunched his eyes closed and sent up another prayer to protect his own skin. *God, whatever happens, don't let Smaug—I mean, Tara—hear that. I'd like to leave tonight with all my body parts intact. Or without being framed for the kidnapping of Reanna.* He could almost see the sadistic joy on Smaug's face as she called the cops on him.

"*He always hated Reanna. He probably killed her and was coming back to try and find a piece of evidence he'd left behind!*"

That was the last straw. Trevor didn't care about Reanna or Adam enough to go to jail for them. He crept upwards, ever vigilant to make sure there were no footsteps in the hallway. As he pulled his hand away from the nightstand, something dug into his skin and drew blood.

Trevor hissed under his breath and dropped back down to his knees, examining the top of the nightstand. The strange teardrop-shaped items shimmered in the darkness, reflecting the moonlight that slipped in…or maybe they produced their own light. Trevor wasn't a gambling man, but he would have bet money that these were fish scales. He wiped his blood from his finger and noticed a few drops on one of the scales as well.

The perpetrator.

The fish scales covered the top of the nightstand and dotted the floor as well. Was Reanna a secret fisherman? Did she have a fish fetish or some other weird obsession? He looked under her bed and found nothing but dust—whatever she was, she definitely wasn't a neat freak. There were no fish decorations around the room, either.

Trevor slid open the first of the nightstand drawers. It was filled to the brim with—what else?—Spider-Man memorabilia. Trevor snorted and closed it to try the second drawer. It only contained a few spiral-bound notebooks—probably her diaries. Trevor almost took them but thought better of it. He shuffled them around instead, just in case they hid any hint or clue. He furrowed his brow as he found a tiny razor blade at the bottom of the drawer. He turned it over, his eyebrows raised as he studied it. He was just about to put it back when he heard Smaug's heated voice.

"Mom, I swear I heard something in the room. What if it's the kidnappers, come back to find some piece of incriminating evidence?"

Trevor jumped up. His blood pounded against his head and dulled his senses.

Without thinking, he shoved the razor into his pocket. There would be no sweet-talking his way out of this one if he stuck around. He raced out of the balcony doors and shut them quietly behind him. Once he was out on the porch, he had a split second to make a decision that might possibly affect the rest of his life. He could either go down the lattice or jump off the balcony.

Trevor climbed over the balcony railing and closed his eyes. He just hoped that he could be out of sight by the time that Tara came. His heart showed no signs of slowing down any time soon, but that was okay. That meant he could count on his adrenaline to keep him going.

Trevor braced himself, opened his eyes, and leapt from the balcony.

He plummeted from the second story to the sand. He reeled forward, collapsed to his knees, and rolled over his shoulder once. He winced and hopped up. Above him, he could hear Smaug opening the door. He careened around the side of the house; please, oh *please*, he hoped she hadn't seen his dark figure. If he didn't look like a kidnapper, he would at least look like a petty thief, and both options sounded unappealing to him.

Trevor's feet hit the pavement, and the abrupt change from sand caught him off guard. He stumbled—nearly fell again—and forced himself to take a breath. His chest heaved, and blood roared in his ears, drowning out everything else. Fear prompted him onward, and he started a slow, painful jog. He knew he needed to go faster in case Smaug decided to take a car and do a once-over around the neighborhood—or fly with her scaly wings, either one.

Oh, c'mon—he would never make it into the pros if he couldn't handle a little midnight escapade. Trevor moaned as his legs burned, but he propelled himself forward, unwilling to be caught, unwilling to pay any attention to the cramp growing in his legs or the stitch in his side. He counted the houses as he passed, and at the third one, he veered toward his stairs—until someone stepped right into his path. Trevor tried to correct himself, but it was no use. He was a train pummeling down a victim. He plowed right over the person, and both train and victim tumbled to the asphalt.

Trevor did an accidental somersault as he hit the road and scraped his elbow as he did so. He yelped and sprang up. All he could think was: *Oh, please God, just don't let it be Tara. She'll add assault to the long list of felonies I didn't do!*

The person on the concrete didn't stir, and Trevor nudged his or her tennis shoe with his own. "Um...hey. I'm sorry about that, but you're not dead, are you?"

"No, but thanks for trying." Adam's voice came from the ground. He grunted and propped himself up on his elbows.

Relieved, Trevor offered his hand to Adam. The younger boy took it, and as soon as Adam was on his feet, Trevor slapped him upside the head. "What were you doing, scaring me like that? I thought the cops were after me!"

Adam rubbed the back of his head and glared at Trevor. In the pale moonlight, Trevor couldn't exactly *see* it, but he could *feel* it.

"Yeah, 'cause if I'm a cop, I'd really go out all by myself without a police car." Adam took a deep breath and exhaled slowly. "Whatever. Did you find anything?"

"I don't know. Maybe. But—where the heck were you? You were supposed to *help* me!"

"My sister—Lily—wouldn't let me leave. She said I would screw something up and that I was messing with things I knew nothing about." Adam scowled, which made the poor kid look a bit like an angry baboon. "So I had to wait until she went off to work to sneak out."

"Yeah, well, I almost got devoured by a dragon thanks to you." Trevor cleared his throat. "I mean, Tara almost called the cops. Anyway—just look at this." Anything to keep Trevor from embarrassing himself more.

With his right hand, Trevor fingered the razor in his pocket. Should he show it to Adam? It could be something that the abductors left behind, or it could just be something Reanna kept around the house. Either way, Trevor felt like he wanted to keep it a secret a bit longer. Instead, he uncurled his left fist and held it up for Adam to see. Three of the fish-like scales rested there, still sparkling.

Adam leaned in closer. "What's that? Did your glitter wand explode all over you?"

Trevor repressed his first instinct of shoving his fist up Adam's nose. "You're so hilarious, Adam. You want me to put you on the flagpole? I can do it, you know. Ask Sean Davis."

Adam didn't reply. Trevor jabbed the toes of one shoe into the gravel. Maybe he wished it was Adam's face, maybe not.

Adam rubbed a fish scale between his fingers. Then he held it up to the moon, squinting like an antique appraiser on one of those PBS shows Trevor's grandma loved.

Adam's eyes widened a bit, like the appraisers did right before they announced that the family's rusting candelabra once belonged to some long-dead king and was worth millions.

Trevor shivered as he waited, but Adam only played with the end of his navy leather jacket.

Another beat.

Trevor tried not to think about all the better things he could be doing with his time, but he couldn't help but ask: "Listen, if you're going to fidget for much longer, just let me know. I've got a full Netflix queue I could be watching."

Adam rolled his eyes, shuffled his feet, and blurted out, "Do you believe in magic?"

"Like the song?" Trevor furrowed his brow.

"No—gosh, how old *are* you that you immediately think of that?" Adam raked his fingers through his shaggy brown hair. He looked like he was about ready to cry again. "I mean *real* magic!"

Trevor crossed his arms over his chest. "My dad's a preacher. If you're involved in the occult, then I'm probably not allowed to associate with you."

Adam snorted. "I'm not talking about *that* kind of magic. I'm talking about *real* magic! Like fairies, and—"

"And Bigfoot, Santa Claus, and the Tooth Fairy?" Trevor snickered. "Those things don't exist."

Adam groaned. "Would you shut up for a second? They may not exist on *Earth*, but where do you think we got the stories from?" Adam's voice gained speed while his hands gesticulated animatedly. "I know where. And I…sort of…know how to get there."

Trevor took a deep breath…and another. This situation kept getting worse and worse. Did mental asylums still exist? Because if they did, Adam had definitely escaped from one. Trevor would never find Reanna if he kept following advice from someone who deserved to be in a straightjacket.

96

Trevor pinched the bridge of his nose. It seemed he did that a lot around Adam. "What does magic have to do with anything, especially Reanna?"

Adam turned around in a circle, his hands resting on top of his head. In the pale moonlight, all that was clearly visible was his bright smile. It kind of reminded Trevor of the Cheshire Cat.

"Because this"—here, Adam shoved the fish scale right up to Trevor's face—"is a mermaid scale! I'd bet my entire life on it!"

"So…Reanna…was abducted…by…*mermaids?*"

Adam opened his mouth—and clamped it shut again. He paced around in another circle like a dog that needed to use the bathroom. "It had to be mermaids! It just has to. It's the only thing that makes sense—I should have *known!*" Adam babbled, mostly to himself, since Trevor had stopped paying attention. "The mermaids abducted her, and there's not going to be a ransom because they're not *ever* going to bring her back!" He turned around and held the supposed mermaid scale underneath Trevor's nose. "You really need to work on your storytelling abilities. I coulda had this cracked— ugh, I'm a moron! All this time, *wasted!*"

Trevor let a moment dangle between them in perfect silence. He hoped the silence was as sarcastic as he intended it to be. Then he pivoted and strode away, which was twice as sarcastic as the silence had been. He'd somehow managed to get entangled in the delusions of someone who played too many video games and thought they were real life.

"No! Wait! Please!" Adam's footfalls thudded against the pavement, and a moment later he latched onto Trevor's arm.

Trevor tried to shake him off, but on top of being a feral cat—boy, would Reanna love this weirdo—Adam apparently had the grip of an anaconda. Heat flooded Trevor's face, and he shoved the younger boy, who staggered back and released Trevor's sweatshirt sleeve.

"Shut up and go home!" Trevor pointed to the road behind Adam. "Reanna's dead, and you're acting like this entire thing is a joke. I shoulda never thought there was even a chance you were serious. I could be really mad at you, but no—half of the blame lies on me for being such a trusting idiot!" Which was precisely one of the things he'd tried to teach Reanna *not* to do, and yet, he'd somehow failed them both.

A street light flickered off and on above their heads and illuminated Adam's face. It didn't do him any favors, but at least it made his death glares easier for Trevor to see. "For once, just shut up!" Adam snapped. "I would *never* joke about this! You're just too stubborn to admit that something strange is going on!"

Trevor snorted and rolled his eyes. "Something *strange* is Reanna going missing. But mermaids? Really? That's *beyond* strange." With those words, he bounded up the stairs to his house two at a time. Adam sprinted up the steps right beside him.

Maybe if Trevor just ignored him, Adam would go away—like a pesky bee or something.

Trevor reached the top and raced for the door, but the smaller boy darted under his arm and reached it first.

Adam plastered his wiry frame against the door. "Please—I love Reanna. I know what happened to her—trust me!" He sucked in a breath. "Maybe I don't know all the details, but that's just a lack in my education. I know I can piece together everything—*please*, just give me a chance! *I need you!* For once in your life, *listen* to me! I need you, and I can do this!"

"Would you keep your voice down? I don't want my dad to hear you." Trevor tried to pry Adam away from the door, but the kid unleashed his inner feral cat. He kicked and scratched at Trevor— maybe even hissed once or twice again. One of the blows caught Trevor across the nose, and he stumbled backward as righteous fury boiled over.

He picked up Adam by his navy jacket collar and slammed the boy against the house. Adam's feet dangled, but he didn't let the simple fact he couldn't touch the ground get in his way. Adam landed a few good kicks on Trevor's knees and shins.

"Look, kid! I just want to be left *alone*. You're a delusional psycho, like one of those fans that kill their idols because they think they're married to each other." Trevor tried his best to keep his voice at a reasonable level, but his face felt flushed—not a good sign for keeping his temper in check. "Mermaids *did not* abduct Reanna, and I don't want to ever see your lousy face again. You know *nothing* about Reanna or the situation!"

Trevor gave Adam another shake for good measure and lowered him to the ground. Adam sniffled and wiped at his eyes, but Trevor still saw the tears that trickled down the boy's pale face. Trevor rubbed the bridge of his nose. Maybe he *had* been a little rough on the kid, but at the same time, Adam was exploiting Reanna's kidnapping to fulfill some weird fantasies, and Trevor couldn't feel sympathy for that.

"I'm not crazy. You have to believe me…they could kill her." Adam swiped away more tears with his sleeve.

Trevor reached past Adam and twisted the knob to open the door.

"Trevor?" someone called from inside the house.

Crap. "Yeah, Dad. It's me." Trevor sighed. "I'm fine."

"What are you doing?" Paul Spencer's voice sounded like he might be coming nearer.

Trevor grunted under his breath and closed the door a smidgen so his dad and Adam couldn't see each other. "I'm just— talking to a new kid. About Reanna. School stuff."

"Well, keep it down. Sounds like you all are a herd of elephants out there, and I'm on the phone."

Trevor grimaced. If his father was talking to Julie's mom this late at night…disgusting.

Trevor shut the door once more and turned around. He'd held on to the blind hope that Adam might disappear during the exchange, but no dice. The kid still stood on the porch.

"You said I didn't know anything, but what do you know?" Adam's voice quivered. "Do you know Reanna's middle name? Quinn."

"Anyone can know that," Trevor muttered. "You just have to look at the yearbook."

Adam continued, his voice quiet. "She kinda likes roller coasters, but she's scared of the dip and sitting next to strangers."

Trevor chewed on his lip. Sounded like her, which might explain why she suddenly clung to the swim team girls on amusement park field trips. Usually she didn't associate with them— or vice versa—outside of practices and meets.

"One of her favorite books is *The Little Prince*, and she cries each time she reads it, and she reads it at least once or twice a year."

That seemed to check out as well; Reanna carried it with her often.

"She has a birthmark on her shoulder that kind of looks like a pear."

Now *that* was a lie.

"It looks like a giant splotch, not a pear." Trevor crossed his arms over his chest.

"If she gets nervous, she starts chewing on whatever she can get her hands on. She loves kittens, is terrified of dolphins, and she gets lethargic when the weather turns too hot," Adam continued.

A thick silence fell between them. Trevor tapped his foot against the patio and digested this new information, piecing it together with what he did know. "How do I know you're not making this stuff up?"

Adam shrugged. "I guess you could think that if you wanted an excuse. But why would I lie about some things and tell the truth about others?"

Trevor returned the shrug.

Adam took a deep breath and glanced over his shoulder. He shifted his weight a few times. Maybe he thought Trevor would ask a question or prod him on. When that didn't happen, Adam huffed and rolled *his* eyes. "The reason she was abducted by mermaids is...is because..." He paused, as if he desperately wanted to say something but couldn't find the words to. "Because...ah...she's from another dimension."

Trevor couldn't help it. He threw back his head and laughed. He laughed so hard tears began to roll down his cheeks, and he had to lean against the house for support. "Right! That—"

"No! She's from a dimension called Gaia. The mermaids want her back because she's one of them!"

Trevor shoved Adam's head and opened the door. "Why don't you just leave me alone and go back to writing weird fantasy fanfiction about Reanna."

He tried to slam the door, but Adam wedged his entire wiry frame into it before he could close it. "I can prove it to you."

"I don't want you to prove anything from your deluded fantasy world."

"You *held* a mermaid scale in your hand! You can't deny that!"

Trevor scoffed. "I held a fish scale."

Adam threw his hands up in the air. He made several jerky, frustrated movements but still wouldn't move out of the doorway. "You are such a *pigheaded jerk*! Why do you have to be so stubborn and set in your ways?"

"It's a talent." Trevor tried to pull the door shut in hopes it would frighten Adam enough to leave. Even when the door hit him in the chest, Adam didn't move. Trevor growled and opened the door wider. He could only pray he would make it through the night without adding murder to the list of crimes he'd committed.

Adam narrowed his blue-gray eyes and stepped into the foyer of the house. The bells of doom tolled in Trevor's head. Wasn't that what they said about vampires—that if you let them in, they'd never leave? "Fine, you want tangible proof? I can get you some proof, because I'm from Gaia, too."

Trevor started to laugh again, but the look on Adam's face stopped him short. Regardless of the veracity or sanity of that statement, Adam believed it: he was from another dimension.

CHAPTER 13

ADAM

EARTH: PANAMA CITY, FLORIDA

Adam couldn't believe he'd blurted out his Gaian heritage. Even worse—he'd spilled it to Trevor Spencer, who currently looked like he was about to enter a catatonic state.

Why had Adam said anything? Lily would be so mad—she'd told him not to say anything, told him not to even come out tonight, but he just *had* to be stubborn.

Trevor still hadn't said anything, but he seemed to be sizing up the younger boy. Adam tried to appear taller, or maybe even bulkier, but it was hopeless. He was no athlete, despite his father's best hopes and wishes. In all honesty, everything that Trevor was, was everything that Adam's father wanted him to be—but that was neither here nor there.

"Prove it."

Adam blinked. Had he misheard? But no, Trevor stood with his arms crossed, eyes still on Adam. He glanced around and shoved Adam back out the door until they both stood on the porch underneath the pale moonlight. It was so silent that Adam could hear the waves as they broke against the shore like a gentle lullaby.

"What?" Adam asked.

Trevor grunted. "I said prove it."

Adam scratched at his nose for a second. "How am I supposed to do that? Show you a Gaian birth certificate or something?"

A light flipped on inside the house. Both boys blinked in the sudden haze, and Trevor growled under his breath. "You have two seconds. If you're from some other mystical Shire, show me. Summon some lightning, turn into an animal—something."

Adam winced. If only he'd kept his mouth shut—Trevor would never believe him now. "Um...I...I don't...I mean—I don't really have powers. Most people do, but I don't."

Of course, Adam could always take Trevor back home and show off Lily's powers, but that would include two things that wouldn't happen: Trevor meeting Lily, and Lily being cooperative and actually showing off her magic. But Lily would sooner kill him than freeze even a popsicle. Adam gripped his hair and paced around in a circle. What proof could he possibly produce that wouldn't end up with him in a graveyard?

Trevor scoffed. "I thought so. I'm done."

"Trevor?" someone called from inside the house. "Trevor, it's getting late."

Trevor opened the door just a crack. "Just give me a second, Dad. I'm almost done."

"Why is your friend out so late? Does he need a ride home? If people are kidnapping kids—" Adam couldn't see Trevor's dad; Trevor's frame blocked most of the opening.

"Everything will be fine, Dad." Trevor kept his voice metered. "Please. Leave us alone for one second."

Trevor's dad sighed. "Well, hurry up. And if your friend *does* need someone to take him home, come get me. And don't be so loud. You're going to wake the entire neighborhood."

"Yeah, yeah. It'll only be one more second. We're almost done." Trevor closed the door. Both Trevor and Adam waited in silence for a moment, but the light in the family room didn't flicker back off.

Trevor grunted. "I'm leaving."

"No! Wait—"

"Keep your voice *down*."

Adam dove for Trevor, but the older boy pushed him away, and they both stumbled.

"You can't prove anything," Trevor hissed. He advanced on Adam like a lion chasing its prey. "Stop whatever game you're playing, because it isn't funny. Stop annoying me, stop attacking me—" Trevor jabbed Adam in the chest with every blow.

Adam held up his hands in surrender. "What if I can open a portal? Will you believe me then?"

Trevor stopped moving, but he didn't remove his finger from Adam's chest. They stood there, and, though Trevor was a good foot taller, Adam tried to stand his ground instead of curling up into the fetal position like he wanted to.

Trevor snickered. "Sure. If you can open up a real portal to another world, I'll have to believe you. But since it doesn't exist..." He ended with a shrug.

"It does exist," Adam said. He could feel his temper rising; the urge to punch Trevor increased exponentially. "It does exist, but—only elves can open one up. You've got to be in a special place, in a special moon phase, or maybe be lucky enough to find residual magic..."

Trevor laughed and groaned all at the same time, an odd combination of sounds. He sank down to the porch and shook his head as he rubbed his temple. Adam knew from experience that a gesture like that meant his antics were driving someone—at this moment, Trevor—up the wall.

"Seriously. I'm going to bed. I don't care about your crazy delusions, but if you manage to open up a portal..." Sarcasm coated every word he said next. "...*then* you can talk to me." He stretched and slipped inside his house.

Adam heard the door lock, and frustration overwhelmed him. Part of him—the insensible, passionate part—wanted to beat on the door and *make* Trevor believe him. But the sensible part of Adam knew that it was over, at least for tonight. He should be lucky he'd gotten Trevor to cooperate for so long.

Adam groaned and gave in to his sleepiness and common sense and left Trevor's porch. He picked up a pebble and launched it into the night. His whole body ached as he climbed down the many, many steps. The exercise only made him angrier—angrier at the world that never seemed to give him a break. Just once, he'd like something to be easy for him, to go his way. But it seemed like ever since his birth, he'd been nothing but a curse, come to cause everyone heartache after heartache...

He trudged back to his house. The dingy apartment was a few blocks away, removed from the nicer beach homes in Panama City. When he and Lily had come here, they only had their savings account money, and that wasn't enough to rent more than a two-room apartment that would never, *ever* be home.

He shoved open the door, which always seemed to stick, and found the apartment still deserted. He had to fight back sleepiness as he scurried to his room. He yawned and booted up his computer.

He'd learned a bit from the elves.... He knew quite a bit about permanent portals, which could connect parts of Gaia or even different worlds with minimal upkeep once set in motion. But the ones between Earth and Gaia had been closed long ago and interdimensional portal travel condemned. Anyway, he didn't need a permanent portal, just a simple temporary one. And he knew portal spells had something to do with moons. Something weird—like the bird—peregrine falcons, or something—no! Perigee moons. That was it. Perigee moons and meridians...

His body sabotaged him. His brain felt dragged two ways at once, his thoughts becoming less and less coherent—why was he picturing a penguin now? He *knew* that wasn't important. No—a manticore wasn't, either… His eyelids drooped.

Adam tapped slowly on some keys, but the words he typed were barely comprehensible. No use. Maybe he should get up and do a jumping jack—no, he didn't have the energy to do that. Instead, he started to swing his chair back and forth as he tried to mentally graph everything.

Aging and time spells needed a perigee-syzygy moon, but any perigee moon would do for transport between Earth and Gaia. That's what the elves had said. But portals could only be opened up along the magnetic fields of meridians. Adam would have to gather supplies…

"A note!" He blurted out his suggestion and cringed. When Lily didn't immediately come into his room to murder him, he continued to mutter his thoughts out loud. "I'll just have to get a note to the elves. There should still be some remnants of an old portal around here somewhere…. That'll work well enough."

He took to pacing. He'd done three laps around his room before he solidified his course of action. Anything he could cobble together on Earth would be too small to get himself through—he needed help from Gaia. And if Trevor saw a note disappear into thin air, he'd have no choice but to believe that magic and Gaia existed and that Reanna had been taken to an alternate dimension.

Gosh. So. Tired.

He yawned. His legs grew heavier beneath him, and every step ached. He flopped face-first onto his bed, his last conscious thought that he hoped he'd remember everything in the morning.

And then it was morning.

Light filtered through his open window blinds. Adam groaned and put his hand over his eyes to protect himself from the stinging light, fighting back a yawn. He adjusted his position and had almost drifted back to sleep again when someone knocked on his door. He lifted his head.

Lily leaned against his door frame, her blonde hair messier than usual. A scowl was etched onto her face, and her blue eyes roamed over his form. "Why aren't you in pajamas?" Her harsh, matter-of-fact tone sounded remarkably like their dad's. Not to mention the cold look in her icy eyes was eerily familiar.

Adam moaned and pulled his mussed covers over his head. "I don't know. I was super tired. On computer. Go away."

Lily grunted and came to sit on the bed. It shifted under her weight, and he rolled over to look at her. She still wore a frown. "Right. Did you happen to sneak off and talk to someone I told you not to talk to?"

Adam let out a pitiful moan and forced a yawn. He tried to turn away, but Lily flipped him back to face her. He would have preferred not to. She looked like some sort of crazed villain. "Adam! I told you to leave it be!"

But instead of tearing his head off and strewing his limbs across miscellaneous parts of Florida, she sighed. She settled down beside him and pressed their foreheads together until their noses met. She smelled like her favorite perfume, a winter scent from Bath and Body Works. Her expression softened a bit as well—or it definitely moved from "enraged" down to "aggravated," at least.

"You need to give it up, all right? There's only so much you can do without screwing everything up." Lily glanced around, as if she thought there might be someone looking for them even now. "Nobody can know we're here. You can't *ever* go back to Gaia. I'm your guardian, and whatever fake powers come with that, I forbid you from ever thinking about it again."

"But—"

Lily tucked a strand of his shaggy hair behind his ear. "But nothing." Her eyes flickered upwards for a moment—but Adam could see that she struggled to fight back tears.

He wrapped his arm around her. "I'm sorry," he whispered. "I'm…I'm so caught up in everything else, sometimes I forget to worry about you."

"You don't need to worry about me. I'm worrying about you, okay?" Lily sat back up, extricating herself from the moment, probably so that she wouldn't be overwhelmed with emotions. That only made Adam's heart ache more for her. "Right now, your lack of sleep is my worry. There're all kinds of problems that lack of sleep can cause to your heart and your mind and—well, you get the picture. So I'm banning all late-night excursions, especially if they relate to Trevor or Reanna."

Adam tried again. "But—"

"No buts, I said!" Lily's expression was back to "mildly aggressive," roughly three or four steps away from where she had begun. "Right now, we're safe, and that's what matters. You can't go digging your nose into everybody's business, hoping to make it better. Put Reanna out of your mind. Everything will end up like it's supposed to be in the end."

"We might be safe, but Reanna's not!" Adam protested.

He sat up, but Lily pushed him back down on the bed.

"That's not our problem right now. Our problem is surviving." She took a deep breath. "Do you want the people who took Reanna to come after you next? You want them to drag your sorry butt to Gaia and try and kill you again?" She coughed, maybe in an attempt to hide her tears. "Please…*please*…try to stay out of trouble. For me." She gave him that puppy-dog look she always denied doing.

Adam sighed. He could never resist that. Lily could probably even get Ebenezer Scrooge to fork over hundreds of dollars by making that face.

But he couldn't leave Reanna without help, either…not when he knew what it was like to be prey.

"All right," Adam said. He wasn't entirely sure if he could go through with their agreement, but he wasn't about to admit that to Lily.

Lily pressed a kiss against his temple—apparently, she bought his act anyway. His stomach twisted up a bit more as his brain accused him of being a big fat liar. But if, in the long run, Adam helped Reanna, wouldn't that make the teensy lie worth it?

Adam's guilty conscience didn't quite think so, but he tried to ignore it.

"Thank you. This'll be better—you'll see." Lily glanced at the clock on her phone and ruffled his hair. "I've got to go to sleep. I hate night shifts. But you stay home, okay? I brought home some breakfast if you want to eat, too. Five-star: McDonald's pancakes."

Lily kissed her fingertips to imitate a chef and slapped his knee as she got up.

Adam gave a grunt in reply and feigned sleep, although he was too awake and guilt-ridden now to truly rest. As soon as Lily was out the door, he snatched a notebook and began to calculate the size of the magnets he needed to buy so he could harness enough energy to get a note into Gaia.

Lily would forgive him in the end, but Reanna…she'd never get the chance to do anything if she died. And somehow, he had to save her from that fate.

PART III

CHAPTER 14

REANNA

GAIA: DISTRICT OF CAPITAL CITY

Reanna screamed, the visions of Atlantis still in her mind as she woke from her sleep. A strange woman approached her, arms outstretched, and Reanna hurled a pillow at the intruder.

"No! Stay back, or—or I'll—I'll—!" Reanna fumbled for a threat, but her poor brain scrambled to make sense of anything. Where *were* they? What had been an awful nightmare, and what had been true?

"Sweetie, calm down," the woman—who looked to be maybe in her late twenties or thirties—cooed as she rounded the bed. "I'm not going to hurt you."

Reanna threw off the soft covers and scrambled from the bed, even though she fell off in her haste. The woman breathed a laugh and flew over to help Reanna up. Literally flew—the woman hovered in midair with her translucent blue wings.

Reanna yelped again and crawled backward. She plastered herself against the wall, her eyes wide with fright. "No, no, no, no, no…."

"What's wrong?" the woman asked. She knelt down in front of Reanna, her face serious.

"I can't be back here! I'm not supposed to be—" Reanna's voice broke, and she couldn't speak through her wails. She buried her head against her knees and sobbed, feeling too much like the little six-year-old who had run away. The distant memories that had suddenly resurfaced ignited all of her fears, and she trembled like a baby.

"Shh. You are Reanna, then? We called you Gilly because none of us were sure."

Reanna felt a touch against her head and wrenched away. She scrambled away as the woman inched closer. If Reanna were a cat, she would have been hissing and caterwauling. As it was, though, those things weren't quite as socially acceptable for a human to do.

For a second, Reanna considered lying. Then she did. "N-no...I'm not Reanna...I-I'm Gilly..."

"Well, Gilly, if you are Reanna, you don't have to worry. The Council has passed an edict that you're not to be harmed, and under no circumstance are you to be handed over to Queen Arana." The woman cleared her throat and perched on the edge of the bed. "I don't know what you've been told, but there's a war right now. Queen Arana ravaged the country of Daspin—"

"Ravaged Daspin?" Reanna's head snapped up. "But—that's where the elves live. Why would she hurt them? They never did anything to anyone!"

"Gilly, hmm?" The woman raised both eyebrows. "You sure know a lot about Gaia if you're just an Earth girl."

Reanna blushed. "I...um...uh..." She glanced up at the woman's crystal-blue eyes only to quickly look back down at the floor.

The woman smoothed out the pink blanket around her. "I promise you. Nobody is going to turn you over to Queen Arana."

Reanna's lips twitched. "Why the elves? What did they do to her? Did they do something to cause the war?"

The woman's tiny mouth twisted into a grimace. "She knew of their powers from the Legend of Thessalonike...how an elf had transformed a human from Earth into a mermaid. Queen Arana began to wonder if the opposite had happened to you." The woman let her gaze surreptitiously go to Reanna's legs, and Reanna tucked them under herself, suddenly self-conscious. "I see you did barter off your tail."

"And powers," Reanna whispered. "It was the only way the elves would let me go to Earth. They said the last time magic had traveled between Earth and Gaia, horrible things happened."

The woman shrugged. "I never liked history much, so I don't know the details. I'm sure they're right, though. My husband probably knows what they're talking about. He might have even lived through those awful things himself." She paused, and her eyes softened. "But the elves are the guardians of the portals, so you had no choice but to trust them."

"There's that, and I was six and running away. If they would have told me to swap my voice and that every step I took would be like walking on knives, I still would have done it." Reanna sniffed and looked around the unfamiliar quarters again. An open window in the left-hand corner revealed a large city with curved brick buildings and large clock towers. Wind flowed in and made the white curtains dance about. For a second, Reanna got lost in the view as she remembered just how beautiful the world of Gaia had been. Beautiful but terrifying.

"How did I get here?" she whispered after a moment.

"Like I said, the Queen barged into Daspin almost a year ago and declared they were harboring a fugitive. They captured all the elves they could, killing the children if the parents didn't obey. Somehow, they tracked down the elf that transformed you. Shaesia, right?"

Reanna moaned. She thumped her head against the wall a few times for extra measure. "How did they find her? She…she was hidden. I didn't even find her! She found me because I was floundering on the shoreline, beached in the summer sun. I was dehydrated and too weak to use my powers. She said I was just pitiful enough that she had to help me."

The woman lowered herself off the bed. This time, Reanna didn't bother to back up. The woman must have taken this as an invitation to invade any other personal bubbles because she reached out to touch Reanna's shoulder. "As kind-hearted as she sounds, apparently she's made quite a few enemies. Most elves are terrified of her for some reason I can't fathom. I'm sure someone turned her in to Arana as a way to protect their own family."

"But she wasn't supposed to tell anyone she helped me!" Reanna bawled. She stuck her sleeve up against her mouth and bit a clump of it. Nothing had changed at all since she was a child. She still messed up everything and caused problems for everyone. First Arana, then Shaesia…why did Reanna even have to be born? Everything would have been so much easier for everyone if she could have died.

The woman's expression drooped. Tears may have even gathered on her bottom lashes—it was as if she genuinely might cry at Reanna's anguish. "I doubt she did. But enough people probably turned on her as a scapegoat."

"Is—is she…d—de…" Reanna choked on the word.

"Oh, sweetie." The woman pressed a kiss against Reanna's temple. Though Reanna typically would have balked at such a blatant invasion of space, the gesture almost felt nice in wake of the devastating announcement. "I…no. I don't think so. Just taken hostage by Arana. The Council is trying to save her—trying to save everyone—but…well, things are bad on Gaia right now."

Reanna whimpered, but that made the woman gather her up in a hug. She ran her fingers through Reanna's mass of unseemly curls and tried to untangle them. Reanna winced every time the woman came across a knot—which was, roughly, every second.

"Atlantis started the war when they captured the elves and forced them to turn the mermaids' tails into legs while they were on land." The woman found another snag, and she jerked particularly hard at it. Reanna let out a sputter of pain and clenched her fists. "The Atlantean soldiers previously had to pull up the ocean tides with them wherever they went, which was good for us, since it required a lot of power. With their new legs, though…well, let's just say they're now bullying us with the weather. They caused a blizzard in the desert of Reggeria earlier in the year, three tidal waves in Daspin, and massive flooding in parts of Kirova. The only people who aren't reporting water-related disasters are the vampires of Simit. They're probably just being their usual anti-social selves, though."

Reanna's eyes fluttered closed. She wished that they would just stay closed forever. Then someone could take her body back to Arana and this would all be over.

"So, as you can imagine—the spellcasters of Reggeria retaliated. The fairies and even some of the werewolves joined the fight, but aside from that…the vampires won't help yet, and the dwarves and gnomes, even though they live in Kirova, aren't good at fighting. But they're trying to help by gathering information, so that's something. They're obsessed with libraries and mines and fishing, and their bodies aren't built for much more."

Reanna wouldn't know; she'd never met a dwarf or a gnome during her six years on Gaia. Not many people wanted to vacation to the depths of Atlantis: not when drowning, maiming, and slavery were more likely to be on the itinerary than sunbathing, souvenir shopping, and surfing.

"So how do I factor into this?" Reanna asked.

"The soldiers captured the elves and…" The woman paused. "Well, you're old enough to know the truth. I'm not going to sugarcoat things. The mermaids have captured the elves in concentration camps and are holding them hostage."

Images of graphic, gruesome pictures from history flashed through Reanna's mind. She covered her mouth and fought back the tide of nausea. She'd known her mother could be abusive, but—that still seemed like a whole new level of depravity.

The fairy grunted as she tried to undo another rat's nest. "The mermaids tortured the elves until they opened a portal between Earth and Gaia. As far as knowing where you were, I think Arana must have some way of divining that, but none of it makes sense to me. I don't know why she let you go for so long or why she's suddenly so desperate to have you back." The fairy sighed. "I'm not privy to all the Council details, either, but what I *do* know is that a spy was the one that opened up the portal and sent a note to the Council to tell them everything. The Atlanteans sent in two soldiers to find you, but my daughter and one of her best friends stopped them on the return trip."

The woman grinned, which felt like a stab through Reanna's heart. She looked so proud of her daughter.

Arana never had that expression on her face when she talked to her own daughter.

"Anyway, the Council is working on things. We're going to get everyone out of those camps, but it's hard to fight when the weather itself isn't on your side." The woman shook her head. "Until then, you're under the official protection of my family—specifically, my daughter, Laile, who's been appointed as your guardian."

The woman paused, perhaps waiting for Reanna to ask some questions, but Reanna's brain felt too sluggish at the moment to think of anything beyond: *this is all my fault* and *I just want to go home.*

Although the last thought made Reanna wince. How could she be so selfish, so uncaring toward the suffering of others? But she couldn't deny it. She couldn't help anyone in a *war*. She just wanted to be shipped back to Earth.

When no questions came, the fairy adjusted her position and continued. "Long story short, when Laile rescued you, you had a powerful memory spell on you which kept you from recalling anything. She accidentally triggered it by mentioning a name, and then you passed out. It must have been a doozy of a memory that the spell tried to repress, though, because you were out for a few days."

Reanna sighed and chewed harder on her sleeve. Through a mouth full of fabric, she blubbered, "I'm sorry I've caused so much trouble for everyone. I don't understand why my mother wants me back so badly. All she ever did was hate me."

The woman paused. Her grip tightened on Reanna, as if this strange woman was going to single-handedly hold back Arana and all her armies. Reanna shuddered—she vaguely remembered the soldiers, dressed in scales that shifted colors between silvers and pastels, as they burst into her house and beat her with water, over and over…

Her mind convulsed. She couldn't think of the attack or Atlantis. Instead, she focused on the fairy in front of her. On her long, dark-brown hair that seemed beautiful enough for a model. It even smelled nice—like cinnamon and honey—as the woman leaned in closer.

The fairy's voice dropped a smidgen, and her bright blue eyes narrowed. "Nobody knows, but it's something sinister if you ask me. Probably some kind of…magic or curse or something. Bloodline black magic is the strongest, though the most forbidden, of all magic, because it requires a blood sacrifice from a relative. That's just a theory of the Council's, of course, but it might explain why she needs you. And depending on what spirit she might make a sacrifice to—well, anything could happen."

"Great." Reanna sucked on her sleeve. "I always knew she'd kill me one day."

"Absolutely not." The fairy gave Reanna another squeeze. "We won't let her. The best dwarves in all of Kirova are scouring their libraries for any information about spirits powerful enough to tempt Arana. If we could possibly assume a motive, we might figure out what her plans are…and that's the way the dwarves prefer to participate, anyway, so it makes them feel useful." The woman smiled as if they hadn't just discussed human sacrifices and concentration camps. Or maybe that stuff happened on a daily basis in Gaia, so the information didn't faze her more than a normal Tuesday. "Don't fret. The only thing better would be to search the legendary Library of Thessalonike. We're going to find out what she wants and stop her. And it may not even have anything to do with bloodline black magic at all."

Ah, always mildly reassuring to know that there was only *some* chance your mother wanted to make you a ritual sacrifice.

Reanna sniffed, wiped at her eyes, and…caught a whiff of herself. She nearly gagged as horror washed over her. She inched away from the woman, afraid to share her scent with anyone else. This was one facet of common courtesy she didn't know—how rude was it to ask someone if you could use their tub when you didn't even know their name?

"Um…ma'am…er, if you don't mind…what's…your name?" That seemed like a logical first step in getting rid of the stench.

"Oh!" The woman's blue eyes grew wide. "I completely forgot to introduce myself, didn't I? I'm Cynerra Úlfur, wife of Council Representative Damien Úlfur." Cynerra smiled and offered her hand to Reanna. "And now that you're safe, why don't we go see to getting you a warm bath?"

CHAPTER 15

LAILE

GAIA: DISTRICT OF CAPITAL CITY

L aile backed away from the door, uttering every Atlantean curse word she knew in her head. Cynerra might have been proud of Laile's guardianship, but she would probably not be so proud of her expansive knowledge of colorful language.

She *knew* coming home was a bad idea. Cynerra had already given Reanna fancy promises of safety and security, which meant that the lost princess would have no desire to blindly follow Laile's loose-on-details plot to rescue the elves—a plan that also lacked the "parental seal of approval"…and the Council's backing.

Flying fig-whits.

She needed a drink before she could do anything.

Still full size, she flew into the kitchen and grabbed her favorite cup from the top shelf. Perks of being one of only two fairy children in the house: she could hide things on the top shelf away from the three werewolf brats.

Typically—though there were exceedingly rare exceptions— when people from different magical races had children, their offspring were born either one or the other. In Laile's family,

Damien's werewolf genetics had proved superior. Only Laile and her older brother, Mionos, had inherited Cynerra's fairy powers. Beyond that, Mionos was the only child that favored Cynerra's pale complexion—though it was a bit darker than their mother's—and even he had Damien's dark eyes.

Her target secured, Laile tapped the top of her faucet to get cold water. It ran solely by spellcaster enchantments, an engineering masterpiece of the Council. Another touch turned it off, and Laile downed about half of her drink in the first gulp as she weighed the options Reanna would soon be faced with.

Option One, per the Council and surrounding adults: Stay in the city with its theater and boutiques, wide parks and museums. Get everything paid for on a pseudo-vacation with bodyguards. And never leave Capital City, which almost guaranteed safety from Arana.

Option Two, per Gregory and Laile: March right into the heart of the battle, break the law, and abandon all security. And she couldn't forget storming Arana's castle as a living sacrifice like Tam Lin to the evil fairy queen of old, Laurel. All for the sake of helping rescue the elves and, simultaneously, all the people of Gaia, a people whom Reanna had no emotional attachment to.

It didn't take a witch doctor to figure out what a traumatized seventeen-year-old girl with no attachments to the continent of Solis would do.

Shake-spear's pen, Laile didn't even know what *she* should do when she put it like that.

But there was always one thing she could do: talk to Gregory.

She flew into the other room and found him deep in some debate with Kal and Mionos. From the snippet Laile overheard, they were going around in circles about the Fiastro colonization. She felt no shame about interrupting this discussion as she beckoned Gregory onto the balcony.

He tapped the back of the couch as he rose. "Anyway, I have more points when I get back."

Wren, one of Laile's youngest twin sisters, made kissing noises as she colored her book on the living room floor. "*Oooh*, going outside with *Laile?*"

"Shut it, or I'll have your werewolf form shaved to look like a poodle." Laile glared at Wren, who stuck her tongue out in return.

Gregory shut the door behind him, probably to prevent any sisterly violence. "Ignore her. She's only nine. She thinks it's fun to tease people."

"She's a brat." Laile rolled her shoulders and took a sip of her water. "Only slightly more annoying than Kal, if you ask me, but I'm getting off-track."

"Yes, I didn't think you called me out here to rant about your siblings in private." Gregory leaned over the wrought-iron fence and threaded his fingers together. He scanned the crowds: witches and wizards scurried through the skies, either levitating themselves or on brooms; fairies zoomed to and fro; and other magical beings—vampires, werewolves, and all the like—walked below.

"Gilly's up. Mom's got her, and she's definitely Reanna." Laile took a swig of her water before she offered it to Gregory. He touched the bottom of the cup, murmured, "*Duplici*," and pulled away an exact copy for himself.

Laile clinked her glass against his.

He pulled the rim away from his lips and swished the liquid around inside the cup. "It seems like we're all good to go, then. Our minor detour has been a success."

"Wrong." Laile slumped against the railing. "Mom's already told Reanna she's under the Council's watch and is not to be harmed under any circumstance."

"Ah." Gregory rested the glass against his lips. "Now I see the conundrum."

"Yeah. Our big plan to go in and save the elves while the Council is bogged down with paperwork? Gone." Laile raised the glass to the sky. "We'll never convince Reanna to come with us now, and even *more* people will die or starve or be tortured in the meantime." She rested the heel of her palm against her eyes. "*Laws*, why did I even try to do something historic and amazing?"

Gregory took a sip of water. "You mean for the greater good, right?"

Laile flushed. No, what she said hadn't sounded okay at all. "Obviously."

Gregory shook his head. "You're so obvious. I know part of your impatience is because you can't stop comparing yourself to your mother."

"She was already out exploring the world and having insane adventures by the time she was my age. And this is *way* more important than some of the stuff she did!" Laile ran her finger around the lip of the cup. "Every time I try to break away from my parents' shadows, I get sucked right back in."

"Oh, yes," Gregory said dryly. "Let's just disregard that you went through sloughs of paperwork, passed your mock guardian trials, *and* were appointed an official guardian at only eighteen. You're right. That is clearly the sign of a person that lives in their parents' shadows."

Laile rolled her eyes. "I want more, Greg. I want to be remembered in history books. My dad will be. The first werewolf representative on the Council, the man who broke through so many barriers and persevered through untold prejudice and injustices. He created a better tomorrow. And my mom—she's been *everywhere*. She's done *everything*. And I'll just be a side note, just a little 'Damien and Cynerra Úlfur had five children' in the history books. Not a name. Not even a gender. I want *more*. I want them to be remembered as *my* parents!"

"And save innocent lives that are being unjustly imprisoned, tortured, and killed by Queen Arana, right?" Gregory raised his eyebrows.

Laile cleared her throat and took another sip. Her face flushed again, and she murmured into her cup, "That, too, of course." Did it make her a bad person, though, if she wanted to be the one who saved them? She waited a few moments for the heat to die away from her cheeks. "But all of that relies on Reanna, and how are we going to convince her?"

"Show her." Gregory's expression hardened, and he stared off into the distance. "Show her all of the dying soldiers. The suffering civilians. The *elves*."

He sighed, and Laile jostled him with her shoulder. "Okay. We'll show her. We'll brainstorm together, but you've been putting me off for too long. Come on. I'm your best friend." And his soon-to-be wife, though he didn't need to know that yet. "Tell me why you're gloomier than normal." Her stomach twisted, and the longer he stayed silent, the more sure Laile became that she was going to throw up.

"It's nothing." His brown eyes shifted over to her instead of the horizon. "Nothing to worry about."

"That's a lie."

"It isn't," Greg said tersely. "I'm fine. Just let it go, okay? Everything's fine."

"Sure, okay. Great talk." Laile patted his shoulder, but her stomach wouldn't unknot. "I just hope that's the truth."

CHAPTER 16

REANNA

GAIA: DISTRICT OF CAPITAL CITY

I t only seemed like a few hours ago that Reanna's biggest problems had been a math test and what Trevor Spencer might say about her puking.

Now she was back in a world that only too clearly reminded her of her psychopathic—in Reanna's humble opinion—mother, wondering what on Earth—excuse her, Gaia—she was going to do.

Reanna let the shower water fall over her for a moment and closed her eyes, imagining, wishing, hoping that she was back in Florida, in her own flower-themed bathroom. She peeked open one eye: no luck.

With a sigh, she shut off the water and exited the bathroom, leaving a trail of drips on the cream-colored carpet. Blue leggings and a floral-patterned white shirt waited for her on the borrowed bed. Reanna felt her heart twist up—she could only hope that Cynerra hadn't done anything to the trusty Spider-Man sweatshirt besides launder it. The woman certainly had an argument that the article of clothing needed to be burned, but Reanna couldn't lose that last bit of home now.

On top of that, the replacement clothes swallowed her whole.

Laile, the rightful owner, had to be a good five inches taller than Reanna, as well as thinner at the hips, and the fabric squeezed Reanna in uncomfortable places. The shirtsleeves reached all the way to her palms, and the leggings were skin-tight and probably showed off every curve and dimple she had.

Hopefully, the Úlfur family wasn't expecting much from a princess of Atlantis. Reanna would only disappoint them.

She took a moment to laugh at her own reflection in the vanity mirror. She swept her damp curls up off her neck and secured them with a hair tie—also borrowed from Laile, judging by the long brown hair still attached to it.

"Reanna! Time for dinner!" Laile knocked once and peeked her head in. "Nice outfit. I have good taste."

Reanna flapped the loose sleeves around. "I look like a shrinking hippie."

"I can only hope a hippie is Earth-slang for someone with good taste. In which case—yes." Laile flew over to Reanna and dragged her out to the dining room for supper—or, as Reanna would later refer to it, the Gauntlet of Úlfur Chaos.

"Come on. Sit here." Laile pulled out a seat for Reanna and claimed the other one. The whole family chattered, laughed, and argued, so loud that Reanna didn't hear Laile talking until the fairy-girl poked her in the side.

"What?" Reanna twisted around so she could look at Laile.

Laile's lips moved, but did she make a sound? Questionable.

"*What?*" Reanna repeated, a little bit louder.

Laile huffed and leaned in closer until her lips pressed against Reanna's ear. "I said, I'll run you through introductions." She gestured to the bronze-skinned, red-headed boy on the other side of Reanna. "That's my older brother, Mionos. He's a fire fairy. He's got a thing for my best friend, too—that is, my best friend *Aimee*, who's from Earth, like you. Not my best friend Greg." Laile snort-laughed, but Reanna couldn't see the humor. "If you get a chance, tell him his hair looks stupid. He dyes it a new color every week, and I told him he looked like a torch this week. Agree with me." Laile pointed to the seat beside her. "Of course, that's Greg. You know him. Beside him, at the head of the table, is my dad, Damien Úlfur." Damien's broad shoulders touched both Greg's and Cynerra's. The Úlfur patriarch wore a brown shirt that almost matched the color of his skin. His dark eyes caught Reanna's, and he smiled as Laile continued to talk. "He's pretty important, actually. He championed for werewolf equality for years to prove that they aren't some mindless beasts. Around twenty-five or so years ago, he finally secured a spot on the Council—the first werewolf to ever do so." Laile's eyes softened as she gazed at her dad.

Reanna shoved down the pang of jealousy. It must have been nice to not have to worry about your dad making out with his secretary—or just not existing in the first place, like her bio-dad.

"Beside him is my mom, Cynerra. You met her. She's a water fairy, and I'm a gem fairy, in case you're wondering." Laile wrinkled her nose at the next two in line: stocky, brown-headed, identical girls that looked like Damien had just cloned himself. Of the children, they alone seemed to favor his wider build—most of the other people that Laile had introduced had inherited Cynerra's tall, willowy frame. "Those are my twin sisters, Wren and Lark. They're werewolves, but, most importantly, they're brats."

One of the twins must have noticed Laile's finger, because she wrapped her arms around her twin protectively and stuck her tongue out at Laile.

"Charming." Laile moved on to the last seat. "And that's Kal, my younger brother. He's a prankster; don't believe anything he says. He's a werewolf, too." Laile made a little *hmm* noise. "I think that's it. Oh—Mionos is twenty-one, I'm *almost* nineteen, Kal is sixteen, and my sisters are nine."

Reanna blinked. Should she offer up a résumé of her own here? Did she introduce herself as a runaway princess of Atlantis, or as Reanna Cook, average high schooler? Somehow, Reanna doubted Laile would be impressed by any of Reanna's swim records or state tournaments.

Reanna settled on the stupidest response. "Uh...cool." She adjusted her drooping shirt and scrambled to think of something else. "I'm seventeen." She dragged her fork through some orange goop with mashed-potato-like consistency and mixed it with the meat on her plate. "So...uh...I heard you say you're my guardian. What exactly does that mean?"

"Oh—it basically means that I'm your bodyguard of sorts. I get to beat up all the bad guys that try and hurt you—and make sure you get to all your Council appointments safely." Laile leaned forward and smiled, crinkling her nose and closing her eyes. Reanna couldn't help but grin, though Laile couldn't see it.

The tender moment ended a bit too abruptly when one of the twins screeched, tackled the other, and the two clattered to the floor.

"*Girls!*" Cynerra sprang up and tried to wrestle them away from each other. The twins shifted and snapped and snarled at each other until their mother doused them both with a waterspout.

Reanna lifted her feet so the rivulets wouldn't wet them. "Um...is this normally what dinner is like for you all?"

Laile bit into a roll and nodded. "Actually, they're on their best behavior right now."

"This is worse than my fights with my sister Tara. And my mom thinks *those* are bad!" Reanna smiled as she imagined Isabella Cook's reaction to this dinner-table scene. "Whenever we had a fight, my mom would always make us apologize and hug each other. Then we had to write a list of ten reasons why we loved each other."

Laile furrowed her brow and swallowed. "I...I didn't think you had a sister. We haven't had any news of Arana having another kid, I mean."

"Oh…" Reanna shook her head. Her happiness fizzled out like all the carbonation leaving a soda. "No…I meant on Earth. In Atlantis, we never had family dinners…it was just me in my room most of the time." She squashed her potatoes beneath her fork and watched them squirt through the slits.

Laile coughed and slammed her fist into her chest a few times. Her cheeks reddened, but she didn't address her blunder. Instead, she shoved another bite of roll in her mouth and chewed.

Reanna scrambled through different conversation topics, but the only one she could settle on was: "It must be interesting, having so many different magic powers under one roof."

Laile bobbed her head, seemingly a bit relieved at Reanna's cover. "Yeah, it's rare. In the old days, different magical races rarely interacted, and half-breeds were considered abominations. Wars were fought over stuff like this." Laile picked at the top of her roll. "It's still uncommon nowadays, but not unheard of."

Reanna nodded her head toward Gregory. "What about him? Does he live here, too?"

"Greg?" Laile's cheeks flushed again. "No, not technically. My parents were friends with his parents until they died in the Great Warlock Uprising ten years ago. Greg has spent a lot of time here ever since, but he technically lives with his grandma and little sister. We didn't adopt him—it's—I mean—that'd make it weird."

Reanna blinked. Make *what* weird? Were they dating? Stuck in the friendzone? In the middle of an unrequited crush? That'd probably be prying, though.

"Oh! I've been meaning to ask you." Laile grasped Reanna's hand. Reanna squeaked and dropped her fork, full of unidentifiable but delicious meat, back onto her plate. "You told us to call you Gilly, because that's what your bracelet said." Laile twisted the silver trinket around Reanna's wrist. "How'd you get that nickname? Gills, as in mermaid gills? Does your Earth family know you're a mermaid?"

131

Reanna shook her head. Her throat constricted. "Uh...no way—because I'm not. Not anymore, I mean. Mom called me Gilly-Goose because there's an old Earth saying called 'silly goose.' But it does come from gills—because I'm on the swim team. Mom always said I took to water like a fish, and when I was little, I'd act all silly whenever she took me down to the beach." Reanna blushed a bit. "It's a dumb nickname, I know. But—go figure, right?"

Laile grabbed another roll. "Nah. I love nicknames and pet names, but nobody ever gives me one. My mom only calls me Laile Reen—my middle name—when I'm in trouble. Otherwise, I'm just plain old Laile."

Reanna dusted off the part of her brain where she stored information about possible new friends and tucked the file away there. Aside from a few mothballs, that cabinet was mostly empty. But if they actually made it past the acquaintance stage, Reanna would brainstorm some nicknames for this fairy-girl.

The conversation lapsed into silence again, and Reanna struggled to find a new topic before her awkward-meter dipped so far into "Danger, Will Robinson" territory that she couldn't come back from it. To give herself more time, she took a bite of her food and hoped Laile wouldn't find her completely rude.

Unfortunately, the silence allowed her brain to *think* once again. Reanna's mind drifted to the elves, especially Shaesia. She couldn't imagine them being held hostage and tortured, all to find her. Her appetite fled as she thought about everyone who was suffering on her account.

She sucked in a breath and put down her fork. She pressed the heels of her palms against her eyes to stop the tears that threatened to come through.

Laile nudged Reanna again. "What's wrong?"

"It's just...I keep thinking about Shaesia and the other elves. Shaesia helped me when I was a fugitive...she doesn't deserve to be held captive. None of the elves do."

Laile sat up straighter even as Reanna's spirit shrank. "Would you be willing to help save them from Arana? If you could?"

Reanna felt the cold, icy water of fear surge through her veins, and she shivered. Arana's face lingered in her mind, as did so many memories. "I...I..." Her tongue suddenly felt too big for her mouth, and the crowded dinner table too constricting.

She subconsciously began rubbing her wrist, digging her fingernails in as the fear overwhelmed her. What could she do against Arana? Nothing—and if Reanna dared to do anything to draw attention to herself, her mother would find out and...and do what? Kill her? Drag her back to Atlantis? A torturous existence with Arana was worse than death.

Breathe. She had to breathe. She had to remember to breathe, to think, to focus on the things she could see in the present, like...like the potatoes on her plate.

"No," Reanna whispered. "I can't do anything. I just wish I could."

Laile slumped back in her seat. "What do you want to do? Stay here?"

"I want to go back home. To my mom and Tara." Reanna blinked back tears. Her throat constricted so much she almost suffocated.

Laile stabbed her roast with her fork. "I wish I could help, but I can't. All the elves that could open up a portal are Arana's prisoners, so we can't get to Earth anymore. Not only that, but now the Atlanteans know where you live. If you go back, you're only putting your mom and sister in danger."

Reanna stilled. She hadn't realized before—she was truly *stuck*. She couldn't go back and couldn't move forward. She would have to live out her days in hiding, staying under Damien and Cynerra's protection, and…doing what? All her dreams back on Earth suddenly evaporated. She was stranded in Gaia forever.

"I never even got to say goodbye," Reanna whispered. She abandoned all manners and shoved her chair away from the table. She raced toward her borrowed bedroom—or was it her permanent bedroom now?—and threw herself onto the comforter. She sobbed, and every time she almost gained composure, she'd think of another face back home and start all over again. Her mother, Tara…she would even put up with Trevor, if only she could get back home.

But there was nothing she could do. She was just as useless as Queen Arana had always said.

CHAPTER 17

LAILE

GAIA: DISTRICT OF CAPITAL CITY

The next morning, Laile found Gregory perched on the edge of the couch, book in hands, the earpiece of his glasses tucked between his teeth. He turned a page but didn't notice her until she splayed her hands out over the ancient words.

"What you said last night—about showing Reanna all the suffering that's going on to convince her to sympathize with us? I think that's the best idea we've got. I talked to her a little last night, and she's got a pure heart. I just know it."

"All right, fair enough. I like hearing that I'm right." Gregory replaced his glasses onto their rightful spot and blinked his brown eyes at her. "What's your plan?"

"Well—I don't want to scare her too badly at first. So I thought we might go out to eat, shop around a bit…" Laile fidgeted with her fingers.

Gregory tucked a bookmark into the page as he closed the cover. "That sounds an awful lot like you're trying to convince her the Council has the best idea—stay here and get pampered."

"No, no." Laile waved him away. "Trust me. That's only the first little bit. I saw her at the table last night. You have to inch her into these things so she doesn't freak out. So after we have a fun girls' day, we'll stop by the catacombs and see all the refugees there."

Gregory winced. "I know you're impatient to get this underway, but it's her first day. I like being right, but you can't just force your own morals onto someone else. Give Reanna time to acclimate—"

Laile poked Gregory's nose, and he sneezed. "Don't you dare back out on me now. We're going to stop this war with Reanna."

He grumbled. "I'm not backing out on you. I'm just trying to help you temper your enthusiasm with a healthy dose of reality."

"Shh." Laile shook her head. "Mark my words. We're going to stop the war soon." She flounced off to retrieve Reanna for their outing. Gregory declined to tag along, but he did give Laile a *remember-what-I-said* look before they left.

And she did think about what he said. She thought about it while she showed Reanna the theater—Laile's favorite spot in town—and the museum that looked like a giant glass pyramid. She pointed out the historic clock, which was one of the oldest structures, and chic boutiques that had taken over the interior of some ancient stone building.

By the time they waited at the manticore bus stop almost two hours later, Laile was fairly certain she'd taken things slow enough to start to ease her way into the bigger issues.

She clutched Reanna's hand as the manticore bus pulled up.

"Wow…" Reanna breathed as the bus's "legs" lowered like a creature crouching on its haunches. As its name implied, the manticore bus was *supposed* to look like the legendary creature, complete with a head on the front and a snake tail on the back. In execution, though, it resembled a toddler's garish drawing.

One of the ribs slid apart, and Laile broke the girl's reverie to tug Reanna inside. "We have three more hours to explore the city before we're due back at the Council." Laile pointed out one of the windows at the stately rotunda that sat in the middle of town. A clock face set into the white marble roof ticked down the time. "It's way past the museum, but you've probably seen glimpses of it all day."

The manticore's legs lifted, and the bus zoomed down the busy streets, kept aloft by levitation spells. Reanna squeaked over every little thing, from the faux fur seats to the chandeliers that rocked back and forth from the ceiling.

Laile stopped by a clothing store next, one more removed from downtown so the prices fared a little better. Reanna still wore Laile's ill-fitting clothes—not something that would make a great impression on anyone, refugee or sitting Council member. Laile ushered Reanna in and out of the nicer boutique. The girl came away with some clothes better suited for her frame—salmon-colored pants and a black t-shirt with a cute witch underneath a full moon. Laile tossed in a cardigan to add a touch of professionalism when her ward met the entire Council.

After that, they visited a tiny café, where Laile bought several extra helpings of meals.

"Where are we taking those?" Reanna peeked into the bags as she ate her sweet bread.

"To the old catacombs."

Reanna blinked. "You feed corpses here?"

Laile chuckled. "No. There are some people I want you to meet—*living* people."

The manticore bus drove them to the outskirts of town. The catacombs spiraled into the skies. Stained glass decorated the very top and reflected beautiful, geometric patterns onto the floor as Laile and Reanna crossed the threshold.

"Word of advice? Don't mention who you are or that you're supposed to be a mermaid," Laile whispered. "Tensions are pretty high right now, and there's some anti-mermaid sentiment. I'm not sure if they'd be angry or happy about who you are."

Reanna tucked her cardigan around her frame and scooted closer to Laile.

They passed through the foyer and into the wide middle room. Rows and rows of sleeping pallets stretched along both sides of the walls, the only beds that hundreds of souls would know. Tired, hungry faces stared up at the girls as they walked between the rows.

A few children darted around the room. They were bursts of happiness in such a dreary landscape—the living embodiments of the pretty glass reflections that danced along the floor in a world of death. Some people slept, while others whispered among themselves, but most of the souls here seemed burdened by weights so heavy they might crumble the catacombs.

"Refugees. There are floods in the desert, droughts on the islands, and blizzards in the floating country of Jenkirre. People come here to escape the mermaids because, so far, we've been blessed to not be physically touched by the war." Laile opened a door which had, at one time, led to an embalmer's office. Now, it served as a kitchen. With a few words, she dropped off her donation and headed back to the front room.

"This isn't even the worst case. I tried to tell you last night…all the elves are in concentration camps. They're being tortured, even killed, because Arana wants to punish them for what Shaesia did for you." Though Reanna had already heard the bare facts from Cynerra, Laile repeated them now that a visible example stood right in front of the princess.

While visible examples *suffered* right in front of Reanna.

The first few tears filled Reanna's gray-green eyes. "I don't understand…I just don't understand how one person could be so cruel. I don't know what she has to gain from all this."

"That's the thing. Arana told the Council from the very beginning that she won't negotiate with anyone until she has you. So nobody knows." Though Laile imagined that the typical megalomaniac motives were a factor.

Reanna sank down onto the floor and brought her knees up to her chin. "But the Council won't let me see her."

"No. They won't. They don't want you to get hurt, and I agree on that point. I don't want to see you get hurt, either."

Reanna chewed on her thumb. "Can...can I call her somehow? You don't have cell phones here, do you?"

Laile furrowed her brow. Vaguely, she remembered her best friend, Aimee, mentioning something like that, but she couldn't remember its purpose. Knowing Aimee, it was probably some kind of mechanical part she needed for an invention. "What's a cell phone?"

"You know—some way that you can talk to people from distances?"

So not a mechanical part Aimee needed. "Oh, yeah! Witch's stones. I wouldn't suggest using it to talk to your mom, though. You can get trapped in witch's stones, or people can steal your soul if you're not careful. My parents wouldn't even let me touch one until I turned fifteen, and even then, I could only visit my best friend Aimee."

Reanna huffed out a sad laugh. "Just when I think this place can't get any more dangerous, you go and tell me there are soul-eating cell phones here."

Laile rested her hand on Reanna's knee. "You know...you can help make it a little less dangerous. Come on. Join us."

"I don't..." Reanna fiddled with her nail against her teeth. "I'm useless, Laile. I don't have my powers. I'm a normal girl who can't do anything. I *want* to help, but I can't." Her breath hitched, and more tears raced down her face. "I'm sorry. I *can't*. It's physically impossible. I'm not some hero; I'm a mermaid without a tail or magic. If I go back to Arana, then she'll probably kill me." Reanna's voice broke, and she dragged her sleeves underneath her eyes as she wept. "I'm sorry. I'm so sorry. I know I'm a disappointment," she bleated. "I just want to go back home."

"And you *can*, once we free the elves!" Laile gave Reanna a squeeze. "Don't you see? You can help us free the elves and everything will be better. If we figure out how you lost your tail and magic, then we can get it back. It can't be *that* hard. Innate magic isn't something you misplace or leave behind on a manticore bus seat. Please, *please*—we have to stop this from happening. We have to go *now*. If you help me, I promise to do everything within my power to get you back to your adopted family."

"Would you listen? I *want* to, but I *can't*!" Reanna shoved Laile away and stood up. She flailed her arms around for a moment before she buried her face in her hands and screamed a little. "Stop, *stop*! I can't *breathe*—you're just making it worse!"

"Making *what* worse?" Laile blinked as Reanna wheezed into her sleeves and gasped for breath.

"I want to go home! I want to go home—I can't help—I can't breathe—I *can't* see my mom…" Reanna's voice was high-pitched and hysterical now. She'd drawn the attention of several people nearby, and Laile hopped up and wrapped the shaking girl into an embrace. Reanna trembled and clutched at Laile's back.

"Okay. I'm sorry for saying anything." Laile rubbed small circles on Reanna's back in an attempt to quell what must have been a bout of panic. "It's okay, Reanna. You don't have to do anything you don't feel capable of. You're safe here; nobody is going to hurt you."

"Not just me," Reanna whispered. "Everyone. Everyone is getting hurt because of *me*."

This small assertion brought forth another round of whimpers, and Laile closed her eyes and rested her cheek against

Reanna's temple. "Shh. Not because of you. You aren't forcing Arana to do anything. Arana is responsible for her own heinous deeds, and she's going to get her comeuppance."

"Excuse me." A third, masculine, voice cut in. Reanna lifted her wet face and tried to wipe away the tears. "Did she say your name was Reanna? As in—*Princess* Reanna?"

Laile studied the newcomer. Definitely an elf, from what she could judge by the point of his ears, his lilting accent, and his height. He looked around Cynerra's age—late thirties or early forties—but elf years were exceedingly deceptive. He could have already passed a few centuries, or maybe even his first millennium, but his face didn't show it. His short, strawberry-blond hair was smoothed back, and he wore the same hollow expression that every other refugee did.

But there was something else. Something small and dangerous that lurked in his violet eyes, like the person that dares not to hope again after all their hopes have been smashed.

Reanna edged closer to Laile, which really didn't work. The only way the poor girl could have gotten any closer was to crawl inside of Laile like some sort of flesh-eater. Still, Reanna nodded, and her grip on Laile tightened.

"Oh, thank the Composer." The elf made a quick sign of religious reverence at the deity's name and bowed his head. "You must help us. Please—my wife—Rosaelina—and daughter are still prisoners to Arana, and my daughter—Maesie—she is ill. I…" His voice broke, and he took a moment to collect himself. "I have done everything I can to keep them safe, even if most people here would hate me for what I have done or call me a traitor to my own kind. But I *must* save them. I promised."

Reanna whimpered. "I want to help, but—"

"No. I have overheard your dilemma, that you have lost your tail and powers. All of us know what Shaesia did, and I can help you."

"How?" Reanna sniffled.

"Our powers cannot just take things away and make them disappear. When Shaesia took your powers, she could not destroy them or release them. Unfettered magic is a danger to the very fabric of reality. She would need to have a safe storage place for them, some charmed item where she stored it. I know that you were small, but— do you remember this?" The elf's voice grew more and more urgent, and he seized Reanna's arm.

Laile flexed her fingers and felt tiny diamonds form between them. She could make a dagger in under five seconds if need be. Elves were powerful, yes, but she was fairly certain she could take this mousy elf on if she had the element of surprise.

Reanna chewed on her thumb. Her eyes drifted between the empty faces around her, and she sniffled some more. But when she spoke, her voice sounded so resigned. "I…I think it was a necklace. A locket."

The man made another sign of reverence but grabbed Reanna's arm again once he finished. "Oh, Composer bless you. Princess Reanna, *please*. Please help save my family. I am merely a violinist, not strong in many advanced magical arts, and certainly not strong enough to take on Arana." Reanna cast a helpless glance at Laile for a moment. Laile drifted closer, the beginning of the dagger already formed in her hand, but her brain raced.

This might be the moment she'd wanted all along. The moment to get Reanna to act.

The elf seemed not to notice Laile's veiled physical threat or Reanna's awkwardness. "But if we find the locket, I can transfer the powers back to you and then cast the same spell that allows Arana and her soldiers to walk on land and swim in the sea. But you must help me save Maesie and Rosaelina if I do so. They are— they are in the concentration camp, along with so many others. Please promise me that you will help me break them out, that you will try anything in your powers once I return your magic to you. Do you swear?"

The loud chime of the Council clock, enhanced with spells to be heard throughout the city, tolled upon the half hour. Every peal resonated in Laile's heart as if to declare: *this moment. Everything hinges on this moment.*

Her heartbeat matched the tune, and her stomach knotted itself around in anxious anticipation. She didn't dare to open her mouth lest she break the spell and interrupt some powerful magic weaving its way into Reanna's heart.

"You can help," the elf repeated. "Please. We can help each other."

Reanna met the man's gaze, and though she never loosened her grip on Laile, her breathless voice didn't quaver as she whispered, "Okay. I promise."

"Thank you." The elf held out his hand, and Reanna clasped it. "My name is Laeserno. I will meet you tonight in Unity Park—midnight."

But when he walked away, Reanna collapsed against Laile and bawled: "What did I just *do?*"

CHAPTER 18

REANNA

GAIA: DISTRICT OF CAPITAL CITY

Reanna carried her promise in her heart, which seemed so heavy that she felt like she'd swallowed a weight. But even though her burden seemed to crush her soul and shoulders, a faint flicker of hope right in the center of her chest helped her carry it—the fact that maybe, for once in her life, she might be able to do some good for someone else. To not be a burden.

But the moment she tried to lean into that belief, the weight crushed her once more.

Who was she to think that she could help the elves?

But Laeserno had been so passionate—or maybe just plain desperate—that she *wanted* to help him. When she'd listened to his pleas, for one solitary moment, all the other voices in her head—the ones that told her she was worthless, useless, unloved, and *broken*—fell silent.

But then she'd said yes, and the voices had gone back to work with even more fervor than before in order to make up for lost time. There had been a solid ten seconds where they hadn't reminded her of her inherent awfulness—what a long vacation.

And the grandness of the Council rotunda didn't help at all. Not with its high, marble arches that made Reanna feel small. All the gilded decorations seemed to yell that she didn't belong, not in the least. Everything from the fancy doorknobs to the golden statues of important magical figures through the ages—people Reanna didn't recognize save by their plaques but certainly couldn't live up to—reinforced those feelings. And so many *living* stately people drifted through the hallways on their way to do important things to stop this war. And Reanna had just promised someone that she could join their ranks as a powerless mermaid?

But Laeserno could help her get her powers back.

Then she had to help him get his wife and daughter back.

There was a distinct possibility Reanna might throw up.

Laile guided Reanna down the curving corridors of the rotunda. "Remind me once again why the Council wants to see me?" Reanna asked.

"Formality. Just some interviews and stuff to make sure you're okay." Laile seemed distracted, and she craned her neck everywhere. "Listen, they're going to try and tell you some stuff in there, but just remember Laeserno. Remember all those refugees." Laile sighed and turned to stare Reanna in the eye. "Look, there's a good chance they won't agree to let us go with Laeserno. That's why we're not going to mention it. We're going to request that they send us to try and free the elves, but if they say no, just keep your mouth shut, and nothing bad will happen."

Reanna shifted uncomfortably. "It sounds like you want me to break the law."

"Not break the law. Just consider it…dodging some paperwork in an extreme circumstance." Laile whirled back around. "Now, come on. Help me look for Greg."

They spotted Greg a few minutes later. He lounged against a wall, a book in hand, his shirt rumpled and his glasses perched on the edge of his nose. Sprigs of wild curls poked up in every direction, and for the first time since Reanna's panic attack, Laile dropped her ward's hand and went over to smooth out Gregory's stray bits of hair.

"How was your girls' day out?" Gregory asked. He made no comment about Laile fixing him up. Maybe he just didn't care that Laile's actions made them seem like an old married couple. Besides, Reanna's awkward-meter didn't sense any danger. The gesture was natural and somewhat cute, even.

Laile straightened his collar out. "Great, actually." She glanced both ways before she patted his shoulders. "But we can't talk here. Mom and Dad might overhear, and we have big news."

"Ah." Gregory raised his eyebrows as he tucked a bookmark between the pages. "A *very* good day, then." He gestured over his shoulder with the ancient leather tome. "Both your parents are in the chamber already. I'm supposed to tell you to go in as soon as you get here."

"All right." Laile straightened her posture and squared her shoulders. "Come on, Reanna."

Reanna nodded and followed Laile as they walked into the wide chamber.

The setup reminded Reanna of a Roman colosseum. Wooden seats curved around a raised dais so that all the important people could look down upon the little people—namely, her—and cast judgments upon them.

Yeah, a colosseum definitely was a great comparison—because Reanna felt like a gladiator facing down a lion for sure. She twisted a curl around her finger and would have stuck it in her mouth, but she remembered Arana's warnings about chewing on things not being appropriate for proper society. "So many people."

"It's the Council." Laile chuckled. "What, did you think it'd be tiny? They have to govern a whole continent."

A wisp of a smile teased Reanna's lips as she remembered a somewhat similarly phrased question posed by a talking beaver once upon a time. "I guess you're right. I just thought it would be tinier."

"Well, no need to be frightened by them." Laile pointed to the far left. "Over there, we have the vampires of Simit. Claudiu is their representative. He's the ancient guy and claims to be a direct descendent of Dracula. He looks old enough to *be* Dracula, in my opinion." He resembled Dracula, too, with pale, wrinkled skin and only a few wisps of white hair left on his otherwise bald head. His pointed ears and small eyes only furthered the resemblance to the Transylvanian bloodsucker. Laile moved a smidge over to the right. "From there, we have the fairies of Jenkirre. My mom's best friend, Kalena, is their representative. And her daughter Aimee is *my* best friend."

Kalena wore a vibrant red dress, which matched the streaks in the long blonde hair that she had gathered in a braid down the side. She seemed to fiddle with it constantly as well. Her eyes were wide and a unique golden brown, which gave her an air of innocent naïvety.

Reanna glanced over her shoulder at Gregory, who seemed immersed in his book once more. "I thought Gregory was your best friend?"

"I've never been one to say that you can only have one best friend. They're *both* my best friends, for different reasons." Laile continued down the line. "Next is Head Mother Viatrix, witch representative from Reggeria." The witch had short, curly black hair pinned back with pearl bobby pins. Her plump lips and dramatic dark eyes reminded Reanna of some devastating fifties starlet—or maybe Hayley Atwell in her Agent Peggy Carter regalia.

"After that…" Laile's face twisted into a grimace. "Corcaelin. He's an elf representative from Daspin who functions as the speaker of the Council, and before you ask—he was here when everything went down, so that's why he's not a prisoner of Arana." Corcaelin reminded Reanna a bit of the asylum doctor in *Beauty and the Beast* and the main lead from *Breaking Bad*. He had long white hair; cragged, sallow cheeks; and sported a close-cropped beard and thin-rimmed glasses.

"He's a jerk," Laile continued. "He hates my parents and has a lot of elf-superiority stuff going on." Laile clenched her free hand into a fist. "He hates werewolves and mermaids—probably puppies and kittens too—so I'd steer clear from him if you want my advice."

Reanna bobbed her head.

Laile pressed on. "Then we have Kirova, the only country to have two representatives—both a dwarf and a gnome one. I forget their names; they both just started their terms." Those two stocky men were barely visible over the edge of the balcony railing; Reanna caught glimpses of brown hair and long beards.

"Gnomes are the second-newest addition, barring only werewolves," Gregory added. Reanna started—he must have been paying more attention than she thought. "They didn't get their rights to be seen as distinct and separate from the dwarves until the Dwarfish-Gnomish War, a little over sixty years ago."

Reanna snorted. "I never knew any of this. You'd think my mother would assume that I would need to learn world politics when I took over the throne, but no."

"To be fair, you *were* six when you ran away. I'm not sure what six-year-old would be interested in this," Gregory said. He tilted his head, and his wild curls fell into his eyes.

Laile rolled her eyes. "Besides you, of course. Growing up, back when we'd play pretend, I always wanted to be Queen Titania, the original queen of the fairies. I *wanted* Greg to be William Shake-spear, legendary magician who could use his storytelling to defeat his enemies and dictate the future with his written words. But he just liked to lecture me on how William Shake-spear was nothing but a myth, how magic rarely works through written word, and then inform me of the *scintillating* true history of Solis' countries."

"All of that is true," Gregory chimed in. "Written magic is so rare and dangerous that most magic-users with that ability are locked up to protect the world. And William Shake-spear is generally agreed to be a myth created by Queen Titania or her court to increase fealty to a leader at a time when tension between nations and races ran high. You want your monarch to seem strong? Give her a powerful nemesis and have her best him and banish him to a different world."

Laile gave him the side-eye. "And that's the same answer you've been giving me since we were six."

"*Hold up.*" Laughter bubbled up inside of Reanna. "You guys think *William Shakespeare* is a myth?"

"He is—" Gregory began.

"He's from Earth!" Reanna cackled. "Imagine that—a fairy and a wizard think *William Shakespeare* is a mythological figure. Oh, that's grand!"

Both Laile and Gregory looked a little too shell-shocked to answer, but Reanna figured that was only natural. After all, that'd be like her going back to Earth and sprouting a tail right in front of the class. More than a few minds would be blown.

Reanna allowed them to compose themselves before her awkward meter flashed bright red in her head. "Sorry. I didn't—that just—well—uh..." She glanced up at the Council representatives. "That's your dad, right, Laile?"

Laile blinked. It must have taken her a minute to register where Reanna was pointing. "Oh...uh, yeah. That's my dad, Damien. He represents the werewolves of Gyranius and officially rounds out the seven representatives of our six countries on Solis." Laile turned her blue eyes back to Reanna. "But, just so we're clear here...William Shake-spear—"

Laile never got to finish her question. The elf representative—Corcaelin, Reanna remembered—cut her off, his words drenched in haughtiness. "Would Princess Reanna Tethys Atlantisi step forward to be introduced to the Council?"

Laile gave Reanna a good shove toward the dais, but Reanna floundered for a hand or something to grab. Laile had already backed away, though.

Ugh.

Reanna did not like fighting gladiatorial matches without so much as a friend to watch her back—or keep her from making an idiot of herself.

"Um…" She winced as her nervous stutter boomed through the chamber. There must have been some enchantment that seized her voice and amplified it for the crowd to hear. "I'm Reanna."

"Yes." Corcaelin threaded his fingers together. "What do you know of the situation in Atlantis, Princess? Do you have any pertinent information to give the Council? Perhaps some insight into your mother's plans?"

"No." Reanna shook her head. "I, um, uh—I don't know what's going on. Just what Laile's told me." Reanna gestured behind her, and Laile raised her hand, though everyone probably knew who she was.

Corcaelin scoffed. "As I thought. Quite useless." He adjusted some papers, and a magic quill, in place of a scribe, floated in midair beside him.

Reanna flushed. The voices in her head shoved all the sacredness of her promise to Laeserno aside so they could agree with Corcaelin's sentiments. Worthless. Useless. A screwup. Reanna had heard it a million times before. She dug her fingernails into her wrist and squeezed until the pain focused her. "Uh—I'm sorry. I don't know, but I'm willing to help. I want to do something."

The crowd sat up straighter, and some of the representatives and their entourages leaned closer to the railings.

"I want to go get my powers back and help the elves." Reanna swallowed as she scanned the crowd.

They whispered among themselves while the magical quill floated near Corcaelin's head and scribbled notes.

"The Council does not think this is a wise decision for many reasons, and therefore moves to deny your request." Corcaelin adjusted his black robes. Apparently, his chunky gold-and-ruby chain on his jacket had gone askew. A few of the representatives nodded their heads. Reanna glanced to Damien, but he didn't catch her gaze. He stared straight ahead, one finger curled around his lips.

"Why? I think it's only fair that I have some hand in stopping this." Reanna lifted her chin—until the fact that she'd back-talked a sitting politician sank in. She slowly drooped and murmured, "I've been told that all Arana wants is me. Maybe it's best if we just turn me over? If I had my powers, at least I could stand a fighting chance."

"Pray tell, how do you plan on getting your powers back? How do you plan on finding Queen Arana?" Corcaelin's voice reached a crescendo as he spoke. "Furthermore, even if you had your powers, you have not trained with your magic since you were six years old. Did you have any training as a child?"

Reanna dug her nails in deeper. "Uh…no."

"Ah, perfect! Which means that you are asking us to send a *civilian* in, with no magical training whatsoever, to fight a war-ready dictator." Corcaelin tucked his hands behind his back. "The whole plan reeks of ignorance and bravado." He muttered that, but the amplification spell still carried throughout the room. Somehow, Reanna doubted he cared. "Do you see why I cannot condone such an action?" the elf finished.

"But—if I had help—" Reanna began.

"If you had *help,* then I would be authorizing the release of untrained soldiers into battle."

"Not if they were already trained!" Reanna glanced over her shoulder at Laile. Her guardian nodded and stepped forward as though she would charge into battle for Reanna's sake. "And I know—"

"Your guardian and her friend do not count as soldiers. Do you realize how imbecilic it is to rely on teenagers to stop wars?" Corcaelin sat back down. The quill stilled as the echoes of his accusations died. "The Council decided your fate before you walked in here. We merely wanted to inform you that we would keep you safe. So, no. We will not send you and your little band of merry misfits into the heart of a very complicated war."

Reanna's cheeks burned as tears bubbled in her eyes. She wasn't sure if they were tears of frustration or shame—or maybe a little of both.

Behind Reanna, Laile whispered: "You just wait until his term's up, Greg. Then my fist will finally get to break his nose."

Gregory's voice was lower than hers, but in the silence of the chamber, Reanna still caught it. "Good luck with that, considering elves live centuries longer than any other race. Even though he's ancient, he'll probably outlive us both and be terrorizing generations to come if he keeps getting re-elected. And since he's been re-elected every time for two hundred years now…your odds don't look very good."

Laile growled under her breath. "I'll live to the end of his term out of pure spite and die right after I sock him a good one."

Reanna could have smiled if she didn't feel so awful.

Corcaelin cleared his throat. "Do you have anything further to add?"

Besides every disagreement Reanna had with this decision? But Laile had told Reanna to keep her mouth shut in this exact circumstance. "No."

"Then I will deliver our verdict." Corcaelin raised his arms. "The Council has unanimously decided that Princess Reanna Tethys

Atlantisi will be placed in a safe house until the end of this war to keep her safe from Queen Arana. She will leave on a dragon ship heading overseas in two days. She will be accompanied by her guardian, Laile Úlfur. Under no circumstances is Princess Reanna allowed to have any contact with Queen Arana, nor shall we give in to her demands to turn the princess over." Corcaelin nodded. "So sayeth the Council."

The six other representatives echoed his opinion, and Reanna stepped down from the dais. Laile scurried over and linked her arm through Reanna's.

"You did fabulously. He's a terrible person who's dooming us all." Bitterness seeped into Laile's every word as she snarled, "*So sayeth the Council.*"

PART IV

CHAPTER 19

ADAM

EARTH: PANAMA CITY, FLORIDA

D*ear elves—my name is Adam, and I request your help. You see, I am the—*

Adam growled under his breath, crumpled up the note, and tossed it into the trash. He proceeded to bang his head on the desk in hopes that it might jar a few of his brain cells into action. "Stupid, stupid, stupid!"

He'd written so many opening lines over the last two days, and none of them would work. It should have been easy to ask for help, but he had to be ridiculously careful. If he spilled too many details and the note fell into the wrong hands, it could lead to him and Lily being captured…or killed. At the very least, they would be in big, big trouble.

So how could he write a letter that would convince the elves that he was trustworthy without screwing everything up? Adam pondered that for a bit and came to the realization that he couldn't. It was impossible.

Taking a deep breath, he picked up another note and hurriedly scribbled down the bare basics of his conundrum and the request for a portal. He was careful to not mention Lily's name;   at least she would be safe if this note got him in trouble. He would take the consequences for whatever happened to him, so long as Reanna and Lily could be safe in the end.

Trembling, he shoved the letter into an envelope and wrote *To The Elves* on the front. There—the deed was halfway done. Now, he just had to go to the hardware store, buy some magnets, and hopefully get home before Lily returned and berated him for leaving the house.

The second part was a bit fuzzier. Adam chewed on his pen as he debated the variables. True, the elves weren't exactly free at the moment, but he remembered there being something about underground networks that helped get some elves to freedom. Or even some elves who had fought so fiercely that they'd never been captured…right? So maybe he could just send it to one of the glens that was sacred to the elves and hope for the best…

He clicked the pen faster against his teeth. It was a bit like shooting into the dark and hoping that he'd hit something, but, more than likely, the thing that he hit would be his own foot.

He was well aware that he could screw something up, that he could get Reanna, himself, or Lily in worse trouble. But there was still the niggling, hopeful feeling that he might actually *help* them all. As long as that chance was there, he wasn't going to waste it.

Adam was halfway to the hardware store when he saw Trevor pull into the gas station across the street. Trevor looked like he had been at football practice after school. He wore a sweaty t-shirt and his hair was plastered to his scalp. Adam rolled his eyes. He couldn't decide whether Trevor was merely a slob or if the guy thought that he was the most attractive man on Earth, and sweat would increase the attention he received.

It actually seemed to be the latter one—and, unfortunately, also seemed to work. A redheaded girl passing by waved at him and stopped to chat. Trevor leaned against the back of his truck, his arms behind his head. Did he really think he was Adonis? He was more like—like…a prat. Adam growled and shook his head. He'd definitely been watching too much BBC lately.

Trevor laughed at something the redhead said, and she took a step toward him. Adam gaped—was Trevor really going to kiss this girl? How could he even *think* about kissing someone when Reanna was kidnapped? He should be bereft, hopeless, maybe even refusing to eat…how could Trevor not even care?

Adam's fiery passion—which sounded much better than *rage*—took over, and he stormed toward Trevor. He was already rehearsing the verbal lambasting he was going to give the arrogant quarterback—and the redhead as well.

But before he could rip into the offenders, the girl commented, "Uh-oh, looks like you're in trouble with your little brother."

Trevor glanced behind him and did a double take. "That's not my brother."

"I'm—"

"No relation to me," Trevor interrupted as he shot Adam a death glare. "I hardly even know the kid."

It was a wonder Trevor could get any words out at all, though, with how tightly his jaw was clenched. It seemed like every tendon in his neck looked ready to pop.

"Well." The redhead shifted her weight and cleared her throat. She took a step backward and waved at Trevor before she jogged away. "See you later, Trevor. Text me sometime!"

Once she was out of earshot, Adam turned his full hostility on Trevor. "*What* was that about?"

"That was *supposed* to be about me getting a date!" Trevor kicked at one of his tires, but Adam knew the tire was probably just a substitution for himself. "But you had to go and ruin it!"

"How can you think about dates at a time like this?" Adam threw his hands up in the air and waved them around for extra emphasis. "You're such a self-absorbed pig-head! Reanna has been kidnapped, and you're not even worried!"

Trevor ignored the barb and removed the gas nozzle from his car, putting it back into its spot. "Listen, I told you to never talk to me again. So, *shoo*."

Adam ignored Trevor and hopped into his passenger seat instead. When Trevor opened the door, his eyes grew wide at the sight of Adam perched there.

"Won't your parents be worried about you riding with strangers?"

"Nah." Adam shrugged. "My dad doesn't care as long as I'm safe. I'm sure he'd trust *you*, for inexplicable reasons."

Trevor sighed and rubbed his temple. Adam knew that it was the start of yet another "Adam-induced headache." He was actually quite pleased with himself.

Trevor started up his engine and muttered, "Well, what are you doing here?"

"I'm opening up a portal to Gaia today," Adam answered matter-of-factly. "And I need to go to the hardware shop."

"Sure you are," Trevor scoffed. Still, that didn't stop him from turning right into traffic, which was away from his house. They drove for three minutes, kept from an awkward silence by a KJ-52 rap song. "You heard any of his stuff?" Trevor asked after a moment. He had one hand on the wheel with his opposite elbow propped against the window so he could rest his head.

Adam chortled. "Yeah. I've heard this song, at least. It's *super* old, though."

Trevor shrugged. "So? This is my childhood on a CD." He turned up the volume, probably thinking it would annoy Adam.

Adam fought back an impish grin—Trevor really thought he'd give up *that* easily—and stared out the window until they reached the hardware store.

"Go on. Get whatever it is you think you need. At least you're not blowing my money." Trevor leaned back in the seat and closed his eyes.

Adam grinned again and ran inside to purchase the magnets. After that was done, he directed Trevor to go to the backyard of Reanna's house.

"I can't," Trevor snapped. "Her sister hates me, and if I'm seen anywhere on their property, I'll probably end up in juvie."

"Your backyard will work," Adam said.

Trevor seemed less than thrilled with this new compromise as well, but at least he put the truck into gear.

"You know, you could just admit that you're worried about Reanna," Adam commented halfway through the ride.

Trevor shoved Adam's head. "Shut up."

"Telling me to shut up isn't a denial, you know."

Trevor turned the music up louder—this time, it did kind of hurt Adam's ears—and began to sing along in a fake falsetto voice.

Adam had seen a lot of torture in his days, but this had to be the worst sort.

Finally, Trevor coasted into his driveway. Adam tumbled out of the car, the music stalking him as he did so. Would it never end? Adam let out a sigh of relief as Trevor finally turned off the truck and climbed out.

Adam stood up straighter. "All right, come with me." He jogged around the beach house, Trevor in tow. Once they were settled in a secluded area, Adam dumped out the four horseshoe magnets he had purchased and positioned them. He pursed his lips and began to arrange them in a diamond.

"Do you need my help?" Trevor asked, seemingly uncertain...and a tad bit grumpy.

Adam snickered but once again decided not to comment. He was an absolute blessed saint today. "Sure. See what I'm doing? We need to arrange these two feet apart, angling inward. They need to be put at the compass points, pointing north, south, east, and west."

It didn't take more than a few seconds for the boys to place the magnets. Adam took in a deep breath as he surveyed his work. It looked good enough—now if only it would serve its purpose.

He withdrew a penny from his pocket and took a deep breath. He flicked it into the center of the magnets, praying fervently. *Oh, God, don't let me screw this up. Let Trevor believe me!*

A small blue circle within the magnets began to pop and twinkle. Electricity sparked from it, and it compacted around the penny. The circle snapped with a great noise and fizzled away with a crackle, leaving nothing in the sand.

"Wh—wha…. Where…" Trevor's eyes grew wide, and he gestured to the spot where the penny used to be as if his stupefied pointing would somehow summon it back.

Adam grinned and reached into his pocket to withdraw the letter. "The penny wasn't even the best part." He gently placed the letter into the center of the magnets and jumped back so he wouldn't be caught in the magical force field. Again, the space around the magnets flickered to life to form a little dome. Then the process repeated itself, and, with another *snap*, the letter evaporated.

CHAPTER 20

TREVOR

EARTH: PANAMA CITY, FLORIDA

Trevor stared at the ground where the letter had disappeared, too dumbstruck to speak. Finally, when he was able to grasp a thought, he whispered, "You are from some other dimension."

Adam stuffed his hands in his pockets. "Yep."

"And so is Reanna?"

"Yep."

Trevor exhaled slowly and crossed his arms over his chest. "Any other major, life-altering bombs you'd like to drop on me?"

Adam paused, as if he was actually considering the notion, but finally shook his head. "Nope." He began to pick up the magnets.

Trevor noted that the strange, dimension-hopping boy was careful not to step into the field. What would happen if Adam did? Would he disappear as well, or would it just kill him? Or would he fly back as if he had walked into a large electrical jolt?

"Why can't we use that thing to go to the other place right now?" Trevor took a step forward.

Adam barely managed to grab him and yank him back before he jumped into the portal. "Careful! You'll get blown to bits if you try to use a portal this small! If I could go myself, don't you think I would have, stupid? That's why I sent the letter over—to get help to open a *bigger* portal so we won't get blown to *smithereens*!" Adam waved his hands around dramatically, although Trevor thought that he was being a *bit* over the top.

"I didn't know!" Trevor rolled his eyes. "Look, it's clear I'm not gonna be any help. Why do you even need me?"

Adam stuffed all the magnets back into the plastic bag and slung it over his shoulder. "Well, I'm a firm believer that everyone has potential—even selfish, arrogant jerks." He smiled, the happiest Trevor had ever seen him. "You never know when a decoy might come in handy."

Trevor snorted. "Oh, you're hilarious, aren't you? I'm not going to be your bait."

"Then don't be bait. If you want to take...I dunno, fencing lessons, you might actually come in handy."

Trevor opened his mouth, closed it, held up a hand, and let it drop. Finally, he just shook his head. "You're *insane*. Fencing lessons? What?"

"Sure. Gaia is full of sorceresses, warlocks and vampires.... Not to mention, there's Queen Arana herself—oh, that's Reanna's mother—and it wouldn't hurt if you could carry your weight in something....especially since you have a lot of weight to carry around."

Trevor reached over and smacked him upside the head. "I'm all muscle, I'll have you know! And I could beat you in any sport, any day."

Adam swung the bag of magnets around and caught Trevor in the stomach. Trevor grunted, his breath momentarily knocked out of him.

Adam laughed wildly, just like a little kid. "You wanna bet? I'll bet I'm a better fencer than you."

"You're really gonna go there, aren't you? Fine! If it'll keep my dignity, I'll take up *fencing*. I can't even say that word without tasting the nerdiness." Trevor grimaced.

"Nerdiness?" Adam tilted his head. His shaggy brown hair fell into his blue-gray eyes—Trevor noted that with the pale-blue shirt Adam had on, they seemed a bit bluer than they had yesterday. Trevor also picked out a few small moles—or would they be freckles?—around Adam's chin and ears.

"Yes. *Nerdiness*," Trevor repeated.

"Are you going to tell all those dudes on the set of *Lord of the Rings* that fencing is *nerdy*?" Adam asked. "Or what about *The Legend of Zelda*? Link wouldn't have been able to be a great swordsman if he didn't practice first."

Dang it—Adam had somehow already pinpointed Trevor's two nerdy loves.

In response, Trevor strode toward his truck. He would not be so easily swayed. No matter how cool he'd look as Aragorn, slicing through countless piles of orcs...or rogue mermaids— *whatever* seemed to be waiting in Gaia.

They reached the vehicle. Adam disappeared around to the passenger side, opened up the door, and slid in. He looked far too comfortable, to Trevor's chagrin. Trevor grumbled under his breath while he climbed in and started the engine.

Trevor tapped out a tune on his steering wheel. "So. Tell me about these supposed creatures I'll have to face. You know, the vampires and the witches and all that jazz."

"Oh." Adam pulled his legs up to his chest. He seemed so scrawny in the seat. "What do you want to know about them?"

"I don't know. What I'm up against? Just trying to figure out what you think I can do if I take up *fencing*." Trevor still spat out the word as if it tasted bad, but he didn't gag as he said it. A definite improvement.

"Well…" Adam fidgeted in his seat, and Trevor had to turn down the static on the radio so he could hear what the kid said next. "Vampires are kind of your traditional vampires. You know, bloodsucking, venomous creatures. The only difference is that they're not dead. They're just…born a vampire. And you don't automatically get turned if they bite you. They have to specifically intend to turn you and inject you with venom." Adam leaned over and flicked Trevor's neck. Trevor jerked away and spluttered out a barely coherent exclamation; Adam only grinned. "Otherwise, if they bite you, it's only to suck your blood. That doesn't necessarily turn you into a dhampir—which is the name for someone injected with vampire venom."

"So…let's say I lose a battle against a vampire, and they inject me with venom. I don't start to glitter or immediately become allergic to garlic, do I?"

Adam snorted. "No to both. Honestly, I'm not too sure where the whole garlic thing got started, but I like to think that one vampire a long time ago had a garlic allergy, and the people of Earth just ran with it. But…that'd be like trying to take out the whole of humanity with peanuts."

Trevor chortled but attempted to cover it with a sneeze. "All right. Go on."

"How about mermaids, since we'll be fighting a lot of them?" Adam's expression turned dour. "They're the most dangerous in my opinion, anyway." He turned away from Trevor to stare out the window. His voice grew quieter. "They can control water. Heat it, freeze it, manipulate the weather—you name it. If they really put their minds to it, they could even manipulate the water in the human body." Adam swallowed; Trevor could see it in the window reflection. "Spellcasters can't come close to that. The only people who can are the fairies. There are several different types of fairies—gem fairies, flora fairies, water fairies, fire fairies, air fairies…all of them have control over different elements, or whatever you wanna call it." Adam rattled off the long list until he had to pause to suck in a breath. "Water fairies have similar powers to mermaids—although most fairies don't need their element to be present to manipulate it. A really powerful water fairy can just *create* water. Mermaids can't do that. The water they manipulate has to be present. But—according to the fairies I've talked to—not all fairies can do that. I don't know if it's technically genetics or some other factor, but some of them just aren't able to spontaneously create their element."

Trevor kept one hand on the steering wheel, propped his elbow up against the glass, and leaned against his fist. "Gotta love how you just casually talk to fairies. No big deal."

"Yeah, and I have breakfast with Bigfoot every Tuesday," Adam said dryly.

"I bet his table manners are awful."

Adam snorted and rolled his eyes. "Dwarves and gnomes don't have magic. That's easy enough to explain. They're mostly known for their skills. Elves and spellcasters are another group of very similar stuff." Adam chewed on his lip as he spoke. "According to my uncle, a long time ago, spellcasters had a lot more powers that no one could use but them: telekinesis, mind speaking and mind reading, using magic with conduits, and prophesying. That kind of stuff. But during one of the wars, spellcasters were almost exterminated, and very few people remained who knew how to teach the skills. So they've died out for the most part, and spellcasters have been relegated to being weaker versions of the elves, honestly. The elves mastered the spells way back when and taught the spellcasters. Oh—and good spellcasters are called witches and wizards. The bad ones...the ones who call upon dark spirits and such...are called warlocks if they're men and sorceresses if they're girls."

Adam sucked in a breath and flopped back against the seat. "Oh, yeah—I think werewolves are the last thing left to cover. I mean, they're pretty much your traditional werewolves. They can shapeshift whenever they want, but they're also forced to shift on a full moon. There. I think I've given you a crash course in the main groups that live on Solis, which is the continent where Reanna's from. There are other races elsewhere, but it's highly unlikely you'll have to face a cannibalistic centaur this time around." Adam paused, only to add, "And if you are, just trust me. Don't fight. Run."

"Seems to me like a centaur might be able to outpace me." Trevor rubbed a finger over his eyebrow. "You know. Horse legs and all."

Adam snorted. "Huh. You talk like you're all in, then. You're really down for helping, even if it means learning fencing?" He leaned in closer, as if whatever he said might seal the deal. "I mean, it technically is the only way to get Reanna back. You'd kinda be a hero here."

Trevor sighed. "I guess. But you better call me Viggo Mortensen from here on out."

PART V

CHAPTER 21

REANNA

GAIA: DISTRICT OF CAPITAL CITY

Outside the Council's meeting room, Reanna clung to Laile's hand as the fairy-girl led her through the curved hallways of the rotunda. A handful of people of different sizes, colors, and magical races loitered in the hallway or scurried about. Some wore street clothes, some were in military uniforms, and some donned elegant, formal robes.

Gregory came up behind them, but even he couldn't stop Laile's march toward the door.

"Of all the…" the fairy muttered under her breath. Reanna could only catch bits and pieces of her guardian's diatribe, but there seemed to be an awful lot of *shabuu* this and *shabuu* that—which Reanna recognized as a favorite swear word in Atlantean—along with other words that she'd heard Arana or the guards often utter in disgust.

"You know an awful lot of Atlantean," Reanna squeaked out after the fourth or fifth insult.

"Laile was obsessed with you when you ran away," Gregory said. Reanna twisted her neck around to catch a glimpse of him; his hands were stuffed in his pockets. "She was seven or eight at the time. She was convinced she'd find you, so she took it upon herself to learn Atlantean."

"Easier to learn than Fae. Mom doesn't even speak that. It's a dead language," Laile responded.

"So…you thought that you'd find me and just hurl insults at me?" Reanna's lips quirked upward in a smile.

"No. It just turns out that I liked their curse words better." Laile twisted around. "Bonus points, my parents didn't know what they meant for a while. Until *Greg* went and tattled on me."

Gregory smirked, and his dimples came out.

"But, anyway—this only complicates things a little." Laile's voice rushed out. "We've just got to sneak away tonight to meet Laeserno—"

"Do you, now?" another female voice cut in.

Laile yelped and thrust Reanna ahead of her—as if Reanna could do anything to protect someone from the wrath of Cynerra.

"*Mom*!" Laile peeked out from behind Reanna's shoulder. "Is Dad with you?"

Cynerra stared blankly at the empty spot to her right. "Yes, he is, in fact. Just practicing some invisibility spells right now."

Reanna giggled but smothered it when Laile offered her a firm pinch. "How much did you hear?" the fairy asked.

"Oh, not much. Something about not obeying the Council's orders, sneaking away to meet someone who I *think* is a strange man…" Cynerra shrugged. "Just the typical things." She crossed her arms over her chest and stared at her daughter. "And when did you think you'd clue me in on your little plan? When I woke up tomorrow morning and found you all gone?"

Laile gripped Reanna's shoulders. Reanna felt a tad bit like a human sacrifice, in more ways than one. "Well, you see—"

"Oh, I know. You hadn't thought that far. Nobody ever thinks of poor moms and dads in these situations." Cynerra sighed, a bit overdramatically, before she chuckled. "Oh, you're so much like me at your age. It's not fun to be the one left behind on adventures."

Laile bristled. "I'm not *just* like you, you know. I'm myself, too."

"Obviously." Cynerra reached into her pocket. A little black ball of fuzz crawled out onto her hand. "I don't think I would have bothered to wait for the Council, for one thing. And you haven't killed anyone yet that I know of, so that's another thing you've got going for you."

Laile gasped. "What—*Mom*—are you—*what?*"

Cynerra didn't answer; instead, she put the little creature down on the floor. It grew until it was roughly the size of a large, muscular black cat. Reanna's eyes widened.

"Whisper!" Laile dropped to her knees. The animal waltzed over to her, head held high, and crawled into her lap and butted her chin with the top of its head. "You bring Whisper with you in your *pocket?*"

"Sometimes, yes. He's kept me safe in more than one perilous situation." Cynerra knelt so she could be face-level with her daughter. Reanna scooted out of the way and bumped right into Gregory. He let out a grunt and steadied her before they both could fall. "Laile, listen. I'm your mom, and—"

"That's the thing. You *are* my mom. But you're also some gigantic figurehead who's apparently *killed* someone—like, what is *that* about?" Laile scratched at the black fur between Whisper's ears.

Cynerra tucked her dark-brown hair behind her ear. She was really gorgeous and had no business being someone's mother—especially not *five* someones. Reanna studied the pair, but the only thing she could see that Laile had inherited from her mother was a pair of bright blue eyes. In every other way—Laile's darker olive skin tone, her mousy-colored hair, her lankiness—Reanna thought her friend favored Damien.

"Keep your voice low, okay? Only your father knows that. I've not even told any of your siblings; I sure don't want these stuffy rule-followers to know about my past." Cynerra reached for Whisper's long tail and stroked it. There seemed to be a sadness that lurked in the back of her eyes, as though she was reliving whatever crimes she'd committed in the past. "Like I was saying: I'm your mom, but that doesn't mean I've completely lost my personality. I hate red tape and bureaucracy more than anyone else. If you were me, we wouldn't even be having this discussion. You'd already be long gone." Cynerra grinned. "But *as* your mom—*and* as someone who sympathizes and agrees with you—I want to keep you safe. And if I can't keep you safe at home, I'm going to give you the one person that kept me safe on my journeys."

With a flourish, Cynerra gestured to the cat.

Reanna blinked.

Laile's brow furrowed. "Whisper? What can he do?"

"Oh, lots." Cynerra held one finger to her lips. "Don't tell anyone, but he's an azernos."

"What?" Laile and Reanna uttered the same response in tandem. Only, Reanna's was bred from sheer confusion, and Laile just seemed angry.

"Mom! That's illegal—you can't just harbor animals from Fiastro inside your house! He could be dangerous!"

Cynerra rolled her eyes. "Ah, yes. And you've been alive how many years? I can tell he's been a real danger to you." She stood up and brushed the dark fur he had shed off her hands. "People fear Fiastro and azernos for the same reason we fear the dark. They're unknown. Whisper's harmless. Quite powerful—but harmless to the people he cares for."

"Does Dad know?" Laile asked.

Cynerra shrugged. "Does your father know that you plan on sneaking out?"

"Excuse me, but *what* is an azernos?" Reanna dearly hoped they wouldn't play the same game as when she'd first arrived—the one where she asked a question only to be ignored a hundred times. Louder, she added, "Why would they be dangerous?"

Laile glanced at Reanna out of the corner of her eye. "Azernos are shapeshifters, taking on the ability of anything they shift into."

Reanna's eyes widened. "So it can turn into me? How do I know *you're* not an azernos? It's like the *Secret Invasion* plotline in the Marvel Comics, with the Skrulls, where—"

Laile blinked. "Excuse me, but what? No. They can't actually *become* a person. They just become a certain magical race, but they'll look like themselves, whatever they look like. So if they have purple skin and pink hair as an elf, they'll have purple skin and pink hair as a fairy—just different powers. But it's why they're so dangerous, because they have the potential to have absolutely any powers they want."

"Or they can stay in their natural form and be a very good bodyguard for a family," Cynerra interjected. "Laile, what I'm getting at here is that, whether anyone likes it or not, your father and I agreed to let you try for your guardianship. With that comes the responsibility of making your own choices and owning up to the responsibility afterward, no matter how awful or illegal they may be. If you think you need to sneak away, then we have to respect you enough to do it."

Reanna balked. If *her* mom—her real mom (her adopted mother, not her biological mother)—ever caught her doing a whiff of something illegal, Reanna would have been grounded for months.

"But I would like to throw out that *if* it's your choice to disobey and go to Daspin, I'm insisting that you take Whisper with you," Cynerra continued.

"Why?" Laile shoved Whisper's head away when it—he?—tried to lick her.

"I've gotten into enough scrapes with Whisper to know that an azernos is worth at least a hundred soldiers in a fight." Cynerra grinned such a mischievous smile that Reanna could easily imagine the fairy-woman as a feckless teenager, bent on causing catastrophes and chaos. "He saved my life more than a few times with that shapeshifting ability." Cynerra tapped a finger against her chin. "Oh, and a little hint: Whatever you do, stay away from Yaester's Swamps in Daspin. Nasty little flesh-eating beasts live there. Nearly lost a toe to them once."

"Wait, what?" Laile hopped up. "Since when did you ever go to Yaester's Swamps? Flesh-eating beasts? Mom? *Mom?*"

Cynerra laughed wickedly as she swept down the hall.

"Your mom is kind of amazing," Reanna commented once the fairy had disappeared. "And…also kind of scary."

"You have no idea," Laile muttered.

CHAPTER 22

REANNA

GAIA: DISTRICT OF CAPITAL CITY

That evening, Reanna found it hard to do anything, productive or not, once the group returned to the Úlfur family penthouse. Laile had told her to catch a last-minute catnap because they would have to travel straight through the night. But Reanna couldn't seem to calm her mind down at all. Every time she closed her eyes, she could still feel the tension and panic that plagued her whenever she thought back to her early years.

Usually, she recoiled from these memories, stuffed them inside her subconscious and locked them away. But now that she was in Gaia, it was like they had stormed the prison walls and were holding her brain hostage, forcing her to relive each and every one of them.

Like, perhaps, the time when she was four years old, stubborn and willful, hidden away in her room…

Reanna put the finishing touch on her seashell crown. She could finally freeze the water between the shells and hook them together, just like a big girl. She'd figured out how to do that last time she sneaked into training. Nobody had seen her at all; she was way too sneaky, just like a spy. She giggled and put her best creation on top of her head. A real crown! Well, a real pretend crown. Arana wouldn't give her a real not-pretend princess tiara even though Reanna asked every day.

She giggled and swam out of her room. She kept her head tilted up, her nose slightly in the air, and tried to look down at all of the soldiers who passed her, just like her mommy did.

"You! Servant!" Reanna snapped her fingers, and a muscular brunette soldier stopped in front of her.

"Yes, Reanna?" The guard seemed slightly bemused.

Reanna patted her crown. It must have real magic powers since the lady didn't pull her hair or laugh in her face. "Get the queen a man. She wants to have a ball!" Reanna clapped her hands to make her request sound more royal.

The soldier shook her head and glanced around the hallway. She crouched down, her voice low and warning. "You should not play such games, Little Highness. These are dangerous games for someone so young."

Reanna blinked. Why did nobody ever listen to her? When her mama said it, *everyone* listened. She put her hands on her hips. "Get me a man—*now!* I want to have a ball, and I am the princess!"

The lady shook her head again but didn't slap Reanna. "No, princess."

It wasn't fair at all! Reanna threw herself down on the floor and slapped her fin and fists against the marble as she wailed, "I want my daddy! I want a ball! I have a crown!" Everyone was so mean, and her tiara wasn't working—why didn't it make everyone listen to her like they listened to her mama? Reanna continued to shriek and holler as she thought of more and more bad things that were happening to her, the worst bad things, because all that ever happened to her were bad things…

The guard stared at Reanna, huffed, and swam off. Reanna calmed herself a bit. Was the woman going to get her daddy? Or any merman? She stared down the hall and waited for her first glimpse of him. Instead, the soldier returned with Arana, who looked very, very, very, *very* mad.

"What do you think you're doing, child?" Arana snapped.

Reanna froze. Arana didn't just seem mad—she seemed *scary* again.

Reanna gulped. "I…I…I was playing that I was going to see my daddy…. Don't you think my crown is p-pretty? I made it…" Her bottom lip quivered, and she stuck her finger in her mouth.

Arana slapped Reanna's finger away with a silver fin. Some of the scales cut into Reanna's hand, and she cried out. Arana knelt down, grabbed Reanna's face, and squeezed it hard.

Reanna whimpered. "Mama! Mama! Stop!"

"I don't ever want to hear any talk of your father, or ballrooms, or men, again. Do you understand? Those are evil words from an evil little girl."

Reanna stuck her thumb back in her mouth. Why was she evil? Was that why nobody loved her, even with her crown on? "B-but…I…Mama…"

"Do you want to know what men do, Reanna?" Arana smacked Reanna's thumb away and gave her wrist a good squeeze. "They kill. They revel in spilling blood! They abuse and destroy mindlessly. They are beasts, every single one of them. I have tamed them to keep you safe from them, and you think that it's a joke!"

Reanna tried to stick her thumb back in her mouth, but Arana batted it away.

"We have to kill men before they kill us. I had to kill your father before he killed you."

"W-why...why did my daddy try to kill me?" Reanna lifted her arms toward her mama for a hug.

Arana shoved her away and growled under her breath. "Because you had a worthless father," she snapped. "And if we aren't careful, you'll end up just like him—so stupid, useless, ignorant—if you aren't already." She stood up and gestured for the friendly guard to come. The soldier glanced behind Arana and sighed when Reanna's mama nodded.

The guard held out her hands, and the water moved at her silent command. Reanna's eyes grew wide. She barely even noticed the fact the water grew tighter and tighter around her.

"Are you going to make some animals for me? Can you make a hippocampus? A pretty one. I saw a pretty one outside my window, and—" Reanna choked. She tried to breathe, but there was something tight around her neck, so tight. She tried to scream, but nothing came out. Ice slithered down her body and trapped her from the neck down in a cold tomb. Her teeth began to chatter. Why wouldn't her mama do anything? It hurt; it hurt so much! But Arana only watched as the once-nice soldier lifted Reanna up and carried her to her room.

Reanna wished the guard would just hit her or pull her hair! Instead, the guard threw Reanna in her closet and shut her in the dark. Reanna sobbed silent tears, but she still couldn't scream. Dresses brushed against her face, but in her mind's eye, she saw them as octopi or sharks or dolphins—creatures eager to steal her away and eat her.

She couldn't move. She couldn't even call for her mama...

Tears dripped down her face as she sat in the dark and tried her hardest to breathe. She couldn't keep track of time properly, but it wouldn't have mattered in that closet anyway. It would have seemed like an eternity no matter how short or long a time it was.

She was so, so cold.

Heavy eyelids finally offered her a reprieve from the arctic temperatures. She nodded off, her dreams filled with dolphins and snow dragons.

Reanna jolted awake when the closet door opened. Her mama stood over her, and she didn't look quite so *scary* anymore. Reanna smiled just a bit. Now her nice mama was here. She would make everything right.

Arana held up her hand. As she lowered it slowly, the ice melted away, freeing Reanna. The princess squeaked and raised her chubby blue arms in a silent request to be held. She tried to speak again, but nothing would come out. Oh well. She didn't need to talk—not when her nice mama was there.

Arana stroked Reanna's hair as she carried her daughter over to the vanity. She picked up Reanna's comb and began to brush the tangled locks. Reanna stared at what was supposed to be herself in the mirror, thinking that she looked very, very strange. Her whole body was blue and red, and she couldn't really feel it when she touched it. She looked up at Arana, who pressed a kiss to Reanna's cheek.

"Oh, Reanna...you know I hate to punish you. But you are so, so evil sometimes...just like your father." Queen Arana sighed as if she had known very many bad men in her lifetime.

Reanna squeaked as Arana tried to jam the comb through a big knot. She wanted to tell her mama she was so, so sorry she was bad and that she loved her more than anything. But she couldn't, not yet, so she just stared at her reflection and hoped that she wouldn't become just like her bad daddy.

Reanna's door banged open. Gasping, she jerked upward and clutched at her chest as her heart slammed against her ribs. Someone else was in the room—she could see their shadow; it was a black spot against the nighttime backdrop and the perfect camouflage.

Fear stole Reanna's voice and kept her prisoner on her bed. Had her mother found her?

That terrified four-year-old was still all too real inside her.

"You ready?" The voice didn't sound like Arana. It took Reanna's sleepy brain a moment to place it, but when she came back to reality, she sagged against the bed.

Laile.

"You scared me," Reanna breathed.

"Sorry," Laile said. "You ready?"

Reanna nodded and went into the bathroom to change back into her new clothes. She even tied her Spider-Man sweatshirt around her waist since it didn't smell like death anymore. Pulling her loose curls into a ponytail, she trudged back into the room. "I don't know what I'm doing, but I guess I'm ready."

Laile crossed the room in the dark and wrapped her arms around Reanna. Reanna stiffened at first, but, after a heartbeat, she allowed herself to relax and sink into Laile's embrace.

"I know. It's scary. Growing up as a whole is kinda scary." Laile sighed. "One moment, I think I'm so ready to be done with this and away from my parents' shadows. I think I just want to live my own life. Then the next minute, all I want is to be little again and able to crawl up into their laps, knowing that they will take care of me when the world feels a little too turbulent and tempestuous and terrifying."

"Yeah. Except my mom *is* the terrifying and turbulent one and stuff." Reanna sighed and pulled away. "Okay. Let's go."

"Oh wait. One second." Laile leaned over, wrapped something around Reanna's waist, and cinched it in the front.

Reanna patted herself down, brow furrowed. "What did you do?"

Laile brought her wings back out so their glow could illuminate the space around the two girls. She so rarely summoned her fairy wings while in human form that their sudden appearance startled Reanna a bit until her brain remembered: *Oh, yes. Laile is a fairy.*

In the light of the glittery wings, Reanna could see a faint sparkle emanating from her own midsection—the glow started at her waist and ended at her knees.

"I put a fairy skirt on you," Laile said. "Fairies use them to carry things on long journeys so that they don't get weighed down when they're flying. Yours is carrying the food we'll need for the journey." Laile reached toward her. It looked like she was going to grasp Reanna's knee, but instead, her hand disappeared. Reanna's eyes widened, but she felt nothing—not even when Laile pulled out an apple and grinned.

"That's amazing!" Reanna reached for the fruit, but Laile lobbed it at the general vicinity of Reanna's knees. Before it hit them, though, it merely evaporated.

"One thing, though. Don't get smart and think that you won't get hit by arrows or something. It only covers you from your hips to your knees, and only the front."

The warning made a shiver run down Reanna's spine. Once again, she was reminded that this journey was far from what she was used to...which was mostly watching Netflix and swimming. This was real, it was dangerous, and she couldn't back out.

The two girls crept out of the penthouse. Gregory waited in the hallway, leaning against the wall with arms crossed. Whisper, his beady eyes trained on Reanna, threaded through Gregory's legs.

Laile jerked her thumb to the right. "Come on. We can't use the elevator; somebody might see us. We've got to take the stairs."

Reanna groaned as she followed the group. Even after eleven years of practice, she still hated stairs. She'd had one too many trips, falls, and slips down the devil-creations during her time on Earth.

But, then again, she was about to rush into a deadly mission to reclaim her tail and set the elves free, all while evading capture from her megalomaniac, narcissistic mother.

First Reanna would conquer the stairs, and then she'd conquer the world.

CHAPTER 23

REANNA

GAIA: DISTRICT OF CAPITAL CITY

Laeserno met the small group of lawbreakers in Unity Park, near a fountain that showed the handful of magical races represented by the Council in various poses. Laeserno was easy enough to find—Reanna assumed few people wanted to take a wartime midnight walk. She briefly wondered if people were even allowed out after a certain hour. But Laile hadn't mentioned a curfew; then again, their group already intended to disobey the Council's orders. Breaking curfew probably held less punishment than disregarding a direct government order.

"You came!" Laeserno made the same act of reverence with his hand he'd made in the catacombs earlier—it reminded Reanna of a Catholic Sign of the Cross, though completely different at the same time. "I started to wonder if you would abandon us."

Reanna shook her head, but Gregory stepped closer to the elf. "No, but if you don't mind, I'd like to place you under a truth spell before we entrust our lives to you." Gregory held out his hands. "Laile told me about what you said, but I still have a few questions."

"I understand." Laeserno touched Gregory's palms with his own.

Gregory tightened his grip on Laeserno's fingers. "*Veritas.*"

A light flashed between them, and Gregory nodded. "All right. Do you plan to lead us into a trap?"

"No." Laeserno locked eyes with Gregory. Reanna shuddered from second-hand embarrassment. Her awkward-meter would have spiked into "Danger, Will Robinson" zones if she had to take either one of their places.

"Do you plan to inflict any harm to us—bodily or otherwise?"

"No."

"Do you solemnly swear that you have only Reanna's—and Solis'—best interests at heart?"

"Yes."

"How did you escape Arana's torture camps?"

Laeserno swallowed, and his gaze flickered down. For the first time, he seemed hesitant to answer, but Reanna assumed the spell dragged the words out of him regardless. "I was never in there."

Gregory shifted his weight, his brow furrowing. "But Laile said you have a wife and daughter in the camp."

"I do."

"How did you get separated?"

Laeserno sighed. His body trembled. "Because I failed them."

"Not an answer. Elaborate—*truthfully,*" Gregory growled. "And why did you tell Reanna and Laile that most elves would consider you a traitor?"

"Because I am." Laeserno's voice cracked. A few tears trickled down his face. "Julius and Violante Festinius approached me." Both Gregory and Laile flinched at the name. Reanna almost thought Violante sounded familiar as well, like a memory of childhood she couldn't quite place. Could she have been a mermaid? One of Arana's friends or associates? "I had some connection with Shaesia, and

Arana had already started rounding up my fellow elves. Violante promised me that she wouldn't hurt me or my family if only I…" Laeserno choked, and he pinched his eyes shut. He shook his head. Sweat beaded down his forehead.

"Gregory, stop the spell," Reanna whispered. "He's in pain."

"He wouldn't be if he'd tell the truth." Gregory's voice sounded curt. "He doesn't want to tell the story."

Laile reached for Gregory's shoulder. "Maybe Reanna is right. We know enough—"

"We don't know if we can trust him just yet. He admitted to being a traitor." Gregory's thumbs pressed even harder on the back of Laeserno's hands. The skin turned white around them, and Reanna wanted to rip the poor elf away from it all. "What did Violante and Julius ask you to do?" Gregory demanded. "What *did* you do?"

"I…" Laeserno gasped. His legs trembled.

Reanna's stomach twisted. She didn't think she wanted to hear the next part. Her brain could fill in the blanks of what he might admit, but her anxiety ramped up the longer he prolonged his inevitable confession. She clenched her fists and dug her nails into her palms to try and refocus herself. In a pinched voice, she croaked, "You turned over Shaesia, didn't you? You betrayed her."

Laeserno turned to face her. Reanna's view blurred through the tears, but she could still see when he buckled over, his knees thudding against the grass.

"*Yes.*" Laeserno shivered and bowed his head. "I am so sorry, Princess Reanna. I falsely believed that my family would be spared, that Shaesia would be enough to buy their freedom." He sobbed; his shoulders shook.

Reanna swiped at her eyes and latched onto Laile before her own knees could give out on her. Reanna's stomach turned and boiled as anxiety and anger warred inside of her. Part of her wanted to scream and shake Laeserno. The other part of her almost understood—if she could save Tara and her mom from any horrible fate by turning in someone else, there was a distinct possibility she would.

"I have lived every day in regret since," Laeserno bleated. "I would give my life to absolve my sins and save my family—and Shaesia."

Gregory dropped the elf's hands. "*Desinmere.*"

Laeserno lowered his head in a pleading position. "Please...*please.* Forgive me."

Reanna sniffled and buried her nose in Laile's shoulder. The fairy-girl reached up and patted Reanna's curls. "There, there," Laile murmured softly.

Recollections of Shaesia threatened to topple what little fortitude Reanna had left. She clung to Laile's forearm, paralyzed by memories. Memories that started with the moment when Shaesia had found a small, shivering mermaid on the beach. For the first time, someone actually treated Reanna with care—Shaesia had plucked the tiny girl up from the beach and carried her all the way home. To young Reanna, Shaesia seemed like a giant—or a fairy-tale goddess come to life—with her elven height, sharp chin and ears, and the long, chocolate-colored hair that trailed past her waist.

Visions crossed Reanna's mind of their short but wonderful days together, when the elf would gather Reanna into her arms and read stories or paint pictures with her. Reanna could still hear Shaesia's voice—dry and no-nonsense—as she tried to imitate the voices of different characters to little avail. Shaesia had often admitted that she was much better suited to teaching facts than fantasies, but she attempted to give in to the whimsical side of childhood after that very first night. Reanna always wondered if Shaesia had seen some of the scars from Arana's cruelties and intentionally softened the pricklier parts of her own personality.

Of course, Shaesia could never fully disregard her penchant for facts and truth. She tried to teach Reanna about many practical matters as well—about life on land, for example; she even gave some basic astronomy lessons on Reanna's very last night in Gaia. Shaesia had held Reanna and whispered the names of constellations and said how they might look different on Earth, but there would be a sun and a moon and stars wherever Reanna might go.

And Laeserno betrayed Shaesia without a thought.

"We need to go," Gregory murmured. "The first thing we have to do is reclaim Reanna's powers. Reanna mentioned that Shaesia used a locket as a conduit; we just need to find it."

"Greg," Laile whispered. "Give them a second."

"What? We don't have time. We can't just wait around because Reanna can't forgive him yet. We know the truth, and if he says he's not going to hurt us, then we need to leave. *Now.*"

Laile sighed and stroked Reanna's curls away from her face. "Do you remember where Shaesia put the locket? We're going to need it for the spell to get your powers back."

Reanna shrugged and took in a shuddery breath. She could visualize the moment in question—how much it had hurt to have her magic, her tail, stripped away from her. She could remember that the silver necklace glowed a little bit as Shaesia lowered it into a…a case of some sort. But that part turned hazy. "I guess her house. I don't know where else…but I think I can identify it if I see it." How hard could it be, really?

Gregory nodded. "Perfect. All right. Laeserno, do you mind getting us a portal? We need to be out of Unity Park before someone gets suspicious."

Laeserno's hands clenched around the grass. "I…I offered my services as a guide and to help give Princess Reanna her powers again. I know the area around the concentration camps and Shaesia's house; I can lead you there, and I remember learning the transference of power spell. But I cannot conjure up a portal."

"What?" Gregory balked. "But—elves are the *guardians* of the portals. Portal magic is what you all are famous for! It's something that you can do that no one else can—"

"I pursued other options in school besides magic." Laeserno didn't lift his head and barely spoke above a whisper. Some strawberry-blond sprigs of his hair had come loose and now curtained his eyes. "I have basic spell knowledge, enough to pass my classes, but I knew early on that I preferred a profession that was not magic-related."

Heat crept up Reanna's neck; her cheeks flushed. She clenched her teeth until her jaw hurt.

Gregory groaned. "What do you mean?"

Laeserno cleared his throat. "I am a *violinist.*"

"What?" Gregory asked, sounding incredulous. His eyebrows rose, which crinkled his forehead.

Laeserno sighed so deeply, Reanna wondered how he had any oxygen left in his lungs. "A violinist. I play music."

"I'm aware of what a violinist does, it's just—I thought you could teleport us."

"No. I can guide you and, most importantly, help Princess Reanna get her powers back. You can do neither of those important things without me."

Laile muttered one of her colorful Atlantean curse words. "Technically, that's all he promised to do in the catacombs. Help us get Reanna's tail."

Gregory massaged the bridge of his nose under his glasses.

"Yeah, but it was implied he'd get us there by portal," Reanna snapped in the harsh tone she usually reserved for Trevor Spencer. Portal travel *hadn't* been implied, but she'd take any ammunition she could get against the man that destroyed Shaesia's life. "What good are you?"

"Reanna," Laile chided softly.

"No—I mean it. He can't even get us there quickly."

"Portal magic is very finicky. I'm fairly certain I told you about the guy who ended up with half his body in Simit and half on some random island." Laile paused. "Then again, you were under the memory spell, so I'm not sure if you remember that. But anyway—Reanna, if he isn't adequately trained, we don't want to risk it."

"Then why don't we just get another elf? One that *isn't* a traitor?" Reanna asked sharply. "And can actually be useful?" She could only see red. Her anger buzzed around her head like a bee and dulled out all other senses—until she really saw Laeserno, still on the ground, shoulders hunched over.

"I am sorry," he whispered. "I wish I could be of more help. But I wish to make amends. I know my offering is small, but…"

She imagined all her accusations piled on top of him like barbells. She imagined his *own* guilt, maybe even heavier than her words. Did he struggle with his own voices inside his head, too? Ones that sounded like hers—that called him useless, vile…worthless?

Some people might say she'd abandoned Gaia, too. Call her a traitor. She ran away at the first opportunity she had, and she didn't even have family to think of. She left out of pure self-preservation, not love.

Reanna's bottom lip quivered. She lifted her head and mopped up the mess her face had become.

She hadn't forgiven him.

She could blame everything on him. Drown him in more grief.

She took a breath.

And reached out her hand.

"I understand." Reanna swallowed. "I…I shouldn't have said what I said."

The hardest half-apology she'd ever uttered in her life.

Laeserno lifted his tear-stained face, and his expression crumpled once more when he saw her proffered hand. "Princess—"

"I'm just Reanna. I'm not a princess." The cracks in Reanna's heart deepened as she gazed on his pitiful expression. "And I'm not my mother. I…" The words clawed at her throat, but Isabella Cook hadn't drummed years of forgiveness into her girls for nothing…even if neither of her daughters could quite forgive one certain father figure in their lives. But that was neither here nor there. "I…I forgive you."

The words seemed to tear at the innermost fiber of Reanna's being, but she still somehow meant them. And she meant them even more when Laeserno grasped her hand, pulled himself up, and drew her into a hug. His tears dripped onto her head as he squeezed her tightly.

"Thank you," he whispered. "I will never forget this."

Reanna nodded. She didn't know if she had any words left inside of her.

Gregory cleared his throat, a very subtle way to cut in. "We still appreciate your offer, and we do need it. I'm afraid none of us know the way to Shaesia's house otherwise. In any case, we have to start walking. We shouldn't risk public transportation here. You never know when someone might have connections to the Council."

Laile nodded. "Sounds fair." She wiped away some more of Reanna's tears. "You okay to walk?"

Ugh. Dealing with her emotions *and* walking? That was a lot to ask of Reanna.

Still, she nodded. "Yeah."

She could only move forward from this point.

They all could.

CHAPTER 24

REANNA

GAIA: DASPIN AND GYRANIUS BORDER

They walked for several hours that night until Gregory finally let them board a manticore bus in a very small town. Reanna managed to nab a few more hours of sleep on board, but she still thought about killing Laile when the fairy shook her awake.

"What?" Reanna rubbed her bleary eyes. Whisper napped on his back, the lucky azernos. She ran her fingers across his sleek fur, and he purred in his sleep as his tail flicked back and forth.

"Greg wants us to walk again. He says there's a good chance the Council might know we're missing by now, and he thinks we should try and avoid crowds. He wants us to take the older, more forested paths instead." Laile's blue eyes roamed around the cabin, which had filled up.

Reanna grumbled and adjusted her sweatshirt. She'd fashioned into a makeshift pillow earlier. "Tell him I hate him, and I need sleep."

"I would love to—especially that first part—but I think he's a little worried." Laile slipped something onto Reanna's lap. Reanna peeked open one eye. A blanket? But it seemed rather heavy for just a blanket.

The fairy bobbed her head toward the gift until Reanna slowly peeked inside the bundle.

A dagger.

Reanna raised her eyebrows and tried to temper her reaction so no one around would think her suspicious. "What..." Her voice trailed off, and she stared at Laile for clarification.

"It's just a precaution. Gregory wants you to be prepared in case we encounter anything. *I'd* much rather you leave the fighting to us, but even I can see the wisdom in it." Laile sighed. "Especially if Julius and Violante are involved. Those two despicable excuses for people are dangerous, so it would make sense for you to have a weapon handy, just in case, since you can't use your powers yet."

Reanna's stomach clenched when her fingers brushed the hilt. "If I put it in my skirt, I get it out again by picturing it, right?"

Laile nodded. "Yep. Just imagine it in your mind or think the word. It doesn't matter. The magic just has to know what you want."

Reanna tucked it in her skirt and waited a moment for any lag period. After enough time passed—just a few seconds—she stuck her hand into the skirt and pictured the dagger. It materialized in her hand, and she pulled it back into the real world.

Useful.

She tossed it into her fairy skirt like she was playing hot potato with someone. "Um, thanks. So...who are Julius and Violante again?"

Laile's lips pursed. "Julius used to be a friend of my father's and Greg's father, but let's just say that friendship ended because we're ninety-nine percent sure Julius killed Greg's parents. Or, at least, he *let* them die if he didn't exactly kill them himself. On top of that, Violante is his wife—and was an instigator in the Great Warlock Uprising, where Greg's parents got killed."

Reanna shuddered. "How is she not in jail?"

"She disappeared to avoid arrest, but I guess she's thrown her lot in with Arana. That doesn't surprise me." Laile's eyes widened. "I bet she's responsible for all of the magic—oh—I'll be right back!" She grinned as if she'd just figured out all the world's mysteries and darted off.

She did not come right back, though. In fact, Reanna didn't see anyone again until Greg came to tell her they'd get off at the next stop.

Reanna shuffled after the group, her head down, while Whisper trotted beside her. She didn't think anyone could recognize her, wherever they were, but she didn't want to take any chances. Were there any shops around here that sold magical disguises? She could see a few log cabins scattered around, all painted bright colors, which made them seem full of personality despite their small height.

Hues of light-blue, purple, and pink still painted the sky as they unloaded. Flowers seemed to wearily poke up their heads, like they, too, protested waking at such an early hour. A few people milled out on their porches—or maybe the porches of establishments; Reanna had no way of knowing. They sat on rocking chairs: some with drinks, some with newspapers, and some with watering cans in hand. One elderly lady with fairy wings waved at the group; Reanna lifted a hand in return but wished for a hoodie so she could hide her eyes. It was far too early to socialize with these morning people.

"Stick together, and stay alert," Gregory said. "We're close to the border of Daspin now. There's a good chance Arana's army could be around here."

"There are tunnels we can take, though, that should help us to stay out of their sight." Laeserno straightened his long sleeves. "The gnomes of Kirova have mined all over this area as well." He motioned them forward with two fingers, and the group set off.

Around midday, they veered into a thick forest, which at least kept the sun off them. Towering evergreen trees blotted out the majority of the sunshine. Some other trees had curved and twisted trunks unlike anything Reanna had seen before. Now and then, they paused to rest on these unusual trees, though they didn't stop as much as Reanna would have liked. Her feet, calves, and shins always hurt if she walked too long, but whether from spending her formative years with a tail or from her penchant for laziness, she couldn't tell.

The only thing that kept her from asking if they were there yet was her deep fear of being seen as a useless child if she whined too much.

But she did think it quite often—especially as the sunlight faded even further and the sun dipped below the horizon to usher in the evening. It reminded Reanna just why she hated hiking—nothing around but a tiny dirt path that wound through evergreen trees and prickly bushes that snagged on her clothes and poked her. Every once in a while, she would hear a branch break and wonder if it was a bird or a serial killer.

Not to mention that, as the elevation rose in parts, she could look to the side and see a sharp drop-off and imagine tripping and falling to her doom. Or when they came to a few creeks and had to hop on rocks to get to the other side, she imagined slipping and cracking her head open. Dying in water—what an ironic way to go for a former mermaid.

They'd come across three babbling brooks and zero serial killers when Laeserno thrust his arm out to the side. "Wait," he said.

Was it too much to hope that he'd found a spot he wanted to rest for the night? The full moon had already risen with its bright beams, and Reanna's feet *ached*.

"I hear something," Laeserno whispered.

She tilted her head. She could almost make out a sound different from the various wildlife she'd heard earlier that day.

It sounded so familiar.... Realization hit her with a jolt and chased away any sleepiness. She tensed, her whole body on edge like a cat ready to jump.

The clinking of armor.

Like back in her bedroom.

"Soldiers!" Reanna hissed.

CHAPTER 25

LAILE

GAIA: DASPIN AND GYRANIUS BORDER

Reanna's words spurred Laile into action. She shrank down to her crystallized form and buzzed toward the soldiers, careful to use the leaves as camouflage. She needed to see the insignia on their uniforms. True, they didn't want to be caught by either the Council or Atlantean armies, but at least the Council's armies probably wouldn't use deadly force against them.

A handful of guards ambled along a gravel road that was far removed from the nearest town. Their armor clinked and glinted in the moonlight. What could they want out here? Laile had only seen rural, backwoods towns and jewel mines thus far on their trip. Could Arana have someone mining for gems? Or was the Council protecting the tunnels so they wouldn't get stolen?

Flying fig-whigs, they stood too far away for her to see. Laile swore under her breath in Atlantean and landed on a branch. She crawled to the end—no good. A gale of wind dislodged her from her perch. She bit back a squawk and flapped her wings, but the gust pushed her down and closer to the soldiers.

She crashed to the ground. The wind beat against her; dark clouds rolled across the sky at a clipped pace.

"Ah, what do we have here?" one of the soldiers asked in English, though he had a thick Atlantean accent.

Laile crystallized two daggers and jabbed them upward as the man swiped at her. But at her size, the weapons could only be the size of toothpicks. The man swore and raised his foot; Laile quickly expanded. He still ended up stomping on her stomach, but at least he didn't kill her.

Laile grunted as his blow knocked all the air out of her. Her weapons had grown with her; she slashed at his leg. He reeled back before she could land a hit, but the other soldier ran toward her, a jagged sword drawn.

Laile thrust out her hands, which began to change color from brown to an unnatural, glittering white hue. She intercepted the blow, wincing as she did. The iron still chipped at her diamond-encrusted skin.

Gregory, Laeserno, and Whisper bounded out of the forest.

"*Ignis!*" Gregory roared. He reared back and hurled a fireball at the first man. A geyser shot out of the earth and diffused the flames.

The soldier with the jagged sword advanced again and hacked at Laile's fingers. Two—maybe three—or maybe four—other thugs rushed to join the fray, but the boys engaged the newcomers as well as the first man. Water flooded the area, and more waterspouts and whirlpools picked up chunks of gravel and blasted Laile with the tiny stones.

Focus. She had to focus on the enemy in front of her, not the ones the boys were dealing with.

The next time Laile's remaining attacker raised his sharp blade, he didn't aim for Laile's arms. Instead, he swung at her legs.

Laile shrank in size; the sword plunged into the ground. She dashed between the man's legs. On the other side, she returned to normal size and clobbered him on the back of the head with her crystallized fist. He howled but didn't tumble.

From behind them, a roar caught her attention. Both she and her opponent turned to see a giant black lion, much bigger than a normal lion should be. It jumped into the air and batted another man down from a Gregory-made tornado. Gregory shouted in complaint, but the lion didn't pay him any attention. It grasped the soldier in its teeth and shook him fiercely before slinging him across the road. The soldier didn't move; meanwhile the lion slowly morphed back into Whisper, who stalked toward Laile's attacker.

Her opponent glanced over at his friend and yelled something in Atlantean. When the second man didn't answer, Laile's soldier smacked the ground; another geyser exploded. He swirled his hands to create a huge whirlpool that lifted him upwards. Laile held up her hands to protect her face from the sharp spray. The wind from the storm still pounded her back, and the vortex whipped her from the front. The water had the force of a raging centaur as it struck her, and Laile staggered and fell. The water kept her plastered to the ground as it hardened into ice; the weight nearly suffocated her.

She jerked, but her body was at such an awkward angle that she couldn't get any force behind her. The ice expanded, up past her neck and down below her feet, until she was sealed in her own icy coffin.

Laile thrashed and screamed, her brain only cognizant of one thing: *new fear discovered—being buried alive.* Desperate, she shrank again, but even her crystallized form couldn't get out—although it was somewhat comforting to finally be able to stand.

She slammed her fist into the icy wall. A thin dent appeared where she'd pounded it. She gritted her teeth and hammered it again—she might be able to break through, but it would be so much quicker if she could make a diamond whip...

The ice beneath her, however, blocked any chance she had of manipulating the dirt and digging her way out. And if she couldn't manipulate the dirt, she couldn't harden it into a diamond, which meant that she'd be back to pounding her way through—which could take *hours*. And the ice above her eliminated any hope of flying out.

She kicked and threw her whole weight into the tomb; though it dented again, it didn't shatter. "Come on!" she screamed. She could see her own breath as fog.

Laile could only hope Reanna would stay safe until her guardian could escape this mess.

REANNA

The dagger felt heavy in Reanna's hand as she watched the battle from the bushes, the scene lit by the bright glow of the moon and the occasional spell from her friends. Laeserno had instructed her to stay put before they all rushed out to engage in battle. She'd thought at first she might just be in the way if she tried to help...except now all of her friends were entombed in ice.

What could Reanna do with one dagger against four—maybe five—elite soldiers? Heck if she knew, but she couldn't just abandon her friends. She charged right into the fray, even as the whirlpool whipped around the clearing. She'd never been allowed to train, but she'd sneaked into enough classes to remember the weakness of a whirlpool.

She could almost hear the teacher's instructions: *Untangle one bottom thread of the whirlpool, and your enemy's weapon will unwind itself.*

On instinct, she thrust out her hand and yanked it back, expecting the water to follow her command.

Ugh.

Shoot.

How could she forget? She didn't have her powers.

So it wouldn't be that easy—but she had to think. Somehow, there had to be a way to disrupt the flow of the whirlpool.

Something huge shattered behind her. She whipped around to see Whisper expand to three times his normal size; broken ice shards lay around him. He unfurled, taking the shape of a giant bear, and swiped his paw at one man. The soldier guided his whirlpool backward, much more agile than he could have been on his feet. But there was one fatal flaw in his plan: it took his eyes off Reanna.

Muttering, "I hope this will work," Reanna ran at the whirlpool and jumped through it. She extended her body across the base so that for a brief second, all the water hit her torso instead of giving power to the whirlpool.

The whirlpool flickered out and collapsed on itself. It whipped the man to the side as it uncoiled at a dizzying speed. The soldier shrieked, and Whisper plucked him out of the deluge and dropped him. The man struggled to get up, but Reanna was there again, sopping wet but still with her wits about her. She'd watched enough movies to know she'd always wanted to try this; she drove the hilt of her dagger against his metal helmet, and he slumped over with a groan.

One down—

Another tomb exploded, and Laeserno pried himself free. He grabbed a shard of ice and hurled it at one of the other soldiers.

Whisper, still ginormous, bit one of the remaining enemies and hoisted him into the air as the man cried out.

Yeah, those two could probably watch Reanna's back as she went to save her guardian.

Reanna dropped to her knees by Laile's prison. "Laile? Can you hear me? I'm going to cut you free, but you have to turn small and get to the top of the cavern. I don't want to impale you. Unless

I'm wrong, I knocked out the soldier that did this to you, which means the ice should be weaker. Right?"

A squeaky voice called back, "Right."

Reanna took a deep breath and slammed the tip of her dagger down. She hacked at the wall several times—right before Laile rocketed out of the ice in her crystalline form. Reanna screeched and dropped the dagger in her shock.

Laile expanded to her regular size, shivering so violently that her knees buckled beneath her.

"You good?" Reanna almost offered a hug to Laile to share warmth, but since Reanna was all wet, too, it wouldn't have helped much.

Laile nodded, though her teeth chattered too much for her to reply. "Th-thanks. I'd almost made my way th-through th-there. Just needed a lit—little help."

"I'm going to go get Gregory out." Reanna patted Laile's shoulder and turned around—but a strange man stood over Gregory's prison.

"Get away from him!" Reanna shrieked as she jumped to her feet.

The man glanced at her and smirked. He flicked a shaggy piece of black hair out of his eyes and placed one finger over his lips in a shushing motion. He muttered something under his breath and snapped his fingers. The ice began to melt, but before it was done, the man vanished—replaced by the odd little creature called Whisper.

Gregory grunted and struggled out of his tomb, a fireball in his hand. "Wha—someone used a fire spell before I could. Laeserno?" Gregory let his flame evaporate. He jerked off his foggy glasses and wiped them on his shirt, his brow furrowed.

Laeserno shook his head. "I just escaped mine a few moments ago." A few bits of fire still lingered on his fingers.

Reanna tried to form words, but she was too fixated on Whisper to make her mouth work. His beady eyes stared back at her, and, if she wasn't mistaken, his mouth quirked into the same smirk the man had worn. But she had to be imagining things, or maybe it was just a weird reflection of the bright full moon.

"Regardless," Gregory answered in a huff when no one offered any ready explanation. "We need to get on our way. These guys were probably scouts for a much bigger troop, and if they don't come back…" He trailed off and shuddered. He strode over to Laile and hoisted her off the ground. "Come here. I'll warm you up." He rubbed his hands over her arm and muttered a spell that Reanna didn't catch. "Is everyone else okay?"

Reanna nodded mutely, and Laile made a sound that somewhat resembled a yes.

"Good. Then we have no time to lose." Gregory raced forward. "Laeserno, lead us to the tunnel."

Laeserno seized the lead, but Reanna held back for a moment to listen. The clink of armor and heavy footfalls piqued her ears. "They're coming!" she hollered to Gregory. She slapped her hand over her mouth a second later, unsure if the enemy soldiers would hear.

"Then come on!" Gregory called over his shoulder.

Reanna and Laile chased after the boys. Laeserno veered off the gravel path and into the woods. The voices grew louder as the group tried to balance speed with silence and ended up doing neither very well.

"Come here, come here!" Laeserno gestured them all closer before he uttered an incantation that Reanna didn't understand. He touched each of them, one by one, and as he made a motion, they flickered out of existence.

Whisper and Gregory went first—then Laile—but Reanna held up a hand to intercept Laeserno before he touched her. "What are you doing?"

"Invisibility spell—and I am sorry, but the only way I know how to do it requires me to touch you," Laeserno whispered. "And I am not as powerful as Shaesia, so it will only buy us a little time." "It's okay." Laile poked Reanna's side. "I'm still here. Just trust him." Trust the man who betrayed Shaesia?

War raged inside Reanna's stomach, and she rubbed her thumbs together.

The new soldiers drew closer. She could almost make out their words now.

"Fine. Do it." She closed her eyes. She felt Laeserno's index finger travel down her forehead and nose, and when she opened her eyes again, she couldn't even see her own body. "What about you?" she whispered.

"If I make myself invisible, how will you follow me?" Laeserno shook out his hands. "Just follow me. I will try and creep past them without engaging in a fight."

Arana's new lackeys burst through the foliage. "There are fresh footprints here," one guard growled. "They came this way."

Laeserno veered away from the path and into the bushes. But even invisible, the rest of the party still made noise. Laeserno's shadowy silhouette shook his head and held up a hand to tell them to stop. He swerved to the left, farther away, and Reanna lost track of him in the bushes.

But now she could see the four remaining guards.

"Something powerful must have knocked them out. Did you see the bite marks it left behind?" one of the men asked. He bent down and stared at the dirt.

Reanna quivered.

"Maybe we should turn back. It could be something wild…" a second one commented.

"Oh, sure! And do you want to be the one to tell General Violante we turned back because someone got *scared*?" the first one snapped.

"I'm not scared, but I'm not willing to die because some exotic animal escaped from Fiastro!" the second hissed back. Reanna bit down on her tongue before she could make a noise and give them away. Had they seen Whisper? Azernos came from Fiastro, but…then again, maybe the man was just using it as an example. The desert wasteland of Fiastro was filled with all sorts of dangerous animals. "And if you tell her, you know what they'll do to me? I'll get shipped off to the palace, forced to be Queen Arana's latest playtoy."

A haunting silence fell between the two men, and Reanna's heart skipped a beat. As a child, she had often been mystified by the fact that mermen only seemed to appear at balls and other functions. It had been like a fairy tale, a skewed version of Cinderella. Now, reflecting on those things with her age, she realized that there had been so much more bubbling beneath the surface of Atlantis—and why these men didn't want to go there.

"Well, I don't see what the problem is," the third man grumbled. His armor clinked as he shifted his weight. "But I'm through with this anyway. Let's just go tell General Violante that it was some wild animal. Maybe a centaur."

The others muttered their agreement, but even when they retraced their steps and left the forest path, Reanna didn't fall for the ploy. She remembered how soldiers used to pretend to leave the room, only to swim out of view and wait for Reanna to reveal herself.

No one else seemed to believe that the soldiers were really gone either. None of them moved or said anything until the first bits of the invisibility spell began to unravel, though Reanna didn't know how long it had been. She held up her hand—she could almost see the shimmering outline of her skin, the place where her body *might* be.

Laeserno crept back to them. He had bits of leaves and twigs stuck to him, including one in his hair that jutted out quite jauntily. "Come on. We should not tarry here."

Reanna fell into step behind the rest of the group—and almost screamed as something furry brushed up against her legs.

She slapped her hand over her mouth before any sound could escape and stared down at the empty spot. In the moonlight, she could make out the faintest glimmer of a feline face. Even more disturbing—what stood out the most in the darkness was Whisper's grin, which looked just like the Cheshire Cat's.

Then—with all the arrogance of a cat—he *winked* at her with one half-visible eye.

CHAPTER 26

LAILE

GAIA: TUNNEL IN DASPIN

They reached the mines by the next daybreak, though they hadn't been able to stop to rest. After the battle, Laile didn't know if she could unwind, and Gregory and Laeserno seemed more concerned about putting space between them and the enemy soldiers. But no one seemed to pursue them, so Laile finally let her tense body relax in the cool underground.

The darkened tunnels rose up and engulfed her. The closeness made her feel smaller than she already felt, even in her crystallized form. The only light came from her own body; she'd shrunk down when they'd gone underground to try and offer some illumination. It bounced off the gems within the dirt walls and showered the tunnel in dim sparkles.

Everyone seemed too tired—or too wary—to speak. They'd been stuck in the tunnel for probably an hour. It was too bad that she couldn't at least sing to keep their spirits high. Moments like this definitely needed a musical interlude to keep the spirits up—and *not* a song about a fat old cat with feet so flat…

Drat. Now it'd be stuck in her head again.

A loud wheeze caught Laile off guard. Gregory took a step toward the noise, his brow furrowed. Laile seized the opportunity to settle on his head and use his curls as protection—one of the many perks of being tiny.

The noise came again. It sounded something like the labored breathing of a creature too big for comfort. Laile gripped Gregory's hair, and he grunted.

"Sorry," she whispered.

He plucked her from his locks and set her down on the floor. She groaned. She didn't really want to fly, not really, but if she expanded to her human form, they'd lose the light. Not to mention her legs felt sluggish, too.

Gregory ushered her onward. "Come on; don't stop. It's an animal. Hurry up."

Laile almost wondered if it was Whisper—but no. Her azernos hadn't left Reanna's side since the fight earlier. In fact, he seemed to have some obsession with her now. Every few minutes, he bumped her legs, tried to trip her, or yowled for her attention. Reanna scooted away or shoved him back every time.

Laile tried to glow brighter, to illuminate the path behind her, but she still didn't see anything.

She did hear footsteps, though, crunching over the hard dirt.

"Laeserno...?" Laile buzzed ahead. Gregory uttered an indignant "Hey" as she left him in the darkness.

She stuck her tongue out at him—not that he noticed the sweet gesture in the darkness.

"Yes?" Laeserno held out his finger, and she perched on it. How considerate—Gregory never thought to do that.

"Are these tunnels abandoned?"

"The last I heard, yes. The gnomes don't want to mine here anymore due to Arana's proximity," Laeserno said. "No one wishes to draw her attention and end up in a concentration camp like the elves."

"So…I have a question."

Laile nearly jumped at the sound of Reanna's unexpected voice; this was the first time the former mermaid had spoken since they'd entered the tunnels.

"What is it?" Laeserno asked.

"Since the elves are so powerful, why can't they just free themselves?"

"Not all elves are powerful." Laeserno chuckled, but Laile noticed the sadness that lurked in his violet eyes. "We have differing levels of powers, just like everyone. I have never pursued magic with as much dedication as some of my peers—I always preferred music—but there are some that are even less trained than me. Compound that with the fact that Arana kidnapped our children first. Anyone that resisted had their family slaughtered." Laeserno's voice broke, and he had to wait a few moments before he could continue. When he did, his voice was quiet—despondent. "I believed that by working with her, I could prevent my family's destruction. Unfortunately, it seems that Arana also lies."

Reanna flinched. Laile left Laeserno's finger and perched on Reanna's shoulder to give the girl a cheek-hug. Even if it was the truth, a certain amount of tact was needed when discussing the utter depravity of one's parents.

Reanna curled her shoulders inward. "That's heinous."

"And that is why I am helping you reclaim your tail and magic." Laeserno kicked a pebble out of his path. "I believe that you can stand up to your mother. And since she wants you, perhaps this makes you the best person to stand up to her."

Reanna stuck the ends of her curls into her mouth. Laile patted her face and just prayed Reanna wouldn't spiral into another bout of panic like she had at the catacombs.

"We'll see," Reanna said after a second, though it was a bit garbled. She still hadn't dropped her hair.

The tunnel rumbled behind them.

Laile screamed and whirled around. The walls shook, and dirt rained down on them. Oh, flying fig-whits—these tunnels *had* to be up to safety codes, right? She lifted her hand and willed the dirt above them to be diamonds. In her head, it made sense: no more dirt could fall down if she crystallized it all.

But, in application, it hurt more as tiny raindrops of diamonds plunked against their skulls.

"Cut it out, Laile!" Gregory yelped as a chunk of crystal broke away and beaned his nose.

The animal cried again, and the noise sounded like a mix between a snort and a horse's whinny combined with a growl.

A giant caramel-colored animal padded down the hall; its long claws gouged at the ground. It bared its pointy teeth and swung its long nose—which had finger-sized red tentacles around the nostril-area—violently. The gems reflected in its dark eyes and made it seem like a rainbow lived inside of the beast. Black and white stripes streaked across its back—and that was as far as Laile got as her fight-or-flight instincts kicked in.

The animal caught sight of the group, stopped, sniffed, and uttered its strange call.

Then, with a wild hiss, it swished its bushy tail back and forth and charged straight at Gregory.

CHAPTER 27

REANNA

GAIA: TUNNEL IN DASPIN

Reanna screamed and thrust out her hands in a pale imitation of the move the Atlantean soldiers had done to create the whirlpool.

Not even a single droplet responded to her call. Back on Earth, she'd never encountered a single problem that made her wish she still had her tail and powers; she'd never really thought about using either except when she played pretend in the pool as a child. Now—well, being surrounded by so many magic-users had awakened her instincts once more…and it would sure be nice to flood the tunnel and stop that *thing* from pursuing them, even as it got closer with every giant stride it took.

Whisper bolted past Reanna with a loud meow. She had to agree with that assessment: Time to start running.

Oof.

She smacked right into the wall as she whirled around to retreat. She moaned; Gregory raced past and grabbed her. He dragged her along until she could gain her footing back.

"Do something, Laile!" Gregory called out.

"I'm trying!" Laile's crystallized form flashed brighter. She held out her hands, and the gems in the walls began to rattle. Laile flung the jewels at the beast—which looked like some weird cross between a mole, badger, skunk, and some other clawed animal—as more dirt rained down above her. The creature shook them off and let out another high-pitched, unidentifiable noise.

"All right, clearly I asked the wrong fairy to do something! Back away!" Gregory muttered a spell underneath his breath. He flung one hand backward and yelled, "Duck!"

The girls obliged—Whisper and Laeserno were too far ahead of them to be bothered—and a wall of flames shot up at the feet of the creature. The flames swiftly engulfed the tunnel as they crawled up the walls. The animal, though, seemed undeterred. It broke through the fiery wall without a thought. Reanna hacked as smoke filled the tunnel and her lungs and stung at her eyes.

"Clearly we asked the wrong wizard to do something!" Laile snapped back at Gregory. She landed on his shoulder and gasped for breath just like Reanna. "Now, not only is the temperature going to rise, but we're also going to be outracing a death by fiery inferno. I'm so glad *you* thought of everything!"

"Okay, okay. I'm sorry." Gregory ran faster, and Reanna struggled to keep pace with him as she limped along thanks to the stitch in her side. "I admit, it wasn't my best idea. I was just trying to think of *something*."

There was water under the ground—Reanna knew that there must be. She could pull it up and extinguish the fire—

Maybe she hadn't imagined a moment where she'd yearn for her powers again, but she also never imagined that there'd come a moment where she wished she'd exercised more, either.

But here she was.

If she was going to be a useless slug, she might as well see if there was anything that Gregory could do.

"There's water underneath our feet," Reanna panted. "Can you call it up?"

Gregory looked at her like she had suddenly grown a third eye. "That's an Atlantean or a water fairy power. Water is the ficklest element to control for spellcasters; it's nigh impossible. But maybe I can do something that I wouldn't necessarily have to control..."

Reanna didn't get to hear what he said next; she tripped over a gem that jutted out of the floor. She staggered and collapsed, scuffing her elbows and forearms as she caught herself. Despite the fact she would probably get eaten now, she was almost relieved to sit down.

Gregory began to mumble—why did he always mumble his spells?—again, and mist filled the chamber.

Reanna shook her head. Now she knew why Arana always boasted about the prowess of Atlantean water manipulation. Reanna's hypothetical flood would have been useful against the creature *and* the flames. But could she be useful? No. As it was, she could only climb back up to her feet and begin their endless race over again. Except this time, it felt like she'd entered some bizarre haunted house, filled with smoke and mist and general darkness, lit only by Laile.

"Can one of you help me out and give me some more light?" Laile shrieked.

Laeserno cleared his throat. "Sorry!" He summoned a *lux* spell to add in more light.

At least the mist did help a bit with the fire. The fog began to condense and turn into thick water droplets, and it almost made it seem like it was raining in the cavern—*almost*.

The creature, though, paid no heed to that either. It surged forward, snarling and calling; Reanna caught sight of a nose here or a claw there as she raced through the haunted maze.

Laile fell back again, her arms poised for another attack. The dirt from the tunnel floor rose and swirled around her. It took on the form of hardened crystal until there was nothing more than a giant gem in the center of the tunnel with Laile trapped inside. The creature slowed as it sniffed this new distraction; it growled and stomped its paw during its inspection.

"Go!" Laile cried from inside the crystal.

"Laile—" Gregory started.

But the crystal that encased Laile flashed red as if in warning. "I said, go!"

The crystal began to unravel, and Reanna saw why Laile had wanted them out of the way. The thing fell apart in sharp knife-like pieces as Laile spun it faster and faster. The pieces tore at the creature and made sharp cuts all over it. The animal growled and lunged at the gem fairy, which only caused it to injure itself.

"Careful, Reanna!" Gregory said. He pulled her back from one shard that barely missed nicking her. She breathed a word of thanks and nudged him backward. She shivered a bit as the condensation turned cooler and raised goose-bumps on her skin. They were still edging farther out of the tunnel when Laile's crystal finished unraveling, and the creature whimpered in pain.

"Ha! Take that, you big dumb beast!" Laile turned and flew back toward Gregory and Reanna.

She never made it, though. The creature lunged at the fairy and caught her between its teeth. It shook her back and forth; Reanna could hear the thump of the creature's nose against the wall, and she imagined Laile being smacked around like a chew toy.

"Laile!" Gregory screamed while he rushed forward. "*Praevolo!*" He shot out his hand. The creature bounded to the left, and Gregory's magic blast hit the wall. The gems that had been lodged there flew up to the roof of the tunnel—he must have been using a levitation spell, Reanna realized.

Gregory yelled the spell again, and this time it hit the mark. The creature slammed into the ceiling. Dirt rained down on Gregory and Reanna, but neither of them stalled their approach. Reanna rushed closer as her mind beat out a simple hope: that her friend hadn't been swallowed, alive or otherwise.

Thank goodness. Laile dangled from the creature's teeth; though limp and more than likely unconscious, she was in one crystallized piece.

Reanna jumped, but her friend remained just out of reach. A water whip would have come in handy…. She gritted her teeth. Where the heck were Laeserno and Whisper? Why had they left three teens alone to fight this animal? "Laile! Can you hear me?" Reanna leapt again, but still couldn't get to Laile.

"Move. I'll get her down," Gregory growled. He shoved past Reanna and lifted his hand.

The ceiling exploded—but through no spell of Gregory's.

The impact tossed Gregory and Reanna back. Reanna's head smacked against the tunnel floor, and sunlight stung her eyes. She inched one eye open, desperate to see their new attacker. Laeserno stood from among the rubble and called up to someone. "Another explosion! Just a few more and we can get them out!"

A dark head peeked over the ledge from outside—the same man who had helped free Gregory last night. Reanna squawked and reached out for Gregory, but her friend's eyes remained closed. She jostled him, and he groaned and tried to mumble something she couldn't understand. At least he was conscious—for the most part—but that didn't help Reanna solve her more immediate problems.

The strange beast bellowed. It swung its giant snout at Laeserno and knocked him back in the tunnel. The elf cried out as the levitation spell carried the monster through the hole and into the open. Reanna didn't know if Gregory's spell had any limitations, but images of Laile and the creature drifting right into space and suffocating in the vast expanse flashed before her eyes.

"Do something!" she shrieked. A scream welled inside the pit of her stomach. Useless, powerless—*nothing*. A waste of space.

The words crashed into her brain and clouded out any sense of rationality. She struggled to keep the inhuman yell contained within her as she staggered to her feet. "One of you, *help her!*" she screeched.

Laeserno pushed himself up. The strange black-haired man reacted quicker than the elf. He lifted his hand as the animal floated higher into the atmosphere. "*Desinmere!*"

The levitation spell evaporated and the creature collapsed. But it landed on the dark-haired stranger with such a force that Reanna just knew Whisper—or whoever the man was—had to be dead.

"No!" She stood under the hole, too short to climb out, unable to do anything but listen to the thundering footsteps of that awful monster as it ran away.

An eerie silence followed.

"What..." Reanna began.

"*Praevolo!*" Laeserno clamped his hands on her shoulders.

Reanna squeaked as she was lifted into the air. She kicked her legs as the hole got closer—soon she'd be at the treetops—then the atmosphere—

"Let me down, let me down!" Reanna pummeled her fist against the air and ended up smacking her skin against the new tunnel exit. But once she cleared it, she heard Laeserno cast the *desinmere* spell again, and she thudded to the ground outside, right next to the strange man.

"Hello there," he wheezed through labored breathing.

"Hi?" Reanna stood and scanned the horizon for Laile's abductor. But she could only see rolling hills, thick with trees, surrounded by dismal plains. Wherever the beast had gone, it had gone there very quickly.

The strange man groaned. He placed one hand over his chest. "*Compositor, sana vulnus hoc.*" He grimaced and gasped, his eyes pinched shut.

Reanna kneeled beside his sweaty head. Her eyes burned from tears, and her bottom lip quivered. "Can I help?" She smoothed back his hair. His body trembled beneath her delicate touch.

He shook his head. He swallowed. Several erratic, painful heartbeats passed in Reanna's chest before the Whisper-man exhaled with a huge *whoosh*. "The only thing that hurts worse than mending broken ribs is getting them broken in the first place." He sat up, though he winced with each movement. "I don't recommend it."

"I'll take your word for it." Reanna wiped at her face before Gregory and Laeserno both floated out—the former looking quite worse for wear. His glasses had shattered, and he squinted at the scene.

"Did *anyone* get Laile?" he snapped.

Laeserno cleared his throat. "Well—I intended to collapse the tunnel behind us to free her, but—"

"She floated through the hole. The animal took her," Reanna said dully.

Gregory whirled on Laeserno. "*You* should have been taking care of her! Or did you think she was disposable, just like Shaesia?" Gregory gripped Laeserno's collar and shook him.

"I—" Laeserno clawed at Gregory's fingers.

Gregory jostled the elf once more. "It's all *your* fault! If you—"

"*Hey!*" Reanna shoved her way between the two and managed to push them apart. She'd swallowed down her own angry words already; she held them both at arm's length and stared at them each in turn. "Gregory, calm *down*! Nobody meant to lose Laile. We're all worried."

The memory of her own outburst in Unity Park kept her temper in check. Though part of her wondered whether or not Laeserno had lost Laile on purpose, or...

No. Gregory had done the spell to test Laeserno's motives, and the elf hadn't let them down since. Reanna had to believe it'd been a horrible accident, though she wouldn't let very many more "accidents" happen before she reevaluated her stance.

Gregory's jaw worked back and forth. Even his nostrils flared, and he whipped off his glasses and muttered something. But he couldn't disguise the tears in his eyes as he stared at his broken spectacles, his long hair hiding his face.

"I am sorry," Laeserno whispered. "I never meant to lose her. I would never betray—" He swallowed. "I would never betray anyone again."

"It'smyfault," Gregory mumbled, and Reanna honestly wasn't sure where one word started or stopped. "Ilosther."

"Imposter?" Reanna's brain struggled to work apart the syllables.

Gregory slumped to the ground like a marionette whose strings had just been severed. The earpiece of his broken glasses hung limply from one hand while he covered his eyes with the other. He must have given up on getting the gummy words out of his mouth because he only sat there, motionless.

"On the bright side, your track record against humans stands just a smidge higher than your track record against animals. Since Arana falls under the humanoid category, we should be safe." The Whisper-man cleared his throat. "How you all will fare against vegetable and mineral is still yet to be seen."

Gregory's head snapped up, and though his eyes were wet, they contained a fire that threatened to incinerate the Whisper-man alive. "Who—"

"Whisper." Whisper-man—or, more appropriately, Whisper *the* man—held out his hand. "Smart boy like you knows azernos are shapeshifters, right? How do you think I helped Cynerra out of as many pinches as I did?" Whisper rose to his feet and adjusted the purple-black jacket he wore.

"You're—you're a *human*?" Gregory blanched. "All this time…?"

"No, I'm an azernos. Although, currently, I've taken the form of a wizard so I can borrow some powers. Seemed a bit more useful than just getting big." Whisper tilted his head to the sky. "I'm going to find Laile. There's no worse scrape that she can get herself into that her mother didn't already get into. Werewolf fights, drowning by sirens…one time she almost got eaten by flesh-eating bugs. That child never sat down." Whisper patted Gregory's shoulder. "I know, boy. I've watched over you enough, too. I know what you're feeling, but I'll get Laile back. You all make it to Shaesia's house. We'll meet up there."

"Do you know where it is?" Laeserno asked.

"I'll find it. I can use a charm to track you once you're there." Whisper touched Reanna's shoulder. A jolt went through her, and when he pulled away, she felt—for a moment—the tug of an invisible string. A wispy pink thread floated between them before it dissipated. Whisper gave them all a nod. "I've attached the charm to Reanna. But I don't want to lose any more time. Neither should you, honestly. Atlantean forces come out in droves in Kirova." Whisper ruffled Gregory's hair. "Maybe when I bring her back, you can give Laile that long-overdue chit-chat she's been wanting."

Gregory jerked his head up. Color rushed back into his pale cheeks. "I—"

"Oh, what do I know? I'm just an azernos, after all." Whisper winked and clucked his tongue before he shifted into a giant crow. The animal croaked once at the group and lifted into the air.

Reanna covered her eyes as the beat of Whisper's wings whipped up some loose dirt particles.

"Well," Laeserno said after a moment. "Perhaps we better make use of the tunnel, just until it ends and we are far away from here. The coverage could still be useful, especially if people come to investigate. Come on."

They all climbed back through the hole. Reanna understood the need for cover, but she still didn't like returning to the tunnel. Even without all the mist and flames, it seemed more like a haunted house without Laile's bubbly presence. The skylight provided enough sunlight to see for the first stretch, but soon enough, Reanna yearned for her fairy friend's shimmering luminescence. She rubbed her chest, which felt hollow and numb all at the same time.

Her mind wouldn't process it. *Couldn't* process it. Laile? Gone?

Never.

No. It *had* happened, and all of them seemed trapped in miserable silence, Gregory especially.

Was Reanna a bad person? She willed herself to cry over Laile's disappearance, willed herself to be as distraught as Gregory, but she couldn't summon the proper emotions. Her body felt numb, and her brain, which usually was all gung-ho for imagining the worst possible scenarios, seemed to be petting her on the head.

It's okay, it said. *Laile's going to be fine. She was taken by a creature, not some mad psychopath. Besides, you don't really know her all that well. It's sad, but it doesn't really concern you. It isn't like Tara or Mom were kidnapped.*

No—Laile wasn't even kidnapped. Temporarily out of sight might be the best way to describe her. Don't panic.

It was all so out of character for Reanna's anxious mind that she wondered if she'd somehow become somebody else. Where had all her empathy gone? She was the type of girl who cried when a sappy commercial played, but now Laile had been kidnapped—

Temporarily out of sight, her mind corrected. *You don't need to panic or cry because nothing's wrong. Laile will be back at any moment.*

Poor Gregory, though—he didn't look like he felt Laile was just "temporarily out of sight." Maybe Reanna ought to tell him that, just to raise his spirits…

For the next several minutes, she worked up the nerve to fall into step with Gregory. He'd repaired his glasses, but he still wore a dour expression.

She took a deep breath and braced herself for social interaction. "I'm sorry...I didn't realize how much you loved her." She brought the sleeve of her Spider-Man sweatshirt up to her mouth and chewed on it as she debated what to do next. She and Gregory weren't close enough for a hug, and a pat on the shoulder would probably send the awkward-meter sky-high again, especially considering their track record. So she settled on repeating her apology, adding, "Whisper will get her back."

Gregory shot her a scathing look. "Laile has been my best friend since childhood. I'm not—I'm not romantically attached to her. At all. But how would you like it if your closest friend was snatched by a monster and taken away to who-knows-where, where the beast will do who-knows-what to her?"

"Oh," Reanna stammered. All her sympathetic thoughts toward him evaporated, replaced in equal doses by mild irritation and social embarrassment. The tears welled up in her eyes again and got caught on her eyelashes. "I...I didn't think about that. I thought, maybe..."

Gregory strode away as if her question had offended him somehow. Ugh, men. Reanna didn't understand them at all. If there was one thing that Arana had been right about, it was that men were confusing and maybe life was better off without them.

Or maybe she needed to apologize once more...

Reanna sighed and ran to catch up with him. "I'm sorry. Why are you upset with me?"

Gregory mumbled something that vaguely sounded like "I'mnotmadatyouI'mmadatmyself"—but, once again, Reanna couldn't understand the gummy words.

Still, she didn't try to get him to repeat it louder. As oblivious as she could be, Reanna knew that whatever he was dealing with, she wasn't allowed to intrude on that private thought.

Reanna had no way to keep track of time, but they walked for what felt like hours in silence. Once the darkness got too overwhelming, Laeserno led the way with a ball of light from a *lux* spell.

Reanna shuffled on. She wasn't sure what conversation topic she could talk to Laeserno about—fond memories of Shaesia before he turned her in?—so she kept her distance. Gregory stared off into space with a glazed expression on his face, and any attempt to speak with him got her one-word answers. At one point, Reanna asked him to wait for her so she could retrieve a water canteen from her fairy skirt. She stopped; when she glanced back up, he was already so far ahead of her she had to jog to catch up. Reanna wiped at her own damp face and took a sip of her drink, even though she would have much rather enjoyed chucking the canteen at his head.

The tunnel seemed to stretch on and on, which encouraged Reanna's thoughts to traipse back to the past. Sometimes she would have nightmares about being caught in a never-ending loop, forced to walk and walk with no end in sight—

Reanna stopped herself before the feeling of utter panic and dread could seize her. They were not caught in a time-loop, nor were they caught in some skewed version of eternal torment. After all, they couldn't be going in circles—they hadn't seen the hole that Laile had disappeared through again.

Then the metaphorical clouds parted, and Reanna heard the "Hallelujah Chorus." The sun shone through the passageway's mouth. She could almost hear the "Chariots of Fire" piano song playing as she raced toward the end of the tunnel. If only the mood hadn't been so dour, she might have raised her hand and pantomimed a slow-motion run.

Grinning wildly, she turned back to see if Gregory and Laeserno were enjoying the sun as well. But they both just plodded on, lost to the world.

Laile's capture.

The elves.

The war.

Everything crashed back into Reanna and sucked away the minuscule amount of humor.

They may have been free, but so many, wherever they may be, weren't.

CHAPTER 28

REANNA

GAIA: FORESTS OF DASPIN

Leaves crunched underneath Reanna's feet as the group plodded on; they were back in the forest once more—only their journey went uphill this time. The noonday sun threatened to burn Reanna's skin, its unflinching rays the only indicator that time had passed. Nothing else had changed: not Gregory's foul mood, not Laeserno's unflinching pace, not Reanna's emotional numbness and physical hunger, and not the fact that Whisper and Laile hadn't returned yet.

"Hey." Reanna's voice cracked from disuse—or parchedness? —when she finally spoke up. "You know, she'll be back. I promise. We'll get her back." After all, Laile was only temporarily out of sight. That was all. Not kidnapped. Temporarily out of sight.

Gregory grunted. It seemed like no matter what she said or did, his funk would not end until Laile came back. Reanna winced and chewed on her sweatshirt. It was all her fault, really…if she hadn't run away…if she'd…

Her stomach interrupted the pity party with a loud rumble. She crossed her arms over her middle to keep it from protesting too much. Gregory must have heard it anyway, though, because he turned around and heaved a sigh. Reanna wanted to snap: *Oh! I'm sorry my hunger is such a burden to you. I can always just die if that'd be more convenient.* But sarcasm probably wouldn't diffuse the situation.

Gregory glanced up at the sky and then to her. "Hey, Laeserno. Stop. We need to eat."

"We will soon." Laeserno wiped the sweat off his brow as he faced them. "On the crest of this hill, there is a safe glen where we can eat. Elves have used it for rituals for years, and the magic there is so potent that even I could easily set a protection barrier. Please hurry."

With a last bolt of energy, Reanna surged forward. Her legs trembled, her side ached, but she'd almost reached the top—

The forest gave way to a clearing. Gleaming white stones made a circle around the exterior. They seemed to be pointing toward the middle, where a large boulder sat as if in a place of honor. The trees were all unnaturally long and bent, forming a canopy over the glen. It looked like they were bowing to the stone in the middle—or protecting it. Long Mandeville vines trailed down with huge pink flowers blossoming on them.

Reanna's breath left her in a puff of wonder. She stepped into the shade. Sparse sunlight filtered in through the tree canopy, but most of the light came through right above the middle stone like a halo. If anything could be angel-blessed, Reanna knew that *this* glen, whatever it was, was truly something special.

Ahead of her, Gregory put his palm against the bark of one of the trees. He shuddered and jerked backward. "You're right—this place reeks of elven magic." He flexed his fingers and shook them out before he let his hand drop to his side. "I can feel the residue seeping through the ground."

"Yes. Be careful. Very powerful and ancient magic has gone on here for several generations—hundreds or thousands of lifetimes, if we go by the shorter lifespans of other races." Laeserno sat down against the rock and tilted his head toward the sun.

Although Reanna didn't possess the same magical affinity as the other two, their descriptions seemed to reinforce her angel-blessed theory. She felt like the glen held too many grand secrets and was about to burst. She gaped up at the canopy of trees, imagining so many magical things that could happen here....

Thud. She grunted as her foot whammed into the boulder in the center of the glen. No—not a boulder, she realized. It was actually flattened on top, like a table, and had an envelope on it. Reanna furrowed her brow and picked up the envelope. It was addressed to the elves in small, somewhat neat, letters.

Gregory stopped his meandering around the perimeter of the circle to look at her. "What is that?"

"I was thinking it's probably a tiara," Reanna said sarcastically. She held up the letter so he could see it.

He snorted and *nearly* smiled. But then it was like the memory of Laile flashed across his mind again, because he grimaced and the forlorn expression came back to his face. When he finally composed himself enough to speak, his voice was barely higher than a mumble and sounded clogged with emotion. "I wouldn't open that if I were you. Elven magic is strange and unpredictable—"

"No need to warn me. I bartered my own tail and powers away with elven magic. Besides, whatever happens here, I'm sure Laeserno can undo it—" Reanna glanced at their leader, who had fallen asleep with mouth agape. "Or, you know, maybe not. Wake him up if I die in a puff of smoke, okay?" With that, she broke the seal and pulled out the letter, which was written on regular old Earthen stationary paper. She scanned over it—and nearly dropped it as she read its contents. Her heartbeat sped up, her tongue doing that inexplicable thing where it seemed it was going to swell inside her mouth. That only happened whenever her heart skipped a beat or her anxiety took full hold…

Gregory reached out to grasp her elbow, maybe to steady her. That was probably good. Reanna swayed, her knees close to buckling underneath her.

Gregory's grip tightened on her. "What? What is it? Let me see!"

He tried to snatch it from her grip, but Reanna backpedaled. She clutched the note to her chest, feeling like a hunted animal. She started as she bumped into one of the trees, momentarily mistaking it for a person, before she whirled around and smacked into another one. Finally she regained her dignity but not her breath.

"Reanna—"

"It's nothing! I swear!" she snapped. Gregory recoiled from her words, so she tried to soften them a bit. Even to her, the tone she had used sounded like a physical punch. "Nothing. I promise. It's just…something that…that Shaesia—yeah—Shaesia needs to read."

"Then why are *you* reading it?"

"Curiosity." Reanna hoped that she could steady her shaking hand. Her whole body seemed to turn to mush, and as she read the letter again, the words didn't make any more sense. Whoever this Adam was, how had he gotten this note across the dimensional boundaries? Nothing about his existence was plausible. He had the most cockamamie explanation…trying to play on sympathies, a poor Gaian boy stuck on Earth…there had to be something sinister about him.

Her face must have gone ashen because Gregory put his hand on her shoulder and steadied her. "Let me see that. It's clearly got you shaken up. Maybe if we show Laeserno—"

"No!" Reanna held it behind her back and shook her head. Her heart threatened to explode within her; her breath came out in little spasms. "I mean, no. You can't."

Gregory crossed his arms over his chest and grunted. "Fine, then put it back."

Reanna shook her head again. "No...I need to get it to Shaesia. It's, uh—for her."

Gregory looked like he was going to protest more, but then he threw his hands into the air. He shrugged and returned to his wanderings, probably grousing about her under his breath. Reanna read the letter once more and slipped it into her fairy skirt. If what this Adam boy had written was true, then Reanna could only trust Shaesia to read it. Only Shaesia could make sense of this confusing situation Adam talked about.

And as for Adam...what had he gotten himself into?

PART VI

CHAPTER 29

ADAM

EARTH: PANAMA CITY, FLORIDA

Adam made his way back to the spot outside Trevor's house where he had sent the note and prayed that a portal would be there. Just like the past few days, it wasn't. He heaved a sigh and sat down to watch the waves lap against the shore. Times like these, his thoughts always turned to his mom—or, more appropriately, what he had been told of her. The fact that she had never held him, never got the chance to, tore into his heart. All he knew about his mom were the little details Lily told him and what they had been able to glean off their father when he wasn't in a mood. Sometimes, when he wasn't feeling especially melancholy, their father would invite them to watch home videos, but those only served to make their father weep and Lily clam up.

In a way, Adam almost felt guilty for missing his mom. Unlike his dad and Lily, he hadn't been able to talk to her, to get to know her or anything. He relied on stories, on those precious moments when people weren't too upset to even breathe her name. Somehow, this made him think that perhaps she wasn't his to miss...or, like Lily sometimes said when she was grumpy, that he only missed a figment of his imagination. Lily and his father...they had known the real thing. They had the true reasons to be upset.

Or, sometimes, his guilt was for his older sister—or lack thereof. Even though she had died with their mom, he couldn't bring himself to miss Rose as much as their mom. Maybe it was because he had Lily as a substitute, or maybe it was simply because even Lily wouldn't say their sister's name. Once, he had dared to ask Lily what she was like, and she had thrown a cup across the room. It had shattered into a million pieces as Lily broke down into hysterics. When she was finally coherent enough to talk, he only got strangled moans out of her.

"I told her I hated her... I wanted to go that day with Mom. They said I wasn't *old* enough, and...I told Rose I wished she had never been born, right as she walked out the door! Why was I so stupid, Adam?"

Adam had never asked again, if only for the sake of Mom's chinaware.

"Hey, you." Trevor's voice interrupted Adam's musings.

Adam turned around, a glare already situated on his face. "What do *you* want?" he demanded.

Trevor scowled. "Aw, did somebody wake up on the wrong side of the bed today?"

Adam sighed and dropped his chin onto his knees. "I don't want to talk about it, so go bother somebody else."

Trevor paused, and Adam wondered if the older boy was actually trying to be sympathetic for once. Then the quarterback had to go and open his mouth. "So is this a bad time to tell you that I joined the fencing club at school? Oh, and do you want to know who takes fencing club? Nobody. Me and some acne-ridden nerd named Dwight."

Despite himself, Adam laughed. "I'm surprised they even have a club with attendance like that."

"Yeah, apparently Dwight's dad is super rich, so he funds Dwight's fantasy sword-fighting club." Trevor rolled his eyes. "But I don't know how this is going to help. So far, I've learned more about Dwight's boring personal life than sword mechanics. We aren't even allowed to use swords. We're using brooms."

Adam snickered. "Maybe you should look into a job as a house cleaner after all this is done. That way, you can beat up any burglars with your broom of doom."

Trevor shoved Adam in the shoulder. "Whatever. Any luck with…the whole Reanna thing?"

Adam picked up a fistful of sand and threw it at the ocean. "I'm at a standstill. The elves won't open a portal, and there's nothing else we can do here."

Trevor stood up and kicked some sand in Adam's direction. "Well, come on, then. If you've got nothing else to do, I *guess* I can teach you some of the broomstick…moves, or whatever they're called."

Adam snorted and fell into step behind Trevor. "I can see your classes are teaching you a *ton*." Oddly enough, Adam felt a sense of brotherhood with Trevor as the older boy led him up the steps and through the door. They weren't adversaries anymore, and Trevor wasn't about to throw him over the railing. They were friends now, or…maybe just acquaintances. Or would it be sparring partners?

"Oh, take your shoes off. Dad's rules." Trevor positioned himself in front of Adam until all shoes were dutifully removed. Not surprisingly, the rest of Trevor's house reflected his dad's Danny-Tanner-like tendencies as well. Everything was meticulously organized and clean. Even the kitchen looked like it was ready to be photographed for one of those fancy, boring house magazines.

Trevor opened up a closet and pulled down a broom and a mop from their conveniently-labeled respective hooks. "Let's go outside," he said. "My dad won't like it if we make a mess or break something."

A brown-headed, bespectacled man entered the kitchen, his ear glued to a phone. When he saw Trevor and Adam armed with cleaning utensils, he shot his son a puzzled glance and said to the person on the phone, "I'm going to have to call you back." After a few more formalities, he hung up and crossed his arms over his chest—just like Trevor often did. "What are you doing, and who is this?" He gestured to Adam, who shrank back and tried to hide himself in his jacket.

"This is a kid from school. Adam. We're…just goofing off."

Adam noticed how Trevor didn't say *friend*. At least Adam knew what to label their relationship now. It was definitely back down to *acquaintance*.

"Hello," Mr. Spencer said. He held out his hand.

Adam shook it nervously and hoped that he wouldn't infect Mr. Spencer with any contagious diseases. It would be just his dumb luck to accidentally pass on the plague or something. "Um…hi." He shuffled his feet and examined both Trevor and Mr. Spencer. They were nearly identical, except that Mr. Spencer's face was older, sharper, and somehow even less friendly. That was saying something, since no one would ever accuse Trevor of having a *friendly* face either.

Mr. Spencer acknowledged Adam with a nod and turned his attention back to Trevor. "What do you think you're doing with my things?"

"Just stuff." Trevor huffed. He banged the broom and mop together. "Can we go?"

"I need your help, Trevor." Mr. Spencer lunged for the mop, but Trevor jerked backward.

"I don't want to help you. I've got things to do, Dad. Important things."

"And they involve taking cleaning supplies outside? Look, Trevor, I'm trying to get things prepared for the banquet and prayer meeting tonight for that missing Reanna girl, and you could show a bit more interest."

Adam's heart skittered at the mention of Reanna. So other people were looking, too? Even if the best private investigator on Earth couldn't find Reanna, it meant a lot to Adam that people were at least trying.

"I *am* helping, Dad!" Trevor made the mistake of glancing at Adam. "I'm helping him, so just leave us alone."

Mr. Spencer turned to glare at Adam. It only took that one nanosecond for Adam to realize where Trevor got all his scariness from. "And what *exactly* do you think you two can do with a *mop* and *broom*?"

Apparently, Trevor had inherited Mr. Spencer's sarcasm as well.

Trevor looked at Adam—what, did the quarterback expect *Adam* to answer? Adam ducked his head. He couldn't tell Mr. Spencer anything without being laughed at, thrown in an asylum, or exposing Gaia.

Trevor growled under his breath when he seemed to realize Adam was just as lost as he was. He shoved the supplies into Adam's hands and whirled back around to face his dad. "Leave me alone, Dad! Why do you think everything I do is stupid?" Trevor put his hands behind his back so he could motion for Adam to leave. Adam crept toward the door as Trevor's voice escalated. "That's why Mom left too! You always made her feel so stupid, and you never, ever give in—ever. Nobody's as stubborn as you!"

Adam couldn't help a snort—but quickly slapped his hand over his mouth.

Thankfully, Mr. Spencer didn't seem to hear Adam over the sound of his own yelling. "Stop being *ridiculous*! Your mother didn't leave because of me. Some people just aren't cut out to be mothers, and *she* was one of them."

Adam reached the door, but he found himself facing an unexpected crisis. Should he pick up his shoes or just run out barefoot? It was probably the most stressful decision he'd had to make in weeks.

"Mom was a *great* mom," Trevor snarled.

Adam knelt down to pick up his shoes and balance them between the mop and the broom.

Trevor didn't let up. "Maybe you should look in the mirror sometime to see who the bad parent is."

Adam finally made it out the door into the free—and probably germy—outdoors. He could still hear the Spencer family going at it inside, although he couldn't make out the specifics anymore. He slipped his apparently filthy shoes back on and rushed down the too-long flight of steps. As he reached the bottom, he heard the door slam shut again and Trevor's heavy footsteps thumping down the steps.

"Let's go," Trevor snapped before he even reached the sand. "He won't look for me for a while." He broke out into a sprint, and Adam groaned. Of course Trevor would run. He didn't even take short-legged people into consideration.

Adam chased after him, already puffing when they passed the next house. By the time they were four houses down, Adam wheezed as though on the verge of death.

Trevor didn't comment as he jerked the mop out of Adam's hand. "All right, get into your stance or whatever. I'm in the mood to beat something up." Without waiting for Adam to even catch his breath, Trevor smacked the mop handle against Adam's head. "Hurry up!"

"Yeesh! Fine, oh Miyagi of the Mop."

Trevor whacked Adam on his opposite shoulder. "Don't think you're getting expensive lessons like this for free."

"What are you going to do? Steal my lunch money?" Adam intercepted the next blow with his broom. He felt a tiny bit like King Arthur...or Donatello, the Ninja Turtle.

"Not even close." Another whack, blocked. Trevor managed to jab Adam in the stomach next. "You heard way too much back there, so now it's your turn to fess up. You and your dad ever have fights like that?"

Adam barked out a laugh, which left him open to a smack on the knee. He staggered backward and fell onto the sand. A few loose granules got into his pants and underwear, and he shifted uncomfortably. "You have no idea. My dad is *crazy*." He chewed on the inside of his lip. "But it's not his fault. My mom and oldest sister died because of me."

This caused a ceasefire in the blows. The mop in Trevor's hand dangled near a tiny dune. "I'm sure it wasn't your fault."

Adam had sand in his eyes—that had to be it. No way hearing Trevor Spencer say the words that Adam had always wanted his dad to say would make him cry. He had to stop this influx of emotions, had to hide it, or else Trevor would probably laugh his head off. "You don't know. It *was* my fault. It was all my fault." Adam let out a gasping sob. He was doing a rotten job of pretending. "And they'll kill me and Lily, too, if they ever find us."

Ugh—crap.

He'd blabbed a little too much.

"They?" Trevor asked.

Adam shook his head. "I can't say."

He expected Trevor to be angry, but the older boy only plopped down in the sand with as much grace as a drunk ballerina. The image made Adam chortle, but it came out all wrong and sounded like a mangled cry.

"All right. Tell me something else, then. What are—uh—were—their names?"

The forbidden words. Adam felt sick to his stomach, the urge to vomit overwhelming him. But instead of losing any contents of his digestive system, he found himself spewing names. "Raven—my mom, I mean. And my sister's name was Rose. And…Dad's name was—I mean, is—Todd—Timothy." Adam hiccuped and licked his lips.

"Todd or Tim? You don't sound real sure."

"Timothy Todd—I am sure. Some people call him Todd, some people call him Timothy…" Adam shrugged. "I don't see why people name their kid one thing if they're just going to call them by their middle name, y'know? It makes it all confusing and stuff and…"

"All right, all right." Trevor brushed the mop handle in the sand, poking holes in the beach. "You know, I don't know your last name."

"East." Adam gulped. "But…please. Don't ask any more questions. There's a lot I can't say. Remember the *they* I mentioned earlier? It's…really dangerous."

Trevor snorted. "What, you think I'm a spy?"

Adam narrowed his gaze on Trevor. "No, but I'm saying there's more magic in the world than you can possibly imagine, and I promised my sister I wouldn't screw anything up or get us caught." He nudged at the sand. "Dad sacrificed a lot to keep us safe the last few months before we came here. I may be an idiot, and he's a jerk, but I'm not taking that safety for granted." Adam sniffed and ran his sleeve underneath his eyes and nose. Trevor didn't push anymore. Perhaps he sensed that Adam needed a moment—

Thump!

Adam winced as he was struck over the head with a weapon—namely, Trevor's cleaning utensil. "What was *that* for?"

"Unh-uh-nun." Trevor leapt up. "C'mon. I'll teach you all of the moves of Dwight. I'm sure we'll be fencing experts in no time."

Adam heaved himself to his feet. It didn't matter—let Trevor act like he was obsessed with training to cover up that he really didn't want to deal with any more emotions.

And that, Adam realized, was fine.

CHAPTER 30

TREVOR

EARTH: PANAMA CITY, FLORIDA

All right. I see your two leaves and raise you two leaves and an acorn." Trevor threw in his bet and wriggled his cards around in front of his face. The sun sank lower beneath the waves as he and Adam sat on Trevor's porch a few days later.

Yet another day without word from Reanna, but they'd decided to play a friendly game of poker after their daily sparring practice.

Adam laid his cards down. He had a five, six, seven, eight, and nine, all of different suits. "Okay, Yahtzee."

Trevor snorted. "Pretty sure that's a different game."

"Okay, whatever. If you're so sure you've got a better hand, show 'em."

Trevor splayed out his hand as well—two fours, an ace, a ten, and a jack. "Booyah."

Adam swept his hair out of his eyes. "Wait...who wins, then?"

Trevor shrugged. "I dunno. I don't know how to play poker." He nudged the rest of his scavenged chips closer to the "pot"—some twigs, a loose feather from maybe a pillow, and another acorn. "Let's play something else."

Adam rubbed at his forehead. "We already played three games of Old Maid and eight of Go Fish. I'm tired of waiting around. Maybe I should just go home."

Trevor scooped up the cards and started to shuffle them. "I'll deal up Speed. You ever played that? You put five cards facedown on either side…"

"Trevor." Adam groaned. "I don't want to play Speed."

"Fine. Memory?"

Adam pushed himself to his feet. "No. My sister might start to worry if I'm gone too long. But…thanks for the offer."

Trevor sighed and arched his hands so that the cards created the rainbow formation. "Don't thank me. I just really don't want to go back inside with my dad. He's been on my case more than usual. He says I'm not showing enough sympathy or whatever about Reanna. Personally, I don't see why spending a copious amount of time with Julie's mom planning prayer vigils counts as showing sympathy. I'd call it more like using grief to get dates, which seems scummy to me, but hey. What do I know? Maybe I should go pick up a girl at her grandma's funeral."

Adam snorted. "You're insane."

"Maybe." Trevor sighed and dealt the cards for Memory. At least he could play that by himself, even if Adam abandoned him. "But I can't defend myself to him. *I* barely believe you about this whole Reanna mermaid fanfic. I know he wouldn't. He'd probably accuse you of being into the occult. Or worse." Trevor smirked. "Harry Potter."

Adam rolled his eyes and hid a yawn behind his hand. "Yeah, it's best not to tell him. I'm wearing my Hufflepuff socks today, so he'd burn me at the stake for sure."

Trevor flipped over two cards. "I should have guessed you'd be a Hufflepuff."

"And proud." Adam waved and headed toward the steps. "I'm heading out. Good luck avoiding your dad. May the odds be in your favor or whatever."

Trevor gathered up the cards just as quickly as he'd dealt them and shoved himself up. "Well—wait a second. At least let me walk you home."

"What a polite date you are," Adam said dryly. "But no thanks. I can make it home by myself."

"Come on. I've got nothing else to do." Trevor tucked the deck of cards into his pocket. "And maybe we should plan some more on what to do when we get Reanna back. After all, finding her is the only chance I have at staving off the budding romance between my dad and Julie's mom."

Adam yawned again. "Would it really be so bad to have a stepmom?"

Trevor caught up with him, and they fell into step beside each other as they descended the stairs. "Yeah. Well—it would if it was Julie's mom. I can't stand her. She's so fake. Both of them are." Trevor rolled his eyes, even though the women in question weren't anywhere in his proximity. "You ever know those people that just, like—I dunno. They act all pious and holier-than-thou? The type of pearl-clutching, good-old-shallow-Southern type of people?" Trevor wrinkled his nose.

Adam nodded. "I mean, I kind of get what you mean. Yeah."

"Yeah, well…that's them." Trevor still felt a bit of rage when he thought of Julie's self-righteous prayer back in class for Reanna—his possible potential step-sister hadn't even been able to remember how to pronounce Reanna's name. Hadn't even cared enough to talk to Reanna, either.

Trevor opened his mouth to launch into a very annoyed diatribe when Adam's voice stopped him. "Are you sure it's not just because it's not your mom?"

"*What?*" Trevor snapped his head to the left to glare at Adam.

Adam stuffed his hands in his pockets and kicked a pebble out of the way. "I dunno. Oh—get ready to turn up ahead to the left.

But—anyway. I mean, my dad never got over my mom when she died. But if he'd tried to, if he'd gone on dates, I probably would have been mad at him. So…are you sure it has less to do with *who* your dad is dating and more to do with the fact he's dating again, period?"

"You don't know them," Trevor snapped. "They're annoying."

"I mean, I kind of do." Adam curved his shoulders in. "A little. Same way I know you and Reanna, that is. So you can discount my knowledge or whatever, but—I mean, they're a little pearl-clutchy, but they seem nice enough."

"They're *shallow.*"

"Just because you don't get along with someone or your personalities don't mesh doesn't mean the other person is shallow necessarily." Adam cocked his head, and a bit of hair fell into his eyes. "I never said I thought you'd be best friends with them."

"Yeah, because I won't."

"And, call me crazy, but I told you some really personal stuff about myself. Dangerous stuff, even." Adam swallowed. "So…if you wanna talk to me about your parents' divorce…or whatever…"

"What's there to talk about? My mom booked it one day." Trevor shrugged. "Dad always picked at her, so I can't blame her. They always fought. But then my aunt—my mom's twin sister—got cancer and passed away. Mom…spiraled. Big time."

As in, yelling, crying, screaming, and throwing things big-time.

"She got so depressed toward the end of it. And instead of trying to help, Dad just nagged at her. Told her she needed to do more to get her mind off it. Told her it wasn't healthy to just lie around. Pointed out that the house was always a wreck. Told her she needed to focus more on her son than herself. Told her not to worry, because she'd see her sister in Heaven." Trevor's voice took on a hard, cynical edge. In retrospect, that was the first time—at least, that he remembered—that he wanted to wring his dad's neck.

"Oh." Adam cast Trevor a sideways glance. "That's rough."

Trevor let out a little puff of air and tried not to quote Zuko from *Avatar: The Last Airbender*. Maybe now wouldn't be the ideal time to hide his uncomfortableness behind pop culture references, but, *man*, was it tempting. "Yeah. Although not as rough as when Mom booked it." His voice wobbled for a second, but he cleared his throat and regained control. One thing he knew for sure—he'd never cry in front of Adam. "I get why she'd want to divorce my dad. I mean, if I was in her shoes, I'd do the same thing. But...I just don't get why she'd want to cut me out of her life completely." He cleared his throat. "I can count on one hand the number of times I've seen her in person since then. She has my number and my e-mail address, but she hardly messages me on either of them. But—it's whatever, I guess. I don't even know where she is now, or if she's got a second family... She didn't fight for custody, either. Or even visitation."

Adam's shoulders drooped further. "I'm...really sorry." His voice hitched a little bit.

"Why are *you* crying?" Trevor snorted, but his own eyes burned. "It's not like it's your mom that ditched you."

"No. It's just..." Adam's shoulders shook. "It's just...I guess...I guess there can be worse parents than my dad. And Lily and I haven't talked to him since...since we had to leave...and I know he's the one that told us to go, because he didn't want us to be killed, but..." Adam suddenly turned and rammed into Trevor.

Trevor uttered an *"Oomph,"* unprepared for the tackle, except—

Except it wasn't a tackle.

Adam's wiry little arms wrapped around Trevor's torso in a tight hug as the strange, feral kid sobbed.

Trevor blinked. Glanced around the street to see if they'd attracted the attention of any neighbors.

How did one deal with a hysterical feral child?

He let out a puff of air and patted Adam on the head three times. That seemed like a reasonable, comforting amount. Trevor even murmured, "There, there," a few times for extra measure.

"I'm sorry," Adam bawled.

"Yeah, yeah—just…" Trevor cut himself short. It seemed kinda rude to tell the kid all would be forgiven if he just let go.

"I'm sorry your mom left, too, I mean," Adam whispered. "I'm sorry."

"Don't worry about it. Not your fault." Trevor swallowed down some more tears. "I'm sorry yours died."

"Not your fault," Adam mumbled.

"Not yours, either." Trevor repeated his sentiment from the other day.

Adam clung tighter to Trevor and blubbered extra-hard.

Trevor rolled his eyes heavenward. He'd apparently adopted this child. This weird, fanfic-writing, emotional, feral Hufflepuff.

There could be worse fates, honestly.

PART VII

CHAPTER 31

LAILE

GAIA: SOMEWHERE IN KIROVA

L aile stirred, vaguely aware that someone was panting above her. She shifted, grateful that she was still in her crystalline form. If she had flesh right now, she'd definitely ache all over. As it was, her body throbbed dully.

She shoved herself upward, half-awake—until something wet dripped on her. Suddenly all-awake, she shrieked and jerked her head up. Her furry abductor stood over her. It drooled like a dog and bared its teeth. It narrowed its eyes, as if afraid she might attack. She backed away, arms outstretched in front of her. "Nice…beast. There you go. Just stay back, and I won't hurt you."

The injured monster growled. Trepidation immobilized Laile's limbs.

"What did you get today, Bolego?" a new person asked. The speaker had a deep voice and a lilting Kirovese countryside accent. A short man, probably no taller than Laile's knee—when she was full size, of course—lumbered over on a cane. He had a short white beard cropped around his chin and wrinkled dark skin.

Bolego nudged Laile and growled. The short man plucked Laile up by the wings and twirled her about. "What do we have here?" he mused.

"Let me go!" Laile thrust out her hands, but he held her too far away from the ground to let her control anything. "Right. Now." She tried to channel her inner Cynerra and use the voice that instilled the fear of the Composer into her children.

"Hmm..." The man squinted at her. "You a gem fairy?" He looked bemused and not at all afraid. "Haven't seen those in years. Not many fairies come to Kirova."

Laile kicked her legs, but her actions did no more damage than a bird beating a window. "And I'm not *supposed* to be here, either!"

She grew full-sized again and dropped out of the man's hand. At least she towered over him this way. This time, when she held out her hands, she could summon the dirt from the ground around her and transfigure it into two diamond daggers. "This is all a little misunderstanding, but I'll be on my way now."

"Say..." The gnome squinted. "Aren't you Damien and Cynerra Úlfur's daughter? I think I saw your face somewhere. Newspaper? Magic-mirror broadcast?"

Laile backed away. No use giving him an answer—

Bolego jumped on her. Her face smacked the ground, and she prayed something hadn't cracked in the impact, though her whole body hurt.

The man cackled. "So, not only are you a gem fairy, you're also a daughter of the werewolf Council representative?" He took a step toward her. "You'll catch a handsome sum for me."

Laile twisted her arm behind her and jabbed Bolego's paw with her dagger. He howled and reeled backward. One of his paws landed on Laile's leg; this time, Laile heard a loud crack—Composer help her, had she heard her own bone snap?—right before pain obliterated her entire body.

She screamed; Bolego roared. The ground shook, and Laile's arms trembled as she shoved herself around.

Maybe if she shrank down—but then she'd have toothpicks for weapons. Her chest heaved as she struggled to catch her breath.

The man whistled, high and shrill. "Capture her, Bolego."

Bolego's nose nudged her. Laile still had enough sense to drive her dagger at the left side of the beast's face. Blood bubbled up from the deep scratch she'd inflicted. She drove her other dagger into the other side of Bolego's face. He snarled and lunged at her, his mouth wide.

She couldn't get out of the way. Couldn't move. Pain. So much pain.

With no other option, Laile screeched and shrank down. The teeth slammed around her, and she found herself inside Bolego's mouth. She banged against his fangs for a moment before she realized how futile that was. Instead, she grew to full size—but instead of bursting through his mouth, she got caught somewhere between the transformation. Her lower body still held its diamond gleam while her upper half turned fleshy. Her head smashed against the roof of Bolego's mouth, and her knees buckled.

Bolego wheezed; Laile's vision whirled from impact and pain. She shrieked and returned to her gem form. She clutched at her leg as she fell, although being diamond helped manage her suffering. "Help! Please," she begged. "I need a healing spell."

The man clucked his tongue. "All right, Bolego. Follow me."

Nausea broiled inside Laile's stomach. She clamped a hand over her mouth to keep it in. She didn't know what made her more nauseous—the stabbing agony in her leg or the smell of Bolego's foul breath.

"Spit her out, Bolego," the man said.

Bolego obeyed his master, and Laile plopped out of his mouth with a load of saliva. The fall jostled her leg; she screamed and rolled to her side. Then the world tilted, and she smacked into a hard surface. Spit coated the bottom of the floor and drenched her. She couldn't even beg for help. The words simply wouldn't come, muffled by the intense pain.

She peeked one eye open and saw her new prison—a glass jar. The man twisted a lid on, probably to prevent her from flying. As if that mattered. Laile could barely stay conscious, let alone flap her wings. If she *could*, she wouldn't be floundering in this mini-ocean of slobber. "Please," she sobbed. "I—I won't press charges. I won't tell my family anything. Just please. *Help.*"

The man stared at her through the warped glass. "How about we strike a deal?"

"Yeah, yeah. What do you want? My firstborn?" Because if he did, he better act fast. Laile would contemplate even that deal right now if it'd fix the excruciating agony. Besides—given her luck with Gregory, she doubted she'd even have a firstborn.

"See, Bolego and I have been working that mine for a long time, and times are hard right now." The man sat and scratched at the hair on his cheek. "Technically, Arana's shut down that mine. Things are getting rough in Kirova. I'd like to head out."

Wouldn't they all?

"Not much anyone can do against her, especially the gnomes and dwarves. We're just not made for fighting." The gnome held up the glass and tapped his cane against it. "So here's my offer. I'll get you to a healer if you promise to make me enough diamonds to get me out of here. I'll specify an amount. You make half of that before we get your leg fixed, and then half after."

"I can barely stay *conscious* right now, and that's your offer?" Laile's vision tinged with blackness.

"It's far less than your firstborn." The gnome frowned. "All I want is enough to get away from Arana and set up a nice house for me and my jurinn."

"Jurinn?" Laile slurred.

"That's what Bolego is. A jurinn—a rare species found only in Fiastro. Picked him up from there myself on one of my travels, back when he was a baby."

Bolego sniffed at the glass. His breath fogged it up as the pink tentacles on his nose brushed against the jar.

A *poacher*. Bolego's owner was nothing more than a filthy poacher who'd gone into Fiastro when the Council had forbidden it and taken protected animals from their natural habitat.

Then again, Cynerra had kept a forbidden azernos at the house for years. Maybe Laile didn't have room to judge. "Okay—okay! Whatever. Just help me. Please."

The gnome began to walk, Bolego following close behind like a dedicated dog. Even his bushy striped tail swished back and forth. "See? I'm not an unreasonable man. You get to work, and I'll get you to a healer."

The gnome knelt in the dirt and buried his hands in it. He dribbled heaps of soil into the tiny air holes he'd poked in the jar until Laile had to fight her way to the top just to breathe. She coughed, spluttered, and climbed until he finished once her prison was half full.

"There we go. That's a start." The man tapped the glass. "I wouldn't wait too long, though. You've got to pay for your healer, after all."

Laile clutched a handful of dirt in her small hand. She willed her magic to enter it, to harden it, but it quaked and refused to fully transform. Her eyes drooped to half-mast as the pain in her leg fought to drown her in a sea of unconsciousness.

Composer help her—she didn't know if there was a way she could get out of this without Him.

CHAPTER 32

LAILE

GAIA: WHIDON, KIROVA

Laile's consciousness bobbed on an unsteady sea. Part of her cursed her own inability to handle this by herself. The second part of her just wished her mother could swoop in and fix everything. Cynerra had been there for Laile through every childhood illness, through every heartache, through every pain—whether emotional or physical.

The glass jar shook, and Laile ended up with a mouthful of dirt and a handful of agony. The world faded to black and came back again as she clutched at her leg.

"Come on. I've called the healer by a witch's stone, but I'll sell you at an auction if you don't make me some gems." Dureg—the gnome, as Laile had learned somewhere in the ocean of pain—tapped against the bottle. "I'd get a pretty good price for a gem fairy, and I don't think many more desperate folks would be as considerate as I am about your leg."

Considerate. Yes, definitely the first word that popped into Laile's head when she thought of her captor. Especially when, in the same breath, he'd threatened to sell her at an auction.

Human auctions had been banned since…Laile couldn't remember the exact date, but she was certain that the ban was almost as old as her father—so really, really old. Still, Damien grumbled about the black market every once in a while. Specifically troubling at the moment was the matter of blood slaves for vampires. There were even rumors that they had infiltrated the Capital, kidnapping "unbitten" people to smuggle to the highest bidder in Simit.

Her family would be *so* ticked if she got sold into slavery, blood or otherwise, on her first solo outing.

Dureg whistled a jaunty tune. The sound rattled inside Laile's brain, and she gritted her teeth. The song wasn't as annoying as "Old Black Cat," but it was certainly a close second.

"Come on now. Don't dawdle." Dureg interrupted his melody. "Work."

Laile clenched some soil in her fist and willed it to harden. Her magic seeped out of her slowly; her tired brain could hardly put forth the effort to transmute it. She held up her hands after a few minutes and let the diamonds leak out between her fingers.

What would Cynerra do in a situation like this?

Mm…no. Laile probably shouldn't kill Dureg, no matter how tempting.

The gnome hit a particularly off-key note on his not-so-merry tune while Bolego whined in harmony.

Well…perhaps no one would notice if she *did* kill them.

When Laile woke again, she found herself under an awning. Bolego slept beside her glass jar while Dureg hummed his song under his breath as he cleaned some mining tools. In front of them sat a wide display of wares, all with prices listed.

"You like my shop?" he asked. Laile didn't answer; she assumed it was rhetorical. "I sell whatever I can find on my journeys. But with the borders all closed up and guarded, Bolego and I have had to go into some old mines to see if there's anything left. Times are tough around here. But I guess they're tough everywhere, aren't they?"

Once again, Laile felt that question was rhetorical.

Beyond Dureg's little shop in the plaza, grand buildings, all made out of gems, glittered in the sunlight. An ornate path wound through the center of town, around a diamond fountain, and up to a lake that sat on a hill. It sparkled just as brightly as any of the bejeweled buildings. Dwarves and gnomes mingled in the plaza. Some sold their wares while others browsed the myriad of goods—books, fishing supplies, and rarities. The former two were geared more for the dwarves, who made their livelihood keeping expansive libraries and selling the abundant variety of fish they caught in the lake.

"All right, Dureg. I received your message." A deep, weary voice caught Laile's attention. "You mentioned that you'd pay well if I came out to your little…knick-knack collection to heal someone?"

All through her childhood, Laile had been taught to pray to the Composer, the One who set harmonies and melodies into being when He created the world. She'd followed her parents' teaching, whether in chapel or by herself, but Laile had never prayed as hard as she did when she saw the figure clad in scarlet before her.

Flying *fig-whits*—Composer have mercy. This man couldn't recognize her.

She would rather be sold as a blood slave than be bought by General Julius Festinius.

Dureg stood up and shook Julius' hand. Julius looked like he'd prefer to amputate his arm than return the greeting; his mouth tilted into a sneer. "I'd like to know how you think you will make this worth my time."

"Oh, I promise it will be." Dureg held up Laile's jar and gave it a little shake. Laile cried out from atop her thin layer of gems. "See, I caught myself a gem fairy. She's going to help me buy my way to freedom."

Julius leaned over Laile's jar. His dark gray eye seemed ginormous in comparison to Laile's own stature. She gulped. He'd always seemed a little larger than life, but this was ridiculous.

"My, my." Julius clucked his tongue. "A gem fairy? Those are a rare breed, indeed. Especially this far from Jenkirre."

"Not just any gem fairy—" Dureg began.

"Shut up, shut up, *shut up!*" Laile hissed.

"—but the daughter of Damien and Cynerra Úlfur. I'm going to get out of Kirova before it descends any further into the sea's madness." Dureg grinned. "Imagine how happy her parents will be when I return their little girl. I bet I'll even get to move into a shiny penthouse and live in the lap of luxury. She's going to make me a rich man."

"I'll tell you what." Julius slipped his white gloves off his hands and tucked them into his pocket. "I'll take her off your hands. You'll get to keep the amount she's already made, and I'll get you into the Capital."

Dureg wrinkled his nose and eyed Julius. "I hope you don't mind me asking, but aren't you—well—aren't you a little disgraced? Under suspicion for being a traitor during the Great Warlock Uprising and all?"

Julius' jaw tensed. The tendons in his neck worked back and forth, but he managed to keep a placid expression. "I was cleared of suspicions, thank you. I merely accepted a remote desk job to be close to my children."

Laile snorted; Julius tipped over her prison. She screeched as she hit the glass and fresh pain seared every nerve in her body. Tears sprang to her eyes as she struggled to breathe.

"Anyway, I'm not looking to sell her." Dureg set the jar back upright and scooted it closer to himself. "Especially not for what she's created. If you heal her, though, you'll get half of the gems she makes."

"Dureg, perhaps I'm not being clear about the situation that we find ourselves in." Julius threaded his long fingers together. "You do realize that you have a member of the Council's daughter, correct? And you are holding her against her will. Even though I only have a remote job overseeing recruitment in this time of war, it would be very easy for me to report this and have you arrested for kidnapping." Julius' eyes slithered over to Bolego. "Not to mention that you've got an illegal creature from Fiastro. Poaching is a serious crime."

"He didn't kidnap me," Laile bleated. "He didn't."

"Ah, so I suppose you *want* to be held prisoner in a bottle until you've created enough gems to buy your ransom? Very interesting." Julius smirked. "Don't listen to her. I'm sure she's just trying to trick you so she can see you punished."

"I am not!" Laile winced as her pain triggered a huge headache. She pressed her thumb and forefinger against the bridge of her nose and wished that action actually helped. "Dureg, please. Don't worry about my leg. Forget it. I'll get back to work; you don't need to heal me." She grabbed a fistful of dirt. The process didn't go any faster, despite her panic—in fact, it almost seemed slower.

Dureg faltered.

"Let me inform you of your position. Not only do I have enough evidence to convict you of two very serious crimes which would get you arrested, I also hold power over you." Julius' lanky frame cast a shadow across Dureg, and the gnome shrank away. "*I* am in charge of drafting soldiers. Give the girl to me, or I will see to it that you are put on the frontlines within a week."

Dureg swallowed; his gaze flittered between Laile and Julius. "Gnomes aren't meant for fighting—"

"Yes, yes. But with a few simple strokes of a pen, I can make it seem like you volunteered out of loyalty to your homeland. And if you so much as breathe a word to anyone, I would expose you and your crimes. I hold your entire life in my hands, Dureg." Julius straightened up and slipped his gloves back on. "Give me the girl."

Bolego whimpered and hid behind his master. Dureg shifted his weight. "Look, I—I'm not trying to cause any trouble. I kept the girl, but I didn't kidnap her. Bolego here brought her to me. I just want to get out of here before things get even worse."

"As do we all." Julius nodded to Laile's jar. "Take what she's made. That's more than enough to book you passage on a dragon ship—or however you choose to travel with your overgrown pet— and I'll see to it that you get a remote house on the outskirts of the Capital. Can't have you getting caught, now, can we?"

"And why should anyone believe the words of a traitor?" Laile snarled.

Julius rattled her cage around, and she covered her mouth with her sleeve so she could bite into the fabric. The waves of unconsciousness swept over the sides of her tiny mental boat, and Laile thought she must have blacked out for a second. Her whole body felt light and heavy all at once, as though her consciousness had crashed back into the shore after a moment of being airborne.

Dureg unscrewed the lid to fish out the gems. Laile knew she should try and escape. If she just grew big now…overpowered them both…but she couldn't work up the will to move. Her heavy limbs resisted, and her mind swirled, lost in the currents. She still hadn't righted herself after Dureg resealed the jar.

"Promise you won't report me? And—that you'll keep your end of the deal? A house and everything?" Dureg wiped the dirt off the gems and tucked them into a pouch.

"Of course." Julius put a hand over his heart. "You have my word." He grabbed the bottle and left. He strode through the crowd, which seemed to part for him. A few people even bowed to him or offered him some small gesture of respect. Laile, on the other hand, rolled over onto her side and coughed up some bile. Her stomach churned while her mind reeled.

Julius would kill her.

He had no intention of fixing her leg. Laile would never see her parents again. Never see her siblings again. She'd never get to see Reanna become a hero and defeat Arana. Never see the end of the blasted war.

Her thoughts circled back to her parents. What had her father done when he found her gone? Did he miss her? Or what about Cynerra? If Laile did die, she hoped her mother wouldn't blame herself.

And what about Mionos, Kal, Wren, and Lark? Maybe Laile had been a little hard on her siblings. They really weren't that bad. In fact, she possessed lots of good memories, all of which bubbled to the surface as the end drew near. So many fun family vacations and so many adventures, such as when she and Kal sneaked out to see a Viscillo Waterfall concert on the outskirts of the Capital. Or when she took the twins on a hippocampus ride, or talked for hours with Mionos, or laughed about his crush on Aimee…

And Gregory. Poor Gregory…if Laile died, she'd never get to marry him. She'd never get to have children with him. It was a pity…they would have had such beautiful babies…

Julius turned onto a deserted side road. Out of everyone's view, he finally acknowledged her. "Well now, Laile. We meet again. You've grown up quite a lot since I last saw you whimpering behind your mother's legs."

There were lots of things Laile wanted to say; lots of accusations she wanted to throw. How Julius had killed Gregory's parents. How he'd tried to have hers assassinated. But that wouldn't help ease her pain or keep her alive, so she closed her eyes and tried to give in to sleep. To try and find one simple bout of relief. Except...

"Where..." Laile licked her lips. She only needed to know one thing. "Where are we going?"

Julius chuckled. "To my estate, where I usually deal with pesky little problems like you."

Laile just prayed someone would find her corpse.

CHAPTER 33

REANNA

GAIA: ELVEN GLEN, DASPIN

Sometime during their meal in the elf glen, the first wave of grief hit Reanna. Her brain had finally un-numbed itself enough, and she experienced a tidal wave of emotions right as she took a bite of her sandwich.

Laile might not just be temporarily out of sight.

She might actually be dead.

And if she was, Reanna was to blame.

Reanna stared at the food that Cynerra had packed until it became blurry with tears. Part of her wanted to regain the emptiness that had kept the depression at bay during the first part of the trek, but now that it was gone, she couldn't just will it back.

Not even Cynerra's mysterious—but delicious—meal could bring an iota of comfort. Reanna tucked her leftovers back into her fairy skirt and removed the letter again. How could she do any of the things she needed to? She'd only get everyone—including this Adam kid—killed before she could even get him *into* Gaia. It might not be a bad idea if she left him on Earth; at least he'd be safe there, and she couldn't hurt him. But she couldn't do anything without Shaesia anyway.

Flipping shark fins, why did everyone believe she could be of any help in the war? She would only disappoint them all. Laeserno. Adam. Laile. Gregory. Even Arana. Reanna had never, ever been good enough to fulfill even one person's desires.

She sniffled and returned the letter back to her skirt.

"I still think you should let me read that." Gregory sat beside Reanna.

She blinked her misty eyes and wiped at the droplets with her sleeve. Apparently, Gregory was the type who dealt with his grief by shoving it down and going, and going, and going until he could fix it or forget it, whichever came first. Whereas she was the type of person who needed a good bed, good food, and a Netflix binge before she was capable of even *starting* to deal with the tidal wave that lived inside her soul and heart.

"I told you. I can't. Shaesia needs to read it." Reanna wrapped her arms around her knees and brought them up to her chin.

Gregory sighed and leaned his head back against the rock. "I suppose it would be hypocritical of me to demand you hand over all your secrets when I can't give up mine."

Reanna furrowed her brow. "What secrets do you have?"

Gregory closed his eyes. "Too many, it feels like. And I can't tell anyone."

Reanna reached out hesitantly and patted his arm. When he didn't protest, she let it linger there. "You can tell me. I'll listen."

"It's not about listening. Laile wants to listen. She's begged me for weeks to tell her." Gregory shoved his glasses up into his curls. "But she wouldn't understand. You know how she is. She'll immediately start trying to fix all my problems and save the world. Some things…can't be fixed. Sometimes, you have to admit that life takes turns you don't want, and you have to face it without slithering out of the bad moments."

Reanna nodded. She had the sudden urge to reach over and wrap Gregory in a hug—and for the first time, she didn't even bother to rank the gesture on the awkward-meter. Maybe their sorrow had finally pushed their relationship into new territory and made them friends.

Weird, awkward friends—but friends nonetheless.

Reanna didn't follow through with her hug plan, but she did lean her head on his shoulder. "This is a bad moment. Well—I mean, not this, right here. Or, maybe it sort of is. But I just meant—Laile being gone. That's a bad moment. And the war. Also a bad moment. Lots of bad moments happening right now."

Gregory snorted. "Yeah. Lots of bad moments happening right now."

Reanna whimpered. She covered her face as the deluge of tears raced down. In the otherwise holy silence of the glen, her grief sounded too noisy. Too messy. She choked on it, coughed, and wished she'd mastered the art of pretty crying. "I'm sorry," she whispered.

Greg cleared his throat and patted her head. "It's okay. When her friend Aimee isn't around, I'm Laile's preferred shoulder to cry on." His voice sounded husky—like Reanna might be *his* shoulder to cry on right now, too.

"I know we need to go," Reanna bleated. "I'm sorry. Again."

"Quit apologizing."

"I just—if I'd had my powers, I could have stopped that monster from taking Laile."

Gregory snorted. "Yeah? I had my powers, and I couldn't. Neither could Laeserno or Whisper. We all failed, and three-fourths of us had magic. Magic doesn't guarantee that you'll be able to fix everything in life. If it could, then my parents would still be alive. Arana wouldn't be rampaging across Solis. Magic isn't a fix-all. It's what you do with it that matters."

Reanna rubbed the ragged sleeves of her Spider-Man sweatshirt; it was still cinched around her waist. The familiarity imbued her with a bit of peace, though she still couldn't stop crying. "And what *you* will do with it is what really matters." Gregory rested his palm on her head. "You're going to use your powers for good. You're going to rescue the elves. You're going to stop your mother. You'll save the world."

Reanna whimpered. "I don't think I can face her."

Gregory huffed. "Sure you can. You're not as weak—"

"It's not that." Reanna's voice fell an octave. "I'm terrified of her. I hate most everything she did to me. But I still can't shake this piece of me inside—like—like some love-forsaken little child of me—that craves her attention. That wants her to be a decent mother for once." Reanna wrapped her arms around his and held his forearm close to her cheek. The fabric of his shirt felt soft against her skin. "I know I should kill her, and there's a very angry, neglected, and bitter part of me that imagines beheading her or stabbing her through the gut with a sword."

Gregory grunted.

"But…the other half of me doesn't want to kill her. At all. It wants her to be better than she's ever been, for us to have a real relationship, for all of this nonsense to stop. I don't want her to be evil. I want her to be a good mom." Reanna's bottom lip quivered. She'd already dampened Gregory's sleeve with her tears. "What if everyone expects me to kill her, and at the end, I chicken out? Because of some misguided, childish desire to have her love me and want to be involved in my life?"

"Then…don't chicken out." Gregory patted her arm. "Do the right thing at the end; see this through. Your mother has committed heinous crimes. Think about those, and see it through."

Reanna slowly disentangled herself from their messy embrace. Her stomach churned even more after his declaration, and a wall of doubt crept up around her heart. That may have been true for him, but he didn't know her. *She* knew herself, kind of. And *she* knew the reality: that a child, desperate for Arana's love, still lurked inside her mind.

A child so desperate, she'd do almost anything to make her mother proud, even if it meant *not* saving the day.

"We should probably wake Laeserno and get back on the path," Reanna said stiffly. She rose and stretched out her muscles so she wouldn't have to make eye contact with Gregory. "We need to get to Shaesia's house soon."

CHAPTER 34

REANNA

GAIA: SHAESIA'S COTTAGE IN OGDEN'S HOLLOW, DASPIN

Reanna's heart pitter-pattered within her chest when Shaesia's house came into view the next morning. Laeserno had guided them through much of the countryside over the night, though they stopped to rest two times. Still, it felt like they'd fallen into a national park—nothing but trees and bushes and flowers grew all around them. Reanna had been tricked on going on a hike once in her life, and the walk to Shaesia's felt like a similar experience.

But her minor annoyances faded away as she stared at Shaesia's abode. Such conflicted emotions settled in the pit of Reanna's stomach that she didn't know what exactly to label them. She had some sweet memories here, but mostly they were so bookended by terrible experiences that her nerves didn't know how to react.

Unlike her feelings, the house itself was uncomplicated—just a small, homey cottage. Except—the door hung ajar with broken hinges. Someone had smashed the windows, and glass littered the front yard.

Reanna stopped and glanced at Laeserno. Warning bells inside her head screamed that it might be a trap, but—no. No one would set a trap and then smash the outside of a house to scare people away.

Right?

She bent down and picked up a piece of broken glass. "When…?"

Laeserno sighed and rested his hand against the door. It gave way as he did and clattered to the ground. Reanna's mixed-up self didn't know whether to laugh or cry at the sight.

Laeserno's expression drooped even more. His pale face looked haggard and exhausted. "I can only assume Arana's forces did this when they came to capture Shaesia. The mermaids are never gentle."

And the inside of the house didn't fare any better. Signs of struggle littered the room: not a single thing was left unturned, and scorch marks blackened the walls.

Gregory brushed his fingertips against the burns; he jerked backward and shook out his hand. "This is *powerful* magic residue."

Laeserno pressed his palm against the mark and scowled. "This feels like Violante."

Gregory winced; his face contorted into a sneer before he smoothed out his expression like an iron running over a wrinkle.

"It would make sense for Arana to send her…and, of course, Shaesia would not go quietly. If you knew her, you would know she fought fang and claw to stay," Laeserno finished.

"Shaesia didn't have fangs or claws." Reanna sniffed.

"It's an expression," Gregory mumbled. "It just means she would have fought hard."

Reanna's cheeks flushed. Of course it was—how stupid could she be?

But Gregory didn't mention it again. Instead, he traced the magic with his finger all the way around the wall. He winced several times but never stopped. "I've never heard of half these spells, but they practically want to jump up off the wall. Dark magic…elven magic…" He dropped his hand. "Violante is evil, but you wouldn't want to make an enemy of *either* of these women."

"And I have made an enemy out of both." Laeserno chuckled ruefully as he righted a high-back leather chair so he could sit in it. "Well, I suggest we do not grow lazy. I know we wished for Laile and Whisper to join us, but, from the looks of things, they have not made it back yet. I suggest we recover Reanna's tail while we wait so we do not grow idle. Then, when Laile is rescued, we can discuss how we will rescue the rest of the elves." Laeserno nodded in Reanna's direction. "Is that suitable with you?"

Reanna swallowed. "I—um—well. Yeah." Her stomach churned. Now that she'd reached the cusp of her choice, uncertainty reared its ugly head. Did she *really* want to be a mermaid? Or did she want to go back to Earth and forget about Gaia, about Solis, about Atlantis? It would be so much nicer to wake up in her bed tomorrow as Reanna Cook, daughter of Isabella Cook, sister to Tara Cook. To live in a world where no one had ever even heard of Arana before.

But that world didn't exist—well, unless a version like it existed in a theoretical multiverse. And the Reanna who *didn't* want to crumble into a puddle of tears knew that she had to recover her powers. Too much hinged on her ability to face her mother and save the world.

Suddenly, that math test and Trevor Spencer didn't seem quite so hard to deal with.

Laeserno nodded. "I think it would be wise if *both* of you had some tutelage while we wait and search. Reanna, you could learn some more about Gaia as a whole—history, customs, even idioms like I used. After a short rest, we will search for your tail."

"Gregory, I could teach you some spells. All the best wizards have some knowledge of elven magic, even if they cannot use all of it. We can translate some of the elven spells into wizard spells, perhaps, and set up a few traps around the house to alert us should a foe come back. Though, I doubt they would come here; everyone knows Shaesia has been captured."

Gregory stood up straighter. "Oh—I need to ask you a question about spellcaster and elf powers, if you don't mind. I once read a fascinating article about the overlap of magical powers among races and the lost powers of the witches and wizards. In the past, apparently we could do all sorts of things—mind speaking, mind reading, telekinesis, most prophesying—I would give my right arm to meet someone that could train me in the lost arts. Do you have any knowledge of that?"

Laeserno chuckled. "I am afraid not. Again, I am a violinist, and that magic was known exclusively by the spellcasters. If they passed it on to any elves, that knowledge has long since died out. But I have heard…"

The two of them delved deep into a conversation about various types of magic, which meant that Reanna lost her usefulness. She wandered off to follow a trail of unlocked memories.

She took a right turn down a narrow hallway. Two doorways sat to her right as well as one to her left and one at the far end. She knew what most of these held; her bedroom would have been the one on the left. Shaesia claimed the second on the right, and they shared the bathroom right before her room.

But the one on the far end beckoned to Reanna. The library held so many cozy memories of whispered stories and books claimed right before bedtime. Did Shaesia still own *The Lonely Dragon*? Or *The Last Unicorn Ride*?

These old friends beckoned Reanna into their sanctuary. She slipped beyond the door and into the large study. Bookcases circled the room, and ivy crawled over the outside of the glass windows. Two large chairs sat next to a fireplace. All of these treasures lay untouched by the battle that had waged in the other room. Reanna inhaled the scent of childhood: succulents, smoldering ashes, and book pages.

"I'm home, Shaesia," she whispered. "I wish you could be here." She reached out a finger and traced the spines of the books—some familiar, some not. She spied legends like *The Library of Thessalonike*. Or history, such as *The Rise of Pallas*—Reanna vaguely remembered the name from what little Atlantean history she had retained—and *A History of the Dwarfish-Gnomish War*.

As she traversed the room, the titles morphed into Atlantean or other languages she didn't recognize. She had almost made a full circle when two books stopped her. The first, a bright, golden one, carried an Atlantean royal seal on the side. The one beside it had nothing more than a white cover with no words or any other decorations.

Intrigued, Reanna pulled out the Atlantean book. She opened it to the first page, where calligraphy-style Atlantean writing curled across the page. She couldn't pick out any of the words except for one name: *Kleassa*.

The name niggled at the back of her consciousness—as if she had somehow heard whispers of it in a past life or something. It reminded her of how it felt to have the memory spell on her: like she could almost recall something, but with no specifics. Oh well. Probably just some long-dead, evil Atlantean.

Reanna slid the Kleassa book back onto the shelf and traded it for the white one.

The room groaned and rumbled.

She jumped back with a squeak. She slapped her hands over her mouth—or, at least, that had been her initial intention. Instead, she conked herself with the book and made her lips ache.

The noise continued to groan while the house convulsed. She half-expected Gregory and Laeserno to run in, demanding to know what she'd done to break the building. But they didn't come, and the house settled back down.

Maybe it had just been a coincidence. Maybe she hadn't actually caused something. Reanna took a step backward—and nearly tumbled into a hole.

She swung her arms in large arcs in an attempt to regain her balance, threw all her body weight forward, and somehow managed to fall on her face instead of backward into the hole. The book squashed underneath her and dug into her ribs. All of her breath left her in a *whoosh*, and she stared at the floor for a second to right herself physically and mentally.

"'S'kay. You made it. You didn't die," she whispered as she sucked in a breath. "That's a start. A good start." She took a few more spasmodic breaths and closed her eyes. She just had to brace herself to look over her shoulder…

The floor had split open behind her, and a spiral staircase descended into oblivion.

Reanna shuddered and gagged. Adrenaline made her whole body participate in the Olympics: her mind ran, her heart raced, and her stomach did gymnastics.

It took a minute for everything inside of her to calm down and for her morbid curiosity to take over.

She kept hold of the chair and craned her neck to peer into the hole. Down, down, down it went…she could just imagine a zombie horde down there, waiting for their time to strike. She pictured them rising up from the ground to gnaw on her brains, tear her limb from limb—

Yeah, maybe she would put "Explore Creepy-Staircase-Possibly-Filled-With-Undead-Monsters" on her list of mysteries to solve on another day.

She dug the book out from under her and scampered back to the bookshelf to shove it in. Just like she predicted, the house groaned again, and this time Reanna watched the floor slide back into position.

She placed an experimental finger on the ancient copy of *The Library of Thessalonike* on the shelf. No telling what might happen if she removed it—the ceiling could collapse, the walls could fall down, or she could make something explode.

Reanna gave it a slight tug. When no one died, she yanked it out and settled down on a chair with it.

Even as a young child, she'd been fascinated with the legend of Thessalonike, and Shaesia encouraged Reanna to learn more. Who knew whether this book, or any of the legends concerning the mermaid, carried any truth; fiction and nonfiction got muddled together where Thessalonike was concerned. Some people said that she was a sea witch who ensnared young knowledge seekers in her library and stole their souls. Others said that she was a kind angel, perfect in every way. The only thing that Reanna knew for sure was that *she* enjoyed reading the legends of the ancient-hermit mermaid, whether or not Thessalonike was an ancient princess from Earth who stumbled through a portal or an ordinary mermaid whose only remarkable quality was her love of wisdom and solitude. Either way, Reanna still loved Thessalonike, and Atlantis revered her.

Reanna opened the book; the musty smell that could only belong to treasured history greeted her. Until Laeserno needed her, she might as well learn as much as she could about powerful mermaids. Maybe something would help her find out how to defeat Queen Arana.

CHAPTER 35

LAILE

GAIA: JULIUS' MANSION IN WHIDON, KIROVA

Two days.

Two days since Laile had been brought into this dungeon.

Two days of *torture*.

Laile grunted and strained against her chains, desperate to get farther away from the basement wall than her bonds would allow. Two concrete blocks encased her legs in a splits-like position. Laile had never been able to do the splits before, but Julius seemed determined to teach her.

Even worse—she couldn't turn into a gem fairy to escape. Her legs were so far apart that it had almost ripped her body in half when she tried. Not to mention her broken leg; Julius hadn't cared enough to set it, but at least the concrete kept it still. That—along with the numbness of being kept immobile for the past two days—at least caused the pain from the break to recede.

The basement door slid open, and two wraith-like forms floated down the steps. A little girl, no older than seven—maybe eight—carried a tray and a jar. An even younger boy followed behind, his hand aglow with the light from a *lux* spell. Julius had introduced them as his children, but either he hadn't given their names, or Laile hadn't cared enough to remember.

"It's time," the little girl said.

"Please." Laile struggled against her bonds. "*Please* let me go. I can't do this anymore. I hurt. Everything hurts."

The girl snorted. Her black hair fell in a long braid past her waist, and she held out the jar, which was filled with only a few granules of dirt. Laile swore under her breath. Still not enough to make a weapon or item that would be of any help. If only Laile could spontaneously create dirt like her mother could create water. But she'd never possessed that ability, a deficit that irked her to no end—especially now.

The child loosened the lid and brushed the lip of the container against Laile's fingertips. "You know the drill. Make some diamonds."

"And don't try and get any funny ideas." The little boy sneered. He looked all of five years old—and far too psychopathic for his age. "My mommy and daddy taught me lotsa spells that would make you unconscious in a second."

Laile gritted her teeth. "Such a lovely family."

Still, she halfheartedly allowed her magic to transmute the dirt into jewels—three of the tiniest diamonds Laile had ever made. But the children seemed satisfied.

"Good. You earned your food." The girl put a tray on a small concrete slab that functioned as a table for Laile. The plate contained a roll, a slice of ham, and a small glass of water. "Daddy says you're making too much noise, and if you're a good little prisoner, he might give you dessert."

"Tell your dad that...that..." Laile frowned, unable to think of anything. Even calling Julius a *shabuu* seemed trite now...and anything else was probably not suited for the ears of children, no matter how deranged they were.

The kids giggled and raced back up the steps, leaving Laile in near-total darkness again; thankfully she had two glow rocks on either side of her cinder block.

Laile groaned as she twisted her hands to try and reach the food. The movement bit at her wrists, reopening raw wounds. Blood pooled beneath the scabs and crawled down her arms.

A weak sob escaped her lips. She couldn't bear to eat another meal like an animal, but she'd already been utterly dehumanized. What else did she have to lose at this point? She leaned over and attempted to eat the food with just her teeth. The movement made her stiff body ache, but she managed to get down a few bites. She just prayed those brats wouldn't come back in and steal her leftovers like they had with her breakfast.

Tears slipped down her face. If only the Composer would answer her prayers. If only someone would show up. Gregory. Her parents. Absolutely *anyone*.

Her imprisonment couldn't get any worse.

"Please, Composer." Laile's voice broke. "Please. I need help."

The door swung open.

She raised her head toward its light. Had her prayers been answered so soon?

But instead of a guardian angel—or Gregory, since they were basically synonyms—Julius strode down the stairs. Everything from his gray, receding hairline to his freshly polished boots gave off the aura of an egotistical, pompous monarch. His tall form already towered over her, but since he looked down his long nose at her so much, his frame made her feel even smaller in comparison.

"Little Laile." Julius nudged her too-sore legs. Laile would have lost her balance, but thankfully her chains kept her from falling. "My daughter said you had a message for me." He leaned in closer until Laile could feel his breath against his ear. "Mind telling me what it is?"

Laile wished she had enough saliva left to spit at his feet. "What do you want from me, Julius? Diamonds? Money? Some sadistic pleasure?"

"Actually, I don't want anything from *you* in particular." Julius smirked and patted her cheek as she withdrew. "It's more what I can get because of you."

Ugh. Laile didn't know whether or not to let him be vague and mysterious or irritate him until he monologued. "I suppose it's money."

Julius snorted. "Hardly. I want my position back. I'm through recruiting. And, I will confess, I'm attracted to the thought of revenge on your family and the Blandinus family for what they did to me."

Laile rolled her eyes. "You have a weird way of getting revenge. My parents didn't do anything, and Gregory's parents are dead."

Julius clasped his hands behind his back. "Oh, Little Laile— how *little* you know." He chuckled as if he'd just made some very impressive wordplay. It only increased Laile's desire to bite him. "I was schoolmates with Cornelia and Titus Blandinus. In fact, Cornelia was engaged to me." His face twisted into a sneer. "Our wedding was no more than a few days out until she *eloped* with my so-called friend, Titus. Imagine the scandal when I found out they'd been secretly seeing each other for months behind my back—not to mention the utter betrayal when she gave birth to your friend just short of six months after her marriage to Titus."

"That's not true!" Laile slumped down as best she could, but she couldn't do much more than crouch. If only she could find some sort of respite and relief from all these uncomfortable positions.

"Isn't it? I'm sure your parents never told you the truth, given their own mechanisms in my downfall. They created some cockamamie story about how *I* was responsible for Cornelia's and

Titus' deaths." Julius sneered. "Their lies cost me everything. And now *I* will take great pleasure in returning the favor."

The gnawing feeling in Laile's stomach grew deeper. "You're *delusional.* I don't know how, but I know you did kill Gregory's parents. My parents *don't* lie." She jerked forward—only to bite down on her tongue to keep from screaming out as the chains bit into her wounded wrists again. Why wouldn't she learn to keep her temper in check? If only she could blame it on some uncontrollable werewolf genetics, but given her mom's checkered past, maybe Cynerra was more to blame for Laile's emotional outbursts. "*Ahckrit xo*, Julius. *Ahckrit* all your delusions of revenge."

The Atlantean slur didn't faze Julius, but it sure made Laile feel better. Her words were the only ammunition in her arsenal right now, and she intended to deliver every blow with them, no matter how ineffectual.

"And you are trapped in the delusion of familial bonds. Despite what you have been told, your parents are not heroes. They're liars, cheats, and manipulators." His voice was measured, every tone clipped with faux formality. "And I'll make them pay for getting me demoted to *drafting*."

"And how exactly do you plan to do that?"

He backhanded her. Laile yelped; she could feel blood trickle down her temple where one of his large, odious rings had cut her. Tears bubbled up in her eyes.

Julius smoothed back his gray hair. "For one, I'll keep you here until your parents report you missing. I won't kill you, but maybe I'll make you wish you'd died like Cornelia and Titus. But after I've bidden my time for just a few more months, I'll sweep in with your battered, tortured body. Don't look so shocked, my dear; you'll still be alive—but barely. I'll say that I found you in the depths of a concentration camp. I daresay your family will be so grateful that they'll rescind their accusations against me. I'll be welcomed back a heroic rescuer and my position at the Capital will be returned to me."

"You're *psycho*." Laile snorted. "Your plans will fail, because you are a pathetic, small, little man. Because I'll tell everyone the truth. That *you* did everything to me."

"But the best part is, you'll be unable to remember. My wife is away at work right now, but when she returns, she'll put a memory spell on you. She's gotten quite good at those." Julius smirked. "We'll implant some false memories, and then all will be complete. You'll have only fond memories of the man who became your savior." He rammed Laile's back into the wall, nearly dragging her legs out of their sockets as they stayed firmly rooted in their concrete blocks. Her breath exploded from her lungs, and the blow made it impossible to draw in any air. The world spun—two Juliuses cackled in front of her.

Composer help her, one was bad enough.

With his hands still on her chin, he raked her head across the sharp, rocky walls behind her. Black spots emerged in her vision; her little boat couldn't handle much more turbulence on the sea of consciousness. Thick liquid seeped down her neck and into her shirt.

She gave in to the blackness, but it didn't last long enough. She came around and found her head still shoved against the wall.

Who knew how long the pain might have lasted if the little girl from before hadn't piped up. Her voice drifted down from above like an angel, even though, in actuality, she only stood on the top of the stairs and her spiritual association was more demonic. "Daddy? I need your help. I just can't get this spell to give someone the death-flu right."

Julius squeezed Laile's cheeks one more time. "Best behave, or I may just let her experiment on you." He released her, and Laile crumpled and tried to force herself into oblivion. Her arms still dangled in the air, her legs still seemed numb, and her lungs still felt deflated. She felt heavy and sluggish, both mentally and physically.

Please, Composer…just keep me alive. Let me get out of this.

The door slammed. Laile couldn't help but think it sounded like a resounding *no* from the Composer.

CHAPTER 36

REANNA

GAIA: SHAESIA'S COTTAGE IN OGDEN'S HOLLOW, DASPIN

Reanna must have fallen asleep reading about Thessalonike, because she vaguely remembered a wedding scene...and then nothing else until Laeserno jostled her awake.

"Are you ready?" he whispered.

She blinked and ran her sleeve underneath her mouth to wipe away all the drool. "Oh—uh. You mean getting my tail, right? We're doing it now?"

"I see no better time, unless you would prefer to rest some more. I left Gregory some studying materials, but I think he fell asleep as well. But...if at all possible, I would like to start soon. For the sake of my wife and daughter." Laeserno's shoulders sagged, and he ran a hand through his scraggly strawberry-blond hair. It looked like he hadn't combed it since their journey began—or maybe since his wife and daughter had been captured.

Reanna scrubbed at her face and nodded. Her brain still felt scattered, tugged between the myths of Thessalonike, Atlantis, and Earth. "All right." Her body protested as she rose from the seat, but she politely told it to shut up. "How do we start?"

"I know that this is unlikely, but do you remember where Shaesia put the locket with your powers? I would have to see it to transfer the magic back to you."

Reanna twisted her fingers together. "Um...not...no. Not really."

Laeserno frowned. "Well, logically, I doubt it would have been in the same place if you did remember. Shaesia guarded her secrets closely." He held one hand out in the air. "Which means that I must use a spell—but at least I use this one quite frequently." The tips of Laeserno's mouth quirked up ever so slightly—that might have been the first attempt at a smile Reanna had seen from him. "It helps me find missing socks. But please, take a step back. I do not wish for you to get hurt."

Magic snapped between his fingers. Sparks of blue, purple, and pink crackled and grew as Laeserno closed his eyes. The words that flowed out of his mouth sounded beautiful and mysterious: Reanna had no idea where one stopped or started; she only knew that with each syllable, the magic pulsed brighter. Soon, a trail of light drifted down from Laeserno's hand. Like a troop of fireflies, the sparks of magic illuminated a path that led...

Straight to the floor.

Laeserno shuddered. His eyes opened, and he lowered his arm. The glow remained, though not on his hands.

"Wow," Reanna whispered.

"It...did not work?" Laeserno phrased his statement as a question. He bent down, his brow furrowed. "I do not understand. I always find my lost socks this way."

"It seemed to work. It was *beautiful*." Reanna brushed her finger through one of the tiny bursts of magic that remained. A zap, almost electrical in nature, coursed through her fingertip. She shivered and smiled. "*So* beautiful."

"That spell was supposed to lead us to the locket. It is a simple locating spell." Laeserno brushed his hand over the floor. "Unless, perhaps, she buried it under the flooring."

Under the flooring.

No—under the flooring!

"That's it!" Reanna grabbed Laeserno's shoulders. "I think I know where the locket is! But, uh, you'll definitely want to move. Go over there." She waved him to a far corner and waited for him to retreat to safety before she went back to the white book. "Watch this."

She yanked it off the shelf. The room shuddered again, and Reanna took great pleasure in watching Laeserno's eyes widen.

The fireflies drifted down into the oblivion where Reanna had almost fallen earlier—the Creepy-Staircase-Possibly-Filled-With-Undead-Monsters.

Guess she'd be exploring it sooner than she wanted to.

She tossed the white book down next to her abandoned biography of Thessalonike. Her eyes locked with Laeserno's, and, for a moment, neither of them said anything. Shivers raced down Reanna's spine and chilled her bloodstream. She wrapped her arms around herself as everything inside her tingled, her excitement mixing with terror. She swallowed and stepped closer to him. He nodded and led the way down a dark, curving stairwell.

Slime seemed to coat almost every step. Reanna shuddered and tried not to touch the disgusting stuff, but sans a guardrail to hold onto, she had no choice but to use the viscous cobblestoned walls. She refused to tumble down into the blackness. She could picture it: one slip on this unidentifiable substance…a headfirst plummet…the *crack, splat,* and *thud* of her body as it crashed to the ground.

Dead.

Sweat beaded on her forehead. She loathed steps. So much.

Out of the darkness, Reanna heard a whisper.

Incompetent, it said. *What a pathetic, worthless, useless girl you are. You can't even walk down stairs without almost having a panic attack. You really think you can save the elves?*

Reanna sucked in a deep breath and tried to recall the tricks her therapist had taught her. How to stay calm when adrenaline and anxiety threatened to send you spiraling into a hole. And Reanna didn't need to spiral into a mental hole—the literal one was enough for her, thank you very much.

"Um…do you think you could give us a little light?" she asked. Her stomach churned as fear crept in, and she clamped one hand over it. Every step made her dread increase tenfold; her mind as it hurtled like a rocket into a brick wall. Her fear might go away if she turned around and went back, but what good would that do anyone?

A light flickered to life in Laeserno's hand. It amplified the glow of the magic.

The mind-rocket altered its course a smidge. Maybe Reanna could stop it completely before it smashed nose-first on a self-destructive course if she drudged up some conversation with Laeserno. "Penny for your thoughts."

Laeserno glanced over his shoulder. "Hmm?" In the glow of his own *lux* spell, his violet eyes seemed hollow. "I am afraid I do not know what that means."

Reanna slowed as they reached a step with a chunk missing. She tip-toed around it and shoved the unhelpful thoughts of, *Don't slip and die, you clumsy idiot,* to the back of her mind before they could seize control of the mind-rocket. She made it around and cleared her throat. "It just means…what are you thinking?"

Laeserno chortled. "A great many things. Mostly how different a man I am than I thought I would be. How different a life path I chose."

Reanna studied his back. The meeting in the park, where he'd confessed to being a traitor, still swirled around her mind. Thanks to him, Shaesia had been attacked and fallen into Arana's clutches. But he'd also led them safely to Shaesia's. Under Gregory's truth spell,

Laeserno had sworn that he didn't mean them any harm, and that everything he'd done had been for his wife and kid.

Reanna swallowed. Maybe she should still hate him. But maybe a broken creature lurked beneath his surface, just like one lurked beneath hers. "Hey. You know…" She stuck a strand of hair into her mouth. She didn't even know if she had the authority to say the words. After all, his actions hadn't been directed at her intentionally, but, nonetheless, she felt she needed to say them. "You know—I forgive you. That is, I mean, if you're looking for my forgiveness. You may not be. But as far as I'm concerned…I think I'm starting to realize why you acted the way you did. Even if I was mad at you for betraying Shaesia and turning her over to Arana, I understand why. I know what it's like to feel hopeless and just want to save the ones you love."

Reanna waited. Their footfalls echoed in the dark room.

Laeserno sniffled. "Thank you," he whispered in a thick voice. "I do appreciate your forgiveness. I do not know if Shaesia herself will give it so quickly, but I know that our troubles now are due to me. We would already know where the locket was—perhaps even have it in our possession—if Shaesia was here instead of me."

"That doesn't matter." Reanna tried to speed up to catch him, but her knees trembled. All right—slow and steady it would be. She wished she knew what to say, but she refused to stoop to pithy platitudes like "Everything will be okay," or "Keep your chin up," or "Be positive." Words like that were so often a blade more than a balm. Instead, she scrambled to find something she *could* honestly say. "I'm glad you're here. So it won't be as easy as it would with Shaesia. So what? We'll still find it."

They lapsed into silence again. Reanna scrambled for a new conversation topic, but her brain came up with nothing.

Something wet dripped onto her nose. She shuddered and swiped it away. Stair gunk—how gross.

"I confess, the life of an adventurer does not appeal to me," Laeserno said after a moment.

Reanna shivered. Even with her jacket on, she could sense the temperature dropping as a chill settled in the deeper they went. "Me neither." She snorted. "I liked my life on Earth just fine." Family vacations, singing in the car with her mom and sister—most often loudly and off-key—Disney movie marathon nights, stargazing and late-night swims… Her throat constricted as her eyes blurred even more from the influx of homesickness.

Laeserno nodded. "And I enjoyed my life as well. I have never had much ambition beyond my music and leading a quiet life with my family. I have never taken an interest in politics or in gaining knowledge just for the sake of knowledge…all of which is considered the societal normalcy for an elf."

Ah—the conversation topic Reanna had been searching for dropped right into her lap. "Is it okay…I mean, could you tell me about your wife?"

The moment hung suspended. It seemed like the past and present had collided as Laeserno appeared to sift through his memories. "Her name is Rosaelina," he said after a moment. The emotion stole Reanna's breath; she could almost feel the unplumbable heartache and inordinate nostalgia and reverence as he spoke. "We met when we were children. Even then—I suppose you could say—well—I was never much to look at, really, and much too…timorous to attract much attention. Even my old school teachers…I doubt they could pick me out from a crowd." He paused and switched his light spell to a fireball. A hint of some scars on his wrist peeked out from underneath his sleeve. They stirred memories up inside of Reanna—the bad sort. The kind that made her feel ashamed for all the pain and turmoil she'd put her mother—Isabella—through as a traumatized adolescent.

Laeserno sighed as if the weight of his spirit, his memories, were too much to hold—or maybe just his adoration for his wife was. "And Rosaelina—Rosaelina was…" He shook his head like her being was ineffable. "She was, and always is, talented beyond measure. She felt like a star, just out of my grasp for the longest time. For—for maybe a hundred years—which, if you are as unfamiliar with elves as you are with most everything in Gaia, is roughly the equivalent of adolescence for elves—I could not fathom why she spared time to talk to me. She was a musician…a top scholar…"

When his voice trailed off, his mind lost somewhere in the murky past, Reanna prodded him on with, "She sounds perfect."

"She certainly tried to be. Her parents were relatively older when she was born, and Rosaelina was their only child. She wanted to be everything for them…not that she did not enjoy her life, but I found that the pressure she put on herself was because she was terrified of disappointing them." Laeserno uttered a single chuckle and ran his hand over his mouth. "I doubt she could have disappointed anyone. She is so vibrant…she is like color in a monochrome world…something that you do not understand, something that you wonder how you are even permitted to grasp…"

His shoulders slumped as his spirit plummeted back to earth like a falling star. "And now…now she is trapped. Because of me. Because I…" Laeserno shook his head. "I do not know. There is a part of me—a very foolish, naïve part—that hopes Violante has left my family alone. That, when I return, Rosaelina will be whole, unharmed, and the first one that we rescue—along with our daughter, Maesie."

Reanna wished she could reach out and pat his shoulder. "They still could be."

Laeserno snorted. "Perhaps you underestimate the vileness that Violante is capable of. But you should not—I have seen the unfathomable atrocities she has committed. And if you do not fear her, if you do not dread what the day will bring when we begin to save my people, then you are blissfully ignorant of the cost of freedom."

CHAPTER 37

REANNA

GAIA: SHAESIA'S LABYRINTH IN OGDEN'S HOLLOW, DASPIN

The stairs eventually opened up into a large cavern, which boasted a mix between man-made and natural features. Reanna gaped at the underground cave. Someone had carved tiny windows periodically throughout the room and filled them with glow stones. A stone column sat in the center and separated the two halves of the room; it would have taken at least three or four Reannas linking hands to circle the circumference of the column, which looked like a stalactite and stalagmite had grown together.

Reanna slipped on the last rock step before the cavern. She reeled and staggered into a pool of stagnant water that reached all the way up to her ankles. Six doors sat on either side of the cavern, but the fireflies led straight to one on the left-hand side.

"Amazing," she breathed as she wandered closer to her goal. "I can't believe Shaesia never showed me this."

"I assume that she did so for your own safety." Laeserno splayed his palm out on the growth in the center of the cavern. "Knowing Shaesia, you were probably better off not knowing what dangers she has hidden in a labyrinth like this one. Especially as a child."

Reanna grasped a doorknob. Behind the wooden frame sat her missing locket—her missing powers. In just a few minutes, she wouldn't be just a girl anymore, but a mermaid. A double life more extreme than Hannah Montana's.

She steadied herself, chastised her queasy stomach, and threw open the door—right as the magical trail disappeared.

A black hole welcomed her, and Reanna squawked and pulled her foot back before she could step through into nothingness. Then a forest came into view like a TV flickering to life. "What—the heck—" she spluttered. It looked *exactly* like the glen she, Gregory, and Laeserno had stopped to eat in.

"Curious," Laeserno muttered. "Look. The magic points over there now." He gestured to a door on the far-right side.

Reanna slammed the forest door. Water soaked her tennis shoes and pant legs and made it difficult to tip-toe to the next door. She paused before she opened it.

The magic flickered out of existence.

It reappeared a moment later, this time pointing to an entrance two doors down.

"The portals shift," Laeserno said. "A real moving labyrinth. Shaesia's skill is truly astounding."

"She *created* this?" Reanna watched as the path flickered again. Instead of chasing after it, she opened the door closest to her.

It opened to the middle of the ocean, where the door hovered a few feet above the tide. A strong gust of wind blew a wave of water at her. She slammed the door before it could reach her. Nope—no way. She would *not* go into that one. But, logically, since she'd closed the door, that meant that if she opened it again, she should find another locale. She opened the door one more time, only to be greeted with another gust of water.

She slammed it shut again before she could be sucked into Atlantis by some whirlpool. Maybe not the most believable sequence of events, but her anxiety played through the scenario rapidly.

Why hadn't the portal shifted? Had she done something wrong?

Reanna cracked the door open a centimeter and yelped when water sloshed over the edge.

"You think they're on a timer or something?" she asked.

"Perhaps," Laeserno replied. "Maybe pause until the magic directs you elsewhere."

She waited for the magic path to shift again and opened the door a fourth time.

A battle raged beyond it.

The Atlantean troops tried to push a battalion of Council soldiers into a retreat. Dead soldiers lay scattered across the blood-soaked ground, and Reanna gasped. Bad move—one of the warrior-mermaids turned around and caught sight of her.

The woman charged at her, yelling in Atlantean, sword hoisted in the air.

Reanna screamed and slammed the door. The tip pierced the wood; splinters rained down on her. She fell into the water and scrambled back, her eyes wide. "Okay, no need to go there." Her voice trembled. In a few seconds, the sword disappeared—though the hole remained—and Reanna climbed back up and peeked through the newfound peephole. She saw an icy tundra filled with glaciers the size of mountains and igloos.

"Yes, please try and stay in one piece. I would hate to get this far and lose Solis' only hope now." Laeserno patted her shoulder before he let his hand drop.

Reanna shook out her trembling hands. Breathe in. Breathe out. Steady. Her heart raced, and her blood felt as cold as the icy wonderland she had seen through the peephole. She knelt down, her knees suddenly weak, and pushed against her temples.

"Those poor people," she murmured. "It's…awful."

"It is war. What did you expect?" Laeserno asked.

Reanna shrugged. What *had* she expected?

"This is why we must fight and all do our part." The elf proffered his hand and guided Reanna over to the next door as soon as the trail switched. "Come on. We must hurry."

Laeserno swung the door open—and the portal edges dimmed.

Instinct took over common sense. Reanna didn't want to have to track the portal down, nor did she want to risk finding the battle again on the other side.

She dove in and landed on her stomach in water the depth of an inflatable kiddie pool. She hacked and spit some of the salty—

Wait.

Salty.

She shuddered. Ocean water. She'd landed in ocean water, and it truly felt like she'd walked right back into Atlantis. She was six years old again, trapped in its unforgiving depths, helpless and afraid.

She stood up and shook herself off. No. She wasn't. She was seventeen, afraid, and still a little bit helpless—but she wasn't in Atlantis yet.

Something hissed right above her head.

She glanced up and shrieked, "Oh, *shoot!*" as she came face-to-beak with a creature straight out of her own bedtime horrors, a vampire's choice pet of the blood-sucking avian variety: a *vampriss*.

CHAPTER 38

REANNA

GAIA: PORTAL CHURCH, UNDETERMINED LOCATION

A cobblestone wall formed one side of the strange waterlogged room. It looked like a tree had punched a hole in the wall many years ago, and the vampriss had picked one of the protruding branches as its throne. The bird's long spiked tail hung down and flicked back and forth as it studied Reanna. Two fangs protruded from its mouth, and its sharp claws curled around the bough. Reanna might have considered it pretty, with its brown, yellow, and red feathers, if it didn't want to rip her body to shreds.

She slapped her hands over her mouth to keep a scream from escaping. She'd always assumed a vampriss was something the guards in Atlantis had conjured up in their macabre imaginations. But here it was, the very creature that had starred in her nightmares. Fear and a little bit of awe overwhelmed her as she gazed at the large bird of prey.

According to the stories, the vampriss was from Simit. And, just like the local vampiric residents, it could bite its victims and inject poison into their bloodstreams. Most vampires used the bird for hunting—it could immobilize prey with its paralyzing venom. The vampires would swoop in next and drain the victim of blood…then the bird of prey would return and eat the remains.

As a child, Reanna hadn't been able to decide whether dolphins or vamprisses were scarier. For a while, she'd given the slight advantage to the dolphins, if only because they were the ones she considered a real threat. As of today, she was going to have to rethink her position.

She instinctively reached into her fairy skirt and prayed her dagger was still somewhere in there.

It didn't come.

No. *No*—where had she left it? Laile had entrusted Reanna with *one* weapon, and she'd gone and lost it. And probably her life, too.

The vampriss hissed and shot into the air. It hovered right below a vaulted ceiling, which was thick with beams and branches as nature fought against the man-made building. The vampriss let out a cry that sounded like a cross between a bird's caw and a snake's hiss. It aimed its claws at Reanna like it intended to rip her heart out.

Reanna screamed and fled the room, any faux bravery she possessed evaporating. She slammed the door shut, but it didn't block out one last loud shriek from her enemy.

Laeserno started as she stumbled back out; it'd probably been mere seconds since she'd entered the room alone. "Did you get the locket so soon?" he asked as he walked over to her.

Reanna gulped in stale cave air and shook her head. "A vampriss. I didn't even *see* the locket, or hardly anything else, for that matter. Just a room that…" Reanna tried to draw a mental picture and couldn't. She'd been too transfixed by the creature. "Uh…I think it was dark in there, but it almost kind of looked like a…church—an old-fashioned one—like, a gothic cathedral, I guess, if you know what I mean. Dark cobblestone, uh…trees. Actually, maybe it wasn't a church. I'm not sure. There was a tree that grew straight from the wall. And the floor was covered with ocean water."

Laeserno shook his head. "I have no idea where you went, but I wonder if perhaps that is somewhere in Simit. That would explain the vampriss, and they do prefer a more gothic and dark architecture style. Though the water confuses me. Perhaps an abandoned church by the sea?"

Reanna buried her face in her hands. "I don't know what to do, Laeserno. I lost my dagger. I couldn't even fight!"

"I will go in your stead." Laeserno patted her head. "If that is okay with you?"

Reanna nodded, and they waited for the door to switch again. When the church portal appeared a few doors down, Laeserno raced into the room—or, at least, before he *tried*. The portal crackled and thrust him back. He slammed into the gathered water and skidded across the floor. He came to rest just a few paces short of the stalactite in the center of the room.

"*What* was that?" Reanna ran over to him and propped his head up.

Laeserno blinked and rubbed his temple. "I...I am not sure..." He stood up again on wobbly legs; Reanna helped balance him until he could find sure footing. "Let me try another portal." He headed back to the same door, which now opened to the middle of the sea. The door hovered above the ground, and salty sea spray sloshed over the threshold and into the cavern. Laeserno gripped the doorframe and inched a hand toward it. They both stiffened, waiting for the blowback, but Laeserno pushed his whole arm through and pulled it back without any repercussions.

The door switched to another scene—a tropical forest—and Laeserno repeated his experiment with the same conclusions. He shut the door and shook his head. "I believe I have an inkling of what Shaesia might have done, but let me test the hypothesis once more." He waited until the locket's door shifted closer to limp over to it. This time, when he pressed his palm against the wood, sparks of electricity shot out from under his hand.

Laeserno shook his head. "Shaesia has this portal locked. I take it she only wanted you—and probably herself—to be able to enter it. Very smart, actually. A final precaution to prevent your powers from being stolen or falling into the wrong hands."

"That's great, except that means *I've* got to fight a vampriss. Alone. Without any magic. And without a weapon." Reanna thumped her fists against her head a few times. "I'm so *stupid*! I must have left the dagger back when I tried to use it to get Laile out of the ice, I guess. That's the last time I remember using it. Besides—you should *see* that thing! A dagger probably wouldn't do diddly-squat against it. A dagger like I had could probably hardly slice cheese!"

Laeserno rolled his violet eyes. "You could easily take a human life with that, should the need arise. Hardly an instrument you would use as kitchen cutlery."

Reanna started to pace. "I need a big sword. Maybe a super fancy one. You know, like heroes in books have. Maybe one that has fire on it, or that's made of lightning—stuff like that."

"An elemental sword?" Laeserno rubbed the back of his neck. "I cannot create that. Magic cannot create something from nothing. If it ever seems that way, the user in question only stole something premade from somewhere else. Regardless—have I mentioned that I am not an adept spell-user? I am a violinist. I know the magic taught in schools; your request requires a high-level spell."

Reanna sighed. She had one idea, but she really, really hated it. "I think I know one place I could get a sword in a hurry."

"Where?" Laeserno swiveled around. "I do not see one down here."

Reanna pointed to the splintered door. "We're going to need that battlefield again. Can you redirect your magic trail to find that?"

"And send you somewhere where you could be killed? Certainly not!" Laeserno said. "Perhaps we can find a way to cripple the vampriss or for me to enter the door…"

Anxiety twisted up in Reanna's gut as she imagined either one of them trying to face that vampriss without a weapon. One wrong move, and—*snap*, immobilized by toxin. Suddenly their corpses would become vampriss food.

She shook her head and hoped it would shake her gruesome daydream away. "No. Come on. If you want to keep me safe, we're going out on that battlefield. Or at least, I am."

"I am not going to leave you alone." Laeserno sighed. He held out his hand, and the trail of magic drifted back to his palm. He whispered something to it, and the fireflies dispersed again, this time to a new door. "You are very stubborn. Has anyone ever told you that?"

If she had to count: her mom, her dad, Trevor, Tara… "Just a few people." Reanna smiled, but it didn't shake the ball that settled in her stomach. In all honesty, she didn't know whether to label it stubbornness or just a deep-seated fear she couldn't get rid of—like a dog so focused on a singular bone that he couldn't shake his desire for it, and any delay in retrieving that bone felt like internal fire.

The doors switched again. Reanna ran to the right side of the room—and nearly fell into the battlefield. A dead soldier lay by the portal; lifeless eyes stared straight up at Reanna, resentment and hatred forever etched in their expression.

The soldier still gripped a sword, though.

"Please forgive me," Reanna whispered. She leaned over and tried to pry it out of their fingers.

Behind her, Laeserno cleared his throat. "Reanna—"

"I'm almost done," she muttered. "Give me a second."

At least the corpse's fingers were still flexible, but—*ew*. Reanna gagged a few times as she leaned in closer to pull the tip of the sword out from under another corpse.

"Reanna!" Laeserno said a bit more urgently.

"Hold on, I've almost got it!" If she could just maneuver it a little bit more, if she could just keep one foot back in the cavern so she wouldn't lose her grip on reality—

A magical burst of ice froze Reanna's hand—*and* the corpse's hand—to the hilt.

Reanna shrieked and tried to pry her fingers away, but to no avail. She glanced toward the attack and saw a mermaid soldier, in full Atlantean armor, standing in the middle of a forest of icicle bodies.

Reanna's eyes locked with the mermaid's.

Puffs of breath escaped the mermaid as she held up another hand. Reanna felt frozen solid again, though no magic held her in place. Just memories, just emotions, kept her prisoner as she recalled what it had been like to be the one trapped as an icy statue—the bone-breaking coldness that had consumed her, even in her mermaid's skin, which was more acclimated to cold weather than these people's were. Being cognizant of everything that happened, but unable to move, unable to talk, unable to break free.

Reanna tried to remember her techniques to control her anxiety, but they were lost. All those soldiers were all experiencing the same torture she'd gone through, except the Atlanteans weren't holding back. This wasn't just a punishment—this was *death*.

Reanna couldn't breathe.

No air.

Knees weak.

Head light.

The mermaid swooped her hand toward the ground, and ice raced toward Reanna.

She'd die. Right here. With these soldiers.

"Reanna!" Laeserno hauled her back through the portal. Reanna stumbled into the cavern, the corpse following suit—at least, it followed until the doorway switched to black again.

As the portal faded, it severed the dead soldier's corpse up to the shoulder of the arm attached to the sword. The rest of the body disappeared into the void; the only proof it had come through at all was the bloody appendage.

With the dead weight suddenly gone, Reanna fell back against Laeserno's chest. They both collapsed into the salty water, the detached arm hoisted straight up like a macabre flag.

Reanna screamed.

Hysterically.

Her breath came in panicked hitches as she stared at the gruesome souvenir still partly attached to her through the ice that bound them. "Get it off get it off get it off get it off *get it off!*" she shrieked as she slammed the sword and ice into the ground. Frozen bits broke off and flew into the water, but they weren't enough to free her or the sword.

"Calm down, calm down! Please, be careful not to behead *me.*" Laeserno grasped her shoulder and wrestled her arm down until she could finally hold it still. She trembled, both from the chilly temperature and the shock.

"Just calm down," Laeserno murmured. He held out his hand away from her. "*Ignis.*" A fireball sprang to life in his palm. He circled around her and knelt by the ice. Slowly, he melted it until Reanna could pull the sword free. She stood there with shaky knees while Laeserno tossed the soldier's hand into the next portal. Reanna's brain didn't process what the landscape looked like on the other side; it only processed how odd it would be for people over there to see a severed arm flying through the air.

Reanna giggled and wheezed, her eyes wide, her brain frantic, her whole body trembling.

"Shh. Calm down." Laeserno gently pried the sword from her grip and let it fall in the water. "Take deep breaths."

"I s-saw them." Reanna's teeth chattered as she tried to get out her thoughts. "They—they f-froze soldiers. The mermaids froze Council soldiers."

Laeserno nodded, his mouth in a thin line. "Yes."

"The—the *hand*," Reanna bawled.

"It is gone." Laeserno gripped her shoulders. "Deep breaths."

Reanna moaned. As the adrenaline retreated from her system, she fell limp, and Laeserno caught her before she could hit the ground. She sniffled and wiped at her eyes. "It—it's awful. What they're doing."

"I know." Laeserno nodded. "It is. Which is why we must do what *we* are doing."

Get the necklace with Reanna's powers. Save the elves. Stop the war.

Reanna nodded. "Yeah." Her voice sounded so unsure, so quiet, despite her best efforts.

They sat in silence for some time. Only Reanna's sniffles and a *drip-drip-drip* from somewhere else in the cave punctured the quiet.

"Okay." She wiped her nose one last time. "I'm okay."

"Are you sure?" Laeserno loosened his grip on her.

She nodded. "Yeah. I'm sure. It's gotta be me that gets the necklace, and I don't want to wait any longer." She couldn't. Every moment she spent in a tailspin or breakdown meant that she could put someone else at risk. She'd endured a shock, but if she stopped moving just because she had—what kind of person would that make her? More importantly: what would it do to everyone else?

No. She couldn't stop here. Couldn't even really pause.

She bent down and picked up the sword from the water. It felt sturdy in her hands—it felt like hope, even. Hope she might be a mermaid again before the day's end.

"All right. Redirect the magic to find the locket room again, please." Reanna took a deep breath. Laeserno's path flickered out of existence before it came back to life a second later, this time pointing at the door on Reanna's right.

She could do this.

"Be careful," Laeserno called. "May the Composer be with you."

Reanna grunted and threw open the door.

From the branch, the vampriss hissed an unwelcome greeting.

CHAPTER 39

LAILE

Laile didn't know how long she'd been trapped in the basement. Days? Months? Years? How did Reanna and Gregory fare? Had they gotten Reanna's tail back? Was the war over?

No, probably not. Julius probably would have said something if all of civilization had crashed and burned.

The door creaked open.

Laile whimpered. She didn't think she could handle another torture session. Earlier, Julius had let his daughter try all manner of odious spells on Laile. She'd thrown up, been burned, gotten knocked unconscious, and faced a bout of the death-flu that had been slightly less-than-lethal—much to the girl-brat's chagrin.

The person at the top of the stairs didn't say anything. Laile closed her eyes and tried to will herself back to sleep to escape the torment of existing. Everything in her body hurt. Her face felt swollen; her body, bruised.

Her eyes snapped back open when she heard a hiss.

"Composer help me." Laile's voice trembled as she stared into the face of a snake. "They're going to poison me next."

The snake flicked out its tongue and raised its body into the air.

If only Laile still had the willpower to cry. As it was, she mustered up some vague disinterest mixed with muted horror as the snake lifted its scaly body further into the air…and arms popped out of its sides.

Oh, never mind. Laile had already died, then, and entered some crazy afterlife hallucination. Not quite the afterlife her parents had taught her about, which tended to be a paradise in the stories, but maybe Laile hadn't made the Composer's short list for the more pleasant option.

The snake grew legs, its body morphed into a suit, and its head turned into a human head full of shaggy black hair. Dark eyes met hers, and then—then the snake spoke person.

"Nasty bit of trouble you've gotten yourself into, hmm, Laile Reen?"

Her broken leg had gone septic. Yes, that was it. Or perhaps Julius had mixed some potent hallucinogenic drugs into her last meal. Death, hallucination, or fever dream—one of them had to be the truth.

And how did one deal with either of those? Did she address the obvious question? Was it considered rude to not answer the figment of your drug trip? Politeness toward hallucinations hadn't exactly been covered in her guardian training.

The snake-person reached out and cupped her cheeks. "I'm going to get you out of here, okay? I'll try and patch you up a bit, but I know from experience that healing spells can be quite painful. I'd much rather get you someplace safe before I start that long process. Because you, Laile-girl, look *rough*."

Laile's eyes crossed and uncrossed as she fought for control over her own body. "Who…"

"Who am I? Someone you've known your whole life, just not in a wizard form." The man who had once been a snake shifted again—

this time into Whisper. Laile might have screamed had it not confirmed her fever dream theory. Her poor mind must have been so broken to put such jumbled pieces of her life together in an attempt to craft a coherent narrative.

Whisper-the-azernos changed into Whisper-the-man again and rested his hands on either side of the chains which bound her wrists. "*Aperidium!*"

The chain gave way, and Laile's arm dropped and hung limply at her side, numb. She gritted her teeth against the painful prickles as blood circulation returned.

The snake-Whisper-man circled to the other chain and repeated the process. It, too, gave way, and the spellcaster caught Laile before she collapsed. She slumped against him despite his strangeness. More than likely, he was an angel come to take her home—but to be fair, even if he wasn't, nothing could be worse than the demons that tortured her in this basement hell.

"There, there," the person murmured. His hand brushed over her spine, up and down. "I'm sorry about this next part. I really don't know how to undo this concrete spell he's used, so I'm just going to have to smash it. It'll hurt you, I know." Snake-Whisper-man paused. "Maybe it's best if I put you to sleep, just until you're out. I'm sorry."

"I—" Laile began.

"*Dormi.*"

She mewled like a pathetic newborn as the snake-Whisper-man climbed the stairs. Every step made her want to puke. She buried her face in his shoulder in an effort to preemptively block out any light that might filter through when he opened the door.

"Stay quiet," the snake-Whisper-man said. "Stay quiet, and as soon as we're out, I'll transform into a gryphon or a dragon or something, and we'll be gone. But I don't want to fight with anyone."

She nodded; her eyes burned with even the small amount of light that trickled in when she peeked up. He tiptoed around a hallway corner. The entire right side of the hallway had floor-to-ceiling windows and elegant scarlet drapes. But they seemed to move and writhe with the beat of Laile's heart—and she heard something heavy that echoed in her ears.

She didn't know if they were footsteps or her own heartbeats.

Whisper muttered something under his breath and stashed Laile behind one of the drapes. But Laile couldn't hold herself upright, so her head slumped against the ground as she splayed out on the floor. Her hiding spot was probably as effective as a toddler playing hide-and-seek and giggling the whole time.

Whisper growled and shoved the curtains together before he switched again, this time to some huge animal. He splayed out in front of her; but she could only see his tail as it wagged back and forth.

"...and then I grabbed a stick and threw it *really* far," a voice said. Laile could almost place it, but her mind couldn't focus enough to make sure. Maybe one of Julius' kids? Or could it be Wren or Lark? ...No, the voice sounded male. Not her sisters. Too young to be Kal or Mionos...

"Impressive," a little girl replied. She didn't *really* seem impressed, though. "I—Sil, did you let in another animal?"

"What? No."

The snake-Whisper-man-dog barked.

"Sil, you can't keep doing this!" the girl hissed again. "Dad hates it when you bring in animals. I thought we agreed that you'd stop?"

"I *did*," Sil insisted.

Another bark.

"Obviously not!" The girl sighed. "Listen—it doesn't matter. You can't have a pet. Help me get it out before Dad sees."

Did Laile sense an iota of fear in the girl's voice? But surely this couldn't be the same little girl who routinely came in to torture

Laile. Surely such a depraved soul, no matter how young, couldn't *fear* someone, right?

"Come on…" The girl grunted. Her feet struggled against the floor, but Laile couldn't see what was going on from behind the curtain. "Get up, you big dumb dog! Ugh!" A few more grunts and growls. "Cooperate, or I'll turn you into a toad and throw you in the basement!"

Now that sounded more like the little girl Laile remembered.

"Don't you dare," Sil snapped.

The two bickered in hushed whispers. Time dragged on…feeling crept back into Laile's extremities, but she couldn't see the people outside her hiding hole from her position. The world still spun, anyway, and every small movement made the waves rock harder inside her brain.

"*Dormi!*" The snake-Whisper-man-dog shifted back into his human self.

The children *thunked* against the floor as they fell into the same magical slumber Laile had experienced.

"I wanted to get out of here without using magic, but those two forced my hand. I wasn't about to waste any more time with their senseless fights." The snake-Whisper-man scooped up Laile and dashed down the hallway. "I just hope that spell lasts longer than it did on you. I'm not the best wizard, you know."

The snake-Whisper-man paused at a window halfway down. "I wonder…" he muttered. "*Aperidium.*" The window flew open, and they vaulted outside. Before they hit the ground, though, the snake-Whisper-man shifted into a gigantic dragon. He lifted a claw and deposited Laile on his wide body; she clutched a protruding spine to keep her balance.

The wind buffeted Laile's injuries and whipped her around as they rose toward the clouds. Away from Julius, away from his psychotic children, Laile finally let herself do the one thing she'd wanted to do all along: scream.

She wailed, the sound carried over the surrounding hills and forests like a banshee's keen.

And then she sobbed.

CHAPTER 40

REANNA

GAIA: PORTAL CHURCH, UNDETERMINED LOCATION

This time, as Reanna stepped into the world of her vampriss foe, she noticed that she hadn't been wrong when she told Laeserno this new location looked like an old church. The inside did resemble a gothic cathedral, and the only light filtered in through stained-glass windows—or the holes where plant life had invaded, whether intentional or not.

Her eyes locked with the bird's. "Listen, why don't we be friends here? You just let me pass and get my locket, and we can be friends. I'll paint your claws, scrub your fangs…what do you think about the name Mina? You know, for Mina Harker? I think it suits you."

With an irate hiss, the bird swooped down from its perch, its claws aimed at her chest.

Reanna held her sword like a baseball bat and prepared to put her one year of softball training to good use. "Okay, my bad. I assume you're a dude, then." She swung the sword at Mina. The vampriss screeched as the flat part of the sword made contact with its side. It fell at an odd angle and crashed to the ground, but Reanna hadn't actually dealt any physical damage.

Mina readied itself again. It flapped its wings, and Reanna tightened her grip on her sword.

Round two.

Mina dropped into a dive. Reanna swung the sword forward like a hammer and managed to nick the very edge of the vampriss' wing. Mina hissed and spat venom; Reanna jumped out of the way.

Mina snarled again and reared up. It flapped furiously with both its wings to compensate for the loss of the feathers.

With shaky hands, Reanna hoisted the sword and leveled it at the vampriss' chest. "Don't you dare come near me, or I'll…I'll…"

If the creature was capable of snorting, Reanna was sure Mina would have done so at her faux threat. Still, Reanna tilted her chin up.

The vampriss flew above her head and charged down at her back, claws outstretched. Mina latched onto some tendrils of Reanna's blonde curls and pulled up, as if the bird intended to lift Reanna into the air and drop her.

Reanna screeched and swung her sword over her shoulder but just caught air. She whirled around—ripping some of her hair out in the process—only to have Mina's spiky tail feathers smack her in the face. Sword and girl clattered to the floor, and Reanna was momentarily jarred by the impact. She swiped at her face and came back with smears of blood; it felt like she'd been scratched by thorns, but at least the injuries didn't seem to be gushing.

Fear urged her to get back on her feet. She jumped up to face Mina, who stared at her. The sword lay useless on the floor. Reanna backed away. The water at her feet sloshed with every movement.

Wait—water!

The locket with her powers was in this room. If Reanna could just find it…

Mina shrieked again and made another pass at her. Reanna dove into the water like she was sliding into first base. She waded forward on her hands and knees until she bumped into the first of two or three steps in front of her that led up to an old-fashioned podium, or whatever they called the stage where a pastor preached.

Mina came again. This time, Reanna flung a bit of water behind her back. The vampriss adjusted its trajectory and flew upwards to dodge while Reanna crawled farther onto the stage. At the back, right under a large stained-glass window depicting a man with some kind of animal fur, she found a tiny music box on a pedestal.

Tears filled her eyes. She had admired this music box during the brief period she had stayed with Shaesia. It always plinked out a traditional elf melody—"Bright Moon" or "Starry Moon" or something like that; Reanna couldn't remember exactly. She gently lifted the lid and listened as the lullaby filled her ears and lifted her spirits a bit. It reminded her of the ethereal but ephemeral nights she'd spent cozied in bed listening to it.

But more pertinent was that the music box contained a locket—a locket deceptively inconsequential in looks, just a small silver heart.

Claws tore at Reanna's neck.

She screeched as panic set in. She elbowed and clawed the creature off her and threw it to the ground. She stomped on its chest—or, at least, attempted to—but the bird swiped at her with its tail and cut her leg. Reanna crashed backward and grabbed the locket from the music box.

"Laeserno! Laeserno!" Reanna scrambled to her feet when Mina charged once more. Who knew if Laeserno could hear Reanna's screams from the other side of the portal, but she shrieked his name hysterically all the same.

All the while, tinkling, lilting notes echoed from the box as Mina chased her.

She could still see the portal and the elf on the other side. But if she ran out, would Mina follow?

Reanna thrust her hand outside. "Change me! Change me quick!"

Laeserno grasped both the necklace and Reanna's hand from the other side. Reanna couldn't hear the words he said, but she could certainly feel it when a jolt of electricity passed through her body. She tumbled backward, the locket still caught in her grip. Her head smacked into the cobblestones.

The jolt sent tingles up and down her spine, from her toes to the tip of her head. Mina dove for Reanna, fangs extended.

It was now or never. Reanna only hoped there wouldn't be a lag period…

She thrust her hands upward and prayed, hoped, *willed* a geyser into existence.

A huge waterspout—large enough to rival Old Faithful—blasted Mina all the way to the ceiling. But when Reanna let her hands drop, the vampriss collapsed to the ground as well.

"Okay—truce?" Reanna offered as she tried to flop farther away from the vampriss. Reanna's legs already felt useless, rigid, and uncomfortable, equal parts achy and numb. She twisted her hips to try and get some momentum going, but without use of her lower extremities, she felt like a literal fish out of water.

Mina picked itself up and hissed.

"Got it, no truce." Reanna let out an "Oof" as she rolled over onto her stomach. On second thought, that probably wasn't her best idea. She'd left her back unguarded—might as well have put a target and bullseye on it for Mina.

Reanna could no longer stand up. When she even tried to control her legs or spread them apart, she glimpsed the new skin that was fusing them together. It felt uncomfortable, prickly, and odd, but not necessarily painful—it felt like what happened when chapped lips got stuck together. And perhaps she should have been scared, but the battle against Mina consumed her brain.

Mina swooped in again. Reanna flung out one hand behind her, her thoughts scattered, and her magic reflected that. The weak blast merely splattered against Mina's wing. The vampriss kept coming, and Reanna scooted out of the way. She threw shards of almost-frozen water over her shoulder—before she felt a pinching sensation in her toes. She craned her neck to catch a glimpse. They must have been midway through the elongating process of shifting into a fluke, because they currently resembled long, flat alien fingers.

She had no memory of taking off her shoes—or her jeans, for that matter—but they'd somehow been "eaten" in the transformation, and now her legs were just a splotchy mass of silver and white.

Mina charged at Reanna and managed to catch some of her shirt in its agile claws. Reanna thrust her hand out to the side, and the water curved over like a wave toward Mina. The vampriss flew up in the air to dodge, dove again, and caught some of Reanna's hair.

Reanna swatted at her foe, which created another wave that crashed over Mina. She rolled onto her back, stomach toward the vampriss, taunting it to go for the heart, so fragile and easy to pierce.

The vampriss fell for the deception and attacked, claws extended toward Reanna's chest. Reanna shoved her arms forward like she was pushing a barbell. A giant geyser attacked Mina and pinned it to the ceiling; the vampriss hissed and spat as Reanna clenched her fists shut to freeze the liquid.

Once she'd trapped the creature, her hands flopped down. Her chest heaved as she tried to suck in air. Mina stared back at Reanna and spat toxin; Reanna rolled away from the vampriss to avoid it.

"Sorry, Mina." Reanna panted. "I'd prefer not to have a duel to the death, because we both know you'd probably win. Take this as a truce. You'll eventually melt your way out of there, but, hopefully, not until I'm long gone."

With one crisis averted, another problem struck Reanna. She'd have to crawl back out the door to Laeserno somehow. But she barely had time to consider that issue when another spasm hit her.

Her legs began to burn as the discoloration there hardened into scales. Reanna clenched her eyes shut and rested her arms over her eyes so she couldn't see Mina's judgmental stares.

Without the adrenaline and battle to keep Reanna occupied, the needle pricks she'd felt before intensified into full-on Charley horses.

She let out a tiny whimper and reached for her waist to bring her trusted Spider-Man sweatshirt up to her mouth—but she wasn't wearing her beloved shirt anymore. Her eyes flew open. Her new, Laile-approved outfit had been replaced with some sort of frilly white shirt clearly meant for a six-year-old; it felt more like a corset on a seventeen-year-old. Reanna could hardly breathe in it, let alone chew on it. She remembered now—when Shaesia had transformed Reanna the original time, the outfit had been "eaten" by the transformation then, too—and Reanna had been left, naked as a jaybird, in Shaesia's library.

She let her hands drift down to her waist where her scales waited. Her toes had fully disappeared, replaced with the fluke she'd been born with.

It was done then. She had her fin back, she had her powers back, and all she'd had to sacrifice was her human existence as she knew it. Oh—and she still didn't know how she could possibly save any elves, stop the war, and fight Arana.

Step one, though? Done.

She reached up to her collarbone; her bare neck reminded her of the locket—the last gift she had from Shaesia. Reanna must have dropped it during the skirmish… She lugged her tail around as she searched in the water. She finally found the locket lodged between two cobblestones. She rubbed her thumb over its carved silver surface as her thoughts turned to Shaesia. "I promise," she whispered. "I'm going to save you, okay?"

Somehow.

Reanna swallowed and donned the little trinket. She felt just like her six-year-old self again—more so in spirit than physically, of course, because she was all too aware that she'd bust out of her outfit if she so much as breathed too deeply.

Now all she had to do was make it through the portal…

Except the faintest whisper of a song filled her heart. It reminded her of a mother's lullaby and mingled with the music box's melody.

The Song of the Sea.

She inhaled deeply, escape temporarily forgotten.

Cha vinseri, cecia
Cha vinseri, cecia
Ane oceanus gann rin xa
Cha vinseri, cecia
Cha vinseri, cecia…

The Song of the Sea could drive every mermaid into its watery arms. It beckoned Reanna to come home, to return to Atlantis…

Reanna snorted. Yeah. Fat chance of that. Even the Song of the Sea couldn't override her fear of Arana.

Reanna caught sight of the portal and surged toward it like some kind of movie monster—she could easily imagine a horror movie villain clawing their way to the hero in the same jerky movements. Closer, closer—she thrust her hand out, and Laeserno yanked her through to the underground cavern. The music dulled in her ears now that she'd left the ocean water behind in the old-fashioned cathedral.

Laeserno pulled her against his chest in a half-awkward, half-fatherly hug and chuckled under his breath. "Welcome back, Princess Reanna."

CHAPTER 41

REANNA

GAIA: SHAESIA'S LABYRINTH IN OGDEN'S HOLLOW, DASPIN

"*Crura si per terram, fin, si per mare.*"

Reanna flinched as a bright white light floated around her body and tail. Unlike the transformation before, this time, under Laeserno's magic, the change from mermaid to human happened painlessly and instantaneously. Reanna patted her trusty Spider-Man sweatshirt, glad to find it back and unharmed. At least she could breathe again with the makeshift corset gone.

"Hurry, on my back." Laeserno knelt down. "That is the same spell the Atlanteans forced my people to use on them. But if you are in any ankle-deep water, you will grow your tail again. And I would rather not carry that up the stairs."

Reanna hopped on his back and shook out her damp shoes. The journey down into the labyrinth had seemed agonizing, but the one back up felt even longer. Eventually, she slid off Laeserno's back and walked by herself; that seemed to be one small mercy she could offer him, no matter if stairs still tortured her.

By the time they emerged back in Shaesia's study, her legs trembled, and she felt like she'd been abused by an elliptical machine. She didn't even bother to greet Gregory; she went straight to a couch and fell asleep.

A crash woke her up several hours later.

"Whoops," someone said immediately after. "Didn't mean to destroy your door. Just wanted to knock."

Reanna screamed and tumbled off her makeshift bed. She knew that voice—that thick accent that almost reminded her of one of those posh black-and-white movie actors, like Cary Grant or Katharine Hepburn. She popped up and dashed for the door.

"Did you get her?" she screamed at Whisper.

The azernos lurked at the door, drenched from an apparent downpour. The world was midnight-dark around him from both the storm and the time of night. He cradled a limp Laile close to his chest.

From Reanna's right, she heard a bellow and madcap steps as Gregory raced into the room, even more disheveled than usual. In fact, he'd forgotten his glasses in his haste and only seemed to realize that when he went to shove them up on his nose and poked himself instead. He shook his head and guided Whisper to the couch.

"What happened? What took you so long?" Gregory choked out. "What—*Composer help us.*" He reached for Laile's legs. Her skin resembled that of a burn victim's. Large red, brown, and black patches covered her from the knees down. Not to mention the odd lump of white that stuck out—Reanna slapped her hands over her mouth so she wouldn't vomit. She refused to believe that could be a *bone* jutting out of Laile's leg.

The rest of the fairy's body didn't fare much better: bruises, cuts, and burns decorated almost every inch of Laile's brown skin.

"Julius." Whisper's voice sounded taut. "He locked her in his basement. Tortured her. I'm not sure what he planned to do with her."

"How'd you find her?" Gregory gathered up the blankets on the couch so that Whisper could put Laile down. Once the azernos deposited her on the sofa, Gregory gently covered her up.

"Traced down the creature first. I found it and its owner making a run for it. Apparently, they were trying to get out of Kirova rather quickly." Whisper brushed his knuckles against Laile's busted cheek. "The gnome informed me he'd given Laile to Julius, supposedly under the assumption the man would heal her." Whisper's nose twitched, and it made him appear even more feline-esque. "As you can see, I don't think Julius was interested in *healing* anything at all."

Gregory smoothed Laile's hair away from her forehead, his touch gentle. He even tucked the blankets in closer around her. Laile didn't stir—if she really did have a huge crush on Gregory, she'd regret not being awake for this.

Tears brewed in Reanna's eyes. She shuffled toward Laile. The fairy's cheekbones were swollen and discolored; parts of her long, beautiful hair had been singed off.

Gregory trembled. He once again reached for his glasses and found them missing; his fingers clenched. "I'm going after Julius. I'm positive this is some part of his perverse vendetta against our families. As if he hasn't done enough already!"

Whisper shook his head. He clamped a hand on Gregory's shoulder. "We came to save the elves, and that's our priority. I'm sure Julius wants you to retaliate so he can kill you." Whisper's eyes flickered. "No, the smarter thing is to go through with your original plan. Now, I hope you've been putting those brains to use while we've been delayed and thought of how to rescue the elves?"

"I got my tail." Reanna held out her hand and tried to extract a few droplets from Whisper's hair. But instead of the cool trick she expected—to try and make a few simple bubbles rotate in midair like a superhero—she somehow made all the dampness that clung to Whisper's skin collapse to the ground in a deluge. He stood there completely dry, but the spray from the downfall splattered Reanna, Gregory, and any nearby furniture.

"Wonderful. Much easier than licking myself clean." Human-Whisper hopped out of the puddle. He shifted into his azernos form and lazily trotted toward Laile. He hopped up onto the arm of the couch, nuzzled her cheek, and settled down on her shoulder. He did, however, lick his paws a few times while he stared at Reanna.

"This is ridiculous," Gregory muttered. "Aside from that, we've accomplished nothing. I'm going to get Laeserno. See if he can help me heal Laile."

Gregory stomped off, leaving Reanna to relay her tail-finding adventure. Whisper listened without interrupting, but that might have been due to the limitations of his current form. When she finished, the azernos hopped up onto the back of the couch and transformed again. He stretched into one of his more humanoid forms and reclined on the top of the backrest.

"Sounds like things are getting worse out there." He glanced down at Laile. "I'm afraid we don't have time for her to recover completely before we put the next phase into action and rescue the elves. Even with magic, I expect she won't be able to walk unassisted for some time. She'll be angrier than—well, her mother—that she missed the action, but she's too injured to participate."

"We just have to figure out *what* to do." Reanna nibbled on her fingernail. "But when I see things like this…what they did to Laile, what they did to all the Council soldiers…it just makes me realize how ruthless our enemies are. They're so well-trained. And what do we have? We're down Laile now. We've got an elf—and a violinist at that—a beginner mermaid, a wizard, and a shapeshifter." Reanna ticked off each of their assets on her fingers as she spoke. "That doesn't seem very promising."

"True. And if our goal was to win the war, it would be nigh impossible. But we're not trying to win the war by ourselves. We're trying to free the elves at the main concentration camp. I do believe a bit of subterfuge, and the element of surprise, might work on our side here."

Reanna stared at her four fingers. The element of surprise *might* give them an advantage so long as they played their cards right. To do that, they'd need to find out more about the location and do some reconnaissance. And if they could find Shaesia in the concentration camp—and *if* she was alive—that would add a fifth player...and the most powerful player on the board. But so far, Arana and the mysterious Violante had kept Shaesia from making any moves.

Reanna wiggled her thumb, the finger that represented Shaesia in the mental chessboard. "What's keeping Shaesia from destroying Arana and Violante?" It occurred to her once more that her powerful mentor might be dead or otherwise incapacitated. But—her brain just couldn't compute that. Wouldn't consider it. They needed Shaesia as a playing piece; she'd be the queen—the most powerful piece on the board.

Anyone like Shaesia just *couldn't* die.

Right?

"I may know the answer to that." Laeserno yawned as he came in, Gregory by his side. The elf's eyes widened when he saw Laile, right before his expression crumpled. He claimed a seat and rubbed his forehead while Gregory sat at Laile's feet. "Composer's music, they don't ever hold back, do they? Julius and his twisted family are capable of anything. It galls me to think of Violante anywhere close to my wife and child, what she might be doing to them right now..." His voice turned bitter and hard, and he practically spat that last sentence.

"They are—and so I'd like to know why you all think *we* have a chance of standing against them." Reanna glanced between the three guys of her party. "And why the most powerful woman I know—leagues more powerful than any of us—can't defeat them."

Laeserno shifted. "I mentioned to you before that Arana has used our familial ties against us. Remember, Violante told me that if I assisted her in finding Shaesia, my wife and child would be spared. Of course, that was but a lie from her blackened tongue, but it is the same with all of us. They kidnap the weak children first, then they weaponize love. '*If you all come quietly, if you do as we say, no one will die. If you disobey, if you fight back...*'" Laeserno sighed. "There are quite a few stories. I remember hearing one story about a little girl, apparently a spitfire in the best way. She and her father tried to escape, and the mother and three brothers were slaughtered. Just rumors, encouraged by the enemy and whispered among the refugees, but do you doubt their veracity after all we have witnessed?"

Reanna shook her head. "No. Not really." She sighed and squeezed her five "assets" into a fist.

How would Queen Arana handle this? As much as Reanna squirmed inwardly at the thought of thinking like her mother, she had to admit that there was a part of her that understood that she needed to. The Atlanteans' twisted actions demanded an equal amount of ruthlessness...or cunning.

Yes—that was it. There was no way that they could win by meeting Arana, Violante, or Julius head-on, which meant that they would have to use subterfuge.

"What about this?" Reanna made eye contact with Whisper, the only man currently looking at her. "What if we snuck—"

"Sneaked," Gregory corrected. He didn't even glance up from Laile as he said it.

Reanna seethed. "*Snuck* into the camp, slowly freeing the elves one by one? It would be like the Underground Railroad."

Whisper tilted his head. "What do you mean?"

Reanna paused. Times like these, she needed something to chew on so she could think. Her thumbnail worked as well as anything else. "In America's history—back on Earth, I mean—there was, um, this Civil War thing." Reanna winced. Yep, way to describe the bloodiest conflict on American soil to date as a "thing." No one else seemed to notice or care, though.

Whisper wrinkled his nose. "Civil wars. Nasty things. My homeland was ripped apart by one."

Gregory jerked his head up. "Fiastro? Fiastro doesn't have enough people to have a civil war."

Whisper shook his head. "There are very few things the countries on Solis know about azernos. They know even less about *me* as an individual." His expression hardened; his eyes turned beady. "But it does no good to focus on past conflict when we've got a *current* crisis on our hands."

"Um, so, yeah." Reanna's gaze flickered between both of them. "Anyway, the country was split, and a bunch of people wanted to free the slaves in the South. So they used these trails, like safe homes and places along the way, to bring the slaves into the North. The conductors—the leaders—like Harriet Tubman—would lead the slaves to freedom. The trails wound up to the North in complete secrecy and were called the Underground Railroad."

Laeserno leaned forward in his seat, his hands clasped. "Did it work?"

Reanna shrugged. "I mean, yes, it helped, though the war itself helped, too." More ideas pinged inside her brain, and she sat up straighter. "And this might help convince the elves to come. If they can't escape because of their family members, if we do it in secret and get the little kids out first, then, well—it might encourage the adults to use their magic. What if, once we get enough of the elves free, we use the freed elves to rescue the rest? We could build our own army!"

Laeserno shook his head. "We should not rely on their help necessarily. If some are willing and able, they may join our cause, but I think we may find most are not in any condition to fight. But at least they might consider escape if they know that their loved ones are safe."

Reanna's shoulders slumped back down. "Oh. You're probably right."

"But it is an admirable idea," Laeserno added. "And I think the four of us might be able to accomplish a lot. For one thing, Arana will not suspect it. She is prepared for all-out war with the Council, and her attention is diverted among the battlefields, like the one we saw."

Reanna smiled despite the thumbnail in her mouth.

Gregory slowly nodded. "I don't see why it couldn't work. Whisper, do you think you could sneak into the camp and find a weak spot? Memorize the layout, report back to us…tell us where the prisoners are held, and so on." Gregory rubbed his thumb along the back of Laile's bruised knuckles. "Laile would have been a good spy, too. Her gem-size would have come in handy. But we can't just throw her in. She'll argue, but we all have to stay firm." Gregory made eye contact with each of them. "No matter what she says, can we agree that she is not coming?"

Reanna shrugged and nodded. "I don't think she's going to get off that couch any time soon, Greg."

Gregory sighed. He seemed extra-gloomy after Reanna's assertion. "You don't know her. She'll still try." He closed his eyes. "My grandmother taught me healing spells. I can try and mend people as they come out—Laeserno, are you well-versed in the healing arts?"

"I passed my tests." Laeserno nodded. "They are necessary for school graduation."

Reanna raised her hand like she was in school again. "Okay, so…that just leaves me. What do you want me to do?"

"We'll probably need you to counteract some of the Atlantean magic—if you think you can handle that, or if you remember anything about your powers at all. That is, if they catch us. Hopefully, we'll be able to not be spotted," Gregory said.

"If we're spotted…" Reanna swallowed. Her stomach churned as she sorted through the possibilities. They needed a contingency plan. And there seemed to be no better contingency plan than to give Arana just what she wanted. "If we're spotted, I'll be the distraction. All I've been told since the moment I've gotten here is that Arana wants me—alive."

Despite her attempt to put on a brave face, her voice hitched on the last note, and her stomach clenched. She squeezed her legs together and bent over a little, arms wrapped around her midsection. She would not throw up here. She would not give in. "I'll be a distraction. You all can continue to sneak the elves out, and I'll get captured."

"Absolutely not!" Laeserno shook his head. "Arana wants you alive, but we do not know *why*. Look at Laile—do you really think that Arana would hesitate to do the same to you? She could want you alive to kill you herself."

"I'm banking a lot on Shaesia's help. Make her priority one and heal her the best you can. If I'm in danger, Shaesia will come. I…I want to trust her." Reanna's voice broke again. Trust—she almost choked on the word. *Did* she trust Shaesia? Yes, but Reanna's version of trust didn't exactly look like other people's. Her version of trust meant that she would give people the chance to prove it, time and time again, but a very large part of her wouldn't be surprised if everyone failed her.

It felt a little bit like holding everyone at arm's length—like Reanna had put someone in a room and told them to stay while she backed away, slowly, never taking her eyes off them.

But Shaesia had risked so much to give Reanna the chance to live. She'd treated Reanna more like a daughter than Arana ever had; she'd given a small, traumatized mermaid a first taste of love and safety. Shaesia had read bedtime stories and played lullabies for Reanna; with every bit of her soul, Reanna wanted to believe that her old savior would come through one last time.

Gregory shifted. "We'll accept that as a contingency, but we're only using it in a worst-case scenario. I don't want you to risk your life the instant something goes wrong."

Reanna nodded. "That's fair enough." Although she wondered if, in the moment, she'd push the sacrifice off. If she would live in denial that things were truly the "worst-case scenario" out of fear until it was too late for her to help.

Too many variables. Too many choices. She didn't even trust *herself*. Did people really have to ask why she didn't trust them?

"Are we all in agreement?" Reanna wondered if she should put her hand out in the middle and start some kind of group chant. Maybe she'd just watched too many *High School Musical* movies.

Slowly, her three friends nodded.

"It's a good tactic," Gregory said. "If your opponent is using brute strength, you counter with wiliness."

Reanna wrinkled her nose. "What happens if they're using wiliness?"

Gregory's brown eyes met hers. "Then you hope you're craftier."

CHAPTER 42

REANNA

The storm raged well into the morning. When Reanna finally woke up the next day—or maybe just several hours later, given that Whisper hadn't arrived until past midnight—it had turned into a full-on thunderstorm outside. Thunder peals ricocheted like artillery; lightning strikes lit through the dull gloom of day.

After they'd all rested and eaten Cynerra's meals, Whisper announced that he'd like to begin his reconnaissance—Laeserno had already given him directions to the camp where Rosaelina and Maesie were being held.

Reanna crumpled up the foil Cynerra had packed the food in. "I guess that's okay. We can't really waste any time. If you start in this weather, they'll never even notice you."

"They'll never notice me in any weather." Whisper smirked, and in a second, all that remained of him was a tiny black mouse. It scampered across the floor, but wizard-Whisper reappeared when he reached the door. He saluted her, although it almost felt like a good-natured jab at her lack of faith. "Tell Gregory and Laeserno to stop dilly-dallying and fix our girl, okay? Cynerra will have my tail if I don't bring her daughter back in one piece."

With that, the azernos slipped out into the storm.

Reanna rolled her eyes and returned to the living room, where Gregory and Laeserno both hovered over Laile. She caught the tail end of the boys' debate—something about whether or not they should try and fix the fairy's wounds naturally before they introduced magic.

"Whisper left to find the camp and figure out a way to get the elves out," Reanna informed them. "Why haven't you guys started?"

"It's a lot more difficult than just casting a spell." Gregory twirled his glasses around by the earpiece. "Firstly, healing spells can be finicky, which is why the best advice is always *don't get hurt.* Second, what if Julius has inflicted some mental pain on her? There's a possibility that I could fix her and…and she wouldn't be the same." Gregory's voice sounded soft, and he swallowed. He reached down and wiped his glasses off on his crumpled shirttail. "And what if we try and fail, and—and she dies?"

Reanna gnawed on a curl. She definitely needed a shower—it had lost that "freshly shampooed" flavor. "She isn't dead yet."

Though there was a fine line between death and Laile's current state.

Gregory snorted. "Oh, yes. Thank you. That just means if she dies, *I* am responsible. Thank you very much." Gregory slid his glasses back into place and pinched the bridge of his nose. "Laeserno, are you sure there are no more potent elven healing spells than what I know?"

"Not that I know. I use the same one spellcasters use. Though I suppose it is not out of the realm of possibility. Again, I am a violinist, *not* an elven doctor." He shook his head. "Nor am I a spellbook with knowledge of all useful magic, though I understand your desire for me to be one."

Gregory muttered something, his words unintelligible.

Reanna rested a hand on his shoulder and squeezed. "I'm sure your spells will work just fine. And didn't you say your grandmother was a healer, Gregory?"

Gregory's grumbles sounded suspiciously like "Ijustdon'twanttogetthiswrongandhurther."

Reanna hesitated, but when her internal awkward-meter didn't warn her not to do so, she wrapped his neck in a gentle hug. "You won't. I promise."

Yes, she, the girl with absolutely no experience, promised.

Regardless, Gregory nodded and reached for the first bruise on Laile's cheek. "*Compositor, sana vulnus hoc,*" he whispered. His hand began to glow, and he slowly massaged the wound. His fingers drifted across her skin, and wherever he touched, the illumination remained. As Gregory's light diminished, so did the matching glow on Laile's wounds. As it faded, it left behind smooth skin.

"Look." Reanna embraced him again. "You did it! I knew you could."

Gregory harrumphed. "It's only a start. That wasn't even the worst of the injuries. Besides, it wasn't really *me*, per se. That healing spell works in conjunction with the Composer. It draws on His power, not my own." Gregory rolled his shoulders, and Reanna released him and took a step back. "There are certain types of spells like that, and they're typically very advanced and, in some cases, very dangerous. Mostly because the Composer is not the only one you can call upon—sorceresses and warlocks call on all sorts of unholy creatures, which is why their destruction is so powerful. Not to mention, some of them are so amoral that things like sacrifices, blood curses, rituals, and summoning do not frighten them. They crave the power those forbidden arts bring them."

The shadows in the room shifted—or maybe Reanna's mind just played tricks on her as she tried not to think about what kind of *unholy creatures* things like that might summon. "My, um, I mean—Arana always called the Composer and stuff like that 'paltry myths.'"

Gregory reached over and brushed his fingers across the other side of Laile's face. He cast the spell and let it work its magic before he replied. "I imagine Queen Arana sees Him as a threat to her authority."

Reanna nibbled on her thumb. Gregory gave her another awkward, soul-searching stare. She tried to scream at him—mentally—to look away, look away, but he didn't seem to be a mind-reader. When he didn't obey her mental commands, Reanna decided to take matters into her own hands. She looked at Laile...the ceiling...the floor. Then she spared one glance at Gregory, who still stared at her.

Ugh—what did he want from her? Did he want to know if she was stupid or not? Maybe he wanted her to say something intelligent so that they could have a deep, philosophical discussion. Maybe he wanted her to ask more questions...or maybe *he* wanted to ask questions about the religious aspect of Atlantis or whether or not she'd ever seen an unholy ritual there.

"Do you know—did Arana ever mention summoning things? Did you ever see any dark magic in the castle? It would be helpful to know ahead of time if we're going to face that," Gregory said after a minute.

Oh, was that all he wanted?

Phew. Much better territory than a philosophical battle of the wits, because Reanna came unarmed for that. She'd never learned much about the Composer in Atlantis; they didn't worship any deity down there. She only knew what little she did—that people who worshipped the Composer believed He had created the world and they could draw upon his power—through either Shaesia or what Gregory had just said.

Reanna's own ruminations on the possible ruler-in-the-sky were vague at best, angry at worst. She lumped the Composer in with the God she'd learned about periodically back on Earth and disregarded them both—just as they, in her opinion, had disregarded her. And on the opposite end of the spectrum, things like ghosts, devils, and demons—or whatever else one wanted to call them—Reanna just preferred to contemplate those other things so she didn't have nightmares.

"I don't know," she said. "I think you overestimate how much my mother talked to me. It wasn't like we had evil teatime every Thursday where she practiced her monologues on me."

Gregory sighed, but at least he turned his attention back to Laile. He cast one sleeping spell over the fairy, even though she hadn't woken up, right before he set her leg. Reanna winced and turned away before she saw him finish; she'd detested the sight of loose teeth, all wiggly and gross. No way could she handle the sight of someone fixing a bone.

With that finished, Gregory moved on and hovered over all the broken and bruised spots on Laile's body, including her arms and legs, and Reanna watched as the skin stitched itself back together.

But it didn't fix everything. Some injuries refused to go away, even if Gregory returned to the spot several times. And many of the worst burns on her legs still scarred or looked odd and discolored. But, on the whole, Laile appeared much healthier than when Whisper had carried her into Shaesia's house.

"How long until she wakes up?" Reanna asked once Gregory finished. She got her question in early so he couldn't return to the discussion about the Composer or demons or whatnot. She didn't like the tiny pinpricks of fear she got whenever things like that came up, even back on Earth when she'd watch hokey ghost-hunter shows. By all accounts, ghosts, demons, and gods seemed scary to her or, at least, vague. And no one could ever come to an agreement. It was almost like the legends of Thessalonike, hard to separate the fact from the fiction.

Gregory reached for Laile's hand again. "Once I lift my spell, and her body registers the healing, she should come right out of it. I'm not sure how long that could take. But I can't guarantee she'll be the same Laile we remember. I've never heard of a healing spell fixing extensive brain damage or personality changes or memory loss brought about by trauma."

"You saved me," Reanna pointed out. "I had memory loss."

"Brought on by a spell. That's different from getting your head bashed in or suffering brain bleeds." Gregory dropped Laile's hand and stood. "I'm going to get a drink."

Laeserno watched the wizard go. "You know, he underestimates himself, I think. In many ways."

"Gregory? Underestimate himself?" Reanna snorted. "I don't think so."

Laeserno smiled. "Sometimes we project the aura of overconfidence to hide our own insecurities; he most likely does not want to face his dearest friend if he did not save her mind *and* body." He stood and patted Reanna's head. "I will go check on him."

Well, regardless of whether or not Laile would be the same when she woke up, it seemed to Reanna that somebody needed to be there when the fairy did revive. Somebody had to be there for Laile—whether or not she remembered them.

CHAPTER 43

REANNA

GAIA: SHAESIA'S COTTAGE IN OGDEN'S HOLLOW, DASPIN

Reanna finished several more chapters in the book about Thessalonike before she heard Laile's first whine. Reanna started and dropped her book; beside her, Laile groaned and flailed her arms. The poor fairy stretched and twitched like a newborn who wasn't sure how to use their appendages.

"Laile!" Reanna shrieked.

Laile didn't reply. Instead, she continued mewling like a cat that needed to be put out of its misery. Reanna seized her friend's hand, but her mind whirled.

Please, please…Reanna hoped Gregory hadn't been right about the extent of Laile's injuries—brain damage and personality loss and all those other scary concepts. The world *needed* Laile's hyper, perky, bunny-like antics.

Reanna needed them.

She sniffled. "Are you okay, Laile? What hurts? I can get Gregory to fix it. I mean, he was really worried about you! I may have even caught him crying a few times, but don't tell him that because he probably wouldn't want me to know…"

Laile tilted her head toward Reanna, blinking like a curious kitten...or maybe an annoyed kitten. "Would you *hush*? I've got a headache, my throat feels like the deserts of Fiastro, and I'm sore all over." Tears welled up in Laile's eyes, and she lurched forward to envelop Reanna in the most pathetic of hugs. "Flying fig-whits—I missed you so much!"

"I missed you, too!" Reanna blubbered as she clung to Laile.

"You would not *believe* what happened," Laile croaked. "But first, I need some water." She swung her long legs off the couch and struggled to get up—only to promptly fall back down, her muscles apparently mushy from disuse.

Gregory stormed into the room with a wild call of something that might have been "Laile!" His face had an ashen pallor, his brown eyes wide behind his glasses.

"What happened?" he demanded. His glasses slid down his nose; he shoved them back up and dropped to his knees beside Laile. He grasped her head and tilted it in different directions. "Well, you don't look hurt." He slumped back and let his hands drop. A slow smile worked its way onto his face. "You're alive."

"Hi to you too." Laile winced as she tried to prop herself up on the couch and stand, but she couldn't make it.

Gregory reached out and helped her back onto the couch. "What is it? Your legs? Can you feel them? Do they still work? I tried to heal them, but you still have some scars and burns, and I'm sor—"

"Relax, Greg." Laile laid her head back down on the pillow. "I'm fine. I just haven't been able to move in a long while." She tried to smile but grimaced instead.

Gregory spiraled into a muttering spree and examined her again. Reanna tucked a curl into her mouth, observing the scene.

Gregory touched one of the bruises; Laile groaned again. She shook him off and stretched her arms out above her head. "Oh, ow.

That hurts, too. Everything feels stiff and sore, but at least I'm in one piece. I assume that's good news, unless it's the afterlife. Is it the afterlife, Greg?"

He shook his head. "No, but you came close to going there." He pulled the covers up to her waist. "Do you need anything else?"

"Water?" Laile closed her eyes. "Just give me a moment to rest, and then I'll be back to normal...especially if you could fix this blasted headache. Oh, and...could you, y'know...tell me about everything I've missed?"

Gregory put his hands on her temple and massaged there. "Well? You heard her. Go get a drink."

Reanna rolled her eyes but trotted off to do so. When she returned, Laile seemed more relaxed. Her smile became more natural, her expression less pained. Gregory recounted some details of the past few days, and Reanna took over at the end to share the "find-the-tail" adventure.

But both of them left out the upcoming elf rescue lest Laile want to join.

At the end, Laile reached out and grasped Reanna's hand. "I'm so proud of you. You were so brave."

"Thanks!" Reanna beamed and shoved her insecurities to the back of her mind. Sure, they still hissed like Gollum and tried to tell her that Laile lied: that Reanna had nothing to be proud of and that she still was an ineffective mermaid. But for just one moment, Reanna wanted to ignore those endless whispers and bask in the praise of a new friend. "Watch this."

She took a deep breath and held her hand out toward Laile's water glass. Just a little bit, a few droplets...Reanna twisted her lips as she tried to guide one or two bubbles out of Laile's cup. Three came; Reanna let them twirl for a bit before she plunked them back into the glass.

Much better than her demonstration with Whisper.

Laile grinned. "Look at my little ward, all grown up and kicking butt. When I'm finally better and we go storm that concentration camp, you'll probably be able to wipe out a whole fleet of mermaids by yourself. Knock 'em flat on their tails, those *shabuus*."

The whispers broke out of their cage and swarmed to the forefront of Reanna's mind. But this time, they didn't bring with them twisted murmurs of insecurity. This time, they carried with them wild guilt that, if the truth came out, Laile would be furious and hurt that they'd conspired to keep her off the mission. That she might even hate Reanna or consider the omittances outright lies.

Reanna glanced at Gregory; he avoided her gaze, though she didn't know whether or not he meant to do it on purpose. But she felt like, from the rigid way he held his shoulders to the fact he changed the subject to ask about what Laile had endured, he didn't want Reanna to press the issue.

If she's mad, you brought this on yourself, the guilt-mongers warned her. *Secrets never lead to anything but hurt feelings.*

Reanna shook her head. True, maybe secrets only led to hurt feelings—but the truth in this matter wouldn't set Laile free.

No—not when scars and burns still crisscrossed the fairy's body and she could hardly stand up on her own. Who knew how long it would be until she recovered enough to stand, and by then…who knew what would happen to Rosaelina, Maesie, and the rest of the elves in the meantime?

No, the truth wouldn't set Laile free at all—it would only get her killed if she tagged along.

CHAPTER 44

LAILE

GAIA: SHAESIA'S COTTAGE IN OGEDEN'S HOLLOW, DASPIN

L aile gasped as she started awake from yet another nightmare about Julius and his twisted torture. She'd been back in the basement as he tried to burn her alive, as he cut off her limbs one by one—

No. It hadn't happened.

She sighed, lowered herself back down on the pillow, and tried to get her pounding heart to realize the danger had passed. Well, sort of. She'd spent the last few days either passed out, in agonizing pain, or trapped in horrific nightmares. Though Gregory had patched her up, her scars and burns still ached and throbbed. Not to mention that her muscles, weak with disuse, protested at every shift.

A hushed voice from the other room piqued her ears. "...so that's what we're looking at."

She strained and tried to twist forward to catch more but hissed under her breath at the stab of pain. That voice sounded familiar, but she couldn't place it.

"Tonight? You think we can do it tonight?"

Laile knew that voice—Gregory. She settled down to debate the merits of trying to go back to sleep…until she heard what her so-called best friend said next.

"I need to know when to put the sleep spell on Laile so she doesn't know."

"Doesn't know *what*?" Laile called.

Silence.

"I heard you guys! Come over here and tell me what it is you don't want me to know." Laile crossed her arms over her chest before two bashful men tiptoed into her line of sight.

One, she knew by heart. The other…

Laile's eyes widened. "*You*! You're the one who rescued me!"

The stranger gave a deep bow. "I've done much more than that, Laile-girl. But I'm glad you remember me, even if it's only vaguely."

Laile grunted. "Who are you again?"

The man flicked his long, shaggy black hair out of his face and grinned. There was something almost feline-esque about the gesture. "Little Laile, you don't recognize me? Such a shame. Then again, your mother was slow on the draw the first time too. But I'm the one you took to bed with you all those nights that you were scared of the dark. You would always rub my back and tell stories to yourself until you fell asleep."

The man winked and vanished. Whisper stood in his place with the same grin on his face. His tail flicked back and forth.

Laile's mouth fell open. She made a few squeaky noises as her brain tried to comprehend. "But—but—"

Whisper shapeshifted again, this time back into a human. "Your mother told you I could shapeshift. I can become any species and take on their special characteristics. This, darling Laile, is a wizard form."

"But—but—I *changed* in front of you!" Laile shuddered. "I probably danced around in my *underwear* in front of you!"

"I assure you, I'm a gentleman. I follow the azernos code of honor and would never watch anything unseemly." Whisper rested one hand on his heart. "Embarrassing, on the other hand…"

Laile moaned and covered her face with one hand. "Ugh. I don't want to think about what you know." She separated two of her fingers to form a slit to stare out at Gregory and Whisper. "And since we're on the subject of surprises, why don't you tell me what you didn't want to tell me? Is this what you've been so upset about, Greg?"

"It's nothing," Greg said curtly. "Just go to sleep."

"Or what? You'll cast a spell on me?" Laile propped herself up on her elbow. She gritted her teeth; her head felt like a balloon about to float off her body. Spots swam around her vision. "Tell me what's up."

"N—" Gregory began.

"Oh, stop protesting. You know the Úlfur women aren't the type of girls easily talked out of something." Whisper crossed his arms over his chest. "We're going to rescue the elves. I found the camp and scoped it out. We've got a plan."

"Sounds great." Laile swung her legs off the couch with a grunt. Her whole body strained in protest. "I'll be ready in a second."

Gregory shook his head and stepped in front of Whisper. "I think you misunderstood Whisper. *We* are going—as in, Reanna, Whisper, Laeserno, and I. *You* are staying here. I'll make sure you're well taken care of. I'll lay out food and water and…"

"What am I, a pet? As *if*," Laile snarled. "Where's Reanna? She'll fight for me."

"No, Laile," Gregory began. "Reanna agrees. She and Laeserno are getting ready, too. None of us want to see you hurt."

Hm. Wow. Some nice *friends* Laile had.

She growled and forced herself up. Her knees trembled underneath her, and dizziness almost drove her to the ground. But she was strong. She wouldn't let Julius ruin any more of her life than he already had. She wouldn't give him any more control—she would get right back on the dragon saddle and get out there to prove he hadn't damaged her beyond repair or made her scared.

Whisper steadied her as she tried to march to the door. But she saw three doors, two floors, and…

Someday, Laile would find Julius and do to him *exactly* what he had done to her. She swore it on Shake-spear's pen.

The floor came up to meet Laile's face as she toppled. She moaned, stretched out on the cold wooden panels. "Just give me a moment and I'll be back on my feet, ready to go. Or wings."

"Absolutely not. Laile, you can't walk *or* fly yet," Gregory said.

Flying fig-whits. Why did he have to go and say that? Now her pride wouldn't let her stop until she tried. Laile shrank into her crystallized form and tried to take off. Her wings faltered; she hadn't flown in so long, it felt like she was lugging five hundred pounds of dead weight inside her tiny body. Her wings, sore and cramped, seized up, and she careened to the floor. She grew back to her regular height at the last second so that she wouldn't have as far to fall. Still, it hurt when her face connected with the floor for a second time.

"Laile!" Gregory dropped to his knees beside her. "Just stop."

He reached out to help her, but Laile glared at him until he froze. Her arm muscles strained as she struggled to push herself up. "Just—just give me a moment…" Laile's arms quivered until they buckled beneath her. Yet again she slammed against the floor.

"Please, Laile. Stop it." Gregory touched her cheek and uttered the healing spell once more. Warmth flowed through Laile, and her skin tingled underneath his caress.

Though maybe she couldn't blame the tingly feeling on the spell.

"Come on." Gregory slipped his arms underneath her armpits. "Please don't fight me."

Laile should have resisted, but that last fall had officially KO'd her pride.

"I know you and your mother have never liked to hear the word *no*, but I believe it falls to me to tell you so now." Whisper crossed his arms over his chest. "Consider me your mother's proxy: *no*. You can't go, and don't cause a fuss. We need to leave soon."

Laile pushed a strand of hair out of her face and shoved Gregory away. She glared at them both while she remained hunched over like some kind of ogre. "Greg and I have planned this for so long. Nobody is going to take this away from me."

Her knees trembled but didn't buckle. She managed to take three large steps without assistance, but after the third, she had to lean against the wall and take a few deep breaths.

"Okay. Looks good," she wheezed. "I'm ready to go."

"No." Gregory's voice didn't leave any room for arguing, but that didn't mean Laile wouldn't try.

"Yes. I'm not staying here alone. What if Julius finds me? You really want me to stay here alone? All alone?" Laile hoped she sounded somewhat pitiful. She treaded a fine line: sounding just pitiful enough that he would take her along but not so pitiful that he decided she needed to be left here for her own protection.

"Impossible. He has no way to follow you. If, by some illogical, miraculous chance, he does, just shrink to your tiny self and hide under the couch. You'll be fine." Gregory looked past her for a moment. He quirked an eyebrow at Whisper, who was watching the ordeal with humor. "Do you have a suggestion, or do you just like smirking at me?"

"Don't flatter yourself. I enjoy smirking in general. It seems to aggravate people." Whisper snickered as he came up behind Laile. "If she's so dead-set on coming, I suggest we take her with us and put her to sleep farther into the forest. Make her take her crystalline form before we do so, then stash her in a bush." Whisper said this flippantly.

Laile grimaced, feeling like Julius had somehow disguised himself as Whisper. "Oh, both of you, *shut up*! I'm a real person, not a dead body!" She balled her fists and would have taken a swing at them...if only she knew which of the four doppelgängers to hit.

"It will keep you safe, though. For the most part." Whisper winked at her. Laile rolled her eyes. "Unless you're trampled on by a rogue animal."

She gritted her teeth. "How about I dump *you* by the side of the road, knocked out, and then run away and leave you all defenseless?"

Gregory rubbed his forehead. "I don't have time for this. We need to get going. *Now*."

"You're right. Silly me. We should go back to Plan A and knock her out now. It'll save us the trouble of stashing her body." Whisper locked his fingers behind his neck. He still wore the irritating smirk Gregory had commented on earlier.

"Why can't you all just shut up and let me fight?" Laile said. "It's *my* choice and *my* decision."

"All right. If you can pin me to the ground once, then you'll go." Gregory held out his arms, inviting her.

Careful to stay out of her crystallized form after her first disastrous flight attempt, Laile noticed a patch of dirt on the floor. She twisted her finger and called it toward her before she stretched it out into a long tendril, shaped it into a baton, and hardened it into a diamond. She tested out its weight in her hand—then swung at Gregory.

He held up his forearm to intercept the baton and batted it away. His movement upset Laile's velocity; she staggered back, and the diamond club hit the ground—hard.

Laile tumbled as well. The fall knocked the breath out of her, and she wheezed, unable to get up. Her heart thudded painfully within her, but she couldn't worry about that when her pride was on the line. She shoved herself back to her feet and heaved the baton upwards. By some miracle, she managed to lift it with her unsteady arms. Laile hefted the baton over her head, intent on bringing it down on Gregory's skull, but it was too heavy to hold aloft.

She stumbled backward with its weight and prepared herself for yet another impact with the floor. Before she could hit, though, Gregory reached out, grabbed her, and jerked her to his chest. She didn't even have time to appreciate the moment because the gesture jostled every muscle in her body. She cried out; the baton dropped from her hand and shattered into dirt.

"Are you okay?" Gregory touched her cheek.

Her heart constricted now for no reason related to a fall. Oh, *flying fig-whits*—she should *not* want to kiss him right now.

Gregory's next words killed her desire.

"You would have been murdered a hundred times over on the battlefield. You're not going. You're going to lie down on the couch and rest until we get back."

Whisper had fled to the door sometime during Laile and Gregory's mock battle. Before Laile could complain or throw a fit, he called, "Gregory, we need to leave *now*."

Gregory nodded and prodded Laile to lie back down on the couch. "Stay here. You're not to move until I come back. Understand? I've got you books to read, some nice snacks—"

"And what if I have to go pee?" Laile snapped. "Don't you dare say you laid out diapers for me."

Gregory pushed his glasses up his nose. "Well, no, but that might actually be a better idea than what I *did* have in mind. But if you can't even make it to the bathroom, shouldn't that tell you that you're not fit for battle?"

Laile pushed down the urge to stick her tongue out at him and call him her father. Instead, she silently got back on the couch and seethed. "Kinda seems like you're a sexist goblin right now. Like maybe you don't want me to go because I'm a girl." Laile crossed her arms and fought back tears—her whole body smarted from that little exercise. "I'm Reanna's actual guardian. I should be out there fighting!"

Gregory took off his glasses and wiped them on his shirt. His brown curls fell across his dark eyes. If she wasn't so mad at him, Laile might have appreciated the view. "If it assuages your ego to think that, sure. Call me whatever you like. You know the truth deep down." His gaze seemed to search for hers, but Laile found she couldn't meet it. Instead, she picked at the blanket. How fuzzy. Scintillating. Pretty.

Gregory sighed. "All right. Be that way."

She could hear his slow footsteps as he retreated from the room. He must have been waiting for her to say something, but she refused to dignify him with a response. She turned to face the back of the couch instead and pulled the covers up over herself.

"Good-bye, Laile."

His footfalls grew faster after he said that, but Laile didn't look. Her breath escaped in hot huffs and ruffled the fabric of the blue-blanket cocoon she'd made. He would regret it. Something would happen, and he would wish that he had a gem fairy around. He'd wish that he had *her* around.

If only he wasn't so *right*. That would make it just a smidge easier to stay angry at him.

Flying fig-whits, it was hot under the throw.

Laile tossed it off her. No way she'd suffocate for the sake of a pity party.

A few tears leaked out of her eyes, and she swiped them away. The first truly dangerous part of their mission, and she'd been forced out of commission before it even began.

"Just keep them safe, Composer," she whispered in the silence of the house. If she couldn't be there, it made her feel a tiny bit better to think that He might be.

CHAPTER 45

REANNA

GAIA: ELVEN CONCENTRATION CAMP, OGDEN'S INLET, DASPIN

Though Reanna had never been a faithful churchgoer on Earth, she couldn't live in the Bible Belt of America and not glean some bit of biblical knowledge. As such, the rain outside reminded her a bit of the story of Noah's Ark. Reanna was sure there was something about the rainbow being the promise of God to not send another global flood to Earth, but this torrent was making her think he'd made no such promise to Gaia.

Mud coated Reanna's legs all the way up to her calves from all the times she'd sank into it. She didn't dare complain, though, for risk of being overheard and of sounding like an ungrateful brat. After all, the people that they were going to rescue had *far* more problems than she did.

Dense trees offered some protection from some of the rain as the group moved underneath them. No one bothered to talk because the din of the heavy raindrops as they connected with the leaves drowned out everything—save the Song of the Sea that thrummed inside Reanna's heart. It pulled her toward the ocean, toward Atlantis, but she stuffed it far down into her soul where she could ignore it. Nobody had time for that today.

Instead, she tried to control the raindrops and keep the group dry, but her inexperience got the best of her. When she couldn't protect all of her friends at the same time, out of fairness, she gave up.

Finally, after the group had traveled for quite some time—and they all looked like wilting, drowned rats—the rain slackened and then stopped.

"Wait a second," Whisper said. Somehow, he managed to look like a glam rock star shooting an artsy music video—compared to Reanna, whose best celebrity lookalike at the moment was one of the *Aristocats* after their butler tried to drown them.

Reanna crouched next to a deep hole and stirred the water inside with her finger.

Whisper picked up a branch that was half-sunk into a mud pit, tested its weight, and began to sketch in the ground. "All right, to recap now that we're closer." He pointed to his sketch. "This is the barrier that prevents anyone from getting into or out of the camp. Very dangerous, and we have to get through it somehow. I'm going to burrow us in, and I think I've calculated the exact distance to get us to the first barrack."

Reanna tried to make sense of the diagram in front of her. An artist Whisper was not—his crude replica of a fence looked more like he was trying to play a very large game of tic-tac-toe.

He tapped the middle space with his pointer wand. "The rows of barracks are here. The children we want to free first are in the far left—right here—that's where I'll break the surface. They're keeping the kids separate from the parents. There are at least two barracks of children, maybe more, but I had to be quick about my reconnaissance."

In Reanna's mind, even though she knew it was probably foolish, she visualized the rows of cabins that she and her family used to camp in back on Earth. That image only lasted for a moment before it was shoved out, replaced with graphic images she'd seen in school of Auschwitz and the malnourished Jews and other prisoners. She prodded at the goop beneath her tennis shoes. Her stomach felt turbulent again. It had taken the Allies years to free everyone. How were four people supposed to rescue a whole civilization? She'd given them the dumb idea of an Underground Railroad system—what if it turned out to be an execution sentence?

"There are guards for each of the barracks and some on patrol," Whisper said. "We'll have to move carefully. But not as many as I thought—Arana has a skeleton crew."

"What about guards outside the perimeter?" Gregory gestured around the tic-tac-toe board.

"They make rounds. Two at a time. It takes about five minutes for one pair of guards to clear a spot before the next ones come. That means, basically, that if we can take out two guards, then we'll have five minutes to hide the bodies and slip in." He looked straight at Reanna, and she blinked, suddenly feeling like the proverbial deer in the headlights. "Reanna and I will take out the guards. You two will be in charge of casting silence spells and keeping them up so no one gets suspicious. Then we'll slip in and the real fun begins." Whisper grinned and stood. "I'll be in charge of taking the kids back out in the tunnel. Laeserno will heal them. Gregory and Laeserno, you were in charge of how to get into the barracks; you don't have to tell me what you decided so long as you do it." He dropped the stick and wiped his hands off on his clothes. "Well, that's all I've got. If anyone wants to comment, say so now."

"I don't know if we should do this," Reanna mumbled.

She wasn't aware she'd voiced her opinion out loud until everyone gawked at her. She tugged a piece of hair in front of her eyes in order to focus on it instead of their gaping mouths.

"This was *your* plan!" Gregory sounded incredulous, and rightly so.

"That's the problem." Louder, she said, "It's just a dumb plan the more I think about it. Two guards? Really? Come on. It's a trap. Moth—Arana—is baiting us."

Gregory leveled his gaze at her. "It's the best we've got, Reanna. The Council can't do anything; they're tied up with the rest of the battles. You heard Whisper say that she's running a skeleton crew here. We have to do this."

His words reminded her of the quote she'd seen on the Internet that went something like, "All that is required for evil to triumph is for good men to do nothing." The only problem was that if they killed themselves, evil would triumph anyway, and no one would remember the four corpses that tried to stop it.

They were all staring at her. Reanna dropped her stringy hair and surrendered once more. "Fine. I just…it just doesn't *feel* right."

Whisper clasped her shoulder. His eyes softened as they met hers, and Reanna turned her attention to the mud. "I know, Reanna. But nothing in a war ever does."

There were some parts of reality that pictures, words, and imagination could never prepare someone for.

Not until Reanna found herself wading in the stench, filth, and despair that permeated even the area around the prison camp did she realize that pictures were worth *only* a thousand words. They were merely a blink in time, a piece of paper that you projected your own feelings and thoughts onto.

Even in real life, Reanna wondered if she had the emotional depth to grasp the scene beyond the concentration camp barrier. Somewhere in there, people wailed, yelled, and cried.

Reanna hated it. She hated all mermaids, even herself. She hated the Council that sat by and did nothing. She hated the injustice of it all. *This* was why Gregory and Laile had been so adamant to do something, anything—why they had sacrificed so much and gone against the rulers of the land to *help*. They had somehow grasped from afar the true atrocities that were happening here, and Reanna had been too self-absorbed to care about much more than her own fears.

She was a mermaid through and through.

While her emotions and thoughts churned about, Reanna absorbed the scene before her in a haze. Dilapidated shanties loomed in front of her, blocked off by a pulsing, water-like pink barrier that crisscrossed the length of the field. She stepped over the trampled-on rubble of what had been there before. The scattered stones and splintered wood—the broken bits of livelihoods and families left to ruin—would only be used as kindling for fires or target practice for soldiers.

The only things missing from this nightmare were the broken bodies of elves. Either the Atlanteans were good about not leaving their corpses out to rot—surely the stench would ruin the festivities, right?—or they didn't execute anyone on the lawn.

Gregory crept closer. Whisper wrenched him backward and gestured to the forcefield-like thing in front of them.

"Careful," the azernos said. He shoved Gregory back into the foliage that they were all using as a hiding spot as they waited to ambush the guards. "I forgot to mention that you'll lose whatever limb you touch the fence with if you try to test your luck." He scowled at the barrier as though it was his personal enemy. "I lost a clump of fur on my tail from that evil contraption."

Reanna shuddered, careful to watch her step. With her luck, she'd probably trip on a stick and tumble headfirst into the barrier. Still, it was hard to imagine how something that appeared so innocuous could be so injurious. It looked like a barbed wire fence made out of bubble gum.

Gregory surveyed the area as he fiddled with his glasses. "All right. I'll stay away from it and cast the silence spells. Laeserno, you work on keeping us invisible so nobody sees us."

Laeserno nodded his agreement and held a finger against his lips. He murmured a spell underneath his breath and touched each of them in turn, minus Whisper, just as he had to make them invisible before. Reanna shivered as her body once again disappeared from sight. Such an awful sensation—not to mention dangerous. Even if it kept them safe from guards, what if they did get into a skirmish and hurt each other? What if she accidentally whacked off Gregory's leg because she couldn't see him?

Two female guards rounded the corner of the fence. They chatted among themselves in Atlantean. Reanna shuddered and reached for a strand of her hair to chew on. She recognized the insignias on their uniforms: these weren't the male soldiers the group had faced before—not the disposable lackeys on the front line. These were Arana's guards, brutal and lethal. The same type of guards that had abused Reanna when she was younger.

She swallowed. Before she could alert the others to her new discovery, Whisper darted out of the bushes.

Her warning fizzled out on her tongue. Her mind yelled at her to move, to join the fray, to not be such a self-centered mermaid. But flashes of memories passed before her eyes: the beatings, the freezings, the stories crafted to instill fear in her. The child inside her trembled, and Reanna held down the puke that threatened to bubble up.

No—come on. She was no longer a child. She refused to have the emotional maturity of one.

She reached out and touched the ground. She closed her eyes for a moment to try and enhance her *magical sixth sense*—if such a thing even existed. She imagined her magic as it crawled forward to the puddle she'd poked earlier. She'd seen Arana teach this move to her guards so many times, but replicating it...

The soldiers laughed together—but it was too late for one of them. Whisper grew into the size of a jaguar and leapt on the closet guard. She screamed as he tackled her to the ground. The second guard held out her hand over a puddle. A handful of droplets rose up, and she hardened them into long thin knives.

Too bad Reanna had just a tad bit more time to prepare.

She jerked her hands up, and several awful copies of the Atlantean guard's daggers rose from another puddle. But with the soldier's focus on jaguar-Whisper, Reanna was free to attack. She thrust her hands forward; the shards flew toward the guard, melting a bit during their flight. When they collided with the woman, they broke into slushy pieces and collapsed to the ground, no more effective than being hit with a Slurpee.

Whoops.

The clock in Reanna's head ticked down like the infamous Tick-Tock Crocodile that hunted Captain Hook. Four minutes until the next two guards arrived...three minutes, fifty-nine seconds...

A fireball burst to life. The spellcaster—Reanna presumed it was Gregory—tossed the ball at the soldier's feet. The guard snapped in Atlantean and hopped away from the inferno before it could attack her. But Gregory—or, perhaps Laeserno, whichever one, if not both—guided the wall of flames around the woman. While Whisper attacked the first soldier, the other boys hemmed in the second until she stood behind a pyre.

A geyser shot up from the second guard's puddle.

"No, no, no," Reanna murmured under her breath.

She held out her hands. She didn't care what happened, whether the water froze or evaporated, as long as *something* did.

This time, when she tried to wriggle her magic into the water, she felt a second, much stronger, consciousness already there—the guard. That second consciousness repelled her and ripped away all control before Reanna could take over anything.

The waterspout doused the flames and spun out into a miniature whirlpool. The soldier—now transformed into her mermaid form—sat atop it. Branches of water snaked out from the whirlpool and scrounged for the invisible attackers.

One thrust toward Whisper.

Reanna squeaked the beginning notes of a warning, but Whisper shrank into a mouse. A giant icicle impaled the ground where he'd sat a moment before—right between the first soldier's feet.

Whisper switched into a fairy next. The ground seemed to tremble; a horrible rumble filled the air. It sounded like loud crunching or crackling—Reanna didn't know how to describe it.

A vine whipped out of the forest and wrapped around the whirlpool soldier's neck.

She cried out and clawed at Whisper's attack. He hovered in the air on translucent green wings.

The whirlpool crashed to the ground as more and more hanging vines slithered up the woman's hands and feet. She kicked and writhed until—

Crack.

Whisper flung her body down next to the first soldier's. The second guard's neck was tilted at an odd angle…

Reanna leaned over and dry heaved.

Whisper landed in the bushes and dusted off his hands. "Come on. That took a little too much time. What were the rest of you doing?"

"I don't know what Laeserno's doing," Gregory said, though Reanna couldn't see where he stood. He sounded close—maybe to her left? "But I'm bleeding. She got me with one of those whip things."

"Heal yourself," Whisper snapped. "We have to hurry."

"You killed them!" Reanna bleated. "I thought we were just supposed to incapacitate them!"

"Not *ideal*, I admit, but since neither one of you seemed capable of landing an attack, I had to do what I had to do." Whisper held out his hand. Tree roots slithered out of the forest to collect the two corpses. "Remember that civil war I mentioned? I may have been an assassin. A dragon-blasted good one, if I do say so myself."

"You…" Reanna's stomach churned.

"Reanna, dear, if you don't want to see me kill anyone else, *get inside the fence*. I don't *like* taking lives, but Cynerra entrusted you all to me, and I will keep you alive to the best of my ability."

Too late.

The next round of guards entered the fray.

"To quote my Laile-girl: flying fig-whits," Whisper muttered. "Gregory, find Laeserno. He may have been hit and is hurt. I've got to burrow us out of here. Reanna will have to handle the next round of guards."

"But—" Reanna began.

"Use that dagger Laile gave you!" Whisper held one wet hand up toward the sky. The ground rumbled beneath them.

"I lost it!" Reanna cried.

"Flying fig-whits," Whisper repeated. Though there were no outward changes, he must have switched into a gem fairy; he held out his hand and formed the mud at their feet into one very shoddy diamond dagger. "There. Not as neat as Laile's, but it'll do the job. Come close so I can give it to you. I can't see you."

"All right. I'm here." Reana reached out to touch Whisper's arm. He shoved the weapon into her hand. The blade wasn't exactly smooth—the edges were jagged, and it kind of resembled a kindergartener's Play-Doh experiment—but it would do in a pinch.

"Thank you," Reanna squeaked. "And—don't kill anyone else." Though Whisper couldn't see her, she turned her pleading eyes toward him. "Please."

"Then I suggest you take the lead." Whisper winked at her—again!—right before hundreds of roots burst through the ground. "I'll even give you a little help before I go."

"I *can't*!" Reanna said pitifully. "I can't do anything! You saw me in that last fight. I'm useless!"

"Then don't complain about my methods." His roots wiggled like tentacles as they shot toward the mermaids. An idea popped into Reanna's head—an awful, stupid idea—but before her mind could talk her out of it, she jumped onto one of the roots as it sped toward the enemy.

If they lived through this, those soldiers would thank her one day.

She collided with the soldier in the front. The roots tore at the guard's armor; sharp scales cut into Reanna's hands.

The Atlantean rolled over and pinned one of Reanna's arms to the ground despite the invisibility spell. Reanna squirmed, but the woman guided water until it conformed to Reanna's body shape.

Reanna was exposed.

The Atlantean pressed her knee into Reanna's diaphragm. "*Faynacore.*"

Reanna gasped for breath and tried to claw at her attacker's face.

A water snake coiled out of the mud and wrapped around Reanna's neck. Reanna choked; the woman grinned.

Reanna swiped at the guard; her fingers—and the rest of her body—flickered into view as Laeserno's spell waned.

The soldier snarled more words in Atlantean; Reanna's vision blurred. She brought her arm up and banged the woman's temple with the hilt of her dagger several times. The blows gained force as frustration and desperation overtook her. The water snake tightened its death grip on Reanna's neck.

She plunged the dagger into the woman's hand.

The soldier screeched; Reanna sobbed at the awful feeling of her weapon meeting bone. The water snake crashed as the woman tried to extricate the blade from her hand. Reanna scrambled to her feet and picked up a large rock. She bashed the woman's helmet several times until the soldier slumped over with the dagger still caught in her palm.

Reanna's chest heaved as she broke into sobs. Her knees trembled, her neck would probably be bruised in the morning, and there was a good possibility she might puke. But she'd kept the woman alive, though the soldier was unconscious.

She staggered back toward Whisper. Gregory's invisibility had worn off as well, and she saw him standing over the unconscious form of another soldier. His shoulders drooped, and a few licks of fire still danced on his fingers. Laeserno was beside him, healing a scrape on Gregory's shoulder. Some fabric dangled loosely around it; apparently Gregory's sleeve had been a minor casualty in the war.

Reanna heaved as her emotions churned in her stomach. She crashed into Gregory and wrapped her arms around him while her whole body trembled. He put a hand on her shoulder as if he didn't know what else to do and gave her a few seconds before he pushed her away.

"I did it," she whispered. "I might hurl, but I did it. Are you okay?"

One side of Gregory's lip curled upward. "I'll be fine. I just got a little nick. If Laile were here, I probably wouldn't have gotten hurt. But don't tell her that. She'll get a big head."

Whisper poked an animalistic head out of the tunnel he'd burrowed, but he shifted into a humanoid form as Reanna watched. With a wave of his hand, more jungle vines carried the bodies away and deep into the forest—a flora fairy's ability. "If everyone's done, could we please hurry before the *next* round comes? I would be very appreciative of that."

Reanna, Laeserno, and Gregory headed into the large tunnel, Reanna at the back of the pack. Whisper caught her by the arm as she passed while the boys each created a *lux* spell to light up the darkness.

Whisper switched into a man and stood. "Good job, you know. See, I knew you could take the lead. You didn't need me."

Wrapping her arms around her stomach to quell the uprising there, she hobbled past him. "Mm." She didn't know if she dared to open her mouth until she'd at least tried to calm the waves of anxiety inside her. Until she could regulate her breathing.

"Wait just one second." Whisper grabbed her shoulder and whirled her around, his dark eyes unreadable even in a humanoid form. "Don't underestimate yourself, Reanna. Just because you are learning how to use your powers and navigate a world you haven't been to in over a decade doesn't mean you are worthless." His words came out clipped and hurried, but they still hit Reanna's heart.

She winced and wiped at her eyes. "But—"

"No. Not a word if you're going to use it to put yourself down." Whisper turned around and began to levitate the dirt. He must have switched to a gem fairy. He maneuvered the ground around as he attempted to fill in the hole. "And…I'm sorry that I had to kill those women."

Reanna sniffled. "Sorry?"

"I can see it disturbed you. I forget not everyone is as used to this as I am." Whisper finished his job and patted her once on the shoulder before he tugged her deeper into the tunnel; she could see Gregory and Laeserno up ahead through their *lux* spells.

"Were you really an assassin?" Reanna dabbed her thumb under her stuffy nose.

"I…" He chuckled under his breath. "And here I said I promised myself I wouldn't yammer on about my past. But, yes. I was. Long before Cynerra found me, back when I still lived in Selah."

"Why?" Reanna whispered.

"Why? We were in a war." Whisper snorted. "War is full of moral ambiguities, Reanna. No—*life* is full of moral ambiguities. At some point you must rationalize what you are willing to do for your beliefs and to help other people."

Reanna shuffled her feet. "But sometimes you forget that your enemies are real people, too."

Whisper smirked. "Ah. You see the conundrum of life, little mermaid." He ruffled her hair as they approached the boys.

"How's your arm?" Reanna asked Gregory.

He rotated it a few times. "Perfect. You know, Laeserno, for a violinist, you do know *some* magic."

In the glow of the light spell, Laeserno smiled. "As I said, I did enough to pass my tests."

Above them, Reanna could hear soldiers laughing as they patrolled. She took a deep breath and grabbed Gregory's sleeve. Dirt dripped onto them as the soldiers tromped around. Reanna's fingers shook, and she clenched her free hand into a fist. Someone overhead cried out for their mother; Gregory's shoulders drooped, and he placed a hand over Reanna's.

In the light of the *lux* spells, Laeserno made the same sign of reverence that he'd done back at the catacombs and Unity Park—the one that reminded Reanna of a Catholic crossing themselves. She caught the tail end of a hushed prayer from the elf, and her heart twisted. Whisper, in his azernos form, strode in front of them with his ears alert and hackles raised.

They'd made it to the concentration camp.

CHAPTER 46

REANNA

GAIA: ELVEN CONCENTRATION CAMP IN OGDEN'S INLET, DASPIN

Laeserno turned the group invisible once again before they resurfaced, with Whisper left visible so everyone had a point of reference to follow. Whisper broke through the ground behind their target, and Reanna felt even sicker when she poked her head out like a tiny groundhog.

The rain had started up again. It pelted the slapdash shanties that sat all around them. The wooden structures must have been hastily constructed because Reanna could peer between the slats of some of them. She swallowed down the bile and wished she could see someone to latch onto as she pulled herself out. Hesitantly, she held out her arm and bumped against someone. She didn't care who it was—she latched onto their sleeve and pulled them closer.

"Careful," Gregory whispered.

Her grip tightened as she let out a puff of air. Ah, so she'd grabbed Gregory.

Meanwhile, Whisper stood tall in his mouse form. He twitched his whiskers, licked his paws, and cleaned his ears while his head swiveled around. He scurried around the corner of the barrack, and though common sense roared at her to stay put, curiosity overtook that sense. Reanna would die just like the proverbial cat, but she released Gregory and army-crawled behind Whisper. They both peered around the edge of the building.

Four guards waited in front of the barrack. One of them dozed on the ground. Another played with the rain as it came down, crafting different shapes and animals with the droplets. A third leaned against the second and clapped for each new shape. The fourth had her back to the rest and gazed, silent, into the distance.

Inside, Reanna could hear the cries of children.

Whisper scampered back to the group, but Reanna paused before she rejoined them. She pressed her eye against one of the gaps between the slats, and her stomach churned again. Children huddled in heaps on the floor. A handful played a game in the center of the room with magic. Some of the younger ones wailed while the older ones tried to comfort them.

Reanna swiped at the tears in her eyes, but the rain mingled with them and made it even harder to see as she rejoined the group.

"All right. Cast the silence spell, Laeserno," Gregory said. "I'll work on my part of the white noise spell."

Though she couldn't see him, Reanna imagined Laeserno with outstretched hands as he intoned, "*Velum Silentium.*"

Nothing remarkable happened, but Reanna knew that a dome of silence had fallen around them and the children inside when the pounding noise of the rain turned into a drizzle, and many of the background noises—the sobs, the whimpers, the pathetic bleatings for missing parents—disappeared.

"Your turn, Gregory," Laeserno said.

Gregory continued to murmur. They'd determined this back at Shaesia's house as well: a simple white noise spell, designed to mimic the general sounds of children. Again, nothing outward happened, but Gregory announced, "Got it." At least the sudden absence of noise wouldn't seem conspicuous. "Now for the next part. *Ignis.*"

A flame erupted on the side of the building.

"Can you try and keep the rain off so I can burn a hole?" he whispered to Reanna.

Could she?

Reanna breathed in and held her hands above them. She tried to reach out and attach her magic onto each individual droplet as it fell, to tell them to move, to go away…

Mouse-Whisper watched the sky as a few droplets scattered, but, on the whole, most still hit Gregory's flame.

The azernos shifted into a dog—a rather large dog that stood just under the height of the shack-sized building—and held out his paw over Gregory.

A puddle squelched near Reanna.

"Keep trying," Laeserno said softly.

Reanna narrowed her eyes at the rain as it splattered against her. She tried to direct her thoughts, to tell the droplets to part right above her. She lifted her hands higher and wrenched them in opposite directions—as if they were curtains she wanted to open.

The rain split but only for a moment.

"Hm. It seems like you can only do magic with over-the-top gestures." Laeserno cleared his throat. "You must work at channeling more magic with smaller effort."

Reanna snorted. "I thought you were a violinist?"

He chuckled. "Finally, one of you remembers."

"All right. We should be good to break through," Gregory said.

Whisper used one of his giant paws to knock over the weakened piece of wood.

Some of the children screamed; others held up their hands as magic sparked on the ends of their fingertips.

"Ghosts!" one of the little ones squeaked.

Reanna stepped forward and held out her hands in a surrendering gesture. It took her a few seconds to remember that these children couldn't see her at all. "Hold on. We're not ghosts— we're not here to hurt you."

"Who are you?" a little boy asked.

"We're…uh, friends of the Council. We're here to get you out, but you have to be quiet." Reanna held up her finger to her lips— again, useless. "My friend is going to make you invisible, and then we're going to sneak you out of the camp. There's a little tunnel right outside here. You all are going to climb in, and my friend Whisper will lead you to the other side. Once we free all of your parents and the adults, we're going to try and transport you guys to safety via a portal, okay? But for now, we have to get on the other side of the force field first." Not to mention rescue an elf that could actually do portal spells. After all, Laeserno was just a violinist.

For the next several minutes, Reanna lined up the kids. Most of them seemed to be unhurt, though a few asked her about missing family members, about where those absent might be, and whether everyone would be okay.

The stories came next. Stories about sisters and brothers who had been taken for experiments, friends that had been killed, and parents that had been separated from their children. Reanna absorbed every hushed, hurried tale like a brick into her soul. They sank down into the pit of her stomach and settled there until she could hardly speak.

She didn't think she could swallow another one, and they'd only partially liberated the first barrack.

Laeserno's invisibility spell flickered off. Without its protection, the children noticed Reanna for the first time—and she felt naked beneath their gazes. She couldn't be anything like what they'd imagined their rescuer to look like. She could only be a disappointment—a wretched, soggy, teenage girl with a Spider-Man sweatshirt tied around her waist as a security blanket.

One of the smaller girls toddled up and grasped Reanna's leg. "Thank you."

Reanna's bottom lip quivered. She sank down to the floor, patted the girl's tangled curls, and brushed the tears away from the child's dirty cheeks. Words failed Reanna; she couldn't shove them past the barricade in her throat, anyway.

"Come on. Follow me." Gregory ushered them out. "Link hands and don't let go."

Whisper, back in fairy form, stood at the front of the line. "I'll look like an animal, okay? You all follow me—the first of you can grasp my tail, but not too hard. Gregory will be in the back. Don't drop a hand, because once the invisibility spell is cast, we won't be able to find you. If you follow me and don't let go, we'll be able to get you to your mummies and daddies and brothers and sisters."

Twenty or so dutiful heads bobbed before Laeserno walked through their ranks and turned them invisible, starting from the smallest up to Reanna.

Whisper and Gregory led the invisible processional out—the only sign that it even existed at all was a tiny squirrel at the head of it.

They expanded their tunnel and repeated the escape route at two more barracks. But after the second time, as Whisper and Gregory led some adults away through the escape route and Laeserno raised the silence dome, a noise louder than any thunder shook the camp.

Reanna froze, only midway to the next barrack, and floundered about until she could find the invisible hand of Laeserno.

"Did you *really* think you could get away with it?" a raspy voice asked. It sounded like it came from the center of camp, just a row over to the left and a few barracks down.

"No," a second person answered. Somehow they seemed steady, strong, even in this heinous place. "I did not think I could get away with anything, but I was unwilling to let my daughter suffer as one of *your* experiments."

Laeserno's grip tightened on Reanna until she thought her knuckles might fall off.

"Rosaelina," he whispered. "My wife."

He dragged Reanna forward through the mud; their footprints squelched with every step, but several other Atlantean guards also seemed intrigued by the turn of events and made their way to the center of camp. The noisy tromps of those guards helped mask Reanna's and Laeserno's careless footfalls.

A small, empty field acted as the center square. A two-storied building stood to Reanna's right. Though still wooden, it seemed somehow nicer than the rest of the camp and actually had windows. People sat outside of it and watched as two women marched away from the building. More figures poured out of the doorway or opened windows; soldiers drifted closer.

The shorter of the women—the one dressed in all black— hauled the second woman behind her: an elf in a torn, ragged gray shirt and pants. The elf had pastel-pink hair that had faded, since concentration camps didn't typically offer salon services to prisoners, but it still reminded Reanna of Laeserno's words as he spoke about his wife, as a burst of color in a black-and-white world.

That had to be Rosaelina.

"Laeserno, who's the other person...?" Reanna whispered. The raven-haired woman looked vaguely familiar, but Reanna just couldn't place her.

Laeserno sounded choked. "*Violante.*"

Images thudded to the front of Reanna's brain, almost painful as every synapse lit up.

Of course—Violante.

Recognition raced through Reanna's body as though someone had blended up an ice cube and shot it through her veins. The woman on the beach. The one who had cast the memory spell on Reanna back on Earth. The one who had orchestrated the whole kidnapping ordeal.

Arana's head sorceress.

CHAPTER 47

REANNA

GAIA: ELVEN CONCENTRATION CAMP IN OGDEN'S INLET, DASPIN

Reanna trembled, her breath suddenly harder to catch.

"My daughter is too ill to survive your treatment." Rosaelina gestured to the large building at the heart of the prison.

"You attacked our scientists," Violante continued. Her voice rose as she addressed the crowd. "This woman—this *elf*—would have murdered one of the top sorceresses in Solis. A woman who is Arana's honored servant." She nodded to the guards. "Open the doors. Let our *prisoners* hear this, just in case they need to be reminded."

Oh, no—if they opened the doors, they'd see that three barracks had already been liberated.

Reanna sucked in a breath. She didn't want to execute Plan B—using herself as a distraction—but she could feel the danger as it breathed on the back of her neck.

Although…if the invisibility spell stayed intact, maybe she could pretend to be a poltergeist? Reanna imagined herself running around the camp, hurling things and screaming, while Violante's troops cowered in fear.

The guards threw open the doors, but many of them stayed with their weapons crossed over the entrances to keep the elves inside.

Violante shook one of Rosaelina's arms and thrust her forward. "Look—this is the wife of the man who betrayed Shaesia. That's right. A traitor to your own kind—so willing to save his skin that he turned in one of his own and abandoned his wife and daughter."

Beside Reanna, Laeserno sucked in a breath. She could feel him tremble in her grip.

Someone shouted from across the camp. "We're missing prisoners!"

"My barrack is empty, too!"

Violante clenched her fists, and sparks of dark magic erupted from between them. "Search the camp! Check all the other barracks. If they've escaped, we'll find them. If we can't find them...I don't think Arana will mind some impromptu executions." She threw Rosaelina to the ground and held out one hand. Black magic leapt between the sorceress' fingers and gathered in a ball in her palm. "What did you plan, you little witch?"

Rosaelina scowled and dusted off her palms as she stared up at Violante. "I did nothing but try to rescue my daughter. I thought it a calculated risk, considering you have no one else to take away from me. *You* have separated me from my husband by your lies. If I could rescue my daughter, then I thought I might stand a chance of escape."

Violante snarled and held her hand over Rosaelina's head. "*Niguinemrum.*" The sorceress' voice sounded like a car tire being dragged over gravel.

Violante's black ball of magic snaked toward Rosaelina and sank into every cranny on her face. The darkness spread throughout the elf's veins and visibly throbbed. She screamed and doubled over as the blood threatened to burst from underneath her skin. Thick, obsidian liquid leaked out from her ears—eyes—nose—mouth.

"*Rosaelina!*" Laeserno cut off his own invisibility spell and rushed forward.

Violante whirled around. "You!"

Reanna glanced behind her—had Whisper and Gregory gotten all the prisoners out? Surely they'd rescued at least a handful of people that could summon a portal to transport the freed elves to Shaesia's, right?

"Laeserno!" Rosaelina yelled. "What—"

"Give me my family back," Laeserno snarled at Violante

"The traitor comes to make demands?" the sorceress scoffed.

"You promised me my family's safety if I cooperated with you." Laeserno dropped to his knees beside his wife and brushed some of the blood away from her nose.

She coughed, and thick, black liquid splattered on the grass.

Violante chuckled—a deep, throaty sound that reminded Reanna of Lauren Bacall. "And you trusted your conquerors? There's your problem." She swept her arm toward the soldiers. "Lock the barracks up. Search the grounds; the escapees couldn't have gotten far. In fact, I think I know who's to blame."

She angled her hand toward Laeserno's head.

Reanna reacted on instinct.

She dove toward Violante and tackled the woman. Laeserno hadn't ended the invisibility spell on Reanna yet, so she used it to her advantage and pummeled Violante's face. No magic necessary—just a classic fistfight.

Violante sputtered and shrieked. She shoved her palm in the air and growled, "*Desinmere!*"

Reanna felt the world ripple as Violante's magic destroyed the invisibility spell.

Violante intercepted Reanna's next blow and captured her wrists. The sorceress' dark eyes sparked. "Oh, look. Arana's brat comes home at last. I've been looking for you. By the time I cleaned up the magical mess back on Earth, you'd up and disappeared and left two of my soldiers locked in your cage. How rude." Violante smirked. "Though I think you'll be pleased to know that they paid for their incompetence."

Reanna thrashed and tried to rip herself free of Violante's grasp.

"Now, now." Violante clucked her tongue. "None of that."

A fireball exploded at Violante's side.

The sorceress shrieked, rolled to the side, and somehow found the momentum to get to her feet. She swung Reanna around in front of her like a human shield to block any further magical attack, pressing a ball of black magic against Reanna's throat. Reanna gagged as her veins started to throb where the magic touched.

"Don't do anything rash," Violante said. "I have the princess. You wouldn't hurt her, would you?" The sorceress' warm breath tickled Reanna's ear. "Of course, if you knew what your mother had planned for you, you just might wish for a quick death at the hands of your friends."

Tree roots shot out of the ground and snagged Violante's ankles.

She swore. Several other branches circled Reanna's waist and ripped her away; the dark magic burned Reanna's neck as it brushed against her skin.

Violante swore again—or maybe those were just her incantations. Black flames erupted from her palms, and she gripped the roots as they crawled up her thighs. But her fire didn't burn the wood as it should have. Instead, the plants shriveled up and turned into something from *The Nightmare Before Christmas*, all gnarled and dead.

Reanna caught sight of Whisper as he stood at the edge of a barrack. He sported green wings again—a flora fairy. Violante's ruinous spell shot through the plants and must have done something to Whisper, too. He doubled over and clutched his chest, and the roots around Reanna curled up and died as well. She tumbled to the ground and rolled.

Arana's soldiers rushed to try and defend Violante, but that left the elves unguarded. Reanna crawled through the melee; some of the healthier-looking elves joined the fray to support Reanna's small band of friends. Not many, but they helped to balance the odds a little.

Ahead of Reanna, Laeserno cradled Rosaelina in his arms. Blood continued to leak from various orifices on her face, staining it and Laeserno's clothes black. Reanna could hardly focus on anything: the melee, Violante, Whisper, Laeserno and his wife—and who could even say where Gregory might be? Reanna's brain whirred with the clamor.

A dead Atlantean soldier collapsed to the ground beside her.

Reanna shrieked and squeezed her eyes shut. She didn't want to think about the blank, open eyes of the fallen woman. She didn't want to think about whether or not that had been the guard at the first shanty, the one that made animals from raindrops. And Reanna *definitely* didn't want to think about what might have happened had these people been given one more chance to change. After all, who knew how Arana had coerced them to commit these deplorable deeds.

She felt a hand against her back, but when she turned, she could only see a faint outline of Gregory. He still looked like a mirage in the desert. "We got the last group out through the tunnel." He adjusted his askew glasses and hurled a fireball at another Atlantean. "These soldiers have made their beds. Now let them sleep in them."

Whisper had expressed similar sentiments before the group had entered the concentration camp. And, on the one hand, Reanna could barely contain her anger at the heinous crimes her people had committed. But on the other hand…

She ducked to avoid an ice dagger. A freed elf engaged the weapon's owner in a battle; Reanna must have been an unintentional target for that attack. She rolled out of the way before she became the *intentional* target of the next blow.

Forget the other hand. Maybe it was best to just focus on the battle instead of the noisy thoughts inside her head.

Gregory ran up and grabbed her hand. "While everyone's distracted—help me free some more barracks."

She clung to him as he pulled her toward one of the barracks. "What about everyone else?"

"A few of the elves in better health got a portal started right on the other side of the fence. We might actually save everyone in this camp." Gregory unlocked one of the doors with magic and they rushed inside—only to stop. The door swung shut behind them, but neither one of them moved.

The urge to go back, to forget what lurked inside this barrack, overwhelmed Reanna.

The majority of the twelve elves in this building were barely more than skeletons. Their bones poked through their ragged, tattered clothes. Even the grooves of their faces were distorted, sunken in. Less than half of them reacted to their visitors—and even those that did could only utter pitiful moans.

Two elves were shackled to the wall, stripped to their underclothes. Whip marks decorated their bare skin; clumps of their hair had either fallen or been ripped out. Dried blood stained their underclothes a garish brown.

Reanna clutched at her throat; her whole body burned and tried to revolt against her.

Gregory sifted through the crowd. He had to pick his way through delicately to avoid the limbs that looked like they would snap like twigs if he so much as breathed on them. He started toward the back wall, toward the two brutally beaten victims. When he got there, he wrapped his hand around the manacle of one of the hanging elves. "*Aperidius.*"

The elf's arm dropped, and he or she cried out weakly. In the state they were in, Reanna had a hard time discerning the gender of anyone in the room.

"Reanna, come help me." Gregory beckoned her over. "You've got to help me hold them so they don't fall."

She edged over to Gregory. Tears blurred her vision. The pain in the room overwhelmed her, threatened to drown her as she absorbed suffering so potent she could choke on it.

"Grab them under their arms." Gregory sniffled, but his voice remained steady. "Just don't let them fall."

Reanna did so; Gregory unlocked the second manacle. Reanna lowered the poor creature down to the floor. Gregory knelt beside them and adjusted his glasses, but he paused, his fingers on the frame.

"I don't even know where to start." His expression twitched as though he might be trying to hold back a deluge of emotions. "They're in so much worse condition than the others. I don't know how to get them out." His voice broke. "Oh, Composer help us."

Reanna reached out for his hand and threaded her fingers through his. In a moment like this, she couldn't bring herself to worry about what was awkward or not. He squeezed her hand; he seemed to understand the meaning of her gesture: a desperate attempt to cling to one thing—to share grief at a time when the aura of pure suffering overwhelmed all else.

"Heal them?" she suggested. "Just like we always planned."

"I know, but—it's so bad."

On the ground, the elf labored to breathe. Around Reanna and Gregory, others moaned.

"You can do this." Reanna scooted closer so she could rest her head on his shoulder. "You can."

Gregory held out his right hand over the elf's cheek. After a moment, Reanna reached forward and put her free left hand over his—she knew her magic couldn't heal, she *knew* it, but she still wanted to will every bit of her power into his by some childish, impossible wish.

"*Compositor, sana vulnus hoc,*" Gregory whispered.

Light flickered to life beneath his fingers.

Reanna closed her eyes. Gregory had said that he called upon the Composer to work a healing spell. Well, maybe it wouldn't hurt, just this once, if she tried to channel some more of the Composer's power into Gregory. *Okay—Composer. I never ask for anything because, frankly, I'm not sure if You're there. But if You are, then all I need is this one little thing. Just let us heal this elf, okay? Just...fix it. Let us fix this all. Do you see everything that's happening here in this concentration camp? It's so cruel. If You care at all...wouldn't You want to fix it, too?*

It almost seemed like the elf smiled. Reanna could feel the warmth in Gregory's hands as it leaked into her. For a moment, she could almost imagine that they'd entered a bubble of just the three of them. No one else existed outside of this warm little cocoon they'd created, a cocoon swathed in this deep warmth.

Peace.

A tiny song bubbled up in the back of Reanna's mind—*peace.* It reminded her of the Song of the Sea, but different. Quieter. Comforting.

Hope flickered to life inside Reanna's chest and fought against the tide of turmoil that filled her. Perhaps...perhaps the Composer had actually listened to them. Perhaps she'd finally been of some use, proved her worth somehow.

Maybe she'd been a good girl just like she'd always craved to be, and had somehow, in some way, earned the love of someone, somewhere.

The elf took a shallow breath…

Exhaled…

But the next breath never came.

Peace.

Reanna waited. She peeked open one eye and saw again the small smile that rested on the elf's face. But something…something was off.

The life, that inexplicable essence of *living*—it'd fled the poor person.

Reanna stared at an empty shell.

Her hands dropped. Numbness seeped through her and replaced all the warmth she'd felt a moment ago.

Peace.

No—there wasn't *peace* here. This was wrong, all wrong. This wasn't peace. This was *wrong*.

"I don't—but—I thought—they were *alive*, just a second ago!" Reanna bleated.

Gregory's shoulders slumped over. "Healing spells aren't always effective, Reanna. And…it was so late…"

"Are you saying the Composer can't heal someone when they're this close to death?" Reanna snarled. Her voice came out harsher than she'd intended. "Doesn't seem very powerful to me, then. Maybe you should call on something else—one of those things Violante uses. Seems like she doesn't have any trouble dealing out pain and destruction."

"Reanna—" Gregory began.

"No! Don't '*Reanna*' me. Don't try and waste any pithy platitudes on me." Tears spilled over. "I hate them. I can't express how much I *hate* them. This isn't for the best, it isn't better this way—" She swallowed more angry words as they bubbled to the top. She'd just prayed empty words again, just like when she'd tried to pray for her adopted dad to come back. "This…" Reanna gestured to the elves around them. "Is not okay."

So what if the Composer hadn't helped them? She was used to it. She was used to doing things on her own, to only relying on herself. She'd never be perfect enough for anyone to love her—not her biological parents, not any supposed deity in the sky.

She'd just have to take matters into her own hands.

Again.

CHAPTER 48

REANNA

GAIA: ELVEN CONCENTRATION CAMP IN OGDEN'S INLET, DASPIN

Reanna stumbled back out into the rain. She shivered, and her foot slipped on mud. She thudded to the ground but picked herself back up. "Violante!"

So many people—Reanna could hardly make sense of anything, and the rain and her tears didn't make it any easier. She swiped the liquid from her eyes and stumbled forward. Laeserno still sat in the middle of the camp holding his wife. Faint traces of blackness wound their way through Rosaelina's body.

So wrong. Everything was wrong.

Reanna cupped her hands around her mouth. "Violante! Stop this. I'll go with you!"

An Atlantean soldier that happened to be near Reanna paused and turned. Their eyes met, and Reanna wondered if the warrior might have been one of the very mermaids that used to work in Arana's palace. Did the woman remember Reanna as a child?

Reanna stood there, shivering, soaked, with a worn-out Spider-Man sweatshirt wrapped around her waist. She cinched it tighter and imagined that the gesture filled her with strength she didn't possess.

"I'm Reanna." Reanna sniffed and swiped her hair out of her face. "The one they're all looking for. The princess. Take me to Violante—uh—*please.*"

The Atlantean scoffed. "*Faynacore.*"

Reanna winced at the favorite Atlantean slur and shuffled her feet.

The Atlantean grabbed her and marched her through the crowd. Violante had moved toward the first row of barracks. Dead elves lay on the ground in her wake. A shield of dark magic must have kept her safe from the elves; the sorceress still held on to a thin layer of black energy that churned in her palm.

"Violante!" Reanna screamed. "Violante, I want to negotiate!"

Violante whirled around. She'd apparently taken at least some damage; a burn marred her neck and shoulder, and her black dress had a charred sleeve. Blood trickled from a deep nick on her cheek. Her expression morphed from agitation—a scowl, eyes narrowed—to smugness.

"Negotiate? What do you have to negotiate with?" The sorceress strode toward Reanna until they were a few feet apart.

Reanna rubbed her arms to generate some heat. "Myself."

Violante raised her eyebrow. "And what would be your terms?"

"You let everyone go." Reanna nodded to indicate everyone in the camp. "You get some healers here to try and fix everything. And...and you fix Rosaelina. Oh—and—and wherever you're keeping Laeserno's daughter, wherever you're doing your experiments—they end now." Reanna sneezed, quite an anticlimactic end to her speech. She couldn't stop shivering, and her teeth chattered together.

388

"And—correct me if I'm wrong—the *only* thing you're offering is yourself?" Violante tapped a long nail against her lips.

"I know my mother wants me. That's what I've been told all along—that this whole war is just to find me. And that the elves are being punished because of *me*." Reanna swallowed. "I want that to end. Mother will get what she wants."

Violante chuckled. She took Reanna's hand from the soldier and guided her over to Laeserno.

Rosaelina still convulsed, but it looked like the dark magic had subsided somewhat.

"Did you hear that?" Violante stared down at Rosaelina. "The little princess has offered herself as a substitute in your place. Don't you feel lucky?"

Rosaelina glared up at the sorceress but didn't speak. Blood stained the elf's face, and though circumstances may have tried to diminish Rosaelina's radiance, something—perhaps Laeserno's glowing testimony—still made the life, the *spirit* inside Rosaelina seem almost tangible.

"She wants me to let your girl go." Violante turned to a few Atlantean soldiers. "All right. Go get their girl. Room Four. Bring her out."

The rain had slacked off a smidge by the time the Atlanteans returned with a little girl in tow—or what remained of a little girl.

She'd withered away to almost nothing. Her bruised, burned arm dangled limply as one of the soldiers carried her. If she'd had long hair before, it had been shorn to a jagged pixie cut that didn't even cover her pointed ears. The nightgown she wore seemed too big for her body and hung off her frame. Reanna could probably count most of the bones in the poor girl's body.

"Maesie—" Laeserno choked.

The Atlantean unceremoniously dropped Maesie into her father's arms. Her head lolled to the side, and she didn't open her eyes.

"If only the princess had been just a tad earlier in her offer. It might have saved your daughter's life." Violante sighed and shrugged her shoulders. "But as it was, your *wife* had to go and make a fool of herself and get her daughter killed." She leaned down and pushed Rosaelina's bangs away from her face. "Look what you made me do. If only you'd not stormed the lab, your daughter would still be alive."

Laeserno's face turned red. Tears spilled down his cheeks, and his whole body trembled. "You—you—"

"Choose your next words very carefully," Violante warned.

Laeserno screamed—an awful, horrible wail that pierced Reanna's brain. She'd never forget that sound of absolute rage and anguish compounded together. She staggered, and Laeserno leaned toward Violante, arm extended, magic crackling beneath his fingertips.

In that moment, he was far more than a violinist—he was a father. A husband.

Violante clucked her tongue. "*Niguinemrum.*"

Rosaelina screamed. Her veins once again pulsed black as midnight beneath her caramel skin.

"Rosaelina!" Laeserno fell back down and attempted to cradle both members of his dying family.

"No! No, wait! I promise!" Reanna screeched and launched herself at Violante. "Stop! Stop, please!"

Violante held her hand up higher. Rosaelina shrieked—

The veins burst.

Black blood gushed out of her body. Laeserno bellowed, and the world seemed to move in slow motion. He gripped Rosaelina's cheeks and shook her, but her eyes stared, unblinking, into the clouds.

The sound faded from Reanna's ears. She could only hear the pounding of her own heart—a steady drumbeat for the horror scene that unfolded before her.

Rosaelina.

Maesie.

Laeserno's wife and child, both dead.

Dead.

Laeserno's mouth moved, but Reanna couldn't comprehend or hear the words that came out. He stretched out a bloodied hand.

"You choose your death, traitor," Violante said. Her words sounded far away and slurred, barely audible over the roar in Reanna's head.

The sorceress raised her hand too.

Reanna had seen this movie before, just a minute or so ago. Laeserno wouldn't stop; he'd lost all common sense in grief. His eyes spelled murder, a literal embodiment of "if looks could kill, Violante would be dead."

But Violante really *would* kill him, no death-glare necessary.

"Stop!" Arms spread out like wings, Reanna dove in front of the sorceress.

"*Niguinem–rum.*" Violante's voice faltered on the last syllable, but she'd already cast most of it before she could react to Reanna's movements.

Reanna's body seized in pain. It felt like someone had injected fiery toxin into her veins and like those veins might just explode from the inside out.

She collapsed to the ground. No Charley horse could compare to this, though the sensations were similar. Her mouth fell open in a silent scream, her fingers and toes twisted on their own accord, and she could feel her pulse as the veins threatened to pop with every heartbeat. Through watery eyes, she caught glimpses of her hand— and the inky varicose veins there.

"*Desinmere.*" Violante lowered her arm.

Reanna's body relaxed as the spell ended. Trickles of blood leaked out of the openings on her face and rolled down her cheeks. "Let them go," she croaked.

"Oh—you see, the trouble with that is…you have nothing to offer me that I can't already take." Violante leaned in closer and pressed her mouth against Reanna's ear. "It doesn't matter whether or not you come willingly. I'm still going to take you to your mother, and your friends are still going to die. You sacrificed yourself for a traitor, but, in the end, that sacrifice means nothing." The sorceress motioned for three guards to come and pick up Reanna. "Take her to the portal to Atlantis. Arana has waited long enough."

Reanna screamed. "No! No—*leave them alone!*" She pummeled her fists against the backs of the guards and kicked and kneed at their stomachs. But her body still hadn't recovered from Violante's spell, and, even if it had, Reanna doubted she could overpower her captors to help her friends.

She had no choice—ready or not, it was time to descend into the depths of Atlantis.

CHAPTER 49

REANNA

GAIA: ATLANTIS

Reanna had only encountered portal travel a handful of times—and being dragged through the one to Atlantis was her least favorite experience. It felt like she was both falling and standing still at the same time. The most similar sensation she could think of was plunging down the hill of a roller coaster. She wanted to throw up, but the ride stopped before anything left her stomach.

The portal had thrust them underwater, right into a living nightmare.

The castle of Atlantis.

Reanna shifted into a mermaid, as did all the Atlantean guards. She slapped her fluke against the one that held her; the woman growled and threw Reanna to the floor. But before Reanna could get away, icy manacles formed around her throat, wrists, and fluke.

The soldiers barked something in Atlantean, and though Reanna didn't remember enough of her original tongue to translate it, she could guess at the meaning from their tone: *don't fight*. She sucked in spasmodic breaths. She'd been on this "swim of shame" so many times before. Panic clawed its way up to her throat, and she screamed—until someone forced an icy gag in her mouth.

Peace.

Underneath the current of terror, that still-small melody played.

Oh, no.

The last time that stupid word had popped into Reanna's head, an elf had died. She wouldn't trust this false peace again. It was probably Arana's way of lulling her into a sense of security.

Reanna thrashed despite the fact she could hardly move. The procession swam out of the small room and into a large hallway.

Even though a decade had passed, the castle almost seemed the same: just as intimidating, just as unwelcoming, and just as stately. But now, instead of mermaids milling around and discussing the latest party, Arana had chained elves to the wall.

Shackles held their arms above them and their legs secured to the floor. Aside from the gentle swaying of their clothes, most of them didn't move.

Reanna's eyes widened, and she struggled against her bonds until someone whipped her. Her shoulders tensed at the blow; a muffled cry escaped past her gag. The pain stole her breath as a thin string of crimson floated up and mixed with the undertow.

Someone prodded her with the butt end of a frozen spear. Again, Reanna didn't need a translator to comprehend: *keep swimming.* She gagged and choked, unable to spit out the vomit that rose in her throat. Surely these couldn't be corpses of elves that Arana kept as trophies. No person could be *that* depraved—right?

An elf shifted to look at them as they passed. His arms were stretched out over his head, held in place by manacles that glowed with some sort of magic.

How was he alive? How could he breathe? Unless—

]\Reanna shuddered. The Siren's Kiss. Any mer could do it—long, *long* ago, it was how mermaids of old stole sailors and brought them down to the ocean. The legends said that the sirens killed the seafarers, but Reanna had witnessed the reality as a child, though she'd been too young to comprehend most of it.

Mermaids didn't capture surface men to kill them. They captured them to enslave them for many nefarious purposes—a fate much, much worse than death.

Before, Reanna hadn't been able to understand why her mother had forbidden her from the grand balls, why the men always seemed so scared. It had upset her even then, but Reanna had only come to realize the *why* behind the depravity of Atlantis as a teenager, as she analyzed her childhood from a more adult understanding of the world.

A new guard swam up to greet the entourage. She barked a few new orders, and the group switched course. Instead of continuing down the hallway to the double doors that concealed the throne room, they turned back around and retraced their path. Past the portraits of Reanna's ancestors on the wall; past the chandeliers fashioned out of coral. Columns of seashells decorated alabaster hallways.

Reanna swallowed as they passed the golden doors engraved with starfish and seahorses—the grand ballroom. The forbidden, sacred sanctuary that her younger self had wanted to visit so badly.

The group swam through a wide hole in the ceiling at the end of the hallway to the second story.

Reanna trembled. She wanted to protest, wanted to beg them not to take her here. She didn't want to be the little princess trapped in her room again. She clawed at the ice they'd use to gag her, but every time she tried to reach out with her own magic and melt it, the soldiers overpowered her.

The hallway ended at her old bedroom with its stately wooden doors carved and painted to resemble large coral formations. Giant pearls functioned as the doorknobs and decorated the rest of the door as well. The soldiers threw open the doors and dragged Reanna inside. One of them froze over the window that Reanna had used as an escape route before. Another clucked like a dolphin and made the rest of the soldiers laugh.

So they *did* remember her.

They dumped her, still shackled, on the floor and slammed the doors behind them as they left.

Reanna quivered.

The tiny, tiny bit of power she'd tried to reclaim from her mother had been ripped away. Tears leaked from her eyes; the saltwater swept them away immediately, but the act of crying carried some sort of cathartic relief.

In the end, her sacrifice hadn't earned them anything. Rosaelina and Maesie—dead. Laeserno, Gregory, and Whisper—who knew. Probably dead since Violante hadn't come to escort Reanna. And Reanna…trapped, just like her six-year-old self.

At least with the Atlanteans out of the room, Reanna could try to melt the ice that kept her bound. She clawed at it and willed her fingers to be hot, to grow hotter—

She growled. The tips of her fingers turned a bright red as they overheated. Her prize for her experiment: ten little indents where her fingers had melted the ice, but not one good thing those marks could do for her.

This had to be some kind of psychological torture method. Just another way for Arana to assert her dominance over her daughter. To remind Reanna who was queen and who was a runaway—

A very, very bad girl.

Reanna closed her eyes to block out the scenes of childhood: the one toy chest she'd hand-painted and decorated with starfish. The salmon-colored walls. The tiny bed crafted to resemble a hippocampus.

The closet on the far-left corner, where Reanna had endured many an awful night locked up and frozen.

She sniffled. No matter how many scenarios she ran through in her head, she couldn't think of anything. She'd tried to take matters into her own hands and failed miserably.

She had nothing to do but think. Philosophize.

Ugh. Times like these were when people typically made crazy bargains with the air, right?

So…Composer. I don't know if You're anything more than a myth—and…I'm still mad at You, but Gregory seems to be a favorite of Yours since You let him draw from your magic, so I hope he can give me a good reference, or whatever.

Did she close her eyes? Open them? And could the Composer really read her mind, or was she just directing her inner monologue toward herself?

Then again, You didn't help Greg that last time. But You possibly did with Laile…unless that was just Gregory's natural talent or some other spirit he called upon. I don't really know. I'm new to this whole magic stuff.

But—if You're really here, could You maybe, I don't know, melt my bonds? Let me get free? Or strike my mother—no, Arana—down with a sudden massive heart attack? Could I get that lucky?

Reanna hoped her specific word usage wouldn't leave any room for error—she had visions of evil genies laughing as they corrupted the wishes of their—*wish-ees?*—whatever the term happened to be. She'd been very specific on which mother she wanted to be struck down. If the Composer were real, He would answer her prayer just as she had asked. Then, maybe, Reanna might start to believe in Him. After all…it would be a miracle, right?

She stewed for a few more minutes. Her skin burned now—not from heat but from ice. She knew from experience that it took a lot for a mermaid to get hypothermia; some merfolk even lived up in the northern waters, where they tamed iceberg dragons. But Reanna was neither a northern mermaid nor accustomed to those temperatures. She might not get hypothermia, but frostnip or mild frostbite were real possibilities.

She tried to melt the ice around her mouth again but earned similar results. Her fingers throbbed, and she had to stop before she caused real damage to herself.

Of course.

Now would be a *real* swell time for the Composer to send that miracle.

Peace.

Shark fins. That song again. Things were about to go even *more* downhill, weren't they?

The door creaked open.

Reanna held her breath as Violante swam in. The blood from the battlefield had washed off in the ocean currents, but that didn't make her any less frightening.

"Oh, Reanna." Violante sighed. So she'd received the Siren's Kiss, too, or else she wouldn't have been able to function underwater…

Reanna squirmed and flapped her fins in a desperate attempt to get away from her enemy. Smirking, the sorceress drifted over—and stomped her foot right on Reanna's fluke.

Reanna winced, unable to scream, as Violante ground her heel into the fluke.

"Don't wriggle," Violante said. "Or I'll do to you what I did to that other little elf. You remember, don't you? What you made me do?" Spurts of black magic appeared between Violante's fingers.

Reanna would have bleated if the guards hadn't muffled her.

Violante crouched down. She traced her long fingernails down Reanna's scales; Reanna's breath came in panicked hitches.

Gregory. Laeserno. Whisper. All the elves. What had happened to them? If Violante had come *here*, did that mean the battle had ended?

"You cost me some good test subjects today." Violante shook her head. "I wonder what your mother will say when I tell her how disobedient you've been?"

Reanna shook her head. Her skin grew colder where the ice rested against her, and she started to shiver.

How stupid had she been to try and call on the Composer? She'd dared to form one prayer, and Violante had materialized. He'd made His disinterest in her very clear throughout her life. Nobody had saved her as a little girl, nobody had kept her adopted parents from divorcing, and nobody had stopped the atrocities of the concentration camp.

Just like no one would save her now.

Violante reached out and touched Reanna's forehead with her nail. "*Famtroire*," Violante whispered.

Reanna shuddered and felt her body give way.

When she opened her eyes again, the world felt and looked different. White fog rolled around in misty swirls, obscuring a black, empty world.

"Hello?" Reanna whispered. She took a step forward and realized that, wherever Violante had sent her, Reanna's tail had disappeared alongside the ice that hadn't allowed her to speak. "Hello?"

"Welcome to your soul, Reanna." Violante chuckled as she stepped out of the mist.

CHAPTER 50

REANNA

GAIA: REANNA'S SOUL

Violante's footsteps reverberated throughout the otherwise empty landscape of Reanna's soul.

Reanna took a step back and tripped over her own tennis shoes. She fell, but in this strange world, she didn't register any physical pain. She just collided with the unnerving whiteness beneath her as though it was solid. Black mist swept over her legs as Violante crept closer.

"Where are my friends?" Reanna asked. She shifted to her knees but didn't rise. "What did you do with them?"

"If you're so worried, you shouldn't have run off and left them. Just like you ran off and left your mother so distraught…even though all you'd ever done before that was cause her anguish and heartbreak." Violante paused a few steps out of reach. "It seems like you can never quite stop being selfish, can you?"

Reanna shook her head and clenched her eyes shut. "No. No—it wasn't selfish. I—I was trying to *help*—"

"Hmm. All you ever try and do is help, isn't it? And look where it gets us." Violante held out her hand and muttered a spell that sounded harsh to Reanna's ears. The words all blurred together, but the mist churned violently until it formed a picture from back on Earth. It looked like a grainy home video.

A window right into the life of young Reanna as she'd watched her adopted father, Alan, bicker with Isabella.

Present-day Reanna grasped at her wrist and squeezed. "I don't want to watch this."

No sound came through, but it didn't have to. Reanna could still hear the angry voices, the snapping words, the yelling.

Violante reached into the memory. The picture rippled as she jerked the younger version of Reanna out. The new, child, version of Reanna buried her face in her hands.

"What did you want to do when you ran away? Were you trying to *help* that family?" Violante asked. "You caused your mother so much heartache and ran away, but you just repeated the process with your new family, didn't you?" Violante snickered as she regarded the scene. Alan stormed out of the house and slammed the door behind him while Isabella tried to hide the tears on her face from her daughters.

Younger-Reanna's shoulders quivered. She lowered her hands and said with a monotone inflection, "But I didn't help anything. I caused their breakup." Her dull, pupil-less eyes flickered up to meet current Reanna's. "*You* caused their breakup."

Reanna swallowed. "I didn't mean to," she whispered.

"You never *mean* to hurt anyone, but you do." Younger-Reanna pointed an accusing finger at her modern-day counterpart. "No one ever says it out loud, but you know they blame you. It doesn't take a brain surgeon to piece together the puzzle pieces. Mom and Dad were happy when they first got married and when they had Tara. But then we come along—*you* come along—and it doesn't take

402

more than four years for everything to collapse." Tears streamed down Younger-Reanna's cheeks, but her words remained acerbic. A mixture of grief and anger that Present-Reanna recognized all too well. "We came along, and all of the sudden, Dad needs *Jade* to be happy again."

"I—" Reanna cut off her own excuse. The past version of herself held too much power, too much influence.

Too much truth—or what seemed like truth.

Guilt twisted around in her stomach—the same guilt she'd had since her father walked away; the same guilt she'd carried for as long as she'd watched her mom struggle as a single parent.

Violante flicked her fingers in midair as though she might be flipping the pages of a scrapbook, but Reanna couldn't see anything. Not until Violante's eyes lit up. "Oh, here's a nice one."

Reanna winced as the memory faded from her father leaving to one of Isabella, crying and screaming, her face red.

Reanna could place this one, too.

"No, *please!*" Her voice came out in a panicked screech. "I don't want to watch this!" She climbed to her feet, but the silent memory played on. The night that the guilt had almost dragged Reanna down to the pits. The guilt of Alan's abandonment, the guilt of disappointing Arana...

The memory-Reanna clutched a razor blade in her hand and brought it down against her wrist. Again and again, until Isabella stormed into the bathroom—Reanna had sworn she'd locked the door at the time, but she must have forgotten—and found her daughter.

Reanna could read her mother's lips on the screen: "*What on earth do you think you're doing, Reanna?*"

And Violante reached into that memory and pulled out another version of Reanna. A version with wrists decorated in crisscrossing wounds that bled in long rivulets.

"What's wrong with you?" Sixteen-year-old Reanna screamed. "Why do you always make such a mess of things? Even when you're trying to make amends, you just screw everything up!" She hurled a razor blade at Reanna. It sliced right into Present-Reanna's heart. Blood gushed from the wound and through Reanna's shirt. She grabbed at the injury, but the crimson liquid spurted out between her fingers. The hole refused to stop gushing, and all her attempts to stop the hemorrhaging resulted in more blood.

Sobs strangled Present-Reanna's throat.

"You should cry!" Sixteen-Year-Old-Reanna shrieked. She lunged for Reanna and brought her fists down on her counterpart's head. "You should *die* for what you put them through. Mom was *bawling* because of you. Because she had an emotional *freak* for a daughter!" The blows came harder and harder. "Who does that? Who cuts themselves so badly they need therapy? Weird emo kids like *you.*"

Reanna covered her left wrist with trembling, blood-stained hands. The true, physical scars had faded—nothing more than barely-there and easy-to-hide white lines that reminded her of a history she'd rather forget. And her therapy—well, it had helped, some...but it hadn't fixed everything. How could it, when Reanna could never tell someone from Earth about her mermaid problems?

"You hurt Mom," Sixteen-Year-Old-Reanna hissed. "I bet she wishes she'd never had a daughter like you. Someone who's so...so...*emotionally volatile* that they would do that."

Reanna winced. The words pierced deep into her chest and ripped off the barely-healed scabs on her heart. More versions of her at different ages stepped out of the mist, and memories crowded around her. From childhood to the present, each of them taunted Reanna with the insults that had wounded her time and time again.

Emotionally volatile.

You're so sensitive, Reanna.

Why do you always act like this?

What's wrong with you?

Searing pain ripped through Reanna's heart and wrist as the comments she'd incurred from Arana slammed against her psyche. They tore open her scars even deeper than the original injuries. She dropped to her knees, her mouth open in silent agony.

Blood cascaded down her hand from a deep slice on her wrist. No—*no*. She hadn't done that. She hadn't cut since the day Isabella had found her over a year ago. She'd promised. And she couldn't break a promise to Isabella; she couldn't add any more hurt to the woman she loved more than anything.

Reanna screamed as she stared at her bloody palms. She rubbed them against her pants, against the white *somethingness* beneath her, but the blood wouldn't come off.

"I didn't do this!" she shrieked. "I didn't!"

Violante slunk over and held Reanna's wrist up so they could both see the cut, which was so deep that Reanna swore she might have seen tendons and muscles. "What a bad girl, Reanna," Violante whispered. "What an awfully bad girl."

The other versions of Reanna echoed the sentiment like awful marionettes under Violante's control, their voices synchronized and flat. More memories flashed behind Violante's head. All of Reanna's mistakes, all of her insecurities…her whole *soul* seemed laid bare before Violante's prying eyes in grainy squares of memory-TV-boxes that swirled around the room.

Violante chuckled, but Reanna couldn't tell which scene the sorceress found humorous. "Look at all these broken memories. No one has ever loved you enough to stick around, have they? The people that have…they just pity you or are stuck with you until you're eighteen—like that woman you call your mother." The pictures spun faster now in a nauseating display of recollections. Violante seemed to absorb them all, and that wicked smile only grew bigger. "You're just a disappointing failure. Like today with the elves. That little girl and her mother—you killed them."

Reanna squeezed her eyes shut, but she couldn't block out the image of Rosaelina's bloodied corpse.

Another one of the Reannas—one that looked more like Present-Reanna—stepped forward. "How do you think *you're* supposed to overcome Arana and Violante? You're powerless. Worthless. You think you can do anything?"

Reanna whimpered.

The Newer-Reanna circled Present-Reanna like a vulture ready to feast on a bleeding carcass. "All you do is make a mess of things, Reanna. If only you weren't born, Laeserno's poor daughter, Maesie, would still be alive."

Another memory flashed; this one was more recent than the others and lacked the grainy quality. In it, the Atlanteans dragged out Maesie, who looked like nothing more than a bundle of bones.

"You couldn't do anything to stop it," Newer-Reanna said. "Just like you can't do anything to stop Violante now. She could trap you in your mind forever, and you'd never get out."

Heat burned Reanna's face. "Well, excuse me. I'm not some all-powerful Composer. You know who you should be mad at? Him, not me! He's the one that has all the power to stop these atrocities. Maesie didn't deserve to die at such a young age, but you know who you should take it up with? The Composer, not me!" The blood on Reanna's chest and arm boiled and burst. Her teeth clenched. Maesie could have been anything when she grew up—she shouldn't have been reduced to a tiny corpse. Not when she had so many choices and mistakes and loves and heartbreaks and adventures in front of her.

What had been her favorite color? What memory did she think of when she was lonely? Her dreams? What had her laugh been like—

"The Composer?" Violante laughed. "Please, what a paltry spirit. I assure you…I can introduce you to *much* more powerful beings." The sorceress leaned in until her lips were right by Reanna's ear. "They could even teach you how to get out of this. But go ahead. Call on your Composer once again. I'm sure He'll answer this time, won't He?"

Reanna choked on a sob. "Why would I even bother?"

A puddle of blood soaked the floor where she sat on her knees. The other versions of herself clawed at her, pulled her hair, beat at her face. They spit at her, drove the razor blade deeper into her heart, tugged at the wound on her wrist.

Pain. Excruciating, never-ending pain. She was trapped in her mind without any hope of salvation.

"Call on your Composer, Reanna," Violante purred. "Go ahead. If you know so much about Him, so much about His magic, call on Him. Let's see what He can do against *me*."

Who even *was* the Composer?

The Composer, the God she'd learned about back on Earth—whether they were one and the same or two unreliable, unrelated deities, she didn't know or understand them. Back when Alan was still around, the Cooks would go to church maybe once a month or every two months. They'd gone to the church where Trevor's dad preached—where Reanna's rivalry with Trevor started when he beaned her in the head with a water balloon after she'd twisted her ankle.

Back then, back when Reanna was gullible and new to everything on Earth, the concept of God had been fascinating. She'd enjoyed the little stories and getting the snacks. Everything about life on Earth, life with legs, seemed like a novelty.

The issue came when she tried to trust an imaginary figment like God.

Regardless of whether or not the Composer and God were the same or two separate beings like with Greek and Roman mythology—it all boiled down to the same end.

There was no Composer. There was no God.

No one to end this torture.

"In this world, you have to look out for yourself." Violante moved from one ear to the other, and Reanna twitched and shuddered as the sorceress' hot breath grazed her neck. "You can't depend on anyone to save a wretch like you."

Despite herself, Reanna nodded. Her old defenses bubbled to the surface again. It was the only way she knew how to cope, the only way to survive: don't give out love and trust freely. Don't hope. She had to expect the worst so she could be pleasantly surprised and didn't have to experience even more pain when something inevitably fell through.

Tears streamed harder down Reanna's face; she felt the dark presence of fear loom over her. The landscape beneath her feet cracked. The other versions of herself dragged her down into the abyss, and she screamed. Fear weighed her down and cut off her air—or maybe that was just the work of the legion of Reannas.

Even if she could swim away from Arana, Violante, Atlantis, and all of the wickedness here, Reanna couldn't run away from the trap of her own mind.

"*Violante.*" A sharp voice entered the mindscape, though a third person didn't appear.

Violante jerked away and swore under her breath. Her mental self disappeared, and the world rippled. The hewn ground stitched itself back together again with a loud *snap*. Reanna collapsed face-first into a puddle of her own blood, alone. Her multiples had disappeared with Violante, the wounds they'd left behind the only proof they'd even existed at all in this black-and-white world.

From outside the mindscape, Reanna heard hushed whispers, but she was unable to make them out.

Until one voice rang out stronger than the other. "I told you—I wanted to be the first one to see my daughter. She's been gone so very long."

Reanna swayed as sickness swept over her. She wanted to puke. *That voice.*

The one that haunted her childhood, her nightmares, her mind.

Arana.

Reanna's mindscape body thudded to the ground. When she opened her eyes back in her childhood bedroom, Arana loomed in front of her.

CHAPTER 51

REANNA

GAIA: ATLANTIS

Reanna's body tensed as her mother swam toward her. No matter how much time had passed, she couldn't forget her childhood. Her fear. Her anxious heart skittered and sent cold blood through her veins. Which version of Arana was this? Would she be pleased to have her daughter back? Infuriated Reanna ran away to begin with?

Both?

Arana glared at Violante and swam past the sorceress. Reanna's heart tried to run away, only to find that it was locked into place inside her chest. She attempted to scream, but, back in reality, the gag around her mouth hadn't melted completely. Instead, she just made some awful muffled noises as she scooted away from her mother.

Their eyes met.

Even though Arana neared—what? something near forty, though Reanna felt ashamed she didn't know her own mother's age—she looked perfect. Streaks as silver as her moonlight-colored tail were woven throughout her loose curls. Her face looked older and even sterner, but no one could overlook the deep beauty in her features. Her high cheekbones, her rounded, Disney-princess-like face…even her gray-green eyes—if one took away the fact that they were somewhat cold and unflinching—were all so glamorous. She reminded Reanna of intimidatingly beautiful black-and-white movie starlets.

"Hello, Reanna dear. It's been a long time, hasn't it?" Arana's voice was every bit as regal as Reanna remembered it. "How have you been?"

Reanna grunted and thrashed her shackled tail.

"Oh, of course." Arana melted the gag away from Reanna's mouth, though the queen left all the other restraints intact. "There. Now, tell me. How have you been?"

Reanna glared at her mother. "Pretty awful since you had me kidnapped and put all my new friends in danger, if you have to know."

Arana went to lounge on the bed. Reanna swiveled around to stare at her mother—and to make sure the queen didn't intend to stab a knife in her daughter's back.

"Sorry if Violante bothered you." Arana turned a pointed look to her sorceress. Violante smiled in return and held up a vial of—

Reanna furrowed her brow. Where had Violante gotten a vial of blood?

Unless…

Reanna glanced at her wrists. Sure enough, she spied a thin scratch there, though it wasn't nearly as deep as it had been in the mindscape. It had mostly stopped bleeding now, but Violante had collected enough to fill a thumb-sized vial.

"I'll see myself out now. I know you and mummy have a lot to catch up on." Violante smirked and half-swam, half-walked out of the room.

"Why did she take my blood?" Reanna snapped. "What do you need it for?"

Arana pursed her lips. "You know Violante's little experiments. She dabbles in several things."

"I don't want to be one of her little experiments." Heat flushed Reanna's face.

Arana leaned forward and traced a long nail over Reanna's cheekbones. Common sense told Reanna to jerk away, but she hesitated, and Arana tucked Reanna's curls behind her ear. "You are much more than an experiment to me, Reanna. Welcome home."

"This is not my home," Reanna snarled. "This is my torture chamber." She yanked her head away and growled like a rabid dog.

"Now, really. Is that the way a princess should behave?"

Reanna scoffed. The question ignited a fire inside her that had smoldered for quite some time. "I haven't been a princess in so long, I've started to forget. Let me see…a princess…that's the thing that cries herself to sleep every night, isn't it? The thing that gets slapped and pushed around for stepping out of line? I must admit, Disney's got it all wrong."

"Who's Disney? One of your little Earth friends? Well, no mind. I can see you're just as dramatic as ever." Arana sighed. "Nothing has changed since you were a child. You always made up such awful tales and twisted everything I did to make me seem so evil. You'd complain all the time about me to anyone who would listen."

"I don't have to make up anything. We're in a war, Mother. Or have you noticed that you've replaced your self-portraits with the bodies of malnourished elves?" Reanna propped herself up and tried to remind herself to be objective in the situation. But still, the small, subjective part of her pondered the truth of Arana's words. Could it possibly be that Reanna's childhood hadn't been that bad? Could Reanna just be the one at fault here—a melodramatic, whiny, insolent brat who could never appreciate what others did for her?

Arana sighed. "A war that you caused. You don't understand the desperation a mother feels when she's lost her child." She lowered herself off the bed and reached for Reanna's cheeks once more. The queen's touch almost seemed delicate as she ran one thumb across Reanna's lips and jaw. "Or do you think that my love for you disappears because you've disobeyed me for so long? A mother's love isn't that fickle, Reanna."

Reanna's lips twitched. She didn't know whether or not she felt abject fear, horror, and loathing or if part of her, deep down inside, liked her mother's feather-light touch.

Maybe both. "I…" Reanna's voice faltered.

Maybe Arana had changed.

No—the elves outside—Rosaelina, Maesie—

"I dislike this affair with the elves, but they knew where you were and how to get to you. People distrust us, Reanna. They distrust us because of our tails, because we are different—more powerful than them." Arana brushed her fingernails over Reanna's nose. "They don't understand our ways, and they fear us. They fear us because our ancestor Pallas once sank Atlantis into the ground, but if you knew the truth, you would agree with Pallas."

Reanna blinked. Shivered. "I don't…"

"Her father intended to sell her off like a bargaining chip, all to keep financial stability and trade routes open. And when Pallas protested, her betrothed raped her. In her anger, she sank Atlantis underneath the waves." Arana's face turned steely. "And that's only a small sliver of the damage men do to our society. There are things you cannot know, things you cannot comprehend, about me, about our family, until the time comes for you to take the throne."

"That—that doesn't make enslaving men—or elves—right."

"There are times when a ruler has to make difficult decisions. If you knew everything I did, if you were in my position, you would understand as well." Arana's smile didn't seem to reach her eyes.

Reanna glanced away, but Arana guided Reanna's chin so that they could stare at each other. "Look at me, darling. This is very important. Please look at me when I'm speaking to you."

Reanna nodded. She swallowed and focused on the tip of Arana's nose.

"If you think I'm wrong, that I'm the monster you've created in your mind, I think I have one person who could tell you the truth." Arana lifted her face and called to the door, "Send in my advisor."

Reanna braced herself for Violante to enter—

Only to audibly gasp when a tall brunette woman—elegant despite the fact she had no tail—swam into the room.

"Shaesia?" Reanna squeaked. Her eyes locked with Shaesia's chestnut ones.

"Hello, Reanna."

"But…" The small amount of trust Reanna had built inside herself crumbled. It was as though her inner stability had been built with Jenga tiles—and somebody had just yanked out the bottom of the pile.

She'd had so many tiles removed over the years. Her whole heart felt full of holes, empty spaces where the people—the building blocks of her Jenga tower—had up and removed themselves.

"No. No—you—I've been to your house! You fought Violante. We saw the—the stuff on the floor, the magic!" Reanna bleated. "You wouldn't—you—"

This couldn't happen. Reanna needed Shaesia on their side. Shaesia had to read the note, to help Reanna get a portal open for that strange Adam boy—

To get free.

"You told me a very twisted version of your mother. Of course I fought when she came to retrieve me." Shaesia's voice sounded just as cold as the manacles that still dug into Reanna's wrists. "But once

I arrived here, and she told me the full story... I understand now why she needs you. She has big plans for you, Reanna. You should be grateful for the part your mother has chosen for you to play in Atlantis' history."

Reanna clutched at her chest. The tower inside her heart crumbled, and she felt each weighty blow. "Did you tell her where I was?"

"I did not know where you were besides Earth. I could not tell her where you were." Shaesia tucked her hands behind her back. She stood straight and stiff, her eyes hard. "So your mother had to turn to some darker forces. Some malevolent spirits are able to cross the borders of dimensions, unlike other locating spells."

Reanna shuddered. "But—the elves. You can't possibly approve of what's going on!"

"Arana and I have our differences, but we at least have a common goal: reuniting you with your mother. There were many things you failed to inform me of when I sent you to Earth, and I strived to keep my kind safe during our search for you."

Arana chuckled. Shaesia didn't move.

Reanna's spirit buckled.

"You see?" Arana twisted one of Reanna's wet curls around a finger. "When people come to understand my side of the story, they realize how insensible you really are. Come now. Don't you think it's time to end your childish temper tantrum and work with me? Work with Shaesia, the elf you love so much? I know you've never been able to admit when you've done something wrong, but Shaesia and I will welcome you back with open arms."

"I—I—" Reanna stuttered.

"Your Majesty." Shaesia stepped forward. "Maybe I should discuss this with Reanna in private. I think she may be a smidgen more cooperative if she hears the truth from me."

Arana sighed and flipped her tail to lift herself off the floor. "Very well. I'll wait outside the door." She eyed Reanna and offered another spine-tingling smile. "I hope you'll take what Shaesia says to heart." She swam out of the room, and the door clicked shut behind her.

Both Reanna and Shaesia waited. One of the many bad things about having a mermaid for a mother was the fact that Reanna had no way to gauge if someone walked away. At least with a human parent, she could listen for the retreating footsteps.

"How could you?" Finally, Reanna had to break the silence. Who cared if her mother listened in—Reanna wouldn't say anything she didn't dare say to Arana face-to-face. "Did Violante put some kind of mind control on you? How could you possibly throw your lot in with Arana?"

For the first time, Shaesia's eyes seemed to soften. She knelt down and crossed her arms on her lap. "Reanna…" Shaesia sighed. "Your mother has very big plans for you. Do you understand?"

"I don't care what her plans are!" Reanna shook with frustration. "I don't care! She's letting all these elves be tortured—she let Laeserno's wife and child be murdered—so many more—I can't believe you're okay with all this!"

"Calm yourself," Shaesia murmured. She glanced toward the door and tapped her fingers against her knee. "Reanna, listen to me. Please." Shaesia leaned in closer. "I know you think you did the right thing, but you did a very wrong thing."

"When? Trusting you?" Reanna snorted. "Tell me about it."

"Whoever convinced you that you had to stop everything was wrong. You do not have to stop everything. People want to take care of you." Shaesia reached for Reanna's cheek. Reanna jerked away, and the elf withdrew. "I want to take care of you."

"How? By giving me right back to my mother?"

"I know you miss your life on Earth—your life with Isabella, Tara, your friends from school, that…that boy from school, Trevor."

"Trevor? I don't miss him, I—" Reanna stopped and only barely caught herself before she sucked in a breath.

She'd never mentioned the names of her mother, sister, or Trevor to anyone in Gaia.

How could Shaesia know? She'd said she had no idea where Reanna was hiding, which was why Arana had to resort to some dark methods or whatever.

"I don't miss him," Reanna mumbled. She glanced toward the door, her brow furrowed. "At all. But I do miss my mom. My sister."

"I know that you would do anything to get back to them, but I implore you, do not do anything rash." Shaesia seemed to reach for her bellybutton—but her hand disappeared.

Reanna's eyes widened. A fairy skirt. Why did Shaesia have on a fairy skirt?

With her still-visible hand, Shaesia put one finger against her lips.

Half of the miniature versions of Reanna that lurked inside her brain all paused and watched, debating among themselves whether or not they should start to rebuild the Jenga tower of trust. The other half scoured over the recent conversation to see if they might find something, any clue, as to a hidden meaning in the conversation.

Could Shaesia still be on Reanna's side after all this? Could the alliance with Arana be a huge hoax?

"Reanna, I need you to calm down." Shaesia continued to make the shushing motion. "Please, do not do anything rash. Your mother has plans for you, and you cannot carry them out if you hurt yourself."

Hurt herself? Reanna glanced down at her wrists as heat flushed her face. "I...I don't hurt myself. I mean, anymore."

Shaesia withdrew a large dagger from her fairy skirt and held it up to her lips. She whispered something low, and the blade began to glow.

Reanna opened her mouth, but Shaesia clamped her hand over it.

"Reanna, what—" Shaesia's voice became more frantic and high-pitched, and she shoved Reanna to the ground. "Stop! Stop—Reanna, please, calm yourself!"

Reanna flapped her tail and tried to get away, but Shaesia pinned her to the ground.

And plunged a dagger through Reanna's abdomen.

Reanna screamed.

Blood immediately tainted the water all around them and turned it a bright crimson. She writhed and clutched at her stomach, at the blade.

"No! Guards—guards!" Shaesia screamed. "Arana!"

Arana threw open the door. Reanna choked on her own blood, spit it into the currents that surrounded her. Pain ripped through her limbs. She couldn't breathe. Blood filled her nostrils, her mouth, everything, and her vision blurred.

"Your Majesty—she—she just killed herself!" Shaesia seemed borderline frantic now. Such a good actor. She'd gained Reanna's trust twice—only to betray her both times. "I tried to stop her—I know—I know nothing will work if you don't have her—the blood curse will destroy Atlantis—"

Reanna couldn't hear much more than that. Not only because of her failing senses but because Arana shrieked incoherently. The queen's hair snapped with electricity above her head, and her eyes glowed a bright gold.

The last word Reanna caught came from Shaesia: "Her *rukarall*!"

That was a funny spell name...Reanna had never heard of that before. Her head lolled back.

Arana moved in front of Reanna's fading vision. The queen's lips moved, her eyes glowed, and she looked like some kind of supervillain from the movies. Or…maybe not.

Reanna's thoughts became less and less coherent.

Arana grabbed Reanna and cradled her like an infant.

How ironic.

Arana had never held her daughter that long before.

PART VIII

CHAPTER 52

TREVOR

EARTH: PANAMA CITY, FLORIDA

Trevor didn't know what woke him up in the middle of the night. Only the fact that he knew somewhere, something had shifted. It was like the hardest piece of a puzzle had just slipped into place and made everything else obvious. Honestly, it was really, really…

Unsettling.

He rubbed his hand over his face and reached for his phone. It buzzed with ten new messages. He furrowed his brow. He may have been popular at school, but not 5:00 a.m.-booty- call-popular. He unlocked his phone.

Every single message came from Adam.

Ah. That made more sense.

The texts were a discombobulated mess, as if Adam's thoughts had poured out faster than his thumbs could type them out. *It's been too long*, the first one said. *For the portal, I meant. I wanted it to be open sooner.* Trevor slid down to the next one. *I'm really worried.*

I can't stop thinking about Reanna.

She's probably scared. Don't you think?

Sorry I'm up. I had too much caffeine, I think.

My dad doesn't usually let me have caffeine after eight. He's pretty smart. You should remember that.

Not that my dad is smart, but about the caffeine thing. You just probably shouldn't have caffeine after eight either.

I hope they get my message soon.

Did you feel that?

The last message had come right as Trevor had stirred. He groaned. The text probably woke him up in the first place.

But he had to admit there was something different. Hesitantly, he erased the first snappy reply he was going to send and decided on, **Yeah. I did. What was it?**

Adam's reply was instantaneous but came in short spurts. *Powerful magic.*

Sometimes it leaks across.

Some—not all—natural disasters are from powerful magic being unleashed in Gaia. After that, there's sometimes residue that can be found.

The text ended there, but just as Trevor tried to reply, Adam began to type again.

I bet there's all kinds of residue. Maybe even enough to open a portal all the way to Gaia.

Trevor tapped out his response. **What about all those stipulations you said had to be in place? And wasn't there some crazy mumbo-jumbo about elves or fairies or something? Just a reminder...it's still weird.**

Adam's next response took so long to get that Trevor almost fell asleep waiting for it.

Gee, I was wondering when the next insult would come. Right on time. It's the elves, by the way. Only the elves can manipulate portals, and even they have special times of the month, and the rules are way too complicated to explain over texting. But I think that was elven magic. Something is happening in Gaia, and if we can harness it, we can hitch a ride on it all the way there. I've seen it before. That's how some Gaians get to Earth, even when the portal is closed. And how some people from this world get to Gaia. The Bermuda Triangle is a hotbed for aftershocks and residues of Gaian magic.

So...you're saying Amelia Earhart... As soon as Trevor sent his question into cyberspace, he knew he'd regret it. Adam would get a big head if he so much as *thought* Trevor believed this crap. Still, it would be pretty cool if...

Let's just say there is a woman named Amelia Heart-of-Air in Gaia who went down in history as one of the greatest military generals the country of Gyranius ever had, who also stood up for werewolf rights.

Trevor snorted. Too bad *that* would never be included in Earth's history books. Stuff like that might actually make history interesting. He yawned and put his cell phone back on the table. The rest of the magic talk could wait until the morning.

Adam, though, apparently had other ideas...none of them as good as sleeping. Trevor's phone lit up, and after five more texts, he angrily snatched it off the nightstand again.

Adam had sent the same message over and over: *I'm going to hunt down a portal. Might be able to find Reanna tonight. Wanna come?*

So Reanna had just become more important than sleep.

How ridiculous.

Still, Trevor threw off his covers and pulled on an oversized gray hoodie, though he left his plaid pajama pants on. Even if they found Reanna, she wasn't someone worth dressing up for, and if they didn't, he could crawl back into bed that much easier.

He sent off one last text: ***Meet me on my porch.***

Trevor crept past his father's room and unlocked the main door. He managed to make it outside without bringing down Paul's wrath upon him—perfect. In fact, Trevor felt so relieved he decided he would reward himself with a nap. He stretched out on the lawn chair and dozed off until someone shook him awake.

"Hmm?" he mumbled through a yawn.

"Let's go."

Adam didn't say anything else but yanked Trevor up. The younger boy darted down the steps while Trevor stumbled his way down and nearly tripped on his own two feet.

"So, how are you going to find these magical wormholes of leftover currents? Or whatever junk it is." Trevor yawned for the second time. His words slurred together a little bit, and he stuffed his hands into the front of his sweatshirt so they wouldn't go numb.

"With magnets. They—I mean, the magical wormholes—will be magnetized, which means that they'll either repel us or attract our magnets, depending on whether they have a positive or negative energy—either one will work. So either our magnets won't be able to go near the leftover magic, or they'll be so drawn to it that nothing we do will stop it. Simple." Adam shrugged.

Trevor rubbed his face. Sure—simple. Because whoever thought interdimensional travel was hard?

Adam offered Trevor a regular horseshoe magnet, probably one of the same ones he had used to make his letter disappear. Then he took out another one for himself and began to sweep the area as though his magnet was a metal detector.

"So…you expect to cover the whole city in a few hours?" Trevor asked.

"Something like that." Adam reached into his pocket and gave Trevor a walkie-talkie. "We'll split up. Stay on channel three. If you find something, let me know. Hopefully one of us will run into some magic before morning is over."

Trevor rolled his eyes but was too tired to think of a magic-based wisecrack. So instead, he reverted to a simple complaint. "People are going to call the cops. They'll complain about our kooky behavior."

"So what if they do? It's perfectly legal to walk around with a magnet at five in the morning." Adam continued to swing his magnet around. If he'd had a tinfoil hat, he could have easily passed for a slightly unhinged alien hunter on a TV show.

"But it's *weird*!" Trevor protested.

"They can't arrest people for being weird!" Adam raced down the first street he saw, his magnet held out in front of him. Trevor rolled his eyes and headed to the opposite end of town.

Just in case, though, he pulled up his shirt's hood, making sure he couldn't be recognized by cops, residents, and potential dates.

CHAPTER 53

ADAM

EARTH: PANAMA CITY, FLORIDA

Adam couldn't get the anxious feeling out of his gut. He knew Trevor felt it too or else he never would have agreed to their midnight excursion. Quite possibly, Trevor might also suspect the cause, too—magic.

Others who didn't understand the concept of magic might have labeled the feeling as something more everyday: déjà vu, dread, excitement, indigestion. All of those were common excuses created by people who had never seen a portal, but Adam knew the truth. That aftershock—something *big* had gone down.

And, oh, how he hoped it didn't mean the worst for Reanna.

Before the shockwave, Adam had been sure that Reanna still lived. It was like he could feel her, and his hope kept her alive. But after the magic rushed in, so potent that it took his breath away for a moment, a hard ball of worry settled in the pit of his stomach and wouldn't dissolve. Whatever had occurred—whatever had shifted—he couldn't shake the gnawing in his stomach that *something* had happened to Reanna.

His phone buzzed in his pocket.

Lily.

You're okay, right? I tried to get off early and they wouldn't let me go. I swear. If it wouldn't give us away, I'd freeze my boss right now and not feel any guilt.

Speaking of guilt… *Yeah. I'm fine. It woke me up, too.*

Lily's response came after a few seconds. *Stay out of trouble or I will hunt you down and kill you myself. You know I will. They could be looking for us.*

Adam puffed his cheeks out, tapped out several responses, and erased them all before he decided what to say back—besides, *Sorry ahead of time for doing exactly what you're warning me not to do. I know, I know.*

There. Technically, he *did* know what his sister wanted him to do.

He just didn't have to do it.

No. He *couldn't* do it—not until he knew that Reanna was okay. That time and space hadn't been completely thrown off its axis.

But even after an hour, he couldn't get the heavy boulder of *nothingness* off his chest, and his "great" idea was turning out to be a monumental failure. He couldn't find any traces of residual magic big enough to open a portal. The sun peeked over the horizon while the sky lightened from black to a navy blue.

The urgency inside of Adam almost suffocated him. How much time had he wasted? He couldn't let the residue's potency evaporate before he found it. The ramifications of losing this chance…suffice to say, it didn't help subdue the overwhelming panic choking him from the inside out.

Adam doubled his speed and scoured several more blocks…until a few pink smears appeared on the horizon. The birds chirped, and he saw a handful of people greet the morning from their porches—people who no doubt wondered what he was doing in their yards.

And Adam still had nothing to show for his late-night goose chase except a bigger sense of loss and heartache.

"Stupid! What made me think that I could do this?" He put his hands behind his back and turned in a circle. "I'm an *idiot*! I can't change anything or help anyone—"

He launched the magnet toward the beach—

And then fell flat on his face to dodge the magnet as it popped right back at him. It had repelled from some strong force on the beach like a bullet from a shotgun and flown right over his head.

Adam dusted bits of loose gravel off his palms, but even the pain from the drop couldn't wipe the grin off his face. He reached into his jacket pocket for the walkie-talkie and announced into it, "Trevor, I'm at…" He glanced at the street signs. "…Hollis Avenue and Rose. I found the portal."

Static filled the airways until Trevor replied, "I'm at Mercedes Avenue. I'll be there in probably thirty minutes or so. Give or take."

"Hurry, please!" As if that wasn't obvious enough.

Adam tucked his walkie-talkie away and went about placing the magnets in the right position, only around a much wider area than he had before—people-sized instead of just paper-sized. The beach was empty this early in the morning, but Adam knew if they didn't hurry, they risked running into morning joggers—and Adam didn't want to accidentally take any of *them* to Gaia with him.

He had just finished setting up the magnets when Trevor got there, panting, his face flushed from running.

"The magic isn't gone yet, is it?" Trevor asked between gulps of air. "You'll never believe the dogs I had to outrun to get here. Apparently, guard dogs don't like people trespassing in their territory, even if it's for a good reason."

Adam laughed and picked up a seashell from the sand. He took aim and threw it in the middle of the magnets, and, just like the letter had days before, it blinked out of existence—or at least, out of the world. Adam pumped his fist and let out a wild whoop.

"Look! Did you see that? Did you *see* that? We're not too late!" He bent over, gasping for breath but grinning. "I'm going through. You should probably think about coming if you want to see Reanna again."

"I don't care about seeing Reanna again," Trevor muttered. "I just want our swim team to have a shot at the State Championships or whatever the heck they're all worked up about."

"Don't worry, Trevor. I won't tell Reanna you have a conscience when we find her."

"Thanks. I've got a reputation to uphold, you know."

Adam only smirked.

He was so ready for this—not just for what waited on the other end but the anticipation of the journey itself. Portal travel was never easy—he knew by firsthand experience—but it always excited him, just like a roller coaster. The panicked, adrenaline-pumping rush wasn't something you could easily replicate at a Six Flags amusement park.

Still bent over, he wiped his sweaty palms on his knees and sprinted toward the portal. He leapt at the center of the magnets, arms outstretched, and the field sucked him up.

In his imagination, this portal-jerk was what a slushie must feel like as someone slurped it up a straw. The portal pulled the breath from his lungs; his stomach twisted. Before the pain could be called unbearable, though, the environment around him shifted, and he found himself in the middle of a clearing in a forest, flat on his back.

He'd knocked the wind out of himself, but he couldn't just stay on the ground and struggle lest he be crushed by Trevor. Adam rolled out of the way, just an inch or two, even though the pain intensified as he did so. He was nearly in tears by the time Trevor thumped down beside him.

They were both silent for a moment.

Then Trevor wheezed, "I take back everything I've ever said about you being crazy."

"Thanks."

Adam struggled to his feet. Instead of a reckless teenager riding a roller coaster, he now felt like a geriatric who could hardly get out of his nursing home bathtub. He rested his hands on his shins, doubled over, as if he were an arthritic man trying to hobble to his wheelchair for some relief.

Trevor sat on the ground, his forehead propped against his knees. He looked even worse than the arthritic man in the nursing home—he looked like a man who was already sealed in a coffin.

Several minutes passed before they could talk to each other again.

Trevor wheezed, coughed, and glanced around. "Where are we, exactly?"

"Not sure. Somewhere in Gaia. Somewhere where there was enough magic to direct the portal."

Trevor pushed himself up and moseyed around. He climbed over boulders and peeked into the forest surrounding the clearing. He seemed to think there was going to be something different about all the flora in Gaia.

"It's not going to eat you," Adam said. "It's just a regular old forest."

"Right! Because everything about this place is *regular*." Trevor scowled and kicked a pebble out of the way. He followed after it as if he intended to kick it again, but he never got the chance.

Instead, Trevor yelped when he found his stone and reeled backward. He promptly leaned over and lost whatever he had eaten recently, and Adam gagged watching him.

The initial disgust, though, gave way to perturbation a moment later. A worried sliver snaked through Adam's spine as he raced over to see the problem.

"Stay back!" Trevor called. He thrust out his hand to try to keep Adam away, but for one beautiful, blessed moment, Trevor's nausea had left him weaker than Adam.

Adam shoved Trevor backward and sent the older boy to the ground on his backside. But as soon as Adam saw what lurked there, he wished Trevor had been able to restrain him.

There, in the grass, lay Reanna, covered in blood.

With a knife in her stomach.

CHAPTER 54

TREVOR

GAIA: ???

Trevor's heart pounded; his head swam. He hated the lightheaded, is-this-real-life feeling in the pit of his stomach. But he hated seeing Reanna like this, her face ashen, her body covered in crimson stains, even more. Somehow, after all of Adam's theories had proven to be true, Trevor had started to expect—or at least, hope—Reanna would be alive. Even though his prediction had come true, his body physically ached.

He'd never hated being right before.

Meanwhile, tears glistened in Adam's eyes, and he kneeled next to Reanna's head. He sat with his hands in his lap, as if he didn't want to touch the corpse even if it was the girl he was head-over-heels for. Trevor wouldn't want to touch a corpse, either, no matter who it was.

After a minute, Adam whispered, "Let's…pull the knife out." He sniffled and wiped his eyes with his jacket sleeve.

"I'm not touching a dead body." Trevor shuddered and took a step back.

Adam shook his head. "Trevor—what—what if she's not dead? We have to check."

"Yeah? She looks pretty dead to me, and I'm not a mortician! I *don't* want to touch a dead body."

The boys bickered back and forth until Trevor came out victorious.

Adam sighed. He tugged at the hilt, and it slid out easily.

The blade was completely clean, without a speck of blood on it—even on the hilt.

"What the…" Trevor's voice trailed off.

Adam squinted at it. "What do you think this means?" He turned the knife around so that Trevor could see. An inscription was burned into the blade, small and cursive but still legible.

Or at least, legible to anyone who spoke Elvish.

Trevor groaned inside his head. He'd meant that to be another Tolkien reference, but in this twisted new reality, it really *could* be some Elvish language. He ran his hand over his face, his reply to Adam muffled. "It looks like gibberish to me. Although it might be Spanish."

Adam scrunched up his nose, which made him look like some sort of gender-swapped version of Samantha from *Bewitched*. "No…I think it's Latin."

After a short pause, Trevor commented, "How do you think that's pronounced?"

"Your guess is as good as mine."

Trevor cleared his throat and squinted at the delicate inscription. "Ego mail-dict two add sim-ill-is some-no more-Tim, in sil-vah con-vall-is don-ek all-e-quiss lect-Tito hawk in-script-to. Two-us vulner-eh-bus airy-ot sane-it-tur et two Volvo excite-toe. Two-us come tangerine—tan-gere—volun-tas audio Mia none-tea-um. Ego volun-tas semper—hey, like Semper Fi?—amo two sim-ill-is Mia adopt-a-bit in fill-ee-um."

Adam snickered. "Actually, I think my guess will probably be better than yours. Let me see." He repeated the phrase, sounding much more professional and less hackneyed than Trevor's pathetic attempt.

Trevor slapped him upside the head. "Well, if you're such a Latin professor, why didn't you just do that from the start?"

Adam smirked, and Trevor assumed the reasoning had something to do with pride and superiority, but Adam never got to verbalize that. The dagger began to glow a pale gold. The inscription flashed and sizzled before it disappeared from the blade. A loud gasp broke the boys' collective astonishment.

Reanna lurched upward, finishing a scream that must have died on her lips at the same time she did. She seemed to recover from her death—and stupor—before they could. "Where *am* I?"

CHAPTER 55

REANNA

GAIA: ELVEN GLEN, DASPIN

The worst part about some naps was that when you woke up from them, you didn't know where you had fallen asleep, let alone what millennium you were in. That was how Reanna felt when she woke up—just slightly better than she had after Laile and Gregory had removed the memory spell.

She stared at the boy on her right for at least a good minute before her mind finally got back from its vacation. "Trevor Spencer!" She blurted it out a little too fast—her silly brain must have still been trying to unpack or something—and forgot to sound nonchalant.

At the same time, the boy next to him whispered, "I'm Adam."

Reanna's brain refused to do work, so she ended up blurting out: "What are *you* doing here?" She intended the question for Trevor, but she realized a little too late that it could have been directed toward them both.

And, while she did truly feel annoyed, she couldn't help thinking her brain had stuffed too much vitriol into one sentence.

Trevor looked like she'd just slapped him across the cheek, and that poor boy—Adam? Why did that sound familiar? —blinked.

"You're not supposed to be alive!" Trevor flailed his arms in her general direction for emphasis, she supposed, though that wasn't really the outcome. "You were dead just a second ago!"

Reanna grunted. "So sorry to disappoint." She struggled to her feet—only to fall down as dizziness swept over her. She nearly slipped right back into the nap or coma or…whatever state she'd lived in for an indeterminate amount of time. She looked at her hand and saw blood smeared all over it—not to mention the huge splotch on her shirt.

Well, that didn't make any sense. "What did you do?" She directed this question at Trevor, too, because that was her rule of thumb. If any unexplained trouble or phenomena happened and Trevor was around, he was always the culprit.

"I didn't—" he began.

Only then realization smacked Reanna upside the head, and she blurted out, "*Shaesia!*"

Trevor blinked—but at least he had the common sense not to say *gesundheit* or something like that. That would have earned him a verbal lashing *and* a punch.

"Shaesia tried to kill me!" Reanna tried to sit up again, but the world flickered to black for a moment, and she slumped to the ground. "We have to get away from here!" She pulled up the hem of her shirt a tad to check if she might be bleeding out. But, aside from copious amounts of blood, she couldn't find a hole or injury at all.

And, come to think of it, why was she in a forest?

She glanced all around, but nothing made sense. She could have sworn she'd been in Atlantis last she checked. It must have been on her third go-around that she finally noticed—truly noticed—the kid crouched next to Trevor. The wiry boy's blue-gray eyes were wide, and his shaggy brown hair fell into his face. Moreover, he stared at her like she had somehow hung the stars, and Reanna couldn't remember ever seeing him before.

"I'm sorry—missed your name."

The boy blinked and peered at the empty spot next to him, apparently flabbergasted she had noticed him at all. When the realization must have sunk in that she had addressed her comment to him, his face turned a bright crimson.

It seemed kinda endearing, Reanna had to admit...

"Oh—uh—my name's Adam."

If Reanna had taken a drink of liquid right before his announcement, she would have done a spit-take. Since she didn't have any water to spew, her mouth opened in a tiny circle as she whipped her head from Adam to Trevor. Both looked rather perplexed at her reaction, and she let out something that might have been called a *meep*.

Adam. He had written the note—that note that she'd found—the poor boy. Should she mention it? She got out the first few syllables of a sentence—something like "I sa—" but cut herself off.

He'd admitted some very private things in that note. Things that made her uncomfortable, so she knew they'd make everyone else feel uncomfortable. She couldn't imagine that Adam wanted her to know what he'd written, let alone anyone else.

She wouldn't embarrass him. She'd just wait and see if he mentioned it to her, and if he did, well...then she'd smack him with the hundreds of questions she had.

Until then, she'd just find a way to subtly prod at him and get him to spill his guts that way.

He cocked his head. He probably thought that he'd broken her somehow.

Reanna rubbed her sweaty, bloody palms on her pants and let out a little puff of air. "Nice to meet you."

"I think—" Trevor began, but before he could continue, Adam cut him off.

"Is that Spider-Man on your sweatshirt?" The younger boy pointed at her sweatshirt, which had fallen from its precarious position on her waist and now sat on the ground like it'd swooned like an old-fashioned Victorian lady.

The image made Reanna smile. Her poor, wounded, overly-dramatic sweatshirt.

She chuckled. "Um…yeah." She snatched it up and patted the faded logo. The trusty superhero had seen better days. "He's my favorite."

Adam's blush deepened. "Oh—mine too! I also really like Iron Man. Who's your favorite Spider-Man actor?"

Trevor started humming under his breath. Reanna recognized the tune right away—"Can You Feel the Love Tonight" from *The Lion King*. She sent him a withering glare, but he only took the moment to be even more annoying.

He rolled his eyes at her annoyed look. "Ah, young nerd love. If you'll excuse me, there may be *something* left in my stomach I didn't previously bring up."

"Shut up." Reanna's voice softened as she addressed Adam next and ignored Trevor's scoff. "Uh—that's a hard choice. But if I had to pick…"

"I hate to break up your first date, but we've got some real problems here. I mean, I, personally, don't want to sit around in this creepy forest where a dead body just came back to flippin' life, but if that's what turns you guys on, go for it." Trevor stuffed his hands in his pockets. "But I'd rather not wait around and see if we unintentionally started the zombie apocalypse here."

"I'm not a zombie." Reanna scowled as her mind filtered through the strange memories. "At least, I don't think so. Shaesia must have put a spell on the dagger before she stabbed me, but—I don't know *why*. Or how she got me here…maybe she teleported me? So that my mother wouldn't get ahold of me?"

She picked up a blade of grass and tore it apart string by string. Grass was one of the few things she refused to chew on after she'd accidentally stuck a piece in her mouth once that had a woolly worm on the end of it.

Reanna sighed. "I don't know *what* she did or whose side she's even on. She said such weird things. I almost get the idea that she meant to send me some kind of coded message. Something about my mother having big plans for me, and blood curses, but I don't know what any of that means." She glanced at Adam. "Do you have any clue?"

Adam pointed at himself. "Me?"

Reanna nodded. "Yeah."

He chuckled and rubbed at the back of his neck. "Uh…no. Not really. Seems kind of vague. But maybe we could look around? See if we can find anyone around here to explain?"

Reanna shrugged. "Even if we don't find Shaesia, we do need to get out of here. I need to find my friends, and…" The final pieces of her brain finally slid back into place. "Oh, *crap*! The concentration camp—Violante—oh, no…" She attempted to get up, but the pain in her abdomen forced her back down. The wound may have been gone, but apparently some of the ache still persisted.

The world spun, and she stared off into the distance, though she didn't see the scenery. Instead, only splotches smeared her vision.

"Hey—you." Trevor nudged her. "You okay? You're suddenly all weird and spacey for no reason."

"I had a reason." Reanna shook her head and tried to reorient herself—and finally got a good look at what Trevor wore. "Do *you* have a good reason for dressing up in your best pajamas?"

"Why, yes, I do. I was forced out of bed at an unholy hour to come look for *you*." Trevor crossed his arms over his chest as if she had just wounded the pride of his night wear.

Reanna snorted. "Whose brilliant idea was that? I don't need you to rescue me. If I had fifty blue-billion choices of who I wanted to look for me, you would be at the bottom of the list. You wouldn't even *make* the list—"

"So original," Trevor shot back. "It's not like I've heard that line a million times before. Come on. Can't you figure out anything better than that?"

"Stop!" Adam crawled between them like they were sparring with their fists instead of words. "Why do you treat each other like this?" He looked like he was about to cry, his eyes wide.

"Come on, I've told you this a million times. Because we're nemeses." Trevor gestured between himself and Reanna.

"That, and because he's evil." Reanna braced herself to get up, but once again, she couldn't even push off the ground. "He's a self-centered egomaniac who likes to think he's funny when he's a bully."

Trevor didn't deny it, so Reanna threw her hands up in the air. "See! He knows it's true. That's why he won't defend himself."

"Actually, *Reanna*—" Trevor said her name so haughtily she could hardly stand it. "I was trying to be the mature person here and not get into a fight. I can pick on you later, but right now, I just need to know where the heck I am and how I get home from here."

"You can't," Reanna and Adam answered together.

Adam chuckled but clammed up, which left Reanna to explain.

"Portals to Earth are hard to come by here. Not like you can just go to the supermarket and buy them ready-made, idiot. You need an elf to make them."

"No, you don't! Adam did it with magnets and a bunch of portal stuff. So let's do it again, *now*." Trevor snapped his fingers in

Reanna's face, and she slapped them away. Ugh—she was so *glad* he hadn't lost any of his rudeness and arrogance while she was gone. The world might suddenly implode if Trevor Spencer could ever be a decent human being.

"We can't just *leave*, though. Well, I can't. You're free to hit the road whenever you want. I've got to stay and find some way to stop this war, and that means finding my friends at a concentration camp."

"Whoa—what? As in…like, World War II? Like what we're studying in history right now, with the Nazis? What kind of jacked up place did we come to?"

"Not any more jacked up than Earth." For a third time, Reanna tried to stand, but once again her actions were futile.

Adam must have taken pity on her, though, because he helped her up. His bony arms wrapped around her as he hefted her to her feet. She only stood an inch or so taller than him, but she would bet money she weighed more than the scrawny thing. He looked like a cat somebody had dumped a bucket of water on.

She smiled. He *was* kinda adorable in a feral-cat kind of way. In the way that made her want to protect him.

Her heart rate skyrocketed. She had to stop thinking. Although she doubted it was physically possible to hear someone else's heartbeat from this distance, if she kept up this train of thought, she knew he would somehow hear hers.

He seemed to eye her with just as much scrutiny. She blushed—did she pass his inspection?

"All right, enough of this," Trevor muttered. "She can *stand* without looking so doe-eyed. I swear—you're babying her."

"Um—hello?" Reanna bit back at him. "I did take a knife to the stomach and practically *die*. That deserves a little babying…even if you can't see the wound anymore."

Adam had that *I'm-about-to-cry* look on his face again. Reanna bit her tongue. She was definitely *not* passing his inspection.

"Stop it!" Adam said. "Arguing doesn't get us anywhere."

"Sure it does." Trevor gestured to both of them in turn. "She argues with me all the time. You argue with me all the time. We somehow ended up here."

Now Adam looked like *he* was the one biting his tongue. He glared at Trevor, probably about five seconds away from hissing and clawing him to death.

Great. They'd all ended up in Gaia, and they'd probably kill each other before they could help anyone.

"Ugh. Never mind." Adam sighed. "So, next—you said we have to locate this concentration camp, right?"

"Yeah." Reanna swallowed. "I need to see if my friends are okay. Or, better yet, I could leave you both here in this glen and make my way back to the concentration camp alone." Reanna realized how that sounded a moment after she said it. "I mean—just to keep you safe. Not because I'm annoyed with you. I'm not annoyed with—well, I'm annoyed with Trevor, but not you, Adam."

"I never asked to cross dimensions to be a third wheel." Trevor scratched his forehead with his thumb.

Reanna rolled her eyes and tried to push herself away from Adam so Trevor would shut up about the whole third wheel thing. She stumbled but managed to catch herself and take a few hesitant steps forward.

"I have an idea. Let's split up." Adam's voice broke her reverie. He gestured to a walkie-talkie hooked to his belt loop. "We'll go this way, and Trevor, you go that way." He motioned behind him. "The radio waves should still function in Gaia like normal, even if cell phones won't work." He tilted his chin forward a bit to indicate the trees in front of them. "Is that okay, Reanna?"

She pursed her lips and nodded. Ugh. Walking. A horrible activity on a normal day, but even worse when she'd just come back to life. But she'd survived her death, and not a lot of people could say that. "Yeah. At least we'll cover more ground that way, and we'll have a better chance of finding something."

"Sure. Let the noob who's never been to any alternate dimensions just hang out here by himself." Trevor chucked a pebble against a tree. "I'll be fine. Hope any ogres don't eat me or whatever."

"Don't worry!" Reanna patted his shoulder. "Ogres don't live on Solis. They're off eating jerks on another continent."

CHAPTER 56

REANNA

GAIA: FORESTS OF DASPIN

Reanna limped through the forest with Adam, her hand over her stomach. Fear for her friends knotted up her insides and made her blood run cold. Her hands shook, and she clenched them tighter against her abdomen. She knew it had to be psychosomatic, but she couldn't forget the sensation of the knife as it entered her body. She winced every time her mind replayed it.

And what about her friends? Had Violante killed them before she'd come to torture Reanna? And how long could it take before they found this stupid concentration camp? Nothing looked familiar; there were just trees upon more trees. They could be days away or in a different world completely—

Ugh. She needed a distraction before she worried herself into a fit of anxiety over the fates of her friends. A nice, light subject—cheery, even...

"Do you know anything about blood curses?" Reanna winced. Ah, yes. A nice, light, and cheery subject, sure to alleviate her anxiety. But she was nothing if not an anxious masochist. Not to mention, if she talked about the scary things, eventually they might not be so scary.

Theoretically.

"Blood curses?" Adam scrunched up his nose. "Uh...let me think."

Reanna wouldn't mention the note, either, but Adam might offer up some information casually in a conversation like this. And she could prod him gently in the right direction. "Did your mom or dad ever tell you anything about blood curses?"

Adam shot her a glance. Had she been too obvious already? She thought she'd been subtle. "My mom died having me. I never got to meet her, so, no. She didn't tell me anything about blood curses."

Reanna swallowed. Her stomach still churned, and she tried to take a few deep breaths to calm herself. "I'm sorry. Did...your dad ever tell you anything about blood curses?"

Adam shook his head. "No." He helped Reanna over the trunk of a huge fallen tree. She winced as more spasms traveled through her body. "He wouldn't tell me anything even if he did know. But, luckily for me, I stopped relying on him to tell me stuff a long time ago."

Reanna winced—not only from the pain but from the bitter tone in Adam's voice. "Do you not get along with your dad?"

"No," Adam said curtly. "Or—well—I guess it's complicated. It's a long story, and I'd prefer to tell you when we don't need to hurry to a concentration camp. But my dad...I don't think he's ever fully forgiven me. I think he blames me for killing her."

"He must be pretty lousy, then." Reanna scowled.

Reanna could almost see the hackles on Adam's neck rise as though he was a feral cat ready to rip something to shreds. "He is *not* lousy."

"But it's not your fault—I mean, you didn't kill your mom."

450

Adam dragged his arm over his eyes. As he did, Reanna caught a flash of something silver on his wrist. A bracelet, maybe? She tucked it away in the back of her head, something else to ask about if she ever got the chance.

A heavy silence fell over them, which, unfortunately, let Reanna's thoughts drift back to her friends. She could imagine a bloodbath with all her friends dead in puddles of black blood, just like Rosalina, courtesy of Violante's heinous spell…

Reanna sucked in a breath. She tried to shove away the images, but the miniature versions of herself seemed all too thrilled to show her another gruesome outcome.

She opened her mouth, desperate to goad Adam into a conversation, but he beat her to it.

"Thanks."

She whipped her head toward him. "Hmm?"

His cheeks colored. "I said, thanks. For saying that I didn't kill my mom. That means a lot to me. But…um…I'm not sure about blood curses. I know they're bad. I know that they usually only end in death because they take a lot of dark magic."

"So only spellcasters or elves could cast them, then?" Reanna leaned on Adam to help her navigate the uneven ground.

"I…I don't think so. I think anyone can; it's not…it's…it's more like alchemy, I guess. Anyone with the right ingredients can do it, I think. And they're potent. Near unbreakable." Adam swallowed. "So I think the best advice is, don't cast them and don't fall under their spell."

Reanna glanced down at her wrist—the very same wrist Violante had drawn blood from. "Adam." Her voice quavered. "Does it take blood to make a blood curse?"

Adam shrugged. "That's pretty much the only ingredient I'm sure of."

Reanna's breath hitched in her throat. "Violante got my blood." Her voice came out in a whisper, but she repeated the thought, louder. "*She got my blood!* What if—what if she's already put me under a blood curse? Or what if she's *going* to? She wants me dead, that's the only thing we know—"

Adam grasped her shoulders and brought their advance to a halt. His blue-gray eyes met hers, a serious expression on his face. "Reanna. Listen to me. Your mother wants you dead, yeah. That's what we know. But if she put a blood curse on you, I *promise* you—I will break it."

Reanna felt her face crumple. "I can't let you do that. I won't. That's—that's not your job."

"So? Maybe I want it to be my job." Adam's hold tightened just slightly. "I promise you. I'll die before I let you die, okay? I didn't come all the way here to just have you die on me from some stupid blood curse. Besides, I said I didn't know everything about them. Maybe I'm just dumb, and there's a super easy way to get out of it."

"But there could not be. And I could already be under one, and—"

"Reanna, stop." Adam sucked in a breath. "I mean what I said. You're not under a blood curse, and even if you get put under one—I promise. I *swear* to you. I won't let anything happen."

"I'm sorry." Reanna swiped at her tears. "I know I'm a disappointment. I don't even really think I'm worth saving, and I definitely don't want you to do it—you don't even know me—if you knew me, you wouldn't…"

"I *would.*" Adam's hands dropped, and he clenched his fingers into fists. "You're not a disappointment. At all."

So many questions boiled up inside of Reanna as though she was a tea kettle about to burst. Every declaration made her want to press him further, to learn everything he knew, to know *how* he knew. How he'd sent the letter, how he'd gotten to Gaia. How much he could tell her about blood curses, himself, *everything*.

She opened her mouth, ready to bubble over with burning curiosity.

Their walkie-talkie crackled to life.

"Hello, children," someone said over the airwaves. Reanna jumped and yelped, which only made her stomach hurt worse. She groaned and dropped to her knees to try and find some comfort after the sudden movement.

"I hope you are well," the person continued. The voice sounded masculine, smooth, and condescending.

Adam pressed the button to respond. "Who is this?"

"Perhaps the better question would be to ask, who are *you*?" the person harrumphed. "Identify yourself. Is Princess Reanna with you?"

Adam twisted up his mouth and glanced between Reanna and the walkie-talkie. The seconds dragged on before he responded. "My name's Adam. Now tell me yours and why you want to know about Reanna."

"Well, *Adam*." Reanna could almost hear the man's sneer. "This is Corcaelin, the elf representative on the Council. Perhaps the princess might remember that—the governing body of Solis that she disobeyed."

Reanna sucked in a breath and held out her hand. Adam gave her the walkie-talkie, and she hit the button. "I remember you." Unfortunately. "But how did you get Trevor's walkie-talkie?"

"I found your friend—Tree-vor, did you say?—wandering around a battlefield. I apprehended him, along with your other partners-in-crime, Laile and Gregory, amidst this disaster."

"Are they alive? All of them? Laile, Gregory, Laeserno, Whisper?"

A pause. "I do not know all the names of your little friends. If you hurry, you can ascertain their safety for yourself. But Laile and Gregory are safe and unharmed."

Reanna swallowed. More tears spilled onto her cheeks, and she had to press the earpiece against her forehead to gather herself.

Her friends.

They were alive.

She steadied her breathing as a knot of anxiety untangled itself in her body and sent a cold rush of relief through her veins. Her head went woozy, and if she hadn't already been crouched down, she probably would have passed out.

"Where—where are you? Where's everyone? Where are my friends?" Her voice cracked.

"Ogden's Inlet. I request you come and meet me. I can give you directions if required." Corcaelin lowered his voice. "Unless you want them to be locked up for your crimes, you will meet us here before sundown."

CHAPTER 57

REANNA

GAIA: LIBERATED ELVEN CONCENTRATION CAMP IN
OGDEN'S INLET, DASPIN

Reanna followed Corcaelin's instructions all the way through the forest until the ground turned softer beneath her feet with every step, and the trees seemed to grow less dense. She could see people in the distance, hear their voices—

And the Song of the Sea.

It stopped her in her tracks.

Reanna hit the "talk" button on the walkie-talkie. "We're here."

She closed her eyes as the crackle of Corcaelin's response was lost to the song of her ancestors. The Song of the Sea was faint, a whisper she could just barely hear. It rustled her hair and sounded like a giggle as it drew her closer and closer to its heartbeat.

Such an intoxicating composition.

The melody bubbled up inside of Reanna, snapped pieces of her soul into place. She paused to take a deep breath, full of music and ocean air. The intoxicating Song might have been quieter when she was fully human, but, looking back, she could see how it had always been there, dormant but persistent. It drove her in swimming competitions, compelled her to take walks along the shoreline in Florida, made her sleep with her balcony doors open so she could hear the chattering waves. And now, it'd been chasing her in Gaia for so long, slowly eroding her defenses like a wave against a rock. Her time in Atlantis had only whet its power.

She took one step forward.

The Song begged her to return to Atlantis, to come home.

Home.

Cha vinseri, cecia

Cha vinseri, cecia

Ane oceanus gann rin xa

Cha vinseri, cecia

Cha vinseri, cecia...

Maybe she should have felt scared that the Song of the Sea compelled her so powerfully, but the melody echoed so firmly in her own soul she couldn't help but follow it.

She started out of her reverie as someone grasped her arm. She yipped and turned to look at Adam. "What?"

"You okay?" His eyes searched her face.

"Yeah." Reanna shifted her weight between her legs. "It's hard to explain, but when I'm this close to the ocean, I can hear the waves singing. Mermaids call it the Song of the Sea. It's supposed to lure people with a seafaring spirit to adventure—mermaids, sometimes even sailors." Reanna hummed a few bars of "Rainbow Connection." "It's dangerous, though. If you're caught unaware by it, it can drown you or make you go crazy." She shrugged.

"You'll be able to keep your head if we keep going, right?" Adam shook his head, which made his swoopy bangs fall to the side.

"Even if I'm not, I can't just leave my friends prisoner to whatever creep is on the other end of this line." Reanna took a deep breath and pretended to stuff cotton in her ears. Maybe she could tune it out if she imagined it was hard to hear.

Cha vinseri, cecia

Cha vinseri, cecia

Ane oceanus gann rin xa

Cha vinseri, cecia

Cha vinseri, cecia...

The ground turned to sand beneath her feet. Tall beach grass swayed in the wind, and as she crested the top of a sand dune, her legs gave out.

She collapsed, tears in her eyes.

There were so many elves.

Granted, they looked haggard and broken still. But she could see healers as they went around and tried to do what they could. Could it be...

"Help me get me down there, please. Quick." Reanna shook Adam a bit. "Hurry."

Adam tightened his grip on her side as they began their descent down the dune. They slipped and slid a few times, but each time he managed to hold Reanna up before she fell.

They finally stopped in the middle of the hubbub. Reanna clutched her chest while tears spilled out. A dozen or so portals were positioned all around the former concentration camp. Soldiers and medics flooded in, all donning Council colors. Had she actually helped free the elves?

Her lip quivered.

Someone tapped her on the shoulder, and she whirled around.

Corcaelin stood behind her, his hands clasped behind his back. He stared down his nose at her, a grimace twisting his gaunt visage. He reminded her of the mortician from *Beauty and the*

Beast—the one who conspired with Gaston to take Maurice captive—except taller and with pointed ears.

"I see you followed my instructions for once," he said.

Reanna nodded. "Look—you said we couldn't do it, but we did it—"

"No, my dear girl." Corcaelin's sneer twisted into a thin-lipped smile. "You did *not* do it. Should the Council not have received intel about your little escapade here, your friends would be dead right now. *You* did not do it. *We* fixed the mangled mess your loyal bunch of *lawbreakers* made."

"What?" Reanna swayed and took a step back.

"You heard correctly. Technically, you are a criminal. Or did you think that you would get out of trouble simply because you are a princess? Or maybe because your little friend, Laile, told you to do what you did?" Corcaelin snorted. "You have disobeyed a direct order from the Council. You disregarded our protections and, quite frankly, almost exposed a discreet undercover agent. Not to mention that if the *trained Council soldiers*—which required an extensive amount of reallocating our assets and left us vulnerable at other key positions—had not arrived when we did, you most assuredly would have lost the battle and many more lives."

"Now hold up a minute." Adam stepped in front of Reanna—as if his thin frame could do an ounce of good against the old man. "I'm sure that Reanna did whatever she did for a good reason."

Corcaelin glared at Adam with such ferocity that Reanna physically pulled the shorter boy back and pushed him behind her. Her knees quaked, but she tried to meet Corcaelin's gaze.

Or at least stare at the tip of his long nose, which didn't seem quite as frightening as his cold, intense eyes.

"I *did*. Laile said that the Council wasn't doing anything to rescue the elves. You didn't have any plans to reclaim my powers, either. We did *both*. We saved the elves, and I got my powers back. I didn't want to just be a useless potato anymore."

"What in all the worlds do you mean?" Corcaelin rolled his eyes. "Oh, never mind. The point is, *Princess* Reanna, that you and your merry band of hooligans cannot just disregard direct orders and not expect any consequences. However things are run in the dimension you came from, here we have law and order. Now." Corcaelin pointed to a tiny cove, where Trevor sat with his hands between his knees. "If you two would go and sit over there, I shall deliver your consequences in a moment. But first, I must see to the instigators of this little rebellion." Corcaelin gestured in the other direction, toward Gregory and Laile. Reanna's knees almost gave out again, and she took a step toward them. Corcaelin grabbed her shoulder and pulled her back before she could even wave or call to them. "And I warn you: if you try to run, your punishment will be even more severe."

CHAPTER 58

LAILE

GAIA: LIBERATED ELVEN CONCENTRATION CAMP IN OGDEN'S INLET, DASPIN

Laile steamed as she sat on the sand like some kind of toddler in time-out. A few hours ago, Corcaelin had opened up a portal to Shaesia's house and barged in with officers and medics. He'd been very sparse on information since then—aside from insinuating that Laile might be arrested for her crimes.

She personally thought that the Atlanteans should be held responsible for their crimes against humanity before she got a little slap on the wrist for her misdemeanors, but—oh well. That might mean the Council would have to admit that their inaction had let atrocities continue for too long, thereby making themselves accomplices by negligence—and no way Corcaelin would ever admit *he* could do something wrong.

Just another reason she'd stay alive until the end of his term just to give him a good sock to the nose.

"Laile." Gregory cleared his throat and poked her in the side. "Laile, please talk to me."

Laile shifted her body away and let the waves lap against her toes. She stared off into the horizon, where the ocean and the sky met. Somewhere beyond, far past where her eye could see, sat the island nation of Cocatrali, then past that, the Regal Archipelago, then the Land of Dragons…

Basically, she could think of several other places she would rather be than held hostage next to her best friend.

"Laile. Come on."

"What? Now you want to talk?" She whirled on Gregory. "I've been trying to get you to talk to me for weeks—months—about what's bugging you, and you won't tell me. At least you know what's bugging me. You didn't take me with you."

Gregory's jaw twitched. "You are the *stubbornest* person I've ever met. You *know* you couldn't go. I'm sorry Julius got his hands on you—I'm *very* sorry—but I didn't tell him to kidnap you. You don't think I was torn up every second you were gone?"

"I don't know." Laile shifted her position and winced. It still hurt to move, and Gregory reached out to grab her.

Flying fig-whits, she wanted to stay mad at him. She didn't want him to go out of his way to be kind to her.

"You do know. Stop being stupid. You're my best friend, Laile." Gregory cleared his throat, released her arms, and adjusted his glasses, though he never took his eyes off her. "I didn't want you to get hurt again."

Laile huffed. Let another moment pass. Then she reached up and brushed her thumb along his cheek. "You've got a cut there."

"Yeah." His voice cracked. "It was bad. The fight, I mean. The conditions—awful. I wanted to tell you what happened."

She sighed and let her hand drop. "All right. Tell me what happened. But make sure you include at least two instances in which you missed me and wished for my expertise."

A hint of a smile tilted Gregory's lips. "I can tell you I wished for it the whole time."

Laile smiled back at him, and for a moment—one sacred, blessed moment—she wondered if she should forget her stinging pride, lean forward, and kiss him.

Until Corcaelin stalked over and greeted them with a condescending: "Hello, children."

Laile sighed. "Come to gripe some more?"

Corcaelin smiled—a very thin-lipped smile. "No. I have met with the Council, and we have decided the punishment for all of you." He pointed at Laile. "You are officially stripped of your guardianship privileges."

"No!" Laile tried to hop up, but the quick movement made her head spin, and Gregory had to catch her before she collapsed back to the sand. "You can't do that—I've worked too hard for this!"

"If you worked so hard, perhaps you would have remembered that all guardians are under the authority of the Council. You are *not* an autonomous deity despite what your teenage brain might tell you."

Laile clenched her fingers into a fist. Sink all consequences to the depths of Atlantis—she'd deck Corcaelin and enjoy it as she got hauled off to prison.

Gregory lowered her back to the sand, placing a hand over hers which kept her pinned to the ground. She bared her teeth and growled, every bit the daughter of a werewolf. "You—you—*you* are not an autonomous deity, either, despite what your fat, egotistical, bloated, narcissistic head might tell you!"

Corcaelin clasped his hands behind his back. "Do you feel better now?"

"No, but if you let me punch you once, I might."

Corcaelin smirked. "Afraid not. You see, I operate with all the authority of a Council Representative, although I make sure to discuss my decisions with the Council beforehand. Sorry that regulations annoy you, but if you commit a crime, then—"

"Wait." Gregory held Laile down before she could spring up. "I'd like to speak on our behalf."

"I fail to see how you could have anything to say."

"I have plenty to say." Gregory cleared his throat. "Laile and I were just trying to help people. We've been helping with the refugees, listening to the news—everything. And day after day, we heard about Arana inflicting unspeakable horrors on her victims, and no one did anything. The war just…raged on and on endlessly, and more people got sucked into her evil vortex." Gregory glanced at Laile. She offered him a small smile to encourage him to go on. "Then Arana kidnapped Reanna. The Council learned of it, and instead of using Reanna to figurehead a rebellion, they wanted to hide her away. Even when Reanna herself expressed interest in helping, the Council told us that we couldn't do anything. But we *could*."

Laile's heart fluttered at Gregory's steady words. He uttered them with such authority that no one could argue with the facts as he piled them, as solid as bricks, on top of each other.

Corcaelin stood still, his expression unreadable.

"We didn't get everyone out." Gregory's voice cracked once more, the only sign of a flaw in his army of facts. "Laile got injured. But we got a lot of people out. Hundreds, even. I'm not—I don't know the population of the elves, but there's got to be a lot here. Maybe even thousands."

"There are not thousands," Corcaelin said. "An official count will be taken when we have transported everyone back to safety, but I would estimate you rescued a good four hundred elves. However, I have not yet been to the camp to see how many you allowed to get slaughtered. Nor do we know how many will die if their injuries are too grievous."

"All the more reason we couldn't wait. You've seen the condition these elves are in. If the Council waited any longer, then—who knows." Gregory took a deep breath. "I'm sorry that we had to break rules, but think of all the good things that have happened because people broke rules in the past. The Dwarfish-Gnomish War. Werewolf rights. Laile's own *father*—"

"Do not bring Damien's name into this fiasco." Corcaelin held up a hand. "As much as I dislike Damien, he lobbied for years for werewolf representation through the *legal* channels. He did not hold the Council hostage until we listened to his demands. He listened to each verdict of the Council and respected them until they fell in his favor."

Gregory sighed. "Okay, well, Laile's mother—"

Corcaelin grunted. "All right, the girl comes by her rule-breaking honestly, I admit."

Gregory chuckled and met Laile's gaze once more.

"And I'm proud of who my mother is, thank you very much." Laile tilted up her chin. "And I'm proud that she taught me to do what I feel is right, no matter what the cost or consequences. Take away the guardianship if it allows me more freedom to follow my convictions. I'm proud that I did the right thing—"

"Except you did not." Corcaelin's eyelid twitched. "You interrupted a very precarious mission. Perhaps you are aware that we have a spy on the inside; they are the one who coordinated the mission that you went on. But what you do *not* know is that they were working on the inside to try and see how deep Arana's claws went. You only somewhat liberated *this* concentration camp—not the dozen or so *other* camps. We knew something went wrong when our spy informed us that Arana had given orders to begin executions of the prisoners thanks to the stunt you pulled here."

Corcaelin sighed and closed his eyes. His shoulders slumped, and for a moment, he almost looked...weak. Vulnerable. Like he might actually have a heart inside his cold, dead chest. Laile gasped and shook her head. She tried to open her mouth, to protest the news, but a simple no couldn't erase the awful truth from existence.

"Our own forces are stretched so thin," Corcaelin continued. His tone sounded softer than it had before. "The vampires of Simit still claim neutrality and refuse to send soldiers to help. The fairies of Jenkirre and the spellcasters of Reggeria make up our dwindling forces, and they are spread very thin. The dwarves and gnomes are suffering nearly as much as the elves, and most of them are untrained, though a few have joined as volunteers. We have to mobilize young recruits, but even with that—we are struggling to send enough soldiers to save the others. What we are looking at is an unprecedented genocide of the elves."

Laile's vision faded to black for a moment as her head went light. She grasped Gregory's arm to keep from tipping backward if she passed out.

Gregory blanched as well. "We…*executions*? But…"

"This is why we do not put children in charge of wars." Corcaelin straightened his shoulders, and the sorrow that his voice had held just a few moments ago dissipated. "You are not privy to the Council's top secret matters of state. I realize that you may feel entitled to some degree of knowledge, considering your father's position and your previous title of Guardian of Reanna, but let me *assure* you—you do not need to know everything. You are to obey when the Council gives you an order, especially on sensitive matters."

"We have to be able to do something," Laile croaked. "We…there's got to be something…"

"You have done quite enough to ruin the Council's plans thus far. But *you*, Gregory Blandinus—*you* could help by reporting to your summons." Corcaelin leveled his finger at Gregory. "You were drafted into the army. You were supposed to report to training two days ago."

"I was a little busy," Gregory muttered. "I planned on going when we got back."

Laile's bottom lip trembled. Her consciousness tottered once again like it had on those miserable days back at Julius' mansion. "What?"

"Gregory received summons months ago. If the two of you were so concerned with the well-being of the elves, then he should have—"

"No." Laile shook her head, and her voice came out no louder than a whisper. Her heart had plummeted to her feet when she heard about the elves, and she naïvely thought at the time it couldn't sink any lower—but somehow it could. "No, that's not true, or Greg would have told me."

Gregory sighed and slipped his glasses off his face so he could clean them on his rumpled shirt. "I knew." He mumbled this so quietly that Laile almost didn't hear him.

The first tear slipped past Laile's defenses as puzzle pieces clicked into place. As the betrayal really sank in. "You mean—all those times when I tried to get you to tell me—all those times when I asked you what was wrong. You knew you'd gotten summoned to the frontlines and..."

Gregory wouldn't meet her eyes. "I didn't see any sense in getting you all upset. Then you'd try and fix everything, and there's simply no solution to this." He fiddled with the earpieces of his glasses, and it looked like he struggled to hold back his emotions as well. "And—it's not fair of me to say I'm worried about the war if I let my fear stop me when I *can* do something..."

"But it's different! It's all different!" Laile gripped his arm. "And you should have *told* me! Greg—" She choked on her own emotions and tried to swallow them down.

"And how is that any different than the stunt you two pulled?" Corcaelin narrowed his eyes at the two of them. "You two marched into danger—"

"We marched *together*! And I knew we could avoid most of the fighting—or at least, I thought we could." Laile pressed her thumb against the cut on Gregory's cheek. "It's just—it's just different!"

The elves. The war. Gregory. Front lines. Laile felt like she might choke on it all. "You should have told me, Greg."

"I didn't want you to get involved, to try and fix the world when some things can't be fixed," Gregory said. "Sometimes they don't need to be fixed. Sometimes you just have to face what comes." He swallowed.

But for a moment, he looked so young.

And, Composer help her, Laile wanted her parents there. Her parents would know how to stop this madness. Because for all her talk, for all her actions that had just ended her up in a worse mess…Laile was only eighteen.

Gregory was only eighteen.

And adulthood—*war*—suddenly seemed far more real than it had before they'd experienced it themselves. Before words like "genocide" and "drafts" and "front lines" had become names and faces, not just ink on a paper.

Maybe Corcaelin had a point all along when he called Laile and Gregory children.

Laile wrapped her arms around herself. Her mind whirled and scrambled for one thread of hope, one measly final grasp at it.

Corcaelin inhaled. She could only imagine he intended to launch into another lecture.

"Wait." Laile grasped Gregory's shoulder. "There's a law. Isn't there a law that says newlyweds can't be drafted?"

Corcaelin rolled his eyes, but his silence carried as much meaning as words. Laile *knew* a honeymoon grace period existed.

She cleared her throat and hoped that she could find the strength in her voice again. "There is—I know it." Laile gripped his sleeve until the fabric bunched up in her fist. "Greg—please. Let's just get married. I can't lose you, too."

Gregory shook his head. "No, Laile. I told you—I don't—"

"It's not fair, and I won't let you go! It isn't right to send boys to the front lines when they didn't ask for it—"

To her surprise, Gregory whirled on her. Without his glasses, she could see the fire in his eyes. "This isn't about that, Laile! You are not marrying me to keep me from fighting. I refuse to be your next bleeding cause."

"What?" Laile's mouth dropped open. She struggled to form any words for several seconds. "What do you mean?"

"I mean just what I say." Gregory shoved her hand off. "You are not going to marry me just because you've found something else in this whole blasted affair that isn't fair. *None* of it is! But you're not going to marry me because you feel *sorry* for me."

"I want to *protect* you—there's a difference!"

"You don't marry someone because you want to protect them, Laile!" Gregory's voice rose a notch.

"Oh, yeah? And why not?" Laile's own voice escalated as well.

"Because! Marriage is a serious thing, and it's not something you do on a whim. Not without proper planning and foresight and—we're *eighteen*! You still sleep with a night-light!"

"I didn't know having a *night-light* disqualifies you from marriage!" Laile wished she could deck him right now. "And—and—" She choked on her own words, the words she so freely admitted in her head. Why could she not just spit them out? It felt like some creature inside her was strangling her vocal chords so those blasted three words wouldn't come out.

She had to find another way to convey how she felt. "You're my best friend, Greg. You think I wouldn't be happy married to you?" She narrowed her eyes. "Unless...you wouldn't be happy married to me?"

"We're getting sidetracked here, Laile." Gregory stood up. "We're not getting married. It's a ridiculous solution. Anyway, look what happened the last time we charged full force with one of your schemes. Those elves..." Gregory clenched his fists. "This is the one way I can fix it."

"One of *my* schemes?" Laile shoved herself up. She tottered for a few seconds and swung her arms around to keep her balance. Gregory reached for her, but she swatted him away. "I thought you believed in us just as much as I did!"

"I did—fine—one of *our* schemes." Gregory sighed.

"Well, I am very glad to see that at least one of you has common sense here." Corcaelin gestured toward the portal. "Take any of these portals and they will lead you back to Capital City. Report to the recruitment department and we shall consider that your punishment for disregarding the Council's orders. As for you, Miss Úlfur—you are to wait here until an escort arrives. I must discuss the punishment with your ward, but you are under house arrest for a very, *very* long time."

Gregory strode toward the portal. He paused at the glowing, twisting ball of pastel colors and glanced over his shoulder. "Bye, Laile."

Tears stung Laile's eyes, and she sniffled. She'd regretted it the last time she hadn't spoken to him right before he left, but here they stood again at the crossroads, and once again, she felt her words fail her. That monster that gripped her vocal chords wouldn't relent; and with the fury and shame writhing inside her, she just couldn't meet his gaze.

"Please don't hate me." Gregory's voice didn't break. In fact, he almost uttered it just as matter-of-factly as he had stated facts earlier. "Please don't."

Laile's heart shattered. "I—" Her head snapped up, but Gregory stepped through the portal before she could finish. She stared at the spot where he'd vanished long after Corcaelin left her side to go censure Reanna.

"No," Laile whispered. She collapsed back to the sand as the tide rolled in. "I don't hate you." A few tears dripped down onto her clenched fists. It seemed the monster that had kept her true feelings hostage saw fit to release them, and they slipped out quietly. "I love you, Gregory."

But she might have just missed the only chance she had to confess them to her best friend.

CHAPTER 59

REANNA

GAIA: LIBERATED ELVEN CONCENTRATION CAMP IN OGDEN'S INLET, DASPIN

Reanna stumbled across the sand. Every footfall hurt, but the pain grew duller the less she thought about it. "Trevor! Trevor Spencer!" Adam raced along beside her toward the star quarterback as Corcaelin went to lecture Laile and Gregory.

Trevor snapped his head up. "*There* you are. Listen, I don't know what's going on, but it's seriously crazy. I feel like I've been transported onto the set of *Lord of the Rings*, but it's all wrong. I can't find a single hot elf-girl around here."

Reanna rolled her eyes and slowed her aching walk. She'd gotten so worked up that she'd forgotten the most important thing—Trevor Spencer wasn't worth her worry. "How classy. These are traumatized war survivors, not some cheerleader you can pass your number to after a lame attempt at flirting."

She felt something knock against her legs; Whisper threaded through them, back in his regular azernos form. "There you are."

Reanna knelt down and patted him between the ears. "At least you're okay."

Whisper chirruped at her. He blinked at her with those beady eyes before he darted away and disappeared among the crowd of soldiers and newly-freed prisoners.

Adam and Reanna situated themselves next to Trevor. The group sat in silence while Reanna watched the waves. The Song of the Sea thrummed in her heart and called her back to Atlantis, back to the homeland she'd once known. Could Arana control its strength like the sirens of old and use it to try and lure her daughter into a trap? For that matter, what plans did she have? And what exactly were blood curses, and why had Shaesia gone out of her way to warn Reanna about them?

Reanna rubbed her temple. So many puzzle pieces, but she didn't have the box as a reference to follow.

"So..." Trevor cleared his throat. "Squirt here says you're a mermaid, but I don't see a tail."

"That's because I'm on land, doofus. My friend had to use a spell on me so that I have feet on land and a tail in the sea."

"Well, excuse me, princess! How was I supposed to know?" Trevor dragged out the word *excuse* and waited a beat. "Ugh, fine. I guess none of you have ever seen the show."

"What show?" Reanna asked.

"I've seen it," Adam answered. "It's just hokey as heck, and that wasn't a good impersonation of the hero."

Trevor growled. "Ugh. I tell ya. Everyone's a critic." He picked up a rock and tossed it into the waves. "Well, if you're a mermaid in the water, show me. I didn't come all the way out here to be told I can't do imitations."

Reanna sighed and winced as she stood. Adam hopped up to help balance her, but she took a few staggering steps without his help. "It's okay. I think I've got it." She marched into the surf and let it swell up over her ankles—

And then fell flat on her bottom as her feet gave way instantaneously to a tail. Trevor cackled; Adam slugged him; Reanna watched it all through a curtain of wet hair.

"All right, all right. Come and get me out." Reanna held up her hand. "I don't want to lug this tail around for your entertainment. You've seen your proof, you cretin."

"I think I've seen a little more than I wanted to see." Trevor hiked up his plaid pants and marched into the water. "*What* the heck are you wearing?"

Reanna winced. Oh, yeah. The white top meant for a six-year-old. She covered the unintentional corset with her arm, even though there was at least enough fabric so that she hadn't flashed them. "Just shut up! I got dressed in this when I was *six*, okay? Sorry if I didn't plan appropriately for the outfit I'd need to wear eleven years later."

"Yeah. What a lack of foresight on your account." Trevor held out his hand for her. "Come on. Let's get you out of here, because you're, like, one step away from going full-on naked siren mode."

"Oh, shut up, Trevor Spencer," Reanna growled. But she seized his hand with her free one, anyway.

Trevor pulled—and his entire face turned red.

He grunted and adjusted his position. This time, he jammed his shoulder into her stomach and tossed her over like a sack of potatoes. He staggered for a moment and winced; she wondered if her sharp scales had bitten into his skin. "You weigh about a couple thousand pounds."

Reanna slapped him with her fluke. "Watch it, mister, or I'll freeze you."

"Yeah, you watch it, or I'll dump you right on your head. You don't want to hit that too many times and lose what precious few brain cells you have."

"You're one to talk, you Neanderthal."

"That's a really great way to talk to the person who just crossed dimensions for you."

Reanna silenced her next verbal barb. Trevor hauled her back to the shore and dumped her between himself and Adam. "I guess— I guess you really did. Thanks." Reanna stared at her fingers. "I didn't know you'd be that worried if I disappeared. Unless nobody else gives you the time of day."

"Nobody gives *me* the time of day?" Trevor sputtered. "Reanna, are you delirious? Which one of us is the popular one? If I disappeared, I guarantee you life at school wouldn't continue as normal—" He clamped his mouth shut, but Reanna already felt the hidden meaning that lurked behind his words.

She grabbed a piece of salty hair and stuck it in her mouth as she stared at her scales until they fizzled and gave way to legs. "So nobody really cares that I'm gone, then."

"I cared." Adam scooted closer. "I cared a lot."

Reanna offered him a small smile. "Thanks."

Trevor cleared his throat. "Excuse me. Still here. I mean, yes, it's pretty much thanks to the kid that I came, but I—I, uh, didn't mean *no one* cared. You were on the news. They even got your dad and step—"

Reanna whirled on Trevor. "She is *not* my stepmother!"

"Okay, okay. Sorry." Trevor held up his hands, but Reanna could see the cogs in his brain as they churned. "You know, I never knew you were adopted, but...if you count your not-stepmother, you've had three mothers and two fathers. You sure blow through parents like I blow through cash."

"Yeah, well, what does that make my average if I've only had one parent that really loved me? One-fifth?" Reanna winced.

"Don't worry. I'm batting zero for two." Trevor looked over Reanna's shoulder at Adam. "What about you?"

Adam scratched at his freckles. "It's complicated."

"All right—enough. I want to know how you guys got to Gaia in the first place. Spill it." Reanna stared at each of them in turn until they opened up.

For the next little bit, they swapped stories of what all had transpired up until this point. Reanna hadn't yet finished when Corcaelin strode up to them.

"I want to go back to Atlantis," Reanna blurted out as the elf stopped. "I saw things there—I mean—I need to go back. There are elves there that need our help."

"While I appreciate the sentiment, I believe it is too late to help those trapped down there." Corcaelin crossed his arms. "Our spy sent word that Arana has ordered the execution of most remaining elves due to the debacle with the head concentration camp. Whatever elves you saw down there are probably slaughtered."

Reanna's brain stalled on his words as if somebody had thrown a wrench into the gears of her brain. Her thoughts rotated around the idea that, if the MCU had taught her anything, it was that the rule of thumb in these situations was that nobody truly died unless they died "on-screen"—aka unless Reanna verified it for herself.

"Haven't you seen *The Princess Bride*?" Reanna clasped her shaking hands together. "The difference between probably slaughtered and really slaughtered is like the difference between *mostly dead* and dead-dead."

Corcaelin looked confounded by her logic.

Adam cleared his throat and reached for her knee. "Reanna, he hasn't seen *The Princess Bride*. That's an Earth movie."

Trevor, on the other hand, whispered under his breath. "*Mawwiage*."

Reanna didn't know whether to laugh or cry. But she didn't want to seem disrespectful or flippant about the fate of the elves.

Especially not when she cared so deeply that her brain found it hard to function without a coping mechanism.

"What is the point to all this nonsense?" Corcaelin raised an eyebrow.

"My point is—I mean—we can't give up on them yet. Let me go back to Atlantis." Reanna pressed her hands together, not above pleading. "Please. Let me try one more time to save everyone."

"And please, tell me how well it worked for you last time? Because that is precisely what you did, and look where we ended up." Corcaelin swept his hands around the beach. "With very few of our elves alive and a much bigger mess to clean up. You caused the deaths of the lives we meant to save."

Reanna's shoulders sank. The air felt leaden as she tried to move it in and out of her lungs. Of course. Worthless. Useless. All she did was mess things up. Why had she even tried?

She pressed her nail into her wrist until she knew it would leave an indent, until it threatened to cut off circulation from her hand. She heard Trevor grunt from behind her, and he captured her fingers and squeezed them together. On her other side, Adam wrapped his arms around her shoulders.

Tears clogged her throat.

"At least she cared enough to try," Adam said. "At least she wasn't some self-absorbed princess who didn't care one iota about the lives of other people."

Corcaelin sniffed. "If she was, those elves might still be alive. Regardless, thanks to you miscreants, Thessalonike reappeared for the first time in three centuries."

"Who?" Trevor asked. He dropped Reanna's hands as if whatever threat he'd sensed had been avoided and he no longer wanted to touch her.

"She's *real?*" Reanna whispered at the same time.

Adam choked and started to cough, which was hard to interpret.

"She is real, yes, and very powerful, though she tends only to leave her library in times of the greatest need." Corcaelin clasped his hands together. "She has requested guardianship of you, and the Council will decide whether or not to send you there after your trial."

"Trial?" Reanna squeaked.

"Of course. You, Laile, and the elf that helped you—the one that was quite inconsolable before he went back to Capital City— will each be tried for the part you had in this debacle. Young Mr. Blandinus had his trial expedited due to the strenuous circumstances; we needed him on the front lines." Corcaelin shook his head. "And now that I see you have two more in your band of merry misfits, we will have to add their names to the defendants as well."

"What? No—you've got it all wrong. I just got here!" Trevor protested. "I don't even know what the heck is going on!"

"I'm pretty sure my sister will kill me if I go on trial," Adam whispered. His whole face had gone pale, and even his freckles had disappeared. "I'm supposed to be keeping a low profile."

"Perhaps you should have thought of that before you threw your lot in with Reanna." Corcaelin glared at both of them. "Now, unless you have further questions, please stay put until I can find you an escort back to Capital City. You three are under house arrest until the trial determines whether or not you will be handed over to Thessalonike for whatever reason she wants you."

CHAPTER 60

REANNA

GAIA: DISTRICT OF CAPITAL CITY

The Song of the Sea dimmed as Reanna headed back through the portal. Capital City was far enough removed from the ocean that the music didn't drown her senses.

But she longed to be in the water even more than she had back on Earth. Luckily, Cynerra and Damien Úlfur had a gigantic tub, and Reanna spent hours inside of it as her house arrest and the trials dragged on.

It had already been a week, and no one had made a decision one way or the other.

Reanna dunked her head under the water and watched the ripples from below. The fluke of her tail hung out over the edge, but she could fit most of her torso—including her new, more age-appropriate top—and the upper bit of her scales into the water.

She exhaled a string of bubbles and let them float to the surface.

She'd made such a mess of things.

Laile still had trouble walking without assistance. Gregory had shipped out for training. Trevor and Adam mostly just sat around and annoyed each other; they'd been allowed to bunk with Laile's brothers. Laeserno had been assigned to a nearby apartment with guards. Reanna visited him at least once a day, but he seemed shattered. He stared out the window, haggard, scarcely touching the food the guards brought or the violin Reanna had requested for him.

But she couldn't leave him alone.

After all, it was her fault his wife and child had died.

Reanna squeezed her eyes shut. Breathe in, breathe out. Focus on things in the real world, not things inside her mind. Go to a happy place. The list of tips and tricks for anxiety flickered across her mind, but not a single one stuck. She jerked on her hair, but even the pain didn't draw her out of the spiral.

A drum beat inside her mind. Worthless. Useless. No good. Harbinger of pain and destruction. Her fault. Her fault. Her fault.

Her fault.

The tune morphed and twisted itself as it became more frantic and louder inside of her. The world might be better off without her. No—all worlds would be better off without her. What benefit did she bring to anyone by continuing to live? She'd exploded her adoptive parents' marriage on Earth. She'd caused the genocide of an entire people on Gaia.

Arana should have just killed Reanna as a child and spared the world the pain of her presence. If Reanna didn't exist, there would be no war. The elves would be alive, and the world would be happy.

Reanna squeezed her thumb into the nerves of her wrist. Pain made her palm and fingers tingle, and she gasped for breath. A few more bubbles exploded from her mouth and floated to the top of the tub.

Such a shame a mermaid couldn't drown. If ever one deserved to, she did.

The chaotic drumbeat intensified inside her soul. In the background, Reanna could make out the Song of the Sea as well, dulled but not gone, not really. She needed a reprieve, needed a break. Needed to shut off her mind before she gave into the dangerous symphony.

Reanna crossed her arms over her stomach. Bile churned inside her, a byproduct of the storm within her mind and body.

The tunes crashed like warring tsunamis. The Song of the Sea, the song of self-doubt. Each fought for dominance with their wicked melodies.

Under the water, Reanna screamed. She needed to be free. Free of the war, free of her mother, free of the prison of a body and mind—

Peace.

The scream trailed off. She gasped and sucked in a breath of water. Her body didn't care; it separated the two hydrogen particles from the oxygen with ease.

Not again. Things couldn't *possibly* get any worse. And Arana was so far away, and, as far as anyone knew, assumed her daughter was dead. If Reanna could just tune out the third melody. It played so softly in the back of her mind; it shouldn't be hard. But the *peace* melody persisted, acting as the undercurrent in the tsunamis. It sliced through the water like a fish, and the churning waters lulled as it passed.

Peace.

Despite the fact her bath had become lukewarm at best, Reanna closed her eyes and soaked in the warmth that came with this new melody. Everything inside of her warned not to trust it, to be on edge, but it felt so good.

Maybe…maybe *peace* hadn't always been bad. Vaguely, she almost recalled this song from her childhood, too. A hazy memory floated to the front of her mind—this song had pulled her through the seas and onto land as a child, so long ago.

Tears mingled with the bathwater. She didn't deserve peace. She didn't deserve to feel comfort when so many were denied it. Where was the peace in the camp? Where was the peace in Laeserno's family dying? In Laile's kidnapping? In Gregory's summons?

She couldn't.

Reanna burst through the water. "Laile!" She screamed the name before her common sense could kick in—Laile didn't need to come. She could hardly walk. No one needed to be bothered by Reanna's problems—not when the fairy had so many of her own.

How stupid. Reanna would just annoy her.

A few minutes trickled by until the lock turned by itself and Laile hobbled in. "Sorry it took me so long! Had to find the bathroom key. Mom hid it a couple months ago because the twins kept stealing it so they could come in here whenever I showered to scare me. I swear, they're the worst."

Reanna's shoulders shook as she burst into heavy sobs. Her breaths hitched, and her nose stuffed up.

Laile's eyes widened. "Reanna! Are you okay?" She shuffled over. Through tears, Reanna saw her former guardian fall once, grab onto the metal shower door handle, and use various bathroom fixtures to hold herself up until she could sit down on the faux brick-style tiles.

"You should be in bed," Reanna mumbled, her voice muffled through tears.

"Actually, I shouldn't be struggling like this in the first place. But here we are." Laile reached out and grabbed Reanna's soaked hand. "What's up? Forget a towel or something? Happens to me all the time. Although I think the twins just *steal* my towel, if we're being honest."

Reanna sniffed. She didn't deserve a friend like Laile. She didn't deserve peace.

But then…why could Reanna still hear that stupid melody in the back of her head?

Peace.

Such a strange concept.

"I…I guess I just wanted to talk?" Reanna whispered. "Or, really, I didn't want to be alone."

Laile traced the veins in Reanna's hand in little curlicues. The fairy followed a winding trail all the way up every single finger and back down. "You don't have to be alone. I've had my fair share of being alone these past few weeks, trust me. We've both been through a dragon-dung ton, I'll tell you that."

"Yeah…" Reanna sniffled. "And it feels like there's still a dragon-dung ton going on in my head."

"I know. Mine too." Laile's fingernail drifted along the dips and curves of Reanna's hand.

"And…" Reanna hesitated. "I don't know. It seems crazy. I never heard it back on Earth, but…I feel like there's more music in my head, too. And it's trying to tell me peace, peace. But it's so quiet, and I…I don't know…" She faltered.

Laile raised her eyebrows. "Interesting." She leaned in closer, as if they were sharing secrets at a slumber party. "Sounds like a Sacred Song. The Composer built this world through music, and those songs still echo throughout Gaia today."

"Sacred Songs? Like the Song of the Sea?"

Laile puckered her lips. "I don't know what that is, but it's more like…bravery when you're feeling scared. Love when you're feeling unloved. Peace when you're in the depths of despair. Stuff like that. The Composer's Sacred Songs."

Except for that to be true, that would require the Composer to actually notice Reanna. But since He'd been absent for most of her life, if the first message He gave her was to *have peace* while the world fell to shambles, well…it seemed patronizing to her.

Reanna licked her lips. "I mean—I'm sorry if this offends you, but—that seems kinda stupid to me. How can we possibly feel peace in war? Peace in suffering, in a world like this? There's nothing *peaceful* or good about any of this."

"It's…surreal. Unnatural, I'll give it that. But that doesn't make it any less potent or true." Laile paused. "You know…I didn't really hear any of the Sacred Songs when Julius had me. But I didn't look for them, either, because I didn't really need peace at that moment. I needed holy fire to rain down from the sky and obliterate Julius, but that's a different story." Laile smirked. "What I mean is—maybe you can hear this song because it's what you need most. You know?"

"No. I don't know. I don't need peace for *me*. I want to bring Rosaelina and Maesie back. I want to bring all the elves back. That would be something *useful*. I don't need or deserve peace. Not after what happened." Reanna rested her chin on the side of the bath. "So many people are dead because of me."

"Don't flatter yourself. There were a lot of choices that put us in this position. Mine included. But don't forget—*Arana* is the one to blame here." Laile flipped over Reanna's hand and began to trace her palm. The movement tickled on the more sensitive skin there, and Reanna twitched.

"I guess." She sighed.

"And you know…yeah, bad stuff happened. Bad stuff will continue to happen. Bad things are happening all around." Laile paused, and her lip quavered. Tears filled her eyes. "But we can't worry about the next moment or the next trial. We don't have a choice in this moment left to make besides carrying on or giving up. And if we carry on, we know that we don't have to live in fear. We just have to exist, to feel that peace, and that's enough."

But was it really?

Enough would have been if the Composer stopped with the melodies and struck down Arana or Violante. If He would have saved all those who died at the concentration camp. His promise of *peace* was too little, too late.

But even Reanna had to admit that the melody relaxed her. And it was the only thing loud enough to drown the twisted lullabies; the Song was as enchanting and dangerous as the Lorelei of Germanic—and Gaian—legends.

Peace.

Peace amidst the chaos.

Peace amidst the uncertainty of what might happen next.

Peace amidst the regret of what had already transpired.

Peace—such a paltry myth, as Violante had said. What if one of her other spirits could give more timely answers than the Composer? What if they could give more than *peace* that was a day late and a dollar short?

Reanna closed her fingers over Laile's hand. "You know, you were a pretty good guardian. But...I think I like you better as a friend. You're—you're a great friend..." Reanna mumbled the next part, unsure of how it would be received. "Lails."

A few tears spilled over Laile's eyelashes. "Wow, would you look at that. My first nickname."

"Do you like it?"

Laile grinned. "Yeah. I love it. Has a nice ring to it, don't you think? *Lails.* Hey, I know. We can be Lails and Tails." She cackled. "I hope you know I am *so* going to use that from now on."

Reanna gave a breathy laugh and dove into Laile's arms. "Fair enough. I'll be your Tails if you'll be my Lails."

The melody still played on in Reanna's head, but it seemed to get louder as the girls hugged. As Reanna snuggled deeper into her new friend's embrace.

Peace.

Sure. Reanna might be scared still, and she might not know what to do next or how to move on from the past. If peace *did* come from the Composer, she still didn't feel like it was enough. But she could try and understand it. And she could try and give *friendship* a shot for the first time in a long time.

After all, these new feelings—friendship and peace—felt kind of nice. Airy.

Light, even.

The only things bright enough to illuminate the dark depths of her soul.

FIN.

ACKNOWLEDGMENTS:

I feel like it's very cliche to begin an acknowledgments section with "where to begin," but it's true. I hardly know where to start when I think about all the people that have supported me on this journey to bring Reanna and friends to life. When I say that this book has taken up a big chunk of my life, I don't mean that lightly. It has. This is one of the most time-consuming projects I have ever worked on. No, scratch that—it is the most time-consuming project I have worked on. I started way back in my teenage years, from the first glimmer of a first draft that hit my mind, back in, oh, maybe 2010 or so. (YEAH. THAT LONG.)

Thank YOU, the reader, for picking up this book and actually making it to the end. (Supposing you have. Sometimes I read the acknowledgments first. No shame if you do, too.) The fact that you actually had a desire to read my book at all means the world to me. For the longest time, I thought no one would care about these characters, but, well YOU do. (Unless you hate them. Then I'm just glad you have a very strong opinion.) I'm sorry for any emotional turmoil I'll put you through, but I hope you'll stick around for the ride. There's still loads left!

I really would love to thank God for all the opportunities He gave to me while writing (and editing, and scrapping, and rewriting, and... well, you get the picture) this book. The road was really tough. All those rejections made me want to give up on this book and throw away these characters. But He saw me through until the glorious end. I guess it's kind of that whole "ruins to redemption" thing played over a million times in my life. I know I'm an ungrateful brat sometimes to the most wonderful Heavenly Father, but hey. You made me, so I guess You're kinda stuck with me for all eternity. Joke's on you. You all have all my enduring love, rants, questions, and worship always.

Mom, Dad, Caleb— Thanks for all your love and support for a starving artist. You inspire me to do better. You're the practical help a writer needs: you give me days off when I'm stressing, you come clean my house, pick up groceries if I beg hard enough... all of those little things that help me to write. Or procrastinate. Mostly write. (Usually.)

To Grandma Pam— Thanks for being my first reader ever. It still warms my heart every time you say, "That's the one I read, isn't it? The one you're finally getting published?" Yes, it is, Grandma. But I hope you'll read it again (or have already read it again), because this time, it's a lot better. And the font isn't bright pink anymore. I'm not sure if that's an upgrade or downgrade.

To Grandpa Francis— Thanks for being the first author in the family and a phenomenal scholar. Your theology always astounds me, and, I know this is fantasy and you prefer devotions, but I hope you'll see a little bit of the wisdom you've taught me reflected in these pages. I'd like to think I inherited my storytelling abilities from you, even if the stories we tell are very different.

To Nana Avonell— Thank you for being such a support. You always buy my books and share them, and you have no idea how much that means to me. Even if no one else comments, I know that you'll be there with a big smile and "love you and this story! Fantastic!" You cheer me on in so many ways. I always love talking about shows, movies, and books with you. I hope once you read this, we'll be able to have a long talk about my characters and who you ship. (Although we both know Olicity will forever be the best ship.)

To Papa Kelly— Thank you for being such a support, too. Just like Nana, I know that you'll always be right there, one of the first people to comment and share anything I like. Bonus: you also have about 300 Facebook accounts, so I get shared on all of them. I'll never forget when you bought about ten of my first short stories just so that you could sell them or give them away. You'll never know how much that touched me.

To Savanna and SnowRidge Press— You will never know how much it meant to me when I pitched this story to you and you enthusiastically wrote back that you wanted it. I may have cried a little bit (or a lot). You have been nothing short of fantastic to work with. But you've become so much more than a publisher: you've also become a friend. From long rants to jokes to philosophy discussions, you've become such a lovely and dear friend of my heart. Your enthusiasm, your belief in Reanna, me, and this book, have made me smile and laugh more times than you know. And it's been a rough road, but you've been there every single step (we won't talk about the cover art process, no, no, no...). I can't thank you enough!

To Nancy Rue— I'll never forget the day that you became my mentor. I mean, after all, it's not every day that your favorite childhood author actually calls you on the phone, right? I don't know if I let on how nervous I was to talk to you, or how I paced the house during our conversation during that first consultation, trying not to break down into happy tears right then. If it weren't for you, I wouldn't have these books. Thank you for editing them, for loving them, and for all your advice on how to become the best writer I can be. Knowing you were on my side gave me the strength to pull these books from my mind to the computer.

To everyone who rejected this novel— I mean this absolutely sincerely. The novel as I pitched it a few years ago, while I thought it was perfect at the time, was not ready. It needed to be sat on and redone just a little bit more, to make it perfect for Savanna. So I'm glad that the doors didn't open then, so that they could swing wide open when the time (and the novel) were just right.

To my beta readers: C.E., Amanda, Beka, Kayla, Maddie, Mariella, Maseeha, and Morgan— Thank you ALL for your hard work in reading this book and giving feedback. I appreciate each and every one of you, and you all really gave me sound advice that helped to fix so many things. This book wouldn't be in its final form without you!

To my writing commune friends— Kayla, Beka, Cass, Anne, Maseeha, and Mariella... you all rule. I can't say thank you enough, and yet, I need to at least try.

To Cass— Thank you for all the inside jokes and cat pictures. They keep me running on days when I'm overwhelmed with writing, editing, life, or all of the above. I'm so glad that you became my mentor in the Writing Games and that we struck up a friendship. You edited for me right up until the deadline (and maybe a little past...) just so that story could be great. And then we won! I'll never forget your e-mail that started it all: ("I was hoping I'd get to mentor you!") Thanks for always picking up those late night phone calls... and for not judging me too much when I turned the wrong way down a one-way street. (Maybe I shouldn't put that in print.)

To Mariella— Thank you for always dreaming up and loving our sassy, murderous babies. You understand me so well, both as a writer and a friend. And you also understand the importance of snarky (and spiteful) people: "If he comes courting, it better be with sass and sarcasm." Thank you for being my first editor. Your comments kept me in stitches... and then frantically shoveling over the plot holes you pointed out. Also, thanks for keeping me from making accidental euphemisms. (Reanna's original last name never leaves between the two of us.)

To Kayla— You were the very first Instagram friend I ever made. I remember being so nervous to try and talk to you when you posted about wanting to review indie authors. I didn't think there was a chance you'd choose to review Seashells-- but then, not only did you, but you also sent me a copy of Metamorphosis. I saw your heart in those poems, and it touched me deeply. I had thought it was a shot in the dark that you'd review me-- but I never imagined we'd become such close friends. And I'm so glad that we are. Thank you for being my oldest and most constant beta reader!

To Maseeha— I think you made over 400 comments in the Depths beta read, and every single one of them made me either laugh, cry (happy tears, of course), or sing. You encourage me to be even more gory, dark, and sarcastic, just because I can't wait to see your reaction. #sorrynotsorry. You are my Senior Oompha Loompa, the Certified Rat Catcher, and Disney Karaoke Partner. Thanks for being a great beta reader and friend. CAN WE FINALLY GIVE THAT DANG RAT A BREAK NOW?? (The answer is absolutely not. We both have too many stories in the fire for him to slack off now. Sorry, Oliver...)

To Anne— Remember that time that it took us 3 hours to read a 9-page short story and I ended up laughing so hard milk came out my nose? Or that time that it took us 6 hours to read 6 chapters of Depths? (I mean, technically, that last one just happened today at the time of writing this, so you'd have really bad amnesia if you forgot.) Thank you for being such a dedicated, yet also hilarious editor. I always feel a hundred times more confident once you edit things, because not only will you be unwaveringly honest ("I don't know what else to say except write better"), but you also encourage me (you know, to not swerve into the other ditch). I hope you notice that I didn't use any em-dashes in this note. It was all for you. Thanks for being "slightly odd."

To Beka— You are my last proofreader on this project, and it only feels fitting that you should be the last thank you in this section. Before we were friends, I was terrified to talk to you. You made me so nervous. But then I posted a picture of Aizawa and you commented, and thus, our friendship and simp-ship was born. ("I'm not cheating; it's called collecting.") Now, my day feels incomplete if we don't chat, either through call or by text. Thank you for being such an avid fan of my characters. Even before you'd edited/read it, you knew about Greg (the best boi and pirate), Laile, and the whole gang, and you loved them all the while. Thanks for being a sister of my heart and soul and the Gus to my Shawn.

I'm so glad I get to cheer each and every one of you on as we share our stories and journeys.

Love,

Hannah

PRONUNCIATION GUIDE

PEOPLE:

REANNA = *Re-ann-uh*

TETHYS = *teh-theez*

ATLANTISI = *At-lan-tis-sea*

LAILE = *Lay-lee*

ÚLFUR = *ull-fur*

GREGORY = *Greg-or-ee*

BLANDINUS = *bland-ee-nus*

TREVOR = *Trev-or*

ADAM = *Ah-dum*

LAESERNO = *Lay-ser-no*

SHAESIA = *Shay-e-see-uh*

CYNERRA = *Sin-err-a*

DAMIEN = *Day-me-un*

MIONOS = *Me-oh-nos*

KAL = *cal*

WREN = *wr-en*

LARK = *lark*

WHISPER = *whis-per*

CORCAELIN = *cor-kay-lin*

KALENA = *ka-lean-uh*

AIMEE = *amy*
VIATRIX = *vee-ah-trix*
ARANA = *uh-ran-ah*
VIOLANTE = *Ve-oh-lant-ay*
JULIUS = *jule-ee-us*
DUREG = *dur-egg*
BOLEGO = *bow-lee-go*
ROSAELINA = *rose-uh-lean-uh*
MAESIE = *may-see*

PLACES:

GAIA = *guy-uh*
ATLANTIS = *at-lan-tiss*
DASPIN = *das-pin*
KIROVA = *keer-oh-vuh*
JENKIRRE = *jen-keer*
SIMIT = *sim-it*
GYRRANIUS = *guy-ran-ee-us*
FIASTRO = *fee-as-tro*
REGGERIA = *reg-jeer-ee-uh*
WHIDON = *why-don*

MISC.:

AZERNOS = *az-er-nos*
JURINN = *jur-inn*
SHABUU = *sha-boo*
NONNIE = *non-knee*
FAYNACORE = *fain-uh-core*

ABOUT THE AUTHOR

HANNAH CARTER IS just a girl who loves to dream and write and still wakes up every day hoping to figure out she's secretly a mermaid. Her short stories and award-winning flash fiction pieces have been published in anthologies such as: SnowRidge Press's *Whispers From Before*, all of Twenty Hill's anthologies, Havok's *Prismatic*—where she won an Editor's Choice Award—and *Casting Call*, as well as other anthologies from Alex Silvius, Effie Joe Stock, and Nightshade Publishing. In 2022, her flash fiction piece, "A Home for Nova," won a Realm Award. Hannah also won a competition with her short story, "Lara." She currently has two published novellas, *Amir and the Moon* and *Seashells*, and *The Depths of Atlantis* is her debut novel. In addition to fiction, she also has had over a dozen devotionals published in various magazines, as well as six devotions published in *Finding God in Anime* and *Finding God in Anime Volume Two*. In her spare time, she's probably either cuddling her cats, drinking tea, reading, or practicing for her imaginary Broadway debut. Connect with her on Instagram at @mermaidhannahwrites.

BOOKS FROM SNOWRIDGE PRESS

PERSUASION DUOLOGY
by Antonia Kane
Persuasion of Deceit
Persuasion of Destiny

THE TALES OF NOTTINGHAM SERIES
by Savanna Roberts
Thief
Merry Men
Archeress

THE DIVINE COURAGE TRILOGY
by C.C. Urie
Defender
Betrayer

BETWEEN SHADE AND FLAME SERIES
by Everly Haywood
Peaceweaver
Grimkeeper

ANTHOLOGY COLLECTIONS
Whispers From Before
Equinox & Solstice

ABOUT THE PUBLISHER

SNOWRIDGE PRESS is a small, hybrid publishing house that offers traditional publishing services for Indie Authors. Specializing in Dystopian and Fantasy Young Adult/New Adult stories, we aim to make self-publishing more accessible, enjoyable, and successful for authors.

For more of our books or to view our author services, please visit our website at snowridgepress.com.

SNOWRIDGE PRESS